Loyal Son

Also by Wayne Diehl

The Boy With No Name

The Midnight Ride of Missy Montaigne

The Snackaholics

Loyal Son

A Novel

By

Wayne Diehl

ISBN 9781657172319
Independently Published

Cover Design by
Jelena Elizia Jovanovic

*For my grandson,
our little German-Irish-Mexican,
Nixon Francisco Salinas*

Prologue

San Ángel, Mexico, August 24, 1847

Jane showed her pass to the guard at the adobe warehouse which had been commandeered by the American army to house their prisoners. She wore an ankle-length embroidered skirt, a low-cut white blouse, and a blue and yellow *rebozo* covering her head and shoulders. Her black hair and olive skin made it easy for her to be taken for a simple peasant woman, as long as she averted her striking, amber-flecked, hazel eyes.

To a man, every American soldier believed the prisoners, members of the Saint Patrick's Battalion, should have been executed on the spot of their capture. Their guards were in no mood to give them any consideration of any kind and Jane didn't want to be turned away by revealing that she was an American, and a reporter, who might be perceived as sympathetic to these Irishmen.

When she first heard about them, Jane shared the opinion of nearly every American that they were despicable cowards and the worst kind of deserters: traitors who joined the enemy and brought death and destruction upon their former comrades. But when she returned to Mexico City after reporting to President Polk that the covert peace mission he sent her on had failed, she met Alicia Salinas Ryan, the young wife of one of those *San Patricios*. Now those feelings had changed to a tender compassion for her and their ill-fated love.

Jane was there to find out if Alicia's beloved Patrick was still alive and, if so, deliver a letter she'd written him. She had given her word to Nicholas Trist not to write about the deserters in order to secure permission for this visit but her curiosity was piqued. She was eager to find out more about them and their leader, John Riley. She would keep her promise but when the time came, she wanted to tell their story.

The sergeant studied the paper with undisguised contempt. It was signed by Trist, the American peace minister, and he had no choice but to let her in. He handed it back to her while openly ogling her breasts. Jane muttered *gracias* and went inside.

The smell hit her like a slap in the face. Human feces mixed with the filth of unwashed bodies made her gag and she covered her mouth and nose with the *rebozo*. It was dark inside, lit only by four small windows on each thick, earthen wall near the ceiling. It took her eyes a few moments to adjust and to recover from the stinging tears the stench caused.

Eventually, the shapes of the men scattered about the room came into view. Most were on the floor with their backs against the wall. All were shackled at their hands and feet. She pulled the scarf away from her mouth and called out, "John Riley?" She felt more than saw their eyes turn toward her but no one answered.

"Major Riley?" she repeated.

"Over here," came a strong baritone voice from the farthest side of the room.

He got slowly to his feet as she approached. He was a giant of a man, well over six feet tall. A shaft of sunlight shone through one of the windows, illuminating his dirt-streaked face, and Jane was struck by his probing sky-blue eyes. She extended her hand which he took with a gentleness that belied his size and strength.

"I'm a reporter, Major Riley. My name is Jane McManus Storm but I write under the name of Montgomery."

"An honor to meet you Miss Storm. I've read some of your articles. You write for the *New York Sun* I believe?"

She was shocked. She didn't know what to expect but it certainly wasn't an intelligent man who was familiar with either her or her work. He noticed her reaction.

"We had access to many newspapers in Corpus Christi when I was with the Americans. And here in Mexico City we received the *Picayune* out of New Orleans as well as the *Sun* on occasion."

"I'd like to speak with you, Major but first I need to ask about one of your men?"

"And who would that be, Miss Storm?"

"Patrick Ryan?"

"Yes. Corporal Ryan it is. The finest of men."

"Is he here with you? I have a letter for him, from his wife."

Riley smiled. "The beautiful Alicia." He motioned with his head to the opposite side of the warehouse. "That's him, in the far corner, against the wall."

"Thank you. May I come talk to you as well afterwards?"

"Yes, but don't wait too long. Like the lot of us, I have an upcoming appointment with the hangman."

Jane marveled at his cavalier attitude. "Thank you, Major," she said. "Under the circumstances, I wish you the best."

He gave her a tight smile and a slight, two-fingered salute before turning and going back to his spot at the other end of the room.

Patrick was slumped forward with his arms and head resting on his knees. He glanced up but made no other move other than to stare vacantly as she approached. Though they had met briefly a few weeks ago he did not remember her. His face and hair were smeared with dried blood, grease and grime, making it impossible for her to recognize him either. She was almost to him when she said, "Patrick?"

His eyes flickered. "Yes?" he said.

"I'm Jane, we met after Mass a couple weeks back. I've brought you a letter from Alicia."

He was immediately alert. His shackles scraped and clanked as he got to his feet.

"You've seen her?" he said. "Is she safe?"

"Yes. An armistice is in place. The Americans have not invaded the city. Perhaps the war is over."

"Thank God," said Patrick. "May I have the letter?"

She took it from a fold in her skirt and handed it to him, watching the tears well up in his eyes as he read it. "She'll be happy to know you're alive, Patrick."

He let out a grunt and said, "Not for long."

"I have a pass, Patrick. And contacts. I may be able to get her here to see you."

The tears had made thin, pallid rivulets down his blackened cheeks. He bit down hard on his lip and his head shook back and forth as he fought with himself. "Please tell her I love her," he said. "But she can't come here. I don't want her to remember me this way."

Jane put a hand on his arm. It was all she could do to keep from crying herself. "I'll tell her, Patrick. And I'll come back to see you again, if I can."

"Thank you. Can you bring a pen and some paper so I can write her and my sister in Philadelphia?"

"Of course. I'll be back as soon as possible. I'm a newspaper reporter and I would like to find out about you and your story."

"My story?"

"Yes. How and why a young Irishman migrates to America and winds up fighting on the side of the Mexicans."

"So that more Americans will despise us?"

"To be honest, it's for my own satisfaction. I'd like to find out more about you and Alicia and to understand what it was that made you do it."

"I'll think about it," said Patrick.

Jane's pass continued to be valid and over the next week while their court-martials were conducted, she visited both Patrick and John Riley. The verdicts were all the same. Without exception, each of them were found guilty of desertion and treason and sentenced "to be hanged by the neck until dead."

Patrick, reluctant at first, eventually opened up and told Jane his story, starting with the day he and his sister Ellen left their family in Ireland and boarded a ship for the Promised Land of America.

Chapter One

Patrick didn't hear the horse and buggy racing up behind him. He was on his way home from visiting Father Muldoon, the pastor and unofficial librarian for their small parish. He walked with his nose in *Oliver Twist*, oblivious to the world around him. His mind also drifted from the page to his conversation with the priest. Was it really a possibility that he could go to college?

When he finally heard it come around the bend, the wagon was already upon him. He jumped out of the way and stumbled into the ditch at the side of the road. The land agent, Preston Wilkes, didn't slow down as he cracked the whip over his horse's ear. Wilkes could only be going one place on this section of road. Patrick got to his feet, checked to make sure the book wasn't damaged, tucked it under his arm, and continued on his way home.

Patrick's father, Thomas Ryan, did see Wilkes coming. He heard the whip snap and the pounding hoofs from the potato garden on the hill above his small farmhouse. He watched the cart approach with a sinking heart. He'd been expecting this visit. Colonel Albritton, like most absentee landowners in London, was dividing up his plots in Ireland and renting them out separately for higher profits. His agent was here to do the dirty work he relished so much.

Wilkes pulled up in front of the house and sat there in his tall hat, expensive greatcoat and silk cravat, and waited with an imperious smirk on his florid face. Thomas shouldered his shovel and walked down the hill through the rows of potatoes. He greeted him at the gate with a tip of his cap.

"Mr. Wilkes."

Wilkes huffed and brushed the dust off his coat, trying to smooth it over his protruding belly.

"Ryan," he said, with an almost imperceptible nod.

"Would you like to come in?" said Thomas. "I can offer you a cup of water."

"I won't be staying. Your lease is up in six months."

"You needn't have come all this way to tell me that."

"I'm here to inform you that these minuscule acres you're renting are going up for auction."

Thomas gripped the shovel's handle and suppressed the desire to crush Wilkes's head with it.

"Did you hear me, Ryan?"

"Aye. But what if I come up with the rent?"

Wilkes laughed and pulled at his coat again.

"You're over a year in arrears, man. Do you expect me to believe that will happen? Why, you can't believe it yourself can you?"

Thomas clenched his jaw and his hands went tighter around the shovel. His two oldest boys, Thomas Jr. and William appeared from behind the house. Preston Wilkes grabbed the reins, preparing to turn and go.

"What is it, Da?" said Tom Junior.

"It's all right. Mr. Wilkes was just leaving."

"I'll have no trouble from you, Ryan, or any of your unruly curs."

"What're we to do then?" said Thomas. "We've nowhere to go."

"That's your problem," said Wilkes. "The workhouse I suppose."

"You didn't answer me about the rent. What if I come up with it?"

Wilkes let out a derisive snort as he turned his horse. "It won't matter, unless you can outbid all the grabbers waiting to claim the land. And then of course there's the small matter of my compensation. You'd have to come up with a little something extra for myself."

Tom and William took a step toward the carriage. Their father put a hand out. "We'll have none of that lads."

"Good advice, Ryan. I'm doing you a favor by letting you know. Next time I'll have the sheriff with me and perhaps a squadron of the 12th Lancers."

They watched the coach go down the road. As Wilkes rounded the corner he nearly ran into Patrick a second time. Patrick raised his hand in a courteous wave. Wilkes ignored him again, flicking the whip once more as he sped down the road.

Patrick reached his father and heard his brother William ask, "What are we going to do, Da?"

"We'll talk about it later. Now, you and Tom get back to work. And what took you so long, Patrick? You were to be gone an hour and it's been more than three."

"Sorry, Da."

"Go help your brothers."

Thomas knew what had to be done. He'd been scrimping and saving farthings and half-pennies for years. There was a chance he could get current on the rent but he'd never be able to outbid anyone else for the land.

Seeing the land agent depart like the Grim Reaper, he gazed over the land he loved and that his grandfather once owned. It struck him like a slash from the Reaper's scythe and he finally accepted the devastating truth.

There was no future here. The only hope his family had was in America. And the only way that could happen was by sending one of his sons to get some of the abundant land that was said to be there for the taking.

It would be his youngest son, Patrick, soon to be eighteen. He was the smartest of his boys if not the hardest working. In fact he was a bit of a dreamer and had to be constantly reminded to get his chores done. But his older sons would fare better here with the trouble that was coming. They were stronger, harder, though much quicker to act before they thought. Patrick could do it. He had to do it.

He would stay with his wife Sarah's sister in Philadelphia until he was able to get some land. Mary Torpey and her husband John had emigrated almost twenty years ago. Mary sent Sarah small amounts of money over the years and now together they had a nest egg of a little over ten pounds. It was a huge amount for people like them. He and Sarah talked long and hard about what to do. Now, they had no more time to waste.

The family sat around the crude wooden dining table in the cramped front room. A picture of Saint Patrick adorned one wall and a crucifix hung on the opposite side over the fireplace which kept the room warm year round. Sarah was already crying and she didn't even know the worst of it yet. She had been keeping the money from her sister a secret and only recently revealed the amount to her husband. He was angry at first but realized they would have spent it had he known. There was never enough and the house was in desperate need of repair. Now, with the extra money his plans changed slightly.

"Why can't we all go, Da?" said Patrick.

"We can't afford for everyone to go."

"But we have ten pounds. Surely that would pay for the ship's passage for all of us."

"The extra money is to buy land. That's the reason you're going. The only reason, son. Never forget that."

Patrick nodded and lowered his eyes in thought, filled with both dread and excitement. He didn't want the responsibility and was afraid he wasn't up to it, but he would be going to America! There wasn't anyone who didn't have a relative or friend who had already gone and the word back was that it was nothing less than the golden door to happiness and prosperity. He wasn't listening to what his father said next. He only heard his mother wail so loud that it startled him.

"No, Thomas," she said. "We didn't talk about that."

Patrick noticed his brother Tom shaking his head and sneering at him.

"Why is it that you get to go?" said Tom.

"Aye," said William, at nineteen, a year and a half younger than Tom. "And Ellen too."

Patrick looked at his little sister, just turned fifteen, the baby of the family. She was crying almost as much as their mother.

"What are you talking about?" he said.

"Are you deaf?" said William. "Sure and you'll be the one to save us. Ellen is going with you."

"Da!" said Patrick. "Ellen's going too?"

"That's what I just said."

Patrick sat there, dumbfounded while the family jabbered all at once. His father slammed his hard, calloused hand down on the table.

"Enough!" he said. "Patrick, you and Ellen will be going to Philadelphia. You'll stay with Mary and John until you're able to buy a plot of farmland. Then, God willing, the rest of us will join you."

"Da," said Patrick. "It isn't safe. What if something happens to Ellen, or me, and I can't take care of her."

"I'll go," said Tom Junior. "It should be me anyway. I'm the oldest. Patrick can hardly take care of himself, let alone Ellen."

"Patrick it is," said Thomas. "And Ellen will go with him. It may be dangerous but what will happen when we lose the farm? We can't feed all of us as it is now. Who'll take care of her then?"

"I'll find work right away," said Patrick. "I'll send money..."

"No, Patrick First you will get us land. If you have to find work to do that, so be it. You'll be taking your sister and you'll be watching over her. I'll hear no more talk about it."

Chapter Two

February 28, 1844

Father Muldoon said Mass and afterward family and friends gathered in the front yard of the Ryan house. It was more like a wake than a going away party. There was drinking, singing and dancing, but the tears, mostly from the older folks, never stopped flowing. Thomas put an arm around his wife.

"It'll be fine Sarah. And we'll be joining them before you know it. You'll see."

"We shouldn't send Ellen, Thomas. I fear I'll never lay eyes on her again. On either of them. I feel it in my bones."

"It's done darlin' and it's for the best. You'll see."

They looked over at their youngest children, each in their own circle of friends, talking and laughing. Everyone always said that if the two of them were closer in height they would have been taken for twins. At five feet eight inches, Patrick was the tallest in the family. Ellen was five inches shorter. They both had luxuriant, mahogany-red hair and eyes of the exact same color as their hair. Their skin was fair and slightly freckled around the nose but Patrick had a ruddy hue to his complexion from working outside all his life.

"You're a lucky one, Patrick," said his cousin Kirin. "What I wouldn't give to be going with you."

"I wish it were so," said Patrick. "It would be much better than having to worry about my little sister all the time."

"I hear the streets of Philadelphia are paved with gold," said Jerry McDonough.

"Land and ladies," said Brendan O'Broin. "There for the taking."

Patrick laughed. "Well, not according to my Uncle John. He's writtenus to be careful when we arrive at New York. The docks are a dangerous place, full of thieves and cutthroats."

"And what will you do when you see them," said his brother William. He was two inches shorter than Patrick but the toughest physically of the Ryan boys. "You're a fast runner, we all know that, but Ellen will be a bit of a load to carry."

"Don't you worry about me, Will," said Patrick. "Worry about Ma. She's not taking this well."

"That's the truth," said William. "She'll be missing Ellen something terrible. But I think she's crying almost as much knowing her little Patrick won't be becoming a priest after all. She always had her heart set on having a bishop in the family."

"You're not still thinking about that are you, Patrick?" said Kirin.

"Not since he was caught kissing Mary Beth McGinnis behind the church last year," said Tom Junior.

Patrick blushed as they laughed at him. He had thought about the priesthood when he was younger. They were needed all over Ireland, ever since Catholic Emancipation. But his piety had decreased with age and the awareness that he did indeed have a desire for the fairer sex. Father Muldoon had kindled his thoughts of college, and the seminary would provide the education he coveted, but that was nothing but a dream after all

He changed the subject when his sister and her friends came over and joined them. "You'd better behave yourself, Ellen," he said.

"I hear all the lads in America are rich and handsome," she said.

Patrick didn't think it was as funny as the rest of them did. "And I hear," he said, "the convents are filled with Irish girls who thought the same thing."

This drew exaggerated "oohs" and tongue clicking from the girls. Ellen feigned being hurt and said, "Tis you who'll be needing looking after, Patrick. Your mind is in the clouds most of the time. I'd feel much better if Tom or Will were taking me to America."

Patrick loved his sister, there was no doubt of that. But having two older brothers who doted on her made it unnecessary for him to do the same. Now the whole family was depending on him to ensure their future and to protect her in the bargain.

Soon it was time to go. Ellen carried a tattered old suitcase that contained a change of clothes for each of them, including their woolen frieze coats. Despite it being late February it was not cold enough to need them but they surely would when they got out to sea. Patrick had a sack slung over his shoulder filled with dried oat cakes, potatoes and a few small pots to cook with on the voyage. He also had the copy of *Oliver Twist* that Father Muldoon told him was now his.

The ten pounds of paper money was in a worn leather wallet his father had given him. It was safely tucked in a pocket his mother had sewn in his shirt. He had enough specie for the passage and any unforeseen expenses secured inside a pouch tied to the rope around his pants.

The entire party, led by Father Muldoon, walked with them the two miles to Uncle Peter's house. Tom and William alternately punched their little brother on the arm and put him in an affectionate headlock. Their mother couldn't stop crying or let go of her daughter's arm.

Patrick and Ellen would spend the night at their uncle's house. In the morning, Peter would hitch up his cart to Molly, his old mare, and take them twelve miles down the road to Buttevant to their cousin Sean's place. Sean would take them another seven miles in his wagon to Mallow. From that point they would be on their own and have to walk or catch a ride the rest of the thirty-plus miles to Cork Harbor.

When they were able to pry Sarah from Ellen, Patrick went to his mother. She grabbed him and held on with all her might. It was remarkable that she still had tears to shed. Patrick's eyes welled up and at that moment he wished with all his heart that he didn't have to go.

"I love you, Patrick. More than life itself."

"I know, Ma. I love you too."

"Take care of your sister. Don't let her out of your sight. Not for one minute."

"Yes, Ma."

His father came to him. His eyes too were wet and red.

"You've a big task, lad."

Patrick nodded. His throat was tight and he feared that if he tried to speak he would break down and cry like a baby.

"We're all counting on you and I know you'll be making us proud. Write as soon as you get to John and Mary's place."

"I will, Da.

Chapter Three

Washington, D.C., February 28, 1844

Jane waited impatiently in front of the Indian Queen Hotel on Pennsylvania Avenue. Her escort, William Marcy, the former governor of New York, was late. The steamship was scheduled to leave in thirty minutes and she did not want to miss it. It was transporting them and over three hundred other passengers, including the president and nearly every politician in the government, to Alexandria to board the *USS Princeton* for a demonstration cruise down the Potomac.

She was in Washington gathering information for an article she was writing for the *New York Sun*, advocating for the immediate annexation of Texas. Her main objective was to interview the President and this excursion was the perfect opportunity.

Marcy's coach turned the corner and clattered to a stop. He stood up and made a move to come down to assist her. She waved him off, gathered her skirts, and climbed aboard.

"Not to worry, Governor, I'm perfectly capable of getting in myself."

He smiled and extended his hand. In her mid-thirties, Jane was as independent and beautiful as ever. Her raven hair and flawless, caramel-colored complexion, as well as her unwavering self-confidence, came from her paternal grandmother, a clan leader of the Mohican Indians. Her petite body and hazel eyes were from her mother's side. Governor Marcy clasped both of his hands over hers. She gave him a peck on the cheek.

"It's good to see you, William. How have you been?"

"Very well. How are you? And your son? Is he with you?"

"No, he's in Galveston with my brother, fighting for our land claims."

"They aren't resolved yet?"

"The Texas government refuses to accept the previous Mexican grants. We've gone to court but the local speculators brought up the whole Burr business again. I was deemed unfit for respectable society, in *Texas* if you can believe that, so I left Robert to sort it out."

Marcy shook his head and sighed. Ten years ago Jane had been named as Aaron Burr's adulteress by his wife in their divorce trial. The maid falsely testified to catching them together in a very compromising position, literally with his pants down. The sensational charge made Jane McManus the most notorious woman in America.

"Will it never end?" she said. "Like you, Aaron was a friend and colleague of my father's. A charming old rascal to be sure, but to suggest we were lovers is outrageous. My God, he was fifty years my senior. But enough of that. I want to thank you again."

"For what, dear?"

"Why for recommending me to Moses Beach. Being able to write for his paper has been a godsend. Until the issues in Texas are settled, I would have no income at all without the work. I know it was a risk for you."

It was unthinkable for a female to be a political writer. One could be a "scribbler" of frivolous novels but no woman could be taken seriously regarding affairs of state or the machinations of power. As a widow with a young son, she wrote to make a living and to convey her firm beliefs, not for prestige or fame. Nevertheless, writing under the pseudonym Montgomery, she was gaining a reputation for insightful, unapologetic opinions on politics, slavery, geographic expansion, republican revolutions around the world and, her most passionate subject, Texas.

"It was no risk at all," said Marcy. "I know your talent and resolve and you've proven me right."

"Bless you, Governor. Now, tell me about this warship and her Captain, Robert Stockton."

Marcy explained that the vessel was fully rigged with sails and also had steam engines. It was the first of its kind to use a screw propeller in place of paddle wheels. The engines were mounted below the water line, concealing them from enemy fire.

"And what about the guns I've heard so much about?"

"Stockton named them the *Peacemaker* and the *Oregon*," said Marcy. "I'm told they can shoot a two hundred pound ball over five miles."

"Astonishing," said Jane. "And the names are interesting aren't they? Between the saber rattling about Texas and the dispute with Britain over the Oregon Territory there's no doubt what message Tyler and Stockton are sending."

John Tyler had deserted the Democrats to join the Whigs as their vice-presidential nominee in the previous election and then controversially assumed the presidency when William Harrison died one month into his term. He promptly alienated his new party by vetoing their bills on the tariff and the bank based on what he deemed a matter of principle.

Henry Clay, the Whig leader, was outraged and banished him, making Tyler a man without a party. He saw territorial expansion, specifically Texas annexation, as the issue that could override party politics and gain him the popular support necessary to become president in his own right.

The day was perfect for a pleasurable sail down the Potomac, warm and not a cloud in the sky. They boarded the steamer for the ride to the *Princeton*. Jane was pleasantly surprised to see the former First Lady, Dolley Madison, among the wives, daughters and girlfriends on board.

Miss Dolley was universally revered ever since she refused to leave the White House when the British invaded in 1814 until the portrait of George Washington was removed and taken to a secure place. She'd been idolized from then on for valiantly saving the image of the Father of the Country from being destroyed and debased by the enemy.

Jane went over to introduce herself. As she approached, a younger woman whispered in Dolley's ear and pointed directly at her. She knew what she must be saying but kept right on going, absently admiring the beautiful celadon silk dress the old woman was wearing, complete with a matching turban and a long yellow feather attached to it. She curtsied when she got to her.

"Hello, Mrs. Madison, please forgive the intrusion."

"Jane! How delightful that we finally meet."

Jane was nearly overcome by her kind reception. "I've wanted to meet you for a very long time," she said. "Aaron spoke so highly of you."

"Poor Burr," said Miss Dolley. "Never has a man been so viciously and wrongly maligned.   Hamilton was the worst. He'd say anything, the more vile the better, in order to ruin the reputation of a rival."

"I suppose it was all about power," said Jane.

"It always is," said Dolley. "Power and vanity. It sickened me when they publicly ridiculed him for proclaiming that women were the intellectual equals of men and for educating his daughter 'as if she were a boy.'"

"He was very good to me," said Jane. "He encouraged me to write and to make my own way in the world."

19

"It was disgusting how you were slandered," said Dolley as she glanced at the woman who had whispered into her ear. "And continue to be. I don't listen to such talk. There is some gossip I *do* pay attention to though. And there's a tantalizing item about you, young lady. Is it true that you're this Montgomery who is writing so adeptly about Texas?"

Jane's face reddened with both pride and appreciation. "How do you know that?" she said.

Dolley laughed. "I may be old, but there isn't much that escapes my attention. Aaron would be so proud of, you, as am I."

"I can't tell you how much that means to me, Mrs. Madison."

"Please call me Dolley, and please keep up the excellent work."

The steamer pulled alongside the warship right at noon. The president appeared from below with the young and vivacious Julia Gardiner on his arm. They were an elegant couple. Julia had dark-hair, fair-skin and by all reports was full of spirit, charm and intelligence. He was the picture of aristocratic breeding: tall and angular with a shock of white hair above a high forehead. His large nose was hawk-like but not in an unpleasing way.

A marine band played an exuberant rendition of the "Star-Spangled Banner" as they were assisted across a plank by a uniformed officer in pristine white pants, a navy blue short-waisted coat and a bicorn hat.

Sailors in their white dress uniforms stood at attention along the deck and up in the rigging. As the president and his lady walked onto the ship they pulled off their hats and gave three boisterous cheers. When they stepped on to the deck the band struck up "Hail to the Chief."

"He may be a man without a party," said Jane. "But Captain

Stockton is making sure he's shown the proper respect."

Once on board, they were met by officers and taken off in small groups to tour the ship. A young ensign named Jones took Jane and Marcy's party. He explained about the ship and the screw propellers and informed them that under both steam and sail, the *Princeton* could reach a speed up to an amazing seven knots.

"And the guns?" asked a congressman who Jane didn't recognize.

"Yes, the guns. We have twelve, forty-two pound cannons placed around the deck but of course those aren't the ones you're here to see. He pointed to the huge gun in front of them. This is the *Peacemaker* and the *Oregon* is at the stern. The *Peacemaker* is slightly larger at fifteen feet long. Both are muzzle loaders with twelve inch bores. They were made using a new process with wrought iron that allows for a lighter, more flexible gun with a far superior trajectory. The range is up to five miles."

Everyone in their group either nodded or shook their heads and murmured to each other in appreciation. The tour ended and the order to get underway was given. The guests were directed below for refreshments and entertainment. The engines started with a deep rumble and sailors hurried to unfurl the sails.

After an hour of cruising, the call came to go topside. They gathered around the *Peacemaker* as it was raised up to firing position. Captain Stockton strode to the *Peacemaker*. He was a small, pompous man with a pile of black curly hair and wooly muttonchop sideburns. He paused dramatically before giving the ready command. He pulled the lanyard and a second later the ship shuddered and the thunderous boom shook Jane to her bones.

When she could hear again the entire crowd was yelling and

applauding. She couldn't see where the ball landed but heard claims that it bounced seven times, some said twelve, on the surface of the water before submerging over four miles downriver.

The guests clamored for Stockton to fire it again. He did so to more cheers of approval. This time Jane had moved to the side of the ship and saw it land. "I don't know how far it actually went," she told Marcy. "But the distance is unbelievable."

The guests wanted more but Stockton declined, sending everyone below for more food and entertainment. The band played, wine and champagne flowed, and toasts were made. Tyler and Julia danced first and then many joined them. The ship turned around at Mount Vernon and soon Stockton was besieged with requests to fire the cannon again. He finally consented and Jane saw her chance when the president lingered behind with Julia. She approached confidently, nodding politely to Julia.

"Mr. Tyler."

He paused, looked into her eyes and waited for her to continue.

"My name is Jane Storm, I write for the *New York Sun* and occasionally the *Democratic Review*."

She saw the surprise register in his eyes. He still didn't respond so she plunged ahead. "I write under the name of Montgomery and am very much in support of annexation."

Now he smiled and his eyes widened further.

"I'm aware of your work Miss Storm but confess I didn't know it was from the pen of a woman. Very good to meet you. May I introduce Miss Julia Gardiner."

They curtsied to each other. Julia studied her closely. Jane was accustomed to the blatant distaste at the knowledge of her occupation, especially from women. But she had the feeling that Julia was more curious, perhaps even impressed, than repulsed by her.

"Sir, is it true," she continued, "that Secretary Upshur has received President Houston's agreement on annexation and that you've promised ships and troops to defend the gulf and the border from an attack by Mexico."

Now he really was caught off guard. "And where did you get that information, Miss Storm?"

Before she could answer, the blast from the *Peacemaker* once more rocked the ship and them. They regained their balance and she started to respond when horrible screams came from above. The president brushed by her and rushed up the ladder. She and Julia followed behind him.

When Jane reached the deck all she could see was smoke and blurred silhouettes careening around in panic and confusion. Through the smoke she saw bodies laying everywhere. The breech of the *Peacemaker* had exploded and split wide open when Stockton pulled the firing lanyard, sending chunks of hot metal through the crowd.

Then, like a ghastly spirit, Captain Stockton appeared covered in black powder. He was hatless and his clothes were shredded. His face was burned clean of eyebrows and facial hair. One of his officers went to him and slowly led him to his cabin.

The president moved about looking for a way to help but like most of them he was stunned and disoriented. The Secretary of War, William Wilkins went to him and said something. Jane watched him go to Julia and speak into her ear. She immediately collapsed in his arms. He picked her up and carried her below. Just then, Jane saw Marcy and he rushed to her.

"Are you all right?" he said

"Yes, yes. I wasn't on deck. How about you?"

"Uninjured, thankfully."

"What happened to Miss Gardiner?" said Jane.

"Her father has been killed in the blast."

"Oh no," said Jane. "How many others?"

"I don't know yet but it's horrible."

The smoke dissipated and bodies that Jane assumed to be corpses stirred and struggled to get up. She saw Senator Thomas Benton being held by two men. Blood flowed from his ears and nostrils. Out on the water, she saw hats and bonnets bobbing and drifting on the gentle swells of the river, like floating tombstones on a watery graveyard.

In all, six lost their lives in the explosion: Secretary of State Upshur, Navy Secretary Gilmer, Beverly Kennon, the head of the Bureau of Construction and Repair, Virgil Maxcy, a lawyer from Maryland, David Gardiner, and the president's slave and personal valet, whose name was Amistead.

The other casualty, though temporary, was the Texas annexation treaty. John Calhoun was named Secretary of State to replace Upshur and he turned the whole process on its ear by making the Texas question a national debate on slavery.

Chapter Four

Cork City, March 1, 1844

Patrick and Ellen walked through the crowded streets of Cork two hours before the steamer was to depart for Liverpool. Cab drivers called out offering cheap fares to the harbor but they ignored them. The noise and traffic increased as they got closer to the docks. While moving among the pushing and shoving bodies, Patrick forgot about his sister. When he realized it and didn't see her anywhere, he whirled around searching, only to be confronted by angry, cursing faces. He heard her shouting before he saw her.

"Patrick! Over here."

He elbowed his way to her. "Ellen! You have to stay with me."

"You were moving too fast."

"I was searching for our boat. Take my hand, and don't let go until we're on board."

They found the steamer and got a spot on the top deck as far from the numerous pens of pigs as possible. It was cold, wet and uncomfortable but the trip was short and Patrick's spirits were high. Ellen was already homesick.

"It'll be all right," he said. "We're on a great adventure."

"I want to go home."

"Well, that's not going to happen Ellen, so we both need to accept it."

They made it to Liverpool just in time to board the *Enterprise*, a converted lumber transport vessel. The departure was delayed until the next morning so they found their berths below deck. Partitions had been set up in the five foot high section between the first and second levels of the ship to accommodate passengers. Crude wooden sleeping bunks with a top and bottom bed lined the sides with room for four adults on each. The families were together as were the single men and women. Patrick requested that he and Ellen be able to share the same berth but it was denied because there wasn't enough room for everyone if only two shared one bunk.

Despite the dank and musty quarters, and the sorrow of leaving their homeland, jubilation permeated the air with everyone looking forward to a new and better life. Once the ship got underway, there was singing, dancing and storytelling. That changed abruptly after a week out when they encountered turbulent seas and unrelenting blankets of rain that came out of the sky sideways. Many got violently seasick, Patrick and Ellen included. Patrick was one of the lucky ones. He stopped vomiting after a few days and was able to stand on his own without falling over.

It took Ellen longer and when she finally got accustomed to the constant pitching and rolling, she succumbed to fever and dysentery from the fetid air, the foul drinking water and the multitude of rats that ran rampant through the entire vessel. The water, which was provided by the captain, was contaminated from being stored in old, rotting containers. Ellen retched just putting the cup to her lips.

"This is horrid," she said. "Is there no other water?"

"Not for us. I don't know about the crew. The grog they receive may satisfy them. All the passengers are enraged but what can we do?"

"I can't drink anymore of it, Patrick. I need fresh water, fresh air, and a cooked meal."

"We can't go on deck because of the storm, and we can't have a cooking fire down here."

He gave her one of the oat cakes which they were both tired of eating. Ellen got progressively worse and Patrick feared for her life. She could only lay in pain and misery, made worse by the constant roiling of the ocean. Water continuously leaked into their berths making it impossible to ever be completely warm or dry. She moved in and out of delirium as her fever repeatedly intensified and subsided. Patrick wished his father had listened to him and agonized over how he could tell him if she didn't make it. He examined her for any sign of the dark purple rash of typhus and, to the relief of both of them, there was none.

Others weren't so lucky. Dozens got the rash and fear spread throughout the ship. Mrs. Kilpatrick and the youngest of her four children, a little girl just two years old, had spots on their necks and chests. Mr. Kilpatrick was frantic. He gathered Patrick and two other men, John Walsh and Aidan O'Malley around one of the two small wooden tables provided for them in the middle of their quarters. Each of the men had family members who had come down with the disease.

"We have to do something," said Kilpatrick. "My wife and baby need good water. We have to go see the captain."

"Wouldn't he have given us better water if they had it?" said Patrick.

"Apparently not," said O'Malley. "It isn't right. The crew has to drink something. They certainly wouldn't tolerate this."

The men pressed Patrick to go with them to confront the captain. They headed up the ladder one at a time. The seas were still turbulent but the heavy torrent of rain had subsided to a wet, dense fog, so thick it was impossible to see more than a few feet ahead. They were confused when they emerged on the main deck. A sailor gave them a contemptuous look as

27

he scurried up the central spar to secure the mainsail. Patrick was in the lead and asked for the captain but the man ignored him.

"You there," came a commanding voice out of the mist.

Patrick strained to see where it came from.

"Over here," said the voice. "State your business."

Like a phantom, a shadowy figure in a tricorn hat appeared above him on a raised deck. Patrick walked toward him with the other three men following behind. He started up the steps.

"Halt right there," said the officer. "No passengers are allowed on the quarter deck."

"We wish to see the captain," said Patrick.

"What about?"

"The drinking water is foul. Fever has broken out and we need fresh water."

"The captain is indisposed and I can assure you there's no other water than what has been provided for you."

"What water are you drinking?" said Patrick.

"That's none of your concern. Your water is in the barrels below and there's plenty of it."

Patrick went forward and started up the few stairs to the deck. From out of nowhere two small, wiry sailors appeared and seized him by the arms. He struggled to free himself. "Easy, Mick," said one of them.

"Let go of me," said Patrick. "I demand to see the captain."

The officer laughed and said, "I'll let him know but don't hold your breath. Now get below before I put all of you in chains."

They never got better water but the rough seas finally diminished a few days later. Passengers were allowed on deck to have fires. Patrick cooked Ellen her first hot meal of potatoes and some beans he was able to procure from Mr. Kilpatrick. He also traded a few potatoes for a ration of oatmeal which eased her nausea and dysentery somewhat. But it wasn't until he made the decision to use some of their money to buy a small ration of pork from one of the crew members that her fever broke. By then, according to scuttlebutt from the sailors, they were about ten days out of New York. It turned out they were correct.

Ellen started feeling better although she was still weak and much too thin. Her appetite returned and she was able to go topside and take in the delicious ocean air. It was just in the nick of time, otherwise she would have been put into quarantine when they landed. As the sun rose on the morning of April the twenty-sixth, 1844, they went on deck and watched, with tremendous relief and gratitude, the city of New York come into view. Their concern now was about Ellen passing the port doctor's examination.

Chapter Five

New York City, April 26, 1844

Patrick and Ellen lined up on the deck of the *Enterprise* with the rest of the passengers and waited to be examined by the doctor. Ellen was pale, emaciated and nervous. If she didn't pass the inspection she would be sent to the quarantine center on Staten Island where the ship was currently docked. She still suffered bouts of nausea and diarrhea but the fever was gone.

Patrick went first. The doctor looked into his mouth and ears and checked for any signs of a rash. Then, without a word, he handed him a document authorizing him to go ashore and said "Next." Ellen moved forward and Patrick held his breath. She looked frightened but their fear was unnecessary. The doctor approved her and motioned to the next in line.

"We've made it Ellen."

"I think I'm going to be sick," she said.

"Not now, please."

Two hours later the ship raised its anchor and proceeded to the harbor. It was late that afternoon when they docked and were finally able to debark. Patrick carried their suitcase and the bundle of cooking utensils. They walked down the gangplank, leaving behind the fear of quarantine and the struggles of the previous two months.

"We're here, Ellen. America! Can you believe it?"

"It's a miracle I think, but we still have to get to Philadelphia."

"There are regular stages from New Jersey. We'll need to take a ferry there first."

"It's getting late," said Ellen. "Will they be running?"

"We'll find out soon enough."

It was after five p.m. when their feet hit the wharf of New York City. They both stumbled and lurched forward. The shock of hitting solid ground after eight weeks on the high seas was too much for their legs. Ellen clutched at Patrick and if he hadn't found and grabbed the rope along the quay they would have fallen face first like drunken sailors.

"I can't walk," said Ellen. "I have no strength below my waist."

"We'll be all right in a bit. Let's stand here until we get our legs back."

They held tight to the rope and edged further away from the gangplank. They had to laugh watching others come down and have the same experience, especially the children who reveled in getting dizzy and falling as if it were a spinning game.

Cork and Liverpool had been impressive and new but they were unprepared for the size and scope of New York. Everywhere they looked there were tall ships, taller buildings, horse drawn freighters and an amazing amount and variety of people, including merchants, dock workers, street hustlers, sailors and new arrivals like themselves. After ten minutes they decided to give it a go. Patrick remembered Uncle John's letter.

"Ellen, stay close. There are pickpockets and swindlers everywhere."

They took a few unsteady steps along the wharf. The feeling was coming back in their legs and they could walk without them buckling. Patrick kept a lookout for a sign or someone to ask about directions to the ferry. The sun was setting and he hoped they could make it to Philadelphia tonight. He heard voices from behind that sounded as familiar as home and in a moment they were descended upon by five rough-looking young men.

"Aye, let me help ya lad," said one.

"A night's lodging for you and the missus," said another. "Just come with us."

A big strapping boy of about seventeen tried to grab the suitcase from his hand. "I'll be helping ya with that, boyo. We'll take ya to Mrs. Fitzsimmons' for a hot meal and a comfortable bed."

It took every ounce of strength Patrick had to prevent him from taking it from him. "Let go!" he said.

"Aye, it'll be all right," said the tough, not releasing his grip. "You'll be needing a place to stay now wontcha?"

"We can take care of ourselves!" said Ellen.

Patrick pulled harder on the case and the boy let go, sending him crashing back on his rear end. The wharf rats laughed long and loud at him as he tumbled to the ground. One of them was putting his hands on Ellen, trying to move her along. He had her by the arm with one hand, the other on the small of her back. Patrick was somehow able to jump to his feet.

"Take your hands off her," he shouted.

Laughing again, they circled around the two of them like a pack of wild dogs smelling the kill. Patrick charged the one manhandling Ellen. He cocked his fist and was about to strike him when the biggest one laid him flat with a blow to the side of his face. He went down in a lump amidst still more laughter. He struggled to clear his head and get back up, ignoring the pain in his jaw. When he got to his feet, he was looking directly at the one who hit him. He was obviously the leader and was now holding their suitcase and bag with a malicious smile on his face.

"Let's just take what they have, Murph," said one of them.

"Yeah, let's get on with it," said another.

"Now, laddie," said Murph, "I'm in a good mood today so I'll give ya both another chance. You'll either come with me to the warm and comfortable lodgings of Mrs. Fitzsimmons, a fine widow from Dublin she is, or we'll just see if you have anything of value in here or maybe hidden somewhere upon you or your fine young lass."

Patrick looked around for help. Hundreds of people crowded the wharf, walking in both directions, but not one paused or even glanced their way. Their attackers were dirty and their clothes were not much more than rags. They were obviously as Irish as he was but there was no pity or compassion whatsoever in them.

"We'll go with you," cried Ellen. "Just leave us alone."

"Aye. That's a good lass," said Murph. "And it will only cost you one U.S. dollar for the convenience."

"We have no dollars," said Patrick.

This caused them all to laugh again. One of the others spoke up. "No problem. We take English sterling. Spanish gold too if need be. We're a regular counting house we are."

"We'll pay you when we get to wherever you're taking us," said Patrick.

"Oh, he's a tough one he is," said Murph. "Since we're all from dear old Ireland, and it's your first day in our fine city, I'm going to allow you to pay on delivery. But the fee just went from five pence to ten."

Patrick started to protest but it was pointless. Murph headed off with their luggage and they had no choice but to follow him. Patrick took Ellen by the arm and hurried to stay close, not knowing if they were really going to a rooming house or into more danger. In a few blocks they were on a street full of seedy wooden structures. They stopped in front of one in need of paint and repair. Patrick thought of trying to grab their things back but by then Murph was already up the short flight of steps and through the door. They started to follow but two of the others got on the steps and blocked them.

After a couple of minutes Murph reappeared, without their bags, and marched directly to Patrick. He got so close their noses were almost touching. His breath was foul and Patrick thought of the stench of the ship they had just departed, which strangely seemed like a long time ago.

"Ten pence, laddie. Now."

He reached into his pocket and pulled out the coin sack. He handed over the money, grabbed Ellen's hand and pushed past him. They went up the steps and into the rooming house as fast as they could move. As the door was closing they heard Murph's voice followed by more laughter.

"Welcome to America."

The bulky form of Mrs. Fitzsimmons greeted them in the parlor. She had gray hair tied in a bun and wore a wide smile that never made it to the dark narrow slits of her eyes.

"Hello, dears," she said, the smile plastered on her face. "Just off the boat are ya? Well you've come to a good safe place to spend the night and get your bearings."

They were exhausted, dirty and angry. Ellen was weak but she'd had enough. "We didn't choose to come here. What is this place, a prison of some sort? How much did you pay those snakes to force us here?"

There was no change in the old woman's expression. "Now, now, lass. Calm yourself. My late husband would be very upset to see a beautiful young redhead from the old country in such a state. I'll be giving you a clean bed and a hot meal for a fair price. Why, there are cheats and liars everywhere. Talk to anyone and they'll tell you that the widow Fitzsimmons is as honest as the day is long."

"We need to get to Philadelphia," said Patrick.

"Of course you do, child. But you'll be needing some nourishment I'm guessing. And a good night's sleep in a bed that doesn't toss and turn with the sea. Now am I right about that?"

Both of them felt the weight of the journey, the experience on the dock, along with a sudden, intense attack of homesickness. Food and sleep were impossible to refuse.

"How much for one night?" said Patrick.

"There's a good lad," said Mrs. Fitzsimmons.

They paid the appalling price of a whole shilling for one night's lodging. Mrs. Fitzsimmons made them get separate rooms despite their insistence that they were brother and sister and couldn't afford two.

They got to their rooms and collapsed on the lumpy mattresses. If the bedclothes had been washed it wasn't recently but it was cleaner and much more comfortable than the ship. Patrick slept like the dead and woke more refreshed than he'd been for the last eight weeks. The morning fare was hotcakes, bacon and coffee. They didn't want to admit it but it was delicious and Ellen was able to eat most of it. After breakfast they asked for directions for the ferry to New Jersey.

"You'll be better off taking the train to Camden," said Mrs. Fitzsimmons. "From there it's a short ferry ride to Philadelphia."

Chapter Six

Kensington, Pennsylvania, April 27, 1844

They followed the directions Mrs. Fitzsimmons gave them to the Camden & Amboy railway station. Patrick got their tickets and they found seats for their first ever train ride. When it lurched out of the station they grabbed hold of each other so as not to fall forward. As it went increasingly faster they couldn't believe how quickly the scenery sped by. Ellen feared that the massive car was going to tip over and kill them. Patrick couldn't help thinking about his brothers and friends back home and how much they would relish taking a ride like this.

"Think about it, Ellen," he said. "We're traveling almost twice the distance from home to Cork Harbor in a matter of hours instead of days. I wish Tom and William were here to see all this."

"I wish they were too," said Ellen. "They could protect us. I'm afraid we'll have more trouble when we get off the train."

"We'll be all right. Make sure you stay right with me."

They arrived in Camden just after noon. It was only a few blocks to the ferry. Patrick kept a sharp lookout for any sign of danger. They fell in with a group of other passengers heading to the wharf. They made it to the ferry and took a place by the railing for the quick trip across the Delaware River.

It was nearly four o'clock when they walked down the ramp and on to the docks of Philadelphia. Patrick declined the shouts of cabbies but did ask one for directions to Germantown Road in Kensington. They went north on Second Street admiring the stately brick homes and buildings of the prosperous City of Brotherly Love. As the sun was setting, they reached the front door of Torpey's Dry Goods.

The store was closed. Patrick banged on the door and after a few moments Uncle John came down from their residence on the upper floors. He greeted them with a big smile and even bigger hugs. He was stocky and shorter than Patrick, with a shiny bald head fringed with a ring of gray hair that still had a few streaks of black running through it. "Ah, it's good to see you children," he said. "Your aunt has been worried sick. She'll be delighted to look upon your faces."

Aunt Mary let out a jubilant squeal as she descended the stairs. She immediately started crying, embracing them repeatedly, all the time asking after their mother, father and every other relative and friend from back home. She didn't stop to hear their answers, until she saw the fatigued expressions on their faces.

"I'm forgetting myself," she said. "Come, children. You'll be wanting a bath and a change of clothes."

"That would be lovely, Aunt Mary," said Ellen.

After they cleaned up, the family gathered around the table. It was way past the dinner hour but Aunt Mary put out some leftover ham and bread. She reminded Ellen so much of her mother. Mary was a bit heavier and older by four years but she had the same brown hair, and pretty, oval face. They didn't know their cousins. Patrick and Ellen were not yet born when the Torpeys left Ireland but it took no time at all before it felt like they'd known each other all their lives.

Robert was twenty-one. He was thin as a rail with black hair and dark brown eyes and the best looking of the Torpey boys. Jimmy was nineteen and greatly resembled his father. His face was just as round and his sandy brown hair was already beginning to thin. He had a ready smile and a constant, mischievous look about him. Nancy, the youngest at seventeen, was slender and beautiful. She had a smooth, ivory complexion and the same dark hair and eyes as her brother, Robert. From the moment they laid eyes on each other, Nancy and Ellen became sisters and best friends. Patrick had a similar connection with Jimmy. The two oldest, Jack and Brian, had their own families. They would meet them tomorrow.

They talked around the table long into the night. Jimmy and Nancy wanted to hear all about the voyage across the ocean. They were the only two in the family that were born in America and they wanted to know every detail. Then Aunt Mary insisted on knowing everything about her sisters, brother, and cousins in Ireland. She cried numerous times over the death of a loved one and over missing her home and family, especially her sister, Sarah.

"They'll be joining us soon, Aunt Mary," said Ellen.

"I can't wait for it to happen. I wish she could have come with you."

"So do I but she'll be so happy that we're here with you."

When it got to be past midnight, Patrick and Ellen could no longer hold their heads up. Right before they went up to bed, the conversation moved to the controversy swirling in Kensington over Bible reading in the public schools. Patrick was surprised and disappointed to learn that there was a virulent, anti-catholic movement here, gaining strength and momentum.

"But isn't there freedom of religion in America?" he said.

"There is, to a certain extent," said Uncle John. "But the Protestants are in control of the schools and only allow the reading of their Bible in class. All we want is for our children to be allowed to read from the

Catholic version."

"It's more than just the Bible reading," said Jimmy. There's a movement of Protestants who call themselves nativists. They think that because they were here first, or that their ancestors were, they have rights that newcomers don't. They want to prevent the likes of you Patrick, from even entering the country."

"When we protest," said Robert, "they shout that we're anti-Bible, or worse, trying to take over the schools and the country. And now, they've scheduled a rally right here in Kensington next week."

Patrick had a hard time believing what he heard. Jimmy noticed it and put a hand on his shoulder.

"Don't worry, Patrick," he said. "We're not taking this lying down. This isn't Ireland and we can, and will, demand our rights. They'll try to prevent you from becoming a citizen and us from getting elected to office because of our religion, but they won't succeed. We'll fight them in the courts and in the streets if we have to."

"That's enough now," said Aunt Mary. "This is a joyous occasion and you're scaring Ellen. No more talk of fighting tonight. Let's get these tired travelers to bed."

Ellen slept with Nancy and Patrick bunked with Robert and Jimmy. The boys continued the discussion from the dinner table. "They're coming here with one intention," said Robert. "To provoke us."

The last thing Patrick heard before sinking into a deep, dreamless sleep, was Jimmy saying, "If it's a fight they want, they're coming to the right place."

In the morning, while the rest of the family was getting ready for church, Uncle John took Patrick aside. They went through a door in the kitchen that led into the store. Patrick was impressed by all the hats, dresses, coats, rolls of fabric, tools and shelves filled with a multitude of other items. Uncle John went to a large glass jar filled with hard candies that was sitting on the long counter. He reached in, took a couple and popped them into his mouth.

"Cinnamon," he said. "I eat them all day long. Your Aunt says I'll be ruining my teeth."

He offered the jar to Patrick. He took one and was unprepared for the sharp, almost bitter taste.

"How much money do you have, lad?" said Uncle John.

"After lodging, and the train and ferry, we've a little over ten pounds."

"Aye. That's not a bad start. You can get maybe fifty acres in one of the remote northwest counties, or in Ohio, for about that much, but you'll need quite a bit more to build a house, buy equipment, stock and the like."

"How much more?"

"I don't rightly know. I'd say a minimum of four times that, plus the money to bring the rest of the family over. Are you sure you want to be a farmer? It's a lot of expense and hard work."

"My father sent me here for land," said Patrick. "It's his dream to have property like our ancestors did, but to keep it forever."

"I understand," said Uncle John. "Why not rent and work existing farm?

"I can't do it, Uncle John. We'll never again be at the mercy of a landlord. My responsibility is to get land. Our own land."

"I think you'll need a steady job for a while before you can afford all you'll need."

"Can I work in the store?"

"Sorry lad but there's no room. Jack and Brian are on their own but the other three work here." Uncle John took another piece of candy, sucked on it for a moment and then said, "One of Jimmy's friends works at his father's shipyard. Donnie is the boy's name. He should be able to get you in to see his father. Hugh Donovan is a difficult man but a respected shipwright. That work would be less of a physical burden than the coal mines and it's right here in town along the wharf. We'll talk to Jimmy about it. In the meantime we should put your money in the store's safe."

Chapter Seven

The family walked the few blocks to St. Michael's and found seats in a pew near the front. The church was ten years old and while not overly ornate, it was larger and more stately than any church Patrick or Ellen had ever been in. Behind the altar was a large, beautiful painting of St. Michael the Archangel brandishing his sword. The pastor, Father Hurley, came out from the sacristy and faced the altar to begin the service.

When it was time for communion, Patrick went up to receive the sacrament. He murmured a short prayer asking for strength to do what he was sent here to do. He experienced the inner glow, as he always did after receiving consecrated wafer representing the flesh and blood of Jesus Christ. It was not something he talked about or completely understood. He knew only that it stirred his soul and make him feel closer to God.

Father Hurley went to the pulpit to give the sermon. He was tall and wide at the shoulders and walked with a slight stoop. His large head, full of stark white hair, contrasted sharply with his broad, ruddy face. Uncle John said he was from County Galway and had been here only a few years. He was loved and respected for the tireless care he gave anyone in need and his strong leadership in defense of their faith. He also possessed the Irishman's gift of gab.

"He could talk the devil out of hell," said Uncle John.

The priest stared out at the congregation for a moment. When he began speaking, he shouted loud enough to shake the rafters. "We've a God-given right! "A God-given right, dears!" he repeated, slamming his fist so hard on the lectern that Patrick thought it might shatter into pieces.

"The right to practice our religion, just as they practice theirs, without interference, bigotry or political maneuverings. Make no mistake, they are heretics, and yet we're not trying to change laws to prevent them from the free expression of their faith. We cannot, stand idly by and allow them to force their beliefs on our children."

A strong undertone of agreement spread through the church.

"We know," he continued, "That they're coming into our midst on Friday. I caution you to act in a reasonable manner. Do not take the bait and resort to violence. That is what they want, to paint us as barbaric and vicious. Let them have their show while we work with Bishop Kendrick, the school board and the legislature to resolve our grievances."

There was another buzzing of voices, though this time Patrick noticed a negative cast to it. Father Hurley let that pass and moved on to other matters: the dangers of excessive drinking, personal penitence and eternal salvation. He ended with an appeal for money, any amount one could give, to help the poor and work towards opening a school of their own. When the service was over he greeted his parishioners on the front steps as they filed out.

"Excellent sermon, Father," said Jimmy. "But don't we have a right to defend ourselves?"

"Let's hope it doesn't come to that, James. There's a council meeting this Wednesday. Please try to make it. We have some ideas about starting our own parish school and petitioning for the same government funds that the Protestant's receive."

"I'll try," said Jimmy.

"The priest smiled at Patrick and Eileen. "And who are these two fine looking young redheads with you?"

Uncle John put his arms around Ellen and Patrick and eased them forward. "This is our niece, Ellen, and her brother, Patrick. They've just arrived from County Cork."

"Pleased to meet you, Father," said he and Ellen at the same time.

"How are you faring in your new home?" said the priest.

"Fine thank you, Father," said Patrick. "But my sister and I are surprised by this conflict with the Protestants."

"It's unfortunate, lad. Old prejudices die a long, slow death and they have been given new life here."

"So it is no different here than in Ireland under the British?"

"Not quite. The extraordinary American Constitution guarantees our freedoms. We have the ability to fight back through peaceful and lawful means. We can organize, protest and, those who are citizens, can vote. That's the power we have to use."

"I was told it takes five years before I can become a citizen."

Uncle John and Father Hurley exchanged glances. Uncle John answered. "The Native Americans, as they call their political party, are attempting to change the law so that it takes much longer."

"Come to our meeting, Patrick," said Father Hurley. "We'll be discussing all of it further there."

When they got home, Ellen was worn out and Aunt Mary made her go upstairs to rest. Patrick was tired too but he realized they hadn't talked about finding work. He mentioned it to Jimmy, who said, "Well, cousin, let's go see Donnie now."

Robert and Jimmy took Patrick around the corner to the Nanny Goat Market. "If I know Donnie Donovan," said Robert, "he'll be at the market trying to find a girl or two to impress."

Patrick stopped when they came upon a flyer posted on the side of a building. It was a nativist broadside denouncing the Irish as alcohol-soaked animals, corrupt papists and sexual deviants. Jimmy ripped it down.

"This is what we're up against, Patrick."

Patrick was instantly disgusted and angry. "I thought this was about Bible reading in the schools."

"Oh, it's much more than that," said Jimmy.

"We'll be having our own meeting about this," said Robert. "We've formed a brotherhood based out of the firehouse. We're calling ourselves The Avengers and we won't take this lying down. You can depend on that."

"You need to join us, Patrick," said Jimmy. "It's about your future even more than ours. They'll try to deport you if they can, or make it impossible for you to vote."

Patrick thought of the last words his father said to him. He didn't want to do anything that might prevent him from his task. "I need work and then I need to find a good piece of land."

"All the more reason for you to be involved," said Jimmy.

Chapter Eight

Jimmy crumpled the flyer and threw it on the ground. They walked across the street to the market. West Kensington bordered the Delaware River and included a section known as Fishtown. There were a few rundown shanties, but for the most part Patrick saw rows of clean, well kept shops and homes. Along the riverfront there were shipbuilders and a constant stream of fishing boats leaving and returning with their catches of the river's abundant shad.

His cousins seemed to know everyone. They were greeted with nods, waves and shouts from friends on the opposite side of the street. They responded mostly with a tip of their tall hats. Patrick wore a shabby, short-brimmed cap which was a hand-me-down from his brother, William. His shirt and pants were just as old and worn. He felt awkward and had a distinct desire for a new hat and clothes. He dismissed it, knowing he needed to make money, not spend it.

The Nanny Goat Market, on the corner of Washington and Master Streets, was the heart of the community. Residents went there to shop, mingle and get the latest news and gossip. The building had a wooden roof and was open at both ends. It ran the length of the entire block. The wide center aisle was lined on both sides with produce, meat, clothing and household items. Like every Sunday, it was noisy and crowded. Out in front, Patrick noticed three pretty young women being entertained by a smartly dressed, dark-haired young man.

"There he is," said Jimmy."

His real name was Hugh Donovan Jr. but ever since he was a boy everyone, except his father, called him Donnie. He had a carefree way about him and was always quick with a smile and a joke. In conversations, he leaned back slightly and tilted his head to one side with an expression of curiosity that indicated he couldn't wait to hear what you had to say next. He saw his friends and waved them over.

"If it isn't the Torpey boys out for a stroll on this fine afternoon. And who do you have there with you? Looks as if he's fresh off the boat."

Jimmy and Robert tipped their hats to the girls, who giggled in response. Patrick shyly did the same. "This is our cousin, Patrick Ryan," said Jimmy. "And you're right. He and his sister, Ellen, just arrived from County Cork."

"And why didn't you bring her around with you then? I'm sure she's the prettier of the lot."

The hair on Patrick's neck pricked up thinking about the thugs at the dock. It must have shown because Donnie smiled and stuck out his hand. "Come on, Pat," he said. "All in good fun. I speak the same way about the beautiful Nancy Torpey and her brothers take it fine."

"That's true enough," said Robert.

"Welcome to the great state of Pennsylvania," said Donnie. "How are you settling in?"

Patrick loosened up and shook his hand. "Good so far."

"He needs a job, Donnie," said Robert.

"Of course he does."

"We thought you could speak to your father about him," said Jimmy.

For a split second, the smile on Donnie's face tightened. He turned to the girls and asked if he could catch up with them later. They gave him mock sad faces and walked into the market. "You boys sure know how to foul up a good thing,"

"Donnie's a desperate man, Patrick," said Jimmy. "Most of the girls run when they see him coming."

"Yes," said Donnie. "They run towards me, begging for my attention."

Robert and Jimmy laughed. Patrick did too, and decided that he liked Donnie Donovan after all.

"Well," said Donnie. "You know my father doesn't think all that much of my abilities or my friends either, for that matter."

"Patrick here is a hard worker," said Jimmy. "He's smart, and steadfast."

"There's plenty of work on the railroad or the canals," said Donnie.

"True," said Robert. "But what kind of family would we be if we couldn't keep him from that back-breaking torment."

"It isn't easy work at the shipyard, boys. He'd be lifting, hauling and hammering all day long. And if he didn't catch on immediately my father would be rid of him and then make my life miserable."

Patrick thought it was time to speak for himself. "I don't know anything about building boats but I'm strong and a quick learner. I'll work like the devil and then some. My family is depending on me to buy land and bring them over so you see Donnie, I can't fail."

"No offense, Pat, but yours is the same story as every other poor beggar streaming into Philadelphia. Our family arrived nearly a hundred years ago and my father's always preaching about our hard-won success and the fear that this new wave of outsiders will somehow set us back."

"So you won't talk to him then?" said Jimmy.

"I didn't say that. I just want you to know that it may not work out. Come round to the wharf tomorrow morning about ten, Pat, and you can have at him. Be on your best behavior."

"Thank you, Donnie," said Patrick. "I'll be there."

Before they left, Robert said, "Will we see you at the meeting at the hose house Tuesday night?"

"You truly want me to provoke the old man don't you? If he finds out I'm involved with you louts he might just sack me, maybe even disown me."

"So you won't be there?"

"I wouldn't miss it for all the tea in India."

They all laughed. Donnie took off into the market looking for his lady friends while the three cousins went to the firehouse to show Patrick around. It was a deep but narrow, four story building made of brick and wood. The bottom floor contained a large pump wagon with stalls in the rear for the horses. There were tall windows on each of the upper three stories. The name Hibernia was carved into the cornice at the top of the building. To be accepted as a volunteer member of the Hibernian Hose Company was a sign of prominence in the neighborhood.

"If you want to join us," said Jimmy, "you'll have to be voted in."

Patrick liked the idea of learning the equipment, meeting the rest of the lads and being a part of something in his new home.

Chapter Nine

In the morning, Jimmy took Patrick down to the wharf to Donovan's Shipyard. They found Donnie in the gaping hull of a merchant ship being built for a Canadian lumber company. Donnie saw them approach and went out to meet them.

"Top o' the mornin' gentlemen," he said.

"Back at ya, Donnie boy," said Jimmy. "Did you talk to your father?"

"I did. He isn't happy about it but we're getting an order for two frigates from the Spanish Government and can use a few more people. Otherwise he wouldn't give you the time of day. As it is you'll probably only have a few minutes Pat, so put your best foot forward."

"I will," he said. All of a sudden he was anxious. He had worked his whole life but it was on a little farm. This was different. They walked from the dry dock into the rear of a large warehouse where there was a narrow staircase.

"You wait here, Jimmy," said Donnie.

Patrick followed him up the stairs. At the top, Donnie knocked on the door and waited to go in until a gruff voice yelled, "Come in."

Behind a long, flat table filled with drawings and plans stood a heavyset man of about fifty-five, though he could have been older. It was hard to tell. He was bent over the desk but his narrow eyes focused on Patrick with a surly, impatient stare. He looked irritated and angry and Patrick's mouth went a little dry.

"Dad," said Donnie. "This is who I was telling you about. His name is Patrick Ryan, John and Mary Torpey's nephew. Patrick, this is my father,

Mr. Hugh Donovan."

"Thank you for seeing me, sir."

Hugh Donovan said nothing. He looked Patrick up and down as if he was a horse he was contemplating buying. The sour expression on his face never changed. He heaved a resigned sigh as if he'd made up his mind about something. A heaviness came over Patrick as he stood there waiting.

"John Torpey," said Mr. Donovan. "Who owns the dry goods store?"

"Yes..." said Donnie but his father held up his hand.

"He can answer for himself."

"Yes, sir. Aunt Mary is my mother's sister. My sister and I got here a few days ago and we're staying with them until we get settled."

"Settled? What does that mean?"

"I have a little savings to buy some land for us to start a farm but we need more money to do that and to bring the family over."

"Hmmm," said Mr. Donovan. "Do you think this is an alms house I run here?"

Patrick started to respond but was cut off.

"You people are overrunning this town and this country. My grandfather started this business and I've worked hard to keep it growing and maintain my reputation. We don't need more shanty Irish coming here, looking for handouts and provoking the good people of Kensington and Philadelphia."

"Mr. Donovan, I assure you..."

"Every last one of you comes here with the same story. Then you wind up on the street, drunk and destitute."

"That's not me, Mr. Donovan."

"John Torpey's an agitator. And those boys of his are troublemakers for sure. I don't need that around here."

"I'll work hard and..."

"How long do you think it will take you to accomplish your goal on the salary you'd be making?

Patrick's cheeks flushed. Hugh Donovan apparently wasn't going to hire him and was only using him to vent his anger. He had to control himself but he wasn't going to be pushed around. The heavy feeling lifted. He stood up straighter and spoke without caring whether he was impressing him or not. "I don't intend to stay at the bottom, sir. I can read and write and I'll learn everything I possibly can in order to improve myself and my station. I was told one can do that in America."

Hugh Donovan's face didn't change but his eyes did. The distaste and derision that were there shifted to something different. Maybe it was respect. As much as he loathed the flood of immigrants invading the country, he was proud of the story of his grandfather who came to America with nothing. Perhaps he recognized a young man with a similar desire. Something he didn't see in his own son.

"This isn't easy work," he said. "You'll get no favors from me. In fact, being a friend of my son's here is not the best recommendation you could have."

Patrick glanced at Donnie, whose face blanched though his expression didn't change. "All right then," said Mr. Donovan. "You've wasted enough of my time. Report to Hugh Jr. tomorrow at seven sharp. If you're late, don't bother coming at all. I'll give you a chance but I will not tolerate tardiness, laziness or trouble of any kind. Understood?"

"Yes, Mr. Donovan. Thank you. I won't disappoint..."

But Hugh Donovan's mind was back on his work, engrossed in the drawings on his desk. Patrick was surprised to say the least. He looked at Donnie who motioned with his head toward the door. When they got down to the shop floor, Jimmy was waiting.

"Well?" he said.

"That was interesting," said Donnie. "I think he actually liked Patrick here, although I can't say why."

Jimmy laughed. "I know he hates me. Well, did you get the job?"

"I did," said Patrick. "I start tomorrow morning."

"Excellent. Let's go home and give my parents and your sister the good news."

"Thank you, Donnie," said Patrick. "I'm in your debt."

"Just work hard, Pat. If you don't the old man will take it out on me."

"I promise you that won't happen."

"See you at the meeting tomorrow, Donnie," said Jimmy.

"Ah, things have changed. I'm going dancing with Catherine Callahan that night."

"You can go dancing anytime Donnie. You said you'd be there. We need every able-bodied man we can get."

"Maybe you should find yourself a good girl, Torpey, and leave the rest of us be."

"You'll be there then?"

"I'll see. I can come before the dance. My father won't like it."

"He doesn't have to know does he?" said Jimmy.

Donnie sighed again. Patrick felt sorry for him and thought of his own father who had always been firm but with an abundance of love and support.

"No, he doesn't" said Donnie, his cocky smile back in place. "I'll see you boys there. Now get out of here. If the tyrant spies us gabbing he'll dock my wages. Don't be one minute late tomorrow Pat, and be prepared for a long, hard day."

Chapter Ten

Philadelphia, April 29, 1844

Isaac Holmes, George Shiffler and Joe Cox passed the whiskey around while they waited for the rest of their friends from the Carrol Fire Brigade. They were across the street from the Fox Temperance Hall where Lewis Levin of the Native American Party was holding tonight's meeting. Isaac took a sip, wiped his mouth and handed the bottle to George.

"The only quarrel I have with Mr. Levin," he said, "is his obsession with abstinence."

"I'll stand with Levin," said George. He's leading the charge against these damn immigrants. Maybe if we ban potatoes and booze they'll just go away. It would be a small price to pay."

Joe laughed and took a long pull on the bottle. "We can handle our drinking. It's the Irish that get falling down drunk, sleep in alleyways and piss themselves."

"The meeting's about to start," said Isaac. "We should go in. We can meet up with the rest of the boys later."

They polished off the whiskey and went inside. The hall was filled to capacity with over three hundred men. Levin ran the nativist newspaper, the *Philadelphia Sun,* which was dedicated to eradicating two things: alcohol from society, and Catholic immigrants from the pure Protestant Republic of America. The fact that no one questioned why a Jew was so adamant about preserving Protestant principles was curious but never came up, or slowed Levin down in the least.

Two speakers preceded Levin to discuss party business and

appointments to various positions. The movement was spreading and gaining members in New York, Baltimore, Boston and even New Orleans. They reminded everyone of the rally this coming Friday in the Third Ward of Kensington to protest the Catholics' attempt at removing the Bible from the public school.

Isaac leaned forward and nodded at George. The meeting was to be held within sight of the Hibernian Hose House. "Let's hope the Torpey boys show up," said Isaac.

"You know they will," said George

Three weeks earlier both fire companies arrived at a house fire on the border of the Second and Third Wards of Kensington. The Hibernians beat the Carrol men by a few minutes. Rival fire departments competed for insurance money and a brawl broke out between them over whose blaze it was. Being the first to respond and extinguish the flames was crucial to getting paid. The Hibernians won the fight that night.

Isaac had been smashed on the head with a club by Robert Torpey and he wanted revenge so much he could taste it. He hated all the Torpeys, but Robert most of all. He was the worst, more arrogant even than his father, who years ago won a dispute in court with Isaac's father over payment for some rugs. The Holmes' were carpet manufacturers, struggling to be successful in a city full of weavers. John Torpey refused to pay for the rugs he purchased, claiming they were defective. After winning the case, the Torpeys never missed an opportunity to besmirch the Holmes' family name.

The Reverend Joshua Campbell from the First Presbyterian Church came out on the stage and led them in the Lord's Prayer. Then he introduced Levin.

"Let us welcome the man who has taken up the righteous banner of our Lord and Savior, Jesus Christ who commanded us to lead his church over all her enemies. Give him your attention, and your commitment to triumph over the ascendency of Popery in our beloved country. Here now is Mr. Lewis Levin, the founder and guiding light of our Native American Party."

Isaac joined the rest of the audience in a rousing ovation as Levin walked to the podium. He was of average height with dark hair and eyes. His sturdy, well proportioned body added to his commanding presence. He raised his hand, which held his reading glasses, and the crowd went quiet.

He put his glasses on and said, "Gentlemen, thank you for coming. These are perilous times. America is in imminent danger. It is to be the battleground to vanquish our Republican institutions from within. If the anti-Christ, who calls himself Pope, is allowed to succeed we will be forced to live in a government where church and state are joined under a single tyrant. If they gain power, the Catholics will unleash another deadly Inquisition right here in our homeland."

He went on about changing the law from five to twenty-one years residency in order to become a citizen. "And no foreign born person," he declared, "should be able to hold office, even if he is already naturalized. Most importantly, no Catholic should be allowed to be elected to anything, ever!"

Isaac, George and Joe stood up and cheered with the rest of the crowd while Levin basked in the applause. When they sat back down, he continued speaking for an hour and a half, emphasizing the importance of voting for nativist candidates in the approaching elections. Lastly, he advised them against drinking.

"Temperance, men. Our work requires a clean body and a clear head.

We cannot be seen to be base and wild like those the Pope has sent here to be plied with alcohol before being directed to the ballot box, still reeking of drink and the stench of steerage from the ships that brought them here. They must be stopped!"

He was given another standing ovation. Before he left the stage he reminded them one more time of the next meeting. "We'll assemble at the State House Friday afternoon and march together to Kensington. The papists will see the force that is aligned against them and the futility of their scheme. It is to be peaceful so I remind you again, no drinking."

After the meeting, Isaac and his friends met up with more of their fellow firemen. "Do you think he's serious about being peaceful?" said Joe.

"It's what he has to say," said Isaac. "But I for one am not going there without the ability to defend myself."

"You know all those Mick bastards will be ready for a fight," said George. "That's all they know anyway."

"Why else are we going there?" said Isaac. "A rally can be held anywhere. I think Mr. Levin knows exactly what he's doing."

"What's that?" said Joe.

"Intimidation," said Isaac.

"What about the drinking part?" said George.

"Well, I can't see how a little nip could hurt, do you?" said Isaac.

Chapter Eleven

Kensington, April 30, 1844

Patrick reported fifteen minutes early for his first day of work at Donovan's Shipyard. Donnie greeted him with a nod and put him right to work with a hammer and nails in the same ship's hull from the day before. He had Patrick follow him up a ladder to a scaffold at the top of the immense bare frame that looked like a giant skeleton of some prehistoric mammoth. Mr. Donovan arrived, scowling and looking for his son. When he saw him he shouted, "Hugh. My office. Now!"

Donnie winked at Patrick as he started down the scaffold. "It's going to be another long day," he said. "Keep on hammering nails into these long boards that connect each side of the frame. If you run out of nails, see Seamus over there."

Patrick followed his outstretched arm to a tiny, emaciated man on the opposite end of the scaffolding. He might have been forty-five or sixty-five. It was impossible to tell. He was not quite five feet tall and couldn't have weighed more than eighty-five pounds. Seamus glared at him with a face that hadn't formed a smile since before Patrick was born.

"Don't worry," said Donnie. "Seamus hates everyone. He's harmless unless he's been drinking, and he's almost always sober on the job."

Patrick went to work and within ten minutes he was drenched in sweat and his back ached from bending over. When he stopped and stretched, he was greeted with a harsh, "Keep hammerin" from Seamus.

By the end of the day he was exhausted. Every muscle hurt and he had the thought that he may never be able to stand up straight again. It was just after five o'clock when he walked out into the cool evening air to find Jimmy waiting for him.

"You look like a crippled old man," said Jimmy. "It's a good thing we didn't find you a job on the railroad now isn't it?"

"I was thinking the same thing. I can't wait for dinner and a nice, comfortable bed."

"Dinner will have to be quick. We're having our meeting at the hose house."

"I'm not feeling up to it, Jimmy."

"You'll get your second wind. Brian specifically asked me to bring you."

The house smelled delicious when they walked inside. Aunt Mary was cooking a pork roast complete with fried potatoes and corn soup. Patrick's two other cousins, Jack and Brian were sitting around the table with the rest of the family. Only Ellen was missing. She tried but nearly fainted coming down the stairs. Aunt Mary made her go back to bed, telling her she'd bring up a tray a little later.

Jack and Brian stood up and shook hands with Patrick. Jack, the oldest, was slender and dark-haired like Robert and Nancy but his nose and freckled face reminded Patrick of his uncle Kevin, back in Ireland. Brian, a year younger than Jack, was slightly taller than his father but with the same build and thin, sandy hair like Jimmy. He exuded strength and confidence. Up until two years ago, Uncle John had been the chief of the Hibernian Hose House, but now Brian was their leader.

Aunt Mary told everyone to sit as she set the food on the table. Patrick dug into the roast like a starving man. Uncle John laughed. "Slow down, lad. You'll make yourself sick."

After asking about his first day on the job, the conversation went to the nativists. Uncle John continued to urge restraint.

"We will, Da," said Brian. "But it won't be easy."

Even though he wanted nothing more than a good night's sleep, Patrick went to the meeting with his cousins. As they walked to the firehouse, the image of their little farm back home came to him and a pang of homesickness mingled with an unbidden rise of resentment for the burden his father put on him. Lost in thought, he didn't hear Jimmy the first time he called his name. Jimmy stopped and said it louder.

"Patrick!"

"Aye?"

"You haven't said a word or given us your opinion."

"I don't know what to think. I wasn't prepared for all this."

"Well," said Jack. "Are you with us?"

"Of course I'm with you. But what about what Uncle John and Father Hurley said? It makes sense to me."

"Probably because you just arrived here," said Brian.

"Yeah," said Jimmy. "My father has done a tremendous amount for our community but he's getting old, and maybe a little soft."

"Don't let him hear you say that, Jimmy boy," said Robert. "He'll show you how soft he is."

"You know what I mean," said Jimmy. "I remember when he was the first one to fight. Now he wants peace."

"Isn't that what we all want?" said Patrick.

"No, cousin," said Jimmy. "We want to show these holier than thou hypocrites that we won't be pushed around."

All twenty-eight members of the Hibernian Hose House were in attendance. The anger in the air was palpable but what shocked Patrick was the stockpile of weapons on the second floor. Against the walls were all manner of muskets, pistols, knives and clubs. A mound of rocks and brickbats took up the center of the room.

Patrick followed his cousins up to the third floor. Brian and Jack led the way through the men amidst loud greetings and thumps on the back. The two of them stepped up on to the platform and Brian moved to the front edge. He raised his hands for everyone to quiet down. He let the silence fill the air before speaking.

"We've been advised to control ourselves."

The room erupted in boos and jeers. Brian waited for quiet. "Listen!" he said. "We *will* defend ourselves. But for now, we'll continue to store our weapons. There'll be guards on the second floor and no one will have access to them unless, and until, it's decided that we have no choice. We won't be the ones to start this fight."

There were grumblings but for the most part the men seem to accept Brian's orders.

Jack raised up a nativist flyer and said, "They'll be gathering across the street. Meet back here Friday no later than five o'clock."

The group slowly dispersed. At the stairs Uncle John greeted the men and encouraged them to stay in control of themselves. When the room was nearly empty, he motioned for Patrick and his sons to stay for a moment.

"That was excellent, Brian," he said.

"I don't know, Da," he said. "They're angry. We're all angry."

"Stay strong, son. The rabble coming here don't represent the majority of Protestants."

"I'm not sure most Protestants don't hate us," said Brian. "And I won't bow to them anymore than the rest of the men will."

When he met Donnie at work the next morning, Patrick realized he hadn't seen him at the meeting. "I was there," he said. "In the back with your uncle and heard Brian and Jack speak. I left as soon as the meeting broke up. If you remember, I had more important things to attend to."

Patrick reported to Seamus for his day's assignment. He worked hard, harder than he ever had before. Not so much physically. He was used to farm labor and the sawing, scraping, sanding and hammering were not that much different. It was the pace. Seamus never let him rest, other than for food in the middle of the day, and even that was rushed. At the end of the day, he dragged himself home, ate dinner, and headed upstairs to bed.

He found his sister at the small desk near the window in Nancy's room. "My letter is finished," said Ellen. "You need to write yours so we can send them together. You know Ma and Da will be beside themselves with worry."

"We've only been here a week, Ellen."

"We should have written as soon as we docked in New York."

"One week isn't going to make that much difference." He looked closer at his sister. "You seem to be improving."

"I do feel better. I'm getting stronger but can't get rid of this horrid flux. When do you think we can bring the family over?"

"I'm not sure. I'll have to tell Da it's going to take longer than we thought. I suppose they could come before we get the farm."

"You need to get a letter to him as soon as possible. He needs to know that."

"I'll get it done by Sunday. I promise."

Chapter Twelve

Kensington, May 3, 1844

Jimmy walked with Patrick to work on Friday morning. There was a noticeable buzz in the air. People on the street were talking about the Protestants coming and Jimmy was galvanized and animated.

"Come directly to the firehouse after work," he said. "And bring Donnie with you. I've been worried about him. I think his father is getting under his skin. Has he said anything to you?"

"I hardly see him. He's all over the shop if he isn't out on errands or upstairs being reprimanded by Mr. Donovan."

"Talk to him today will you? We need to be completely united."

He saw Donnie as soon as he walked into the shipyard. "Morning, Pat. How are things? Seamus says you aren't terrible. That's a good sign."

"Thanks, Donnie. Jimmy wants to know if you'll be coming to the firehouse this evening."

"I want to be there, but the old man's been all over me. He's adamant that I not get involved. And I'll tell you this. If he finds out that you're part of it, you'll be out of a job."

Patrick's stomach tightened. He needed the money and he also liked learning this new craft. But the idea that he might be punished for standing up for his family got to him.

At the lunch hour, Mr. Donovan had the entire crew assemble at the bottom of the stairs to his office. "There's going to be some trouble in town today," he said. "If I find out that any of you are involved, you'll no longer be welcome here."

Patrick thought he was talking directly to him. "My family and I," continued Mr. Donovan, "have worked too long and too hard and I'll not have any drunks in my employ do anything to destroy what we've achieved."

Patrick didn't like being threatened. He couldn't stop himself from speaking. "Begging your pardon, sir, but what exactly do you mean?"

Mr. Donovan was not accustomed to being questioned. His face flushed and contorted in anger. "I mean, Mr. Ryan, that if you, or anyone else here, participates in any violent action against these people who are coming here in a legal assembly, you'll be dismissed from my employment immediately."

Patrick wanted to ask more. He wanted to understand why Mr. Donovan would be on the side of people who despised his religion and his fellow Irishmen. But he held his tongue and glanced at Donnie, raising his eyebrows to ask what he was going to do. Donnie just curled his lip in disgust as he turned and went about other business.

At the end of the day Patrick put away his tools and headed out on to the street. He stopped off at home before going to the hose house. Aunt Mary, Ellen and Nancy were the only ones there. They were sitting in the kitchen, upset and worried.

"We're glad you're home," said Nancy.

"I'm not staying," he said.

Ellen took hold of his arm above the elbow. "Don't go, Patrick."

"I have to."

"You'll only get in trouble, or hurt. Please don't."

"What kind of man would I be then? Would Uncle John and our cousins ever respect me again?"

"What about the rest of us?" said Ellen. "Ma, Da, and everyone back home who are counting on you?"

"I think they'd want me to be a man first, Ellen. Don't you see? I have to stand with them. Enough talk. I'll see you later."

On his way to the hose house he saw a crowd of two hundred nativists mingling and setting up a platform for their speakers. Across the street a throng of men and boys with clubs and brickbats in their hands congregated in and around the Nanny Goat market.

Patrick met Jimmy and Robert on the second floor. The weapons were still piled there but there were less of them now. They heard shouts from outside and went to the window just as the nativists began to scatter and run. Screaming and cursing locals chased after them, swinging their clubs until they were completely out of the neighborhood.

"That was easy," said Robert.

"Too easy," said Jimmy. "There'll be a lot more of them next time."

At breakfast the following morning, Robert read aloud from an article in the *Sun* announcing that they would indeed be back.

The American Republicans of Philadelphia, who support the NATIVE AMERICANS in their Constitutional Rights of peaceably assembling to express their opinions on Public Policy, and to Protest the Assaults by ALIENS AND FOREIGNERS are requested to assemble on Monday Afternoon, May 6th, at 3 o'clock, at the corner of Master and Second street, in Kensington, to express their indignation at the outrage perpetrated by the Irish Catholics, in tearing and trampling of the American Flag, and to take the necessary steps to prevent a repetition of it.

Chapter Thirteen

May 6, 1844

On Monday morning Patrick worked with Donnie who showed him how a hull is structured and secured together. Then he got a chance to help with the critical job of caulking. At half past noon, Mr. Donovan shouted from the top of the stairs of his office for everyone to gather together.

"He's going to send everyone home," said Donnie. "He's afraid for the safety of the yard. Only a few of us will remain to guard the place."

When the crew was assembled, Mr. Donovan addressed them. "I'm closing down for the day. You'll be paid for half a days work. Go home and stay indoors. I remind you again that if I find you're participating in any sort of violence you will no longer work here."

"What are you going to do, Donnie?" asked Patrick.

"I have to stay here. I'd go if I could. Tell Jimmy and the boys that, won't you, Pat?"

Patrick nodded.

"And you'd better hope the old man doesn't find out you're involved," said Donnie.

Every store was closed and houses were shut up tight. The streets were filled with men and boys carrying every kind of weapon. Despite the sky darkening with the clouds of an incoming storm, Patrick sensed a festive feeling, especially among the boys, as if it was a holiday of some sort.

On the way up the stairs of the hose house he noticed that the stacked weapons were gone. All that remained was the pile of rocks. The third floor was filled with men, shouting, and pacing back and forth brandishing their muskets and handguns. Patrick joined Jimmy and Robert who were at the windows. Jimmy pointed up the street and Patrick saw a horde stretching back as far as he could see marching toward them.

"Here they come," said Jimmy.

The sky swirled and rolled with billows of menacing, black clouds rumbling directly towards Kensington. Three thousand native-born Protestants, and at least one Jew, marched in unison up Second Street. It looked as if they were bringing the tempest with them. A sickening bile rose from Patrick's stomach to the back of his mouth.

"The bastards are singing," said Jack.

Patrick recognized the tune. It was "The Boyne Water" which celebrated the victory of the Protestant, William of Orange over the Catholic James II in 1690. It struck him hard that this was a war that had been going on for centuries. He dropped any doubt about joining the fight. It was being brought to him anyway, maybe by God himself judging by the turbulent sky. Just when he realized he had no weapon, Jimmy opened his jacket and brought out a large handgun.

"It's a Colt revolver," he said. "Just pull the trigger."

"I've never fired a gun before, Jimmy."

"Just aim and shoot but remember you only have five bullets."

The Protestants arrived and crammed into the lot. Another small platform had been assembled and Louis Levin stepped up on it. When he started speaking, three neighborhood men with wheelbarrows full of wet manure bulled to the front of the crowd. They dumped their loads and were immediately descended upon and beaten to the ground. The melee was on. As if on cue, the skies opened up and a torrent of rain poured down.

Many of the Protestants ran for the Nanny Goat Market, the closest shelter, to escape the downpour. It was filled with Catholics, who saw their arrival as a battle charge. Swarms of men armed with clubs and pikes clashed together, moving and fighting in every direction. Bricks soared at the hose house and Patrick crouched to avoid being struck by the shattering glass. A shot rang out like a bolt of lightning from somewhere down on the street.

"That's it," shouted Brian. "Let 'em have it!"

Musket fire exploded from inside the building and Protestants down below returned fire. Patrick raised his pistol and shot down into the mob. He lowered his head after firing, then rose up and shot again, never sure if he actually hit anyone. After a few times, he stopped and scanned the scene. Amidst the pandemonium, he saw his uncle trying to get through to the firehouse. Two laughing, teenaged boys descended on him with their clubs, knocking him over.

Patrick shouted for Jimmy and pointed out his father who was struggling to get up and fight back. Jimmy cursed, called out to Robert and they both jumped up and ran to the stairs. Patrick followed behind them.

Outside, it was impossible to see anything but bodies running in every direction. Stones and brickbats flew at the Protestants still in the lot while vicious combat went on between individuals with fists and clubs. Shots pinged off the building walls and thudded into bodies. Patrick almost lost sight of his cousins as they waded into the mob. When he caught up to them they were picking their father up off the ground. His left eye was half shut and swollen and his nose was bleeding profusely. His right ear was cut, the lobe dangling by a thread, but he was alive.

"I'm all right, boys," he said. "They're trying to get to St. Michael's to burn it down. We have to get over there."

"Get into the firehouse, Da," said Jimmy.

"Let's get him home," said Robert, "so Ma can take care of him."

Jimmy held him by one arm and Patrick grabbed the other. Robert's face twisted with fury. He picked up his father's hat and handed it to him. "I'm going to get the bastards who did this," he said.

"Do you know who they were?" said Patrick.

"I saw Isaac Holmes here on the street."

"Are you sure it was him?" said Jimmy."

"It doesn't matter. Some other nativist can pay for it."

"Wait for us, Robert," said Jimmy. "We'll get Da cleaned up and head over to the church."

Robert bent over and picked up a long pike that was laying on the ground. "I'm not waiting," he said. "I'll find you later." Patrick watched him weigh into the crowd, striking at any and every nativist within his reach.

The Torpey place was only around the corner but it took a long time to drag Uncle John through the mayhem. Their street was quiet and they made it to the house and took him upstairs and into bed. Aunt Mary was frantic at first but then took charge, ordering Nancy to get bandages and Ellen to fetch some water and antiseptic. She cleaned the gash on his head and wrapped it and his ear up.

Jimmy looked at Patrick and said, "Let's go."

Jimmy led the way through an alley that connected Germantown and Cadwalader Streets, avoiding the area of the market and the firehouse. They headed west on Jefferson. The rioting had not yet made it to this section though the gunshots and uproar from the few blocks away sounded like a full scale war. When they reached the church, Father Hurley was on the front steps, directing women and children inside, hoping the sanctuary of the

70

building would keep them out of harm's way.

"Are you all right, Father?" asked Jimmy.

"Yes. Are they coming this way?"

"Not yet. We'll send some of the boys back over to guard the church as soon as we can."

"Thanks, lads. Be careful."

They headed back toward the firehouse, stopping first at the market. Defiant Protestants remained in the lot, armed and formed up like a squad of soldiers. Patrick saw the American Flag still waving where it had been planted for their assembly.

"That's Holmes," said Jimmy, "and the rest of the Carrol House brigade."

Patrick didn't know who they were and at that moment didn't care. He spied Robert and some of the other Hibernian boys firing muskets at them from the sides of the market and the nearby buildings. Holmes, wearing a military frock and a feathered hat, was in command. He stood to one side of their formation and pointed his sword. In one deafening blast the front group fired, then went to the rear. The next line moved forward and raised their weapons. Before they could get off their volley, shots were returned from every window, alley, and corner.

A couple of the Carrol men went down and their resolve weakened. George Schiffler grabbed the flag, and they began to retreat from the area. As they ran Catholics fired and Patrick saw Schiffler fall and the flag with him. Holmes bent over to help him up. He couldn't do it himself. His friend was dead. He grabbed him by the arms while another man grabbed his legs. They struggled to carry him back down Cadwalader Street and out of the battle zone.

Patrick and Jimmy ran over to join Robert in front of the market. For the moment, there was a lull in the fighting. The rain picked up again, coming down in sheets, and most of the nativists fled for shelter and to regroup.

"We should check back on the family," said Patrick.

"You two go," said Robert. "I'll go meet up with Brian and Jack."

"Have Brian send some of the boys to guard St. Michael's," said Jimmy.

"I will. See you back at the hose house," said Robert.

Chapter Fourteen

Uncle John was in bed, angry for not being out there helping his sons and neighbors. When they walked in he tried to get up.

"Stay there," said Aunt Mary with a force that surprised everyone, especially her husband, who did as he was told.

"What's going on?" he asked.

"It's calmed down for now," said Jimmy. "But it isn't over."

"Did you get to the church?"

"Yes. The Protestants haven't got there yet. Robert is going to get some of the boys to go over."

"Good," said Uncle John. "I'll be up and about soon."

"No you won't, John," said Aunt Mary. "You can't even stand without falling over."

"Rest up, Da," said Jimmy. "We'll come back later and let you know what's happening."

Back out on the street the rain had slackened. The injured and wounded were carried off or cared for where they sat on the ground. Patrick saw houses where all the windows had been smashed and furniture and personal belongings were broken and scattered in the street. Residents were loading wagons with their children and valuables and getting out of town. The image of neighbors back in Ireland being evicted from their farms came to his mind.

When they got to the firehouse, Donnie was out in front of the building. "Have I missed it all then?" he asked.

"Only the beginning, Donnie," said Jimmy.

"Does your father know you're here?" said Patrick.

"To hell with him. I belong with you boys. Besides, most of the builders on the wharf are old Swedes and Dutch. These nativists have no quarrel with them. The shipyard will be safe."

"I never doubted you for a minute," said Jimmy.

Donnie let out a loud laugh. Jimmy pounded him on the back and the three of them went inside and upstairs. Jimmy told Jack and Brian what happened to their father and asked if they'd seen Robert.

"Not since we were all here last time," said Jack.

"Where'd he go?" asked Brian.

"He said he was coming here," said Jimmy.

Patrick had a bad feeling. "We need to find him," he said.

"When you do," said Brian, "bring him back here. We'll need to be ready for the next attack."

Jimmy, Donnie and Patrick went back out on the wet and muddy streets. It was almost dark and the rain had stopped. Jimmy asked everyone they came upon if they had seen Robert. After searching for over an hour someone said they saw him being carried to Ahern's Apothecary near St. Michael's.

On their way Patrick saw a large group gathered around a monstrous bonfire down on Second Street. He heard a roar as a hundred nativists came running up the street carrying torches. Their target was the convent of the Sisters of Charity. When they reached the front gate, a nun, not believing anyone would be so depraved as to attack a convent, opened the door to confront them. She was instantly struck on the head by a rock and dragged back inside by two other sisters.

The mob struck their torches to the wooden fence that surrounded the grounds, lighting it ablaze. When they attempted to rush the building, a dozen muskets fired from the roof of Griffin's Grocery Store across the street where Catholics were stationed just for the purpose of defending the convent.

Patrick pulled the gun from his jacket pocket as they ran to join the fight. By the time they got there the Protestants were driven back by the guards at the store. They tried to mount a second attack but after another hail of bullets, three of them fell. They fled back to the safety of their bonfire. Two of their wounded were able to limp to safety. One lay dead in the street. He would stay there until just before dawn when his friends were able to retrieve his body.

Patrick was relieved. As angry as he was, he wanted this madness to be over. He wasn't sure if there were any more bullets in the gun and he would be fine never to have to shoot it again. He watched Jimmy aim his pistol and fire at the escaping Protestants.

"How's your ammunition, Patrick?" he asked.

"I'm not sure how many times I've fired it. Maybe three or four.

"Let's take a look."

He handed him the Colt and Jimmy checked the chamber. "You have one left." He took the pistol from Patrick, reached into his pocket and pulled out a handful of bullets. He carefully loaded them and handed it back.

They left the area of the convent and continued on to the apothecary. A small group mingled out front with minor injuries. Inside, two men were being tended to by Mr. Ahern. He was doing the best he could but his knowledge was of medications and herbal mixtures, not the removal of bullets. When he saw Jimmy enter his store his look of concern for his patients changed to one of pity.

Jimmy went to him. "We've been told my brother Robert may have

75

been brought here. Have you seen him?"

Patrick followed Mr. Ahern's eyes as they darted to the rear corner of the room. An icy numbness came over him. There on a table was a body, covered with a sheet. Mr. Ahern went closer to Jimmy and put a hand on his shoulder. "I'm sorry, son," he said.

"Sorry about what?" said Jimmy.

Mr. Ahern gently guided Jimmy to the table in the corner. He lifted the sheet and Jimmy gasped and his knees buckled. Donnie rushed to his side and held him up by the arm. Patrick couldn't move. His entire body was paralyzed. There lay Robert, his radiant black hair stark against his lifeless, ashen face and the clean white sheet. Just below his temple was a rusty red splotch of dried blood where the bullet had entered his skull.

Patrick heard Jimmy howl as he threw himself on top of his brother. He had his head on Robert's chest and his arms around him trying to shake him back to life. "Get up, Robert. Wake up! We have to go home now."

Mr. Ahern loaned them his small cart to take Robert home. At the door, Jimmy fumbled with the key. His hand was shaking so much he couldn't unlock it. Donnie took the key and did it for him. They went inside and laid Robert down on a large cutting table in the back of the store. They heard footsteps coming down the stairs. Patrick saw the amber light of the candle and the fluttering shadow of Aunt Mary, calling out
before she came into view.

"What's happened?" she said.

When she saw her son, Aunt Mary dropped the candle and would have collapsed to the floor if Patrick hadn't caught her. Uncle John followed her down and the shock turned him to stone. Jimmy couldn't stand still. He paced back and forth, as his mother's cries turned to wracking sobs.

No one could do anything but cry and attempt to comprehend how and why this horrible thing had happened. Finally, it was Ellen who took charge. She didn't know where she found the strength. She just had to help ease her aunt and uncle's pain. Mary was bent over, cradling Robert's head in her arms, slowly rocking him, her body convulsing with every motion. Ellen put her arms around her shoulders and tried to get her to let go of her son.

"Aunt Mary," said Ellen. "Please, let me take care of him."

"Don't touch him!" she said, her eyes wild.

Ellen stroked her back and spoke softly, almost in a whisper. "We have to cleanse and prepare his body. And we should get a priest as soon as possible."

Aunt Mary gained some composure. "We need Father Hurley," she said to no one in particular.

Ellen looked at Patrick. He was in his own state of shock but she didn't need to ask. It was a relief to have something to do. He went back out on the streets, which were now ghostly quiet. He passed small groups getting themselves organized with weapons and moving into positions on rooftops, in second story windows and behind makeshift barricades, preparing for the next assault.

Before he got all the way to the church, he ran into Father Hurley in his black cassock and biretta walking the streets. He was visiting the wounded and dying, doing his best to get to those who needed him before they took their final breath.

"Father, you must come to the Torpey house."

"I heard," said the priest. "Robert is dead then?"

"Yes, Father."

77

"Terrible. Just terrible. Tell John and Mary that I will be there as soon as I can, lad."

When Patrick got back, Robert had been moved to a smaller table. Nancy and Ellen had removed his clothes and got him into a clean white nightshirt. Aunt Mary washed his face, hands and feet, then combed his hair. She was wrapping him in her very best linen sheets when Father Hurley arrived. He anointed Robert's forehead with fragrant holy oil and gave a final blessing.

"I'm so sorry, Mary," he said.

"Thank you for coming, Father," said Mary, the words muttered and barely discernible.

"I know how hard this is dear, but we must bury him right away. The mob has already attacked the convent. It won't be long before they come after the church."

"But what about a proper wake and funeral? Will he not have a Mass said for him?"

"There'll be time for that later. It's best to lay him to rest right away. I'll have a grave prepared first thing in the morning."

This brought Uncle John out of his stupor. He started crying and his body shook. Jimmy went to him and put an arm over his shoulder. He led his father to a chair and had him sit down. The rest of them stood there, unable to think or speak until Ellen again stepped forward.

"What time should we have him there, Father?" she asked.

"As early as possible. No later than eight."

Chapter Fifteen

May 7, 1844

A dismal gray fog shrouded the silent streets of Kensington as they took Robert to St. Michael's cemetery. The family, Donnie Donovan, and a small group of friends walked behind Mr. Ahern's wagon. Patrick watched his cousin being lowered into the ground with an overwhelming loss and bitterness. After the brief service, Father Hurley put his arms around Mary trying to console her. "He's with the Lord now, Mary."

She had to be held up by Jack and Brian and lifted back into the wagon. Uncle John was dazed and uncomprehending. He threw up his arms in anger when Patrick and Jimmy tried to help him into the wagon.

"I'll walk," he said

They trudged home through the waking neighborhood. More people were packing up valuables and leaving town. Patrick saw American flags that some had placed on their doors in an attempt to appease the attackers and avoid having their homes destroyed. It was a nightmarish scene with the loss of Robert, the smoldering remains of burnt houses, and the fear hanging over the neighborhood.

When they got home, Ellen and Nancy tried to get Aunt Mary to lie down. She fought them, wanting to make breakfast but they finally got her upstairs. Brian was concerned for his father. He looked drained and lifeless.

"We have to get to the hose house, Da," he said.

"I'll be all right. I need to stay here with your mother. Be safe boys. Promise me that. She won't be able to overcome another loss."

"We will, Da" said Brian.

79

On the third floor of the firehouse, Brian called the men to order. There were only nineteen present. The others were taking care of their homes and families.

"Boys," he said, his voice cracking. "We buried my brother, Robert this morning."

There was a brief, incredulous silence, followed by an outcry so strong, Brian had to calm them down or they would have stormed out of the building to go on the attack. "We have to wait for them to come back," he said. "If we go after them we'll be crushed."

He asked for reports from around the neighborhood and they were informed of the damage and the fact that the Protestants were still on the outskirts with their bonfire raging. Jack updated them on the convent. "There are still men on the roof of Griffin's store across the street. We need to find ammunition for them. Does anyone know where we can get some?"

Jimmy knew where to find more muskets and bullets and he left to get them. Jack took five men with him to guard St. Michaels. Patrick and Donnie were assigned to the second floor windows as lookouts. The minutes crawled by and after an hour of sitting and staring down the street, Patrick asked Brian if there wasn't something else he could do.

"Can I go check on Aunt Mary and the rest of them?"

"I can't spare you right now," said Brian. It's almost three and the Protestants will no doubt he here soon."

Forty-five minutes later Jimmy returned with a dozen more muskets. As soon as he joined Patrick and Donnie at their posts, they heard the mob approaching. Shivers ran up Patrick's arms and neck. He leaned forward out the window to look down the street where he saw thousands of incensed nativists shouting, singing, carrying signs and waving effigies of Irishmen decorated with potatoes and empty whiskey bottles.

"Hold your fire!" shouted Brian.

Patrick gripped the revolver tighter. As they marched closer, the nativists hurled rocks at the windows of the houses and building on the street. Some broke from the ranks and smashed open doors. Once inside they ransacked homes, stealing money or jewelry and destroying everything else.

They kept coming, like a monstrous snake winding relentlessly up Cadwalader Street. When they got to the Nanny Goat Market, a man tried to plant another flag at the southern entrance. At that moment, out of doorways and alleys, local men appeared and opened fire.

Inside the firehouse they obeyed Brian and held fast. Patrick saw a few Protestants fall and the front of the mob dispersed in every direction. A formation lined up in their place. "Holmes!" said Jimmy.

Isaac Holmes led the group. He directed a line of eight across to aim into the Market. They discharged their muskets and Brian finally gave the command to fire. Holmes remained in place with his squad. While the front group went to the rear to reload, the second row, at his command, raised their rifles and fired.

A counter attack came from every alley, corner and rooftop. The neighborhood was responding with guns, rocks and brickbats, along with the volley of fire from the hose house. The Protestants were driven back, diving to find cover wherever they could.

The explosion of weapons going off at the same time nearly deafened Patrick. For a few minutes the only thing he could hear was a high pitched ringing in his head. He shot randomly into the crowd below. He had to duck down as rocks smashed through the windows followed by a hail of bullets.

Jimmy put his musket on the sill to get a better aim. He fired and ducked down to reload as fast as he could. Patrick peeked up and saw a group with torches rushing the building. He stopped shooting randomly and took aim at individuals. He fired again and again until there were no bullets left.

A ball of fire flew through the window and rolled to the center of the room. Donnie went to put it out when another one crashed in right behind it. They were bunches of oil-soaked rags and despite Donnie's stamping on them, they refused to go out. Soon two more soared in and the room was filling with smoke and flames.

"We have to get out of here," shouted Jimmy.

Patrick held his breath, crouched low, and hurried down the stairs. A handful of men were defending the front entrance from the mob's attempt to break down the doors. Running out meant heading right into a barrage of bricks and bullets. It was suicide to try it but soon there would be no choice. The second and third floors were in flames and outside, lit torches were being tossed at the base of the building.

"Let's go," shouted Jimmy and they charged as if one body, out into the street, swinging clubs and shooting their weapons. It was like running from purgatory directly into hell.

Patrick pulled the trigger on his gun while running, but he was out of ammunition. It was probably a blessing since he couldn't tell Catholics from Protestants at that moment. He put his head down and ran without any thought whatsoever other than getting somewhere safe. The only place he could think of was his aunt and uncle's house.

He looked about for Jimmy and Donnie but they were nowhere to be seen. He was smack in the middle of a free-for-all. As he tried to get through he was bashed on the side of the head and went down in a semi-conscious heap. He struggled to one knee. When he tried getting to his feet he was knocked over by bodies running and falling over him. It took every ounce of strength he had before he managed to stand up. The whole world had gone silent. Everything and everybody moved in slow motion like in a bad dream.

His hearing returned all at once with a sound like an enormous wave crashing on the shore. He saw Jimmy and Donnie. Both were fighting for their lives. He moved toward them, picking up a club as he went. He smashed it into Jimmy's attacker, sending him to the ground. Then he swung it at the man fighting Donnie and he ran off.

The hose house was engulfed in flames. Smoke filled the streets and alleys nearby. Houses and buildings were burning and collapsing amidst crackling flames and the constant roar of the mob. Patrick's only thought now was for Ellen.

Jimmy, thinking about the family too, was running toward his house, along with Donnie and four other boys from the firehouse. Patrick followed close behind them. When they turned the corner to his street Patrick heard Jimmy shout "No!" He looked up the block and saw that all the houses were either burning or being set on fire.

A small group of nativists were in front of Uncle John's house laughing as they shattered their belongings they had pulled out into the street. Jimmy stopped, took aim and fired his musket. One of them dropped to the ground and the rest scattered, dragging their fallen comrade with them.

Patrick frantically scanned the street for his sister. He ran inside the house calling out for her. There was no answer. Flames licked up the walls as he rushed up the smoke-filled stairs. He choked from the fumes while screaming her name. In a moment Jimmy was behind him, pulling at his arm. "They're all safe," he said. "Come on. We need to get out of here."

That's when he remembered his money. He had neglected to store it in Uncle John's safe, putting it under the mattress instead. He went to the bedroom and didn't want to believe what he saw. The mattress was ripped to shreds and the bed frame had been tossed out the window. He knew immediately that his wallet and money pouch were gone. He stood there gaping as the heat from the growing flames singed his hair and face. Jimmy pulled him back. "Now, Patrick!"

He never recalled going down the stairs or out of the house. He fell to his knees screaming and cursing. Everything he and his family ever wanted was lost, and it was his fault. Jimmy and Donnie picked him up and dragged him away from the inferno. He went down on all fours. His eyes burned and when he tried to breathe he coughed violently, the pain wracking deep in his chest. Ellen found him and ran to his side. She bent down and put her face to his. "Thank God you're alive," she said.

He tried to speak but couldn't. Hot tears from the smoke and fire mixed with the tears of loss and rage. "Gone," he managed to say.

"What?" said Ellen.

"All gone."

"I know, Patrick. The house is burning to the ground."

"Our money, Ellen. It's all gone."

Ellen helped him to his his feet. They took in the sight of the house roaring in flames and the broken furniture littering the street. Patrick rocked back and forth on the balls of his feet, shaking his head.

"Come on, Patrick," said Jimmy, coming over and putting an arm around his waist. "We have to get the family out of here."

Patrick took one last look at the crumbling house. He wanted to do something; shoot someone or smash somebody's skull. But at the moment there wasn't any fight left in him. He said nothing, only able to move, stiff-legged and numb at the side of his cousin.

Chapter Sixteen

Columbia, Tennessee, May 11, 1844

James Polk and his wife, Sarah were taking tea in the front parlor of their elegant but modest home when the first of two pressing letters arrived. He sat at his rolltop desk catching up on correspondence while she sat on the settee reading the article in the newspaper explaining Martin Van Buren's declaration that he was against the annexation of Texas.

The first letter was from Andrew Jackson's adopted son and personal secretary, Andrew Jackson Donelson. Polk opened it and read it silently.

It is important that you see us without delay. The division in our ranks threatened by conflicting views about the annexation question must be obviated before the convention in Baltimore.

After a cursory glance at the rest of his mail, he went upstairs to pack. He would leave first thing in the morning for the fifty mile ride to the Hermitage, Jackson's home outside of Nashville. Another letter arrived by courier before he finished getting ready. This one was from Robert Armstrong, the Postmaster in Nashville and longtime friend of the General's. Sarah brought it upstairs and read it to her husband as he laid out his clothes.

"It is important that you be here, James. General Jackson wants to see you as soon as possible. Start on receipt of this and you can be here by Sunday evening." Sarah paused and raised an eyebrow at her husband before continuing. "I cannot see how the South and West can now support Van Buren. He ought to have paid some little respect to the Old Chief's opinions."

James stopped what he was doing for a moment but said nothing. Sarah watched him and waited. He was a spare, intense and serious man. She loved and respected him for his integrity and dedication and she recognized the significance of the situation, but to her, religion had a higher place than politics. "Surely it can wait until after the Sabbath, James. Start out Monday morning."

He sighed and smiled at his wife. She was his strength and support in everything he did. They were a childless couple but rather than pulling them apart, it had, over time, forged an unbreakable bond between them.

"Don't you think the Lord is more important than Andrew Jackson?" she said.

"Yes, but the Lord may be taking him soon. He called for me, Sarah, and I must go. Besides, Van Buren has just changed everything."

"Do you think," she said, "he'll abandon his support of Mr. Van Buren?"

"I have no doubt of it."

"Then who will he promote in his stead?"

The question hung in the air. He and Jackson had been carefully and discreetly campaigning the last few years, for James to be the vice-presidential nominee in the upcoming election. He was only forty-nine years old and neither he nor his wife had entertained the thought that this would be the year for his run at the presidency.

"It's too early to speculate," he said.

"Not if you're ignoring the Sabbath to run off and discuss it."

He went to her and brushed back a piece of dark hair that had fallen across her large, beautiful eyes. He kissed her softly on the forehead. "Make sure," she said with a resigned smile, "to give him my love and affection."

At daybreak, James walked down the porch to the barefoot, teenaged slave holding his horse. He got up in the saddle, feeling the familiar discomfort from the crude and painful operation he had as a boy of sixteen. With only brandy for his anesthetic, the doctor cut through his scrotum and removed urinary stones from his bladder. Though they never spoke of it, there was little doubt the surgery was the reason he and Sarah could never conceive the children they had so ardently desired.

He arrived in Nashville that evening and stayed with Armstrong. They departed the next morning for the ten mile ride to the Hermitage. On the way, James asked after the general's health. "I hope he hasn't taken a turn for the worse."

"On the contrary," said Armstrong. "There's a glint in his eye we haven't seen in a long time. He's very anxious to see you, James."

It was nearly noon when they cantered up the cedar lined drive of Jackson's beautiful sand colored mansion. A stout, unsmiling negress in a faded calico dress and a white kerchief wrapped around her head met them on the steps of the expansive portico. James handed her his hat, riding gloves and overnight bag.

"He's in the garden, Massa," she said.

Old Hickory was sitting next to the gravestone of his wife Rachel. He had a blanket covering his legs. From the angle James saw him he looked like his old self. The long, angular face and plume of white hair appeared to be no different than it had for the last twenty years. But as he got closer, the frail body and the deep, rugged lines in his face told a different story.

Jackson noticed his protege approach and rose slowly from his chair. The small black boy attending him tried to help but the General snarled at him and he backed away. James hurried over and shook his hand, as much to steady him as to greet him.

"Thank you for coming, James. Have you seen Van Buren's letter?"

"Yes, sir, I have," said Polk. "I was shocked."

"He must believe he no longer needs my support," said Jackson. "He will regret it."

"What can we do, General?"

He clapped James on the back and left his arm draped over his shoulder. James supported him around his waist as they walked towards the house. "We'll show him the error of his ways at the convention. He has destroyed himself but we won't let the party go down with him. Are you ready to take the reins, young Mr. Polk?"

"Isn't that a bit premature, General?"

"Not any longer. We need a strong, Southern, expansion man with solid relationships with our Northern friends and a reputation for hard work, dedication and virtue. And that of course, James, is you."

"Would it not be better with an expansion man from the North and continue with our plan for me as his running mate?"

"We had that man but he has just deserted us. No, we need a Southerner who the abolitionists won't despise and who'll save the country from that puffed up rooster, Clay. And now we need to discuss our strategy to make that happen."

Chapter Seventeen

Philadelphia, May 11, 1844

The National Guard and militia units under the command of General George Cadwalader finally restored calm but not before another day of destruction and violence. The nativists got to St. Michaels, and set it ablaze. It was completely destroyed, along with the rectory, two factories and five other houses nearby. When there was little more to burn, the nativists slowly withdrew. In their wake, they burnt another Catholic church, St. Augustines in Philadelphia

At least twenty-four deaths occurred during the three days of violence but there were many more unreported as bodies were still being pulled from the burned homes days after the rioting stopped. The grand jury was called and arrest warrants were issued, almost all of them for residents of Kensington.

The next Saturday afternoon, the Sheriff and three deputies came to Brian's house. Patrick and Jimmy had just returned from bringing the family back from Carmac Woods where they had fled when the house was destroyed. Uncle John, Aunt Mary and the two girls moved in with Jack while he and Jimmy stayed with Brian.

They were upstairs drinking whiskey with Donnie when Jimmy looked out the window and saw them coming. They had been drinking nonstop for the last two days but it hadn't done much to ease Patrick's guilt or anger. Jimmy thought about escaping out the back as McMichaels pounded on the front door, until he saw two deputies posted in the rear of the house.

Brian went to the door. He had an idea what the sheriff was there for but demanded to know why anyway.

"I've come for your brother and your cousin," said McMichaels. "I'm told they're staying with you."

"Are they under arrest?"

"Yes, are they here?"

Patrick and Jimmy came up behind Brian. "Out of all the people involved in this," said Brian, "you've singled out these two? That's ludicrous, Sheriff, and you know it."

"A witness claims that Jimmy killed George Shiffler and your cousin is accused of gunning down a man named Joe Cox." McMichaels looked past Brian and said, "Will you two come quietly?"

They all stood there for a moment, with Brian blocking the doorway."What will happen to them?" he asked.

"That's out of my hands," said the Sheriff. "I can tell you that there have been so many arrests bail is being granted to nearly everyone and trials have been put off for a later date."

"We're innocent," said Jimmy. "We were the ones being attacked and you know it, Sheriff."

"Maybe I do, and maybe I don't. My job is to bring you in, with or without your cooperation."

For a moment, Patrick thought there would be a fight. But Jimmy grabbed his coat and hat and went outside. Patrick followed behind him, his head down, hoping Ellen wouldn't see him from across the street. The deputies came from the back of the house and put them in the wagon with three other prisoners. As they pulled away down the street, Brian looked at Donnie and said, "Let's go."

"Where?" said Donnie.

"To the courthouse. We need to see what happens."

An hour later Jimmy and Patrick were taken in the side entrance of the court with ten other prisoners. They sat down next to each other in the third row of benches to await their arraignment. Patrick was anxious and disconsolate. Jimmy's smoldering anger could hardly be contained when he saw Isaac Holmes standing at the defense table directly under the gaze of Judge Andrew Young. Next to him was Peter Browne, his expensive lawyer provided by the Native American Party. Holmes was accused of arson and rioting but he was being released for lack of evidence. The judge hammered down his gavel and the words "case dismissed" thundered through the packed courtroom.

The Catholics in the court and those among the large group of spectators outside howled in protest. Judge Young banged his gavel repeatedly and threatened the entire room with prison if order wasn't restored. When it was, the proceedings continued. Each of the accused was brought in front of him and the charges were read. Only a few had attorneys but it didn't seem to matter. If there wasn't more than one accuser or witness, the defendants were released with a trial date.

Holmes remained in the court to testify against Jimmy and Patrick, claiming to see both of them murdering his friends in cold blood. But he was the only witness and Judge Young was fair enough to allow both of them to go free with the promise to appear at the appointed time. Their court dates were set for July tenth and they were released.

Outside, Holmes confronted Jimmy. "You're going to like the penitentiary, Torpey. I hear you need a place to stay anyway."

Jimmy lunged at him and landed a punch to the side of his jaw. They grappled and fell to the ground rolling and pummeling each other. The Philadelphia police were in full force around the building and two of them appeared instantly, wielding clubs. They beat the two of them until they each curled up in a ball to protect themselves. Four more policemen bulled their way through the crowd, formed a small ring around them and yanked them to their feet. If they hadn't intervened, another full-scale riot would have ignited right on the steps of the courthouse.

"I'm coming for you, Holmes," said Jimmy. "You're a coward and a murderer."

Holmes smiled. "I'm shaking in my boots," he said. "Too bad you don't have your brother to help you anymore."

Brian and Donnie grabbed on to Jimmy's arms and held tightly. Patrick followed behind them until they had walked a couple of blocks and Jimmy finally quit saying over and over again, "I'm going to kill him."

They stopped for a moment to let Jimmy calm down a little more. Donnie put a hand on his friend's shoulder and said. "I think a drink is in order."

Chapter Eighteen

Kensington, May 27, 1844

Patrick got dressed to go out one more time to look for work. He wore Robert's clothes that Aunt Mary had managed to salvage before the house burned down. Over the last two weeks he had dutifully gone out every day. This morning he stopped by Jack's house to grab a biscuit before leaving and when Mary saw him the tears brimmed in her eyes.

"I shouldn't wear these," he said.

Mary brushed at some lint on his shoulder. "Yes you should, Patrick," she said. "You've nothing else."

"Maybe Jack or Brian have some to spare."

She brushed at a nonexistent piece of dirt on the other shoulder, took hold of his arms in both her hands and looked into his eyes. "You're taller than they are," she said. "Like Robert. I want you to have them."

Robert had always been the best dressed of the Torpey brothers. The pants and jacket were a bit tight but Patrick no longer looked as if he just arrived from Ireland. The tall black beaver hat was especially stylish with a gray felt band around it. But it didn't do anything to get him employed.

There was no work locally. The Third Ward of Kensington resembled a sacked city after Napoleon's army had laid siege to it. Half of the buildings were burnt to the ground and many of the remaining ones had boarded up windows and bullet holes in the walls. Patrick had gone to the shipyard but he wasn't allowed on the premises. Donnie warned him not to even try. Since his own father had fired him, he certainly wouldn't allow Patrick back.

Each morning he extended his search further out. He'd already gone through Southwark and into Philadelphia only to find that where there were help wanted signs, they all had "No Irish" written in big letters underneath. Today he ventured into Moyamensing along the Schuylkill River where there were textile mills and brick factories. With no experience with the textile machines, he was turned away at each of them.

The only available work was in a brickyard but it paid next to nothing. He grew more and more despondent. He had failed his family and he had no hope of ever making it right. He sat for a long time on the bank of the river and considered walking out and letting it take him away forever. When he couldn't do it, he thought *I don't even have the courage to kill myself.*

He got up and walked back to Kensington. It was after three o'clock and he knew Jimmy and Donnie would be at O'Toole's Tavern, one of the few establishments that had survived the riots. The bar ran nearly the length of the building, with tables lining the opposite wall. There was a large painting behind the bar of ships in Cork Harbor which always made Patrick homesick. He found them at a table near the back, already feeling no pain.

"Any luck?" said Jimmy.

"The foreman at one of the brickyards said he'd hire me but it was for pennies and the workday is fourteen hours. I have to find something better than that."

Donnie ordered him a beer and a whiskey. He drained the whiskey and sipped the beer. He took off his hat and placed it on an empty chair next to him. His mood improved slightly and he asked Donnie, "Will your Da ever let you back at the shipyard?"

"I doubt it," said Donnie. "I don't want to go back anyway. It's a relief not to be screamed at every hour."

"What are you going to do then?"

"Don't know yet. I'm staying at my aunt's house in Southwark. She'll let me be there as long as I want. I'm thinking of going to Pittsburgh. There's a thriving ship building business there and I'm sure I can find work."

The drinks kept coming and soon Patrick was thoroughly drunk. He laid his head down on the table, resting it on his crossed arms, to try to stop the room from spinning.

"I have to leave," said Jimmy. "And Patrick needs to come with me. They're convicting most of the Catholics. Michael Magee was just sent to Eastern Penitentiary for three years. I can't go there."

"Where will you go?" said Donnie.

"West," he said. "Oregon, maybe."

Patrick raised his head. A long, slender strand of saliva stayed connected from his mouth to his hand, breaking off to dangle on his chin when he spoke. "Whassin Orgon?" he said.

Donnie laughed and Jimmy nearly spit out a mouthful of beer.

Patrick stared dully at Jimmy, waiting for an answer. "Land, cousin," said Jimmy. "That's what's in Oregon. Lots of land, there for the taking."

"You can't be serious," said Donnie. "You'll have to get there and that will take food, equipment, mules...which means money. Lots of money."

"Come with me, then. We'll be partners."

"I'm not going to Oregon," said Donnie. "What is it, three thousand miles? Is there even a road there?"

"There is," said Jimmy. "And thousands of people are heading out each month."

"I don't want to fight savages or get lost in the mountains." He shook Patrick's shoulder and asked "What are you going to do, Pat?"

Patrick didn't answer. His head was back down on his arms and he was snoring slightly. He had no idea how long he stayed in that position but when Jimmy woke him he had a stabbing pain behind his eyes and thought that any second he would puke. Jimmy handed him a glass of whiskey and he downed it in one gulp. The pain didn't go completely away but it helped a bit. All he wanted was to go to bed and sleep it off.

Jimmy stood up and said, "Come on." He staggered after him into the dark night. Donnie was no longer with them but two Avengers were, Tom Shelby and Kirin McDougal. Both were carrying clubs.

After a few blocks they were joined by Francis Burke and Nick Murray. They too had clubs, stuck in their belts, and Murray had a bottle of rum. Patrick declined a drink. "Let's go home," he said.

"We'll go soon enough," said Jimmy. Ten minutes later, they stopped at a corner where there were rows of neat houses in both directions.

"What are we doing?" said Patrick.

"Paying a visit on Richard Strand," said Jimmy. "A nativist running for Constable. We're going to give him our vote."

Patrick didn't like it. He hadn't been sober one day since the riots and now his headache and nausea were back in full force. Most nights over the last couple of weeks, Jimmy looked for Holmes on the streets but never found him. They chased after small groups of nativists but it was mostly rock throwing and an occasional fist fight. This was more serious.

"Patrick," said Jimmy, "You and Tom stay here. Call out if anyone approaches." The rest of them crept up the street. When they got to the house, Murray went to the opposite side of the street as another lookout. The other three went up on the porch. Jimmy knocked hard on the door and took a step back. In a moment Patrick saw the door swing open and Richard Strand step outside.

Burke and McDougal grabbed him and pulled him off the porch out into the street. Patrick heard the smack when Jimmy punched him in the face. The other two beat him with their clubs and he heard Richards groan as he went down. Murray rushed over and got a few licks in before Jimmy kicked him in the head and once more in the stomach. Then all of them whooped as they ran towards Patrick, who stood there gaping at the lifeless figure, hoping he wasn't dead.

"Go!" shouted Jimmy as they rushed by him.

Chapter Nineteen

Jimmy and Patrick didn't go home after beating up Richard Strand. They stayed at Tom Shelby's place on the north end of town near the docks. In the morning they walked home to Brian's house. It was after ten when they reached the front steps. Ellen spotted them from across the street and rushed over before they could get inside.

"Patrick, what in God's name are you doing?"

He didn't say anything. He tried to walk around her but she blocked his way. His clothes were rumpled and dirty and his eyes were red and swollen. His neck hurt and the sour taste in his mouth was like a combination of spoiled meat and the pine tar resin he used to caulk with at the shipyard.

Ellen stuck her finger out, inches from his face. "Out drinking till all hours," she said. "Did you spend the night in a ditch?"

He wouldn't look directly at her. "I'm going in," said Jimmy." Patrick started to follow him.

"Don't walk away from me, Patrick," she said, her voice quivering. He stopped and turned toward her. For an instant she took pity on him. He looked lost and defeated, but then her anger returned. They were in this together and he had been avoiding and ignoring her over the last few weeks. "Have you found work?" she said.

"No."

"Have you even tried?"

He finally held her eyes, gritting his teeth as he tried to control himself. "I've been all over the city and beyond," he said. "No one is hiring any Irish."

"We have to do something," she said. "Drinking and fighting every night isn't going to get us anything but more trouble."

"What do you want me to do, Ellen? I'm probably going to prison anyway. It's hopeless."

"Stop pitying yourself for one thing. And find work. I have."

His head went back in surprise. "What kind of work?"

"Piece work for one of the textile mills. Nancy and I make skeins of yarn on a hand loom that Jack was kind enough to buy for us. It's in the basement and we alternate shifts. It's long, hard work and pays little but it's better than nothing."

Her eyes bore into him. The shame that was never far away returned in a flood. He turned from her again and headed toward the front steps. "I'm trying," he said over his shoulder.

"Take a look at yourself, Patrick. A long, hard look." He didn't answer her. She stomped her foot, turned and walked away.

When Patrick got inside, Jimmy and Brian were in a heated discussion in the front room. Brian was leaning in close, their noses almost touching.

"The sheriff was by again an hour ago looking for you," said Brian.

"What about?" said Jimmy.

"A man was taken from his house last night and beaten nearly to death. He named you and Kirin McDougal as two of the men who did it." Brian turned his attention to Patrick. "I'm assuming you were with him?"

When neither of them responded, Brian went on. "Your trials are in six weeks. This isn't going to help you. You have to know that."

"I'll be out of your hair soon enough," said Jimmy.

"What does that mean?"

"It means I'll not let them put me in prison."

"You won't have a choice if the sheriff catches you for last night."

"I don't have much of a choice as it is, do I? They're going to convict me for something I didn't do anyway. Patrick too. We both know that."

Brian backed away from his brother and paced in front of the bookcase at the rear wall. "You might have gotten off for the murder," he said. "But now, with this man you assaulted identifying you..."

"I'll pack my things," said Jimmy.

"Where will you go?"

"For now, I'll go to Tom Shelby's, or one of the other boys from the hose house. Then I'll be heading out for Oregon."

Now it was Brian who said nothing. He could only shake his head in disbelief or despair, perhaps both.

"Donnie, Patrick and I will be going to Pittsburgh first, to get work and make some money."

Brian saw the surprise on his cousin's face. Patrick vaguely remembered talking about it last night. No one spoke for a moment. Brian went to Jimmy and put an arm over his shoulder. "Listen," he said. "It seems the ones who are getting off have lawyers. We'll get you both one. Da and I have already talked about it."

"I can't let you do that," said Jimmy. "Da's going to need every cent he has left to rebuild the house and the store."

"I don't think he'll rebuild the store. He sits on Jack's porch all day and stares off in the distance. Ma isn't much better. If you leave, it'll only make things worse."

"Worse than having their son in the penitentiary?"

"Neither you nor Patrick have a pot to piss in," said Brian, "And

101

you're talking about making it across an entire continent?"

"We'll get jobs in Pittsburgh," said Jimmy, "until we make enough to get to Missouri. We can hire on with a wagon train heading west."

Brian was exasperated. He looked from his brother to his cousin. "What do you have to say about all this, Patrick?"

He hesitated before answering. "There's no work here for me, Brian. Not that will get me land any time soon. And if we're convicted..."

He didn't finish the sentence. Brian exhaled a long slow breath. "You really can't stay here, Jimmy. The sheriff will be back soon enough."

"Did he say anything about me?" said Patrick.

"No. But if I were you I'd be careful about being seen out on the street."

Chapter Twenty

Jane checked in at the Barnum Hotel in Baltimore. The city was even more crowded than it was for the Whig Convention which she attended a month ago. Not only were the Democrats there to choose their candidates, President Tyler had also organized his own convention to gather support for his third party candidacy. Tyler men mingled on the streets and in the hotels, displaying their pro-annexation, "Texas Lone Star" badges and were even more rowdy than the Democrats.

Jane met Governor Marcy for dinner in the hotel's opulent restaurant. They sat at a table in the center of the room under a dazzling, crystal chandelier. They dined on fish chowder, venison, oysters and collard greens and talked of family, mutual acquaintances and eventually, Jane's work.

"Moses gives me full liberty to express my opinions," she said "He takes no political contributions so I can criticize politicians and their shortsighted policies or support those I believe are on the right path. I've also had a few more pieces accepted by Mr. O'Sullivan at the *Democratic Review*."

"Very impressive, Jane. I liked what you wrote about gaining Texas without going to war, but do you think it's truly possible?"

"I do, Governor. Mexico has already lost Texas and they've mortgaged California to British holders of Mexican bonds. It's jealousy and the conceit of their politicians and generals, along with the prodding of the English intriguers, that makes them threaten war. California can be purchased, I'm sure of it. And there are enough Mexican republicans who admire our independence and institutions and desire, like Texas, to be part of the United States."

Over dessert of cheese cake and coffee the conversation went to the business at hand. "Can Van Buren still secure the nomination?" she asked.

"Our party is in disarray," said Marcy. "As a New York delegate, my vote is committed to him but there's an effort by General Jackson's men to require a two-thirds majority to gain the nomination. If that goes through, he'll have a serious challenge."

"I know you agree with me about supporting annexation, Governor. Why is it that Van Buren doesn't?"

"He won't alienate the anti-slavery movement in the north or those who abhor the idea of war for territory. But you know all that, Jane."

She took a sip of coffee before responding. "Slavery isn't going away. Not yet anyway. It's more important to spread our way of life across the continent and let slavery die a natural death. With the colonization movement and the advancements of science and industry on agriculture, it must surely and eventually disappear."

"But in the meantime," said Marcy, "Adding another slave state, or four since Texas is big enough to be broken into numerous pieces, would completely tip the balance of power to the South."

"He has no vision and neither does Clay," said Jane. "If we buy California and resolve the Oregon border with Britain there would be two additional free states and the balance restored."

Marcy took a bite of cheese cake. Jane continued. "What do you think of President Tyler's efforts? He got Texas to sign the treaty for annexation. If Congress approves it, that might be enough to get him elected."

"He has little chance. General Jackson will no doubt want a southerner and a true Democrat in the top spot to counter Clay."

"What about Calhoun?" said Jane.

"Jackson hates him almost as much as he despises Clay. He's the one who has brought slavery to the forefront by declaring in no uncertain terms, that annexing Texas is precisely for the advancement of slavery. Many in the North are incensed over it."

"The only way to defeat Clay is by coming out strongly for Texas *and* Oregon. I don't know what's wrong with Van Buren."

They finished their coffee and dessert. They gave each other a quick embrace. "Thank you for dinner, William," said Jane. "And for the convention ticket."

In the morning, Jane walked to the Odd Fellows Hall on the west side of Gay Street between Fayette and Saratoga. It was a handsome brick building, built ten years earlier. The convention was being held in The Egyptian Salon, a grand ballroom on the second floor. Paintings of pharos, pyramids and scenes from the River Nile adorned the walls and alcoves. It was the largest available room in the city but it was readily apparent that it was not big enough for the two hundred sixty-six delegates and over one hundred spectators. As she found her seat in the packed gallery there was already an air of animosity and confrontation with jostling and raised voices coming from the floor below.

The proceedings began at noon when the gavel was dropped by the chairman, Hendrick Wright of Pennsylvania. Immediately, Romulus Saunders from North Carolina rose to propose the two-thirds rule. Shouts of approval and objection greeted him. Vehement arguments both pro and con erupted, nearly escalating into physical brawls.

The debate raged until six-thirty when the meeting was blessedly adjourned, though it continued in the hotels and saloons of Baltimore all through the night. It wasn't until the next afternoon that the two-thirds rule was approved by a vote of 148-118.

The voting to decide the candidate began that afternoon at three-thirty. After seven ballots and more heated and passionate arguments, Van Buren was losing ground with no other candidate rising to take control. The convention was recessed until the following day.

Things happened rapidly once the convention reconvened. Just as Jane sat down, the vote was called for. As usual they went in geographical order with Maine going first and sticking, with the exception of one vote, with Van Buren. They cast seven votes for him and one for Cass. Next up was New Hampshire. Their spokesman got to his feet and cast all of their six votes for James Polk of Tennessee. By the end of the eighth ballot, James Polk had 44 votes. Lewis Cass from Michigan had 114, Van Buren, 104 and James Buchanan from Pennsylvania and Calhoun from South Carolina had 2 each.

Bedlam again consumed the assembly. Delegations removed themselves to meet and decide how to proceed. On the floor, representatives demanded to be recognized to speak. But by the end of the day the tide had turned. From her place in the balcony, Jane noticed that a wave of enthusiasm had replaced the contention and discord.

After the ninth ballot, Polk had 233 votes to Cass's 29. The dissenting votes were recast and James Polk was unanimously selected to be the Democrat's presidential candidate. Later that day, George Dallas, the former Mayor of Philadelphia, became the vice-presidential candidate. Now it was time to unify the party and attack Henry Clay and the Whigs.

Chapter Twenty-One

Philadelphia, July 4th, 1844

Over the next four weeks, Jimmy kept moving from one house to another of his fellow Avengers. Patrick stayed at Brian's but he gave up trying to find work. He didn't want to run away but saw no other option. Maybe he could find a decent job in Pittsburgh and be able to send money back home to at least get the family to Philadelphia. As for Oregon, he'd need money no matter how available land was there. He couldn't bring himself to talk with Ellen about it. He was never able to get out from under the black shroud of guilt that engulfed him.

The three of them discussed their plans one night in Donnie's bedroom at his aunt's house. Their trials were in two weeks and they had to do something before then.

"We'll stay to celebrate the fourth," said Jimmy. "And then go."

"How will we get there?" said Patrick.

"We can take the train," said Donnie.

"The sheriff will be be able to track us if we do that," said Jimmy. "He'll know where we went. It only goes to Lancaster anyway."

Then we'll take the packet boat," said Donnie. "The canal system can get us all the way to Pittsburgh in five days. Or we can ride the stage which is only a couple days longer."

"Both easy trails to follow, just like the railroad," said Jimmy. "I think we'll have to walk."

"Walk?" said Donnie. "It's three hundred miles!"

"It'll be an adventure, Donnie boy."

"How about if I meet you there."

Patrick laughed. "Do what you want," said Jimmy. "I'll be walking."

He raised his eyebrows and looked at his cousin. Patrick put a hand up to his forehead and moved it slowly over his hair to rub the back of his neck. He had roamed over the rolling, green hills of Ireland his whole life before coming to America. Walking would be no problem for him.

"I have no money for a train or anything else," he said. "I'm for walking."

By the fourth of July, Jimmy still hadn't told his parents and Patrick hadn't said anything to Ellen. They decided to do it that morning before going out to see the parade.

Aunt Mary and Uncle John sat at the kitchen table drinking coffee. Patrick heard Ellen and Nancy upstairs getting dressed, chirping and giggling as they got ready for the day's festivities. For the first time since they arrived in America, his sister sounded happy. The girls came down the stairs, looking pretty in their pastel cotton dresses and matching bonnets decorated with red, white and blue ribbons.

"We have something to tell you," said Jimmy.

The air went out of the room. Uncle John stared vacantly and Aunt Mary held her breath. Ellen glared daggers at Patrick. He held her gaze for a moment, then looked away. Jimmy forged ahead. "Patrick and I will be leaving in a few days."

"Leaving for where?" said Ellen.

"Pittsburgh," said Jimmy. "Then Oregon, after we've made enough money."

"No, James," said his mother.

"I have to, Ma. If I don't, they'll send me to the penitentiary."

She knew this to be true but it did nothing to ease her heartache. She put her head in her hands.

"Why do you have to go, Patrick?" said Ellen.

"If I stay I'll wind up in jail too, Ellen. I can't let that happen. Donnie says we'll find work in the shipyards in Pittsburgh. I'll send you money as soon as I get a job."

"Donnie's going with you?"

"Yes. With his experience, he's sure we can all find something."

Ellen wanted to say more. She wanted to scream. At that moment, more than anything, she wanted to be back home with her mother. Instead, she turned her back and ran up the stairs. Patrick hesitated, then followed after her. Up in her room, she whirled on him, her face contorted and her eyes swimming in tears. She hammered her fists against his chest until he was able to grab her wrists. "Why didn't you tell me? We should have talked about it."

"I wanted to, many times, but I wasn't sure about leaving."

"And you are now? Not everyone is being sent to jail."

"No, but I can't take the chance."

"What about me, Patrick? What about Ma and Da?"

"I'll find work. I'll send money."

"Are you really going to Oregon?"

"I don't know. That's Jimmy's dream, not mine. I've heard land is cheaper west of Pittsburgh, in the Ohio Valley. I'll find something there for us."

They were both exhausted. They'd been in America for only two months and the prospects of a better life began to unravel the moment they stepped off the ship. "You've never written home have you?" said Ellen.

"I've tried but can't find the words. You did, didn't you?"

"Yes, before all the violence. I told them we made it safe and sound. You have to write them now. They need to know what's happened and what you're doing. It's not your fault, Patrick. I know you believe it is but no one could have expected the house would be burned to the ground."

"It is my fault, Ellen. Uncle John told me to put the money in the safe and I didn't."

"Running away won't make it better, or bring the money back."

Neither of them wanted to go to a parade now. He went downstairs to tell Jimmy they would stay home. "Come on," said Jimmy. "It's your first Fourth of July in America. The celebration will take your mind off things."

Jimmy talked him into it but Ellen refused to go. They met up with Donnie and a few other of the Avengers and walked into the city. The day was warm, sunny and bright; a perfect summer day for a parade. The streets were lined three and four people deep holding small flags. Young women waving handkerchiefs filled the windows and balconies.

As soon as the first float appeared, it became apparent that the day was little more than a call to arms to the Native American cause. Magnificent teams of horses pulled expensive carriages of different sizes and styles. All were decorated with banners, ribbons and signs with nativist messages.

There were life-size images of George Washington and nearly full-scale replicas of many different kinds of ships. On the bow of one was a gigantic open Bible. A contingent of ships carpenters walked in front of it carrying a sign that said, "Our fathers gave us the Bible. We will not yield it to a foreign land."

Patrick got more anxious and angry with each successive exhibit. Next came a dozen men waving the same despicable effigies he had seen during the riots. Stuffed with old clothes and straw, the "Paddies" hung on poles by their necks. They had strings of potatoes dangling from their shirts, pipes stuck in their mouths, and bottles placed in one hand and drinking glasses in the other.

Patrick had seen enough. "Let's get out of here," he said.

"I'm staying," said Jimmy. "You can go if you want to."

Right after the "Paddies" came a barouche carrying Lewis Levin. His popularity as the leader of the nativist movement was growing by leaps and bounds. They had recently changed the name of the party to attract more members. In a broad sign on both sides of his coach he announced his candidacy for congress with the newly designated American Republican Party. Patrick saw Jimmy reach inside his jacket and caught a glimpse of his pistol.

"What are you doing, Jimmy?" he said.

"Don't worry about it. Go ahead and go home."

"We're leaving in a few days. Don't do anything stupid."

"I have some business to take care of before we go and fortunately for Levin, it isn't with him."

"I don't care who it's with," said Patrick. "This isn't the way to do it. Or the time or place. These people will be on us like a pack of wolves."

Following Levin came a wagon with a flag draped across it that was purported to be the one George Schiffler was holding when he was killed. Escorting the wagon was a company of local militia in full, grandiose uniforms. Leading them, the brass buttons of his navy blue uniform and the oversized golden epaulets on his shoulders gleaming in the morning sun, was Isaac Holmes. He made eye contact with Jimmy and doffed his tricorn hat with a venomous smile. Jimmy reached into his jacket.

Patrick reacted without thinking. He tackled Jimmy and they both fell to the ground. The crowd around them moved back, causing a circle of onlookers watching what they assumed to be a couple of Irish drunks. Patrick was on top of him, holding him down with all his might. "Dammit, let me up," shouted Jimmy.

Patrick wouldn't release his grip. He didn't let go until Holmes and his militia unit passed by. Jimmy jumped up. He was so angry he spit when he spoke. "You shouldn't have done that, Patrick. You're lucky I don't shoot you."

He regretted it as soon as the words were out of his mouth.

"You'd kill me Jimmy? You're letting your hatred overcome you. We're surrounded by an ocean of Protestants. There'd be no escape if you shot Holmes. They'd hang you for it, and the rest of us as well."

"He's getting away with it," said Jimmy. "They're all getting away with it."

"And killing Holmes will make it better? It would only bring more grief and trouble for you and the family."

"I have to do something," said Jimmy, still boiling. The people around them grumbled and pointed. Angry voices grew louder about the Irish scum ruining the Fourth of July. They needed to get out of there.

Donnie suggested they go around the corner to St. Philips church. The pastor there was the brother of one of the Avengers, Francis Dunn and the priest was worried about violence against his church during the parade. Jimmy had arranged for a wagonload of muskets to be delivered to the church for its protection. They calmed Jimmy down and with his friend on one side of him, and his cousin on the other, they walked to the church.

Father Dunn told them all was quiet but the next day word got out that St. Philip's had a stockpile of weapons and a nativist gang showed up to demand they be removed. The Avengers were alerted and they rushed to the scene. They armed themselves with the muskets and took positions around the church. Patrick stood on the front steps, nervous but ready, going over in his mind how to reload his gun if it came to that.

Father Dunn had already sent for the sheriff, who called for the state militia and this time they responded timely. General Cadwalader took control, replacing the Avengers with his troops. He forced them to leave after taking away their muskets. As they made their way to Kensington they were shot at and chased. They could do nothing but run, being mostly unarmed and greatly outnumbered.

The mob wanted to search the church and when they were refused, they pelted the soldiers with stones and bricks. Cadwalader ordered a cannon to be fired into their midst, sending them for cover, but not into submission.

Over the next two days the nativists continued hurling bricks and bottles and shooting muskets. They acquired their own cannon from somewhere down at the docks. They had no balls but used anything they could find; nails, scrap iron, broken glass, and fired them on the soldiers.

Lewis Levin arrived at the scene and worked with Cadwalader to defuse the situation. The fighting ended on the eighth but not before fifteen people were killed and over fifty more were injured. As in Kensington, a grand jury blamed the Irish Catholics for inciting the trouble.

Chapter Twenty-Two

Kensington, July 10, 1844

Donnie arrived at Jack's house before sunrise. The family was awake and quiet in the muted yellow of the candlelit kitchen. Jimmy and Patrick were packed and ready to go. They carried a bedroll, a canteen, a sack with a change of clothes and fresh biscuits Aunt Mary made for them. Patrick made sure to pack *Oliver Twist* which he hadn't yet finished.

In the few months Patrick had been there, the Torpeys became as close as his own family. This was like leaving his home in Ireland all over again, coupled with the nagging thought that he was abandoning not only his sister, but his promise to his father.

Ellen went to her aunt, who took her in her arms and rocked her as if she was a small child. They both cried softly. "We'll take good care of her, Patrick," said Mary. "Don't you worry about that."

"Thank you, Aunt Mary. I'll be sending money soon."

"We know you will. Promise me you'll watch over Jimmy."

"I will."

"Off with you now," she said. "Before I wrap my arms around the three of you and never let you go."

Uncle John's face was blank. He was still a lost soul. He stood up and shook hands with Donnie. His eyes were wet when he embraced Jimmy. Then he hugged Patrick, pulling him close to whisper in his ear. "I'm so sorry, lad. It shouldn't be like this."

"Thank you for taking us in, Uncle John."

"Keep an eye on Jimmy will ya? He's a hothead like his father, but without a good woman to calm him down."

"I will, Uncle John."

Ellen was losing control. She grabbed hold of her brother and cried into his chest. "I'll never see you again, Patrick."

"Stop that, Ellen. I'll be back for you in no time and we'll get the farm." He reached into his shirt pocket and pulled out an envelope. "I've written Da. I told him everything, the riots, the money, and that I'm going to Pittsburgh. Will you mail it for me?"

"Of course."

"I will be back for you, Ellen. Don't lose faith." He turned and hurried out the front door. Jimmy and Donnie followed after him.

In the end, Donnie convinced them to take the train the eighty miles to Lancaster. The sheriff, if he decided to pursue them, wouldn't know where they went after that. They would be there in eight hours at the cost of two dollars per person. He paid for it and refused to take any money from either of them.

The train departed from the Philadelphia and Columbia Rail station three miles from Kensington. They arrived in plenty of time. Donnie got the tickets and they settled in for the first leg of the trip that would wind up taking them close to seven weeks. The whistle shrieked and gusts of black smoke billowed from the stack as the train pulled out of the station heading north. Clouds of steam hissed from the rods connected to the wheels, blowing a thick mist past the window where Patrick sat.

Once it was out of the city and after climbing a mile long incline, the train picked up speed. Patrick was amazed at how fast it moved, nearly twenty miles an hour at times. It made objects in the foreground blurry but did nothing to obscure the bucolic scenery of grassy hills, farm fields and forests in the distance.

They made ten stops in towns along the way, arriving at the station in Columbia right at six o'clock. The small town lies on the east bank of the Susquehanna River just past the city of Lancaster. From there they could have traveled via the Main Line Canal all the way to Pittsburgh, and arriving, Donnie said, in four or five days. Instead they took the ferry across the river and walked west, taking advantage of what little daylight was left.

When it was nearly dark, they bedded down in a grove of trees a hundred yards off the road. Donnie was already complaining. "It's cold, and this ground is harder than a ship's deck," he said. "Whatever made me decide to do this?"

"It's not cold, Donnie," said Jimmy. "It's July for God's sake. But the ground is hard."

"I'm missing my nice feather bed and soft pillow right about now," said Donnie.

Patrick didn't say anything. He pulled his blanket up and looked at the stars beginning to appear in the fading light. He thought about what his brothers might be doing back in Ireland. He drifted off to sleep hoping his parents were well and that his letter wouldn't cause them too much suffering. They were back on the road at daybreak with Patrick setting a brisk pace. By dusk they had traveled nearly twenty miles and came to a farm on the outskirts of Harrisburg.

They asked the farmer if they could spend the night in his barn in return for work. The farmer, Mr. Schneider, said yes and they stayed there two days digging out stumps and moving boulders until his field was ready to till. The back breaking work reminded Patrick fondly of home on the one hand and his unfulfilled promise on the other. On the morning they left, Mrs.

Schneider gave them bacon and fresh baked bread for the road.

During their journey they found odd jobs for food and shelter where they could. They stayed in Carlisle for six days, getting work on the turnpike, repairing and resurfacing a section of the macadam road. At night they slept in a large tent that served as a makeshift barracks. With every passing mile, Patrick's spirits improved. The havoc and violence of Philadelphia were behind him. Guilt remained his constant companion but he allowed himself to believe things would get better.

Pittsburgh, August 20, 1844 - May 22, 1845

Five weeks after leaving Kensington they reached the town of Bedford. Donnie wanted to use the money they earned working on the turnpike to ride the packet boat over the mountains by way of the Allegheny Portage, a combination of canals, railroad, mules and a stationary steam engine that pulled boats and wagons up and over the mountains. It cut the time to get over the rugged thirty-six mile trail down from two days to six hours.

"How much would it cost?" said Patrick.

"I don't know," said Donnie. "Maybe eight dollars each."

"I have three dollars to my name, Donnie and I won't be indebted to you."

Jimmy agreed and Donnie gave up arguing about it. They continued heading northwest on the old Forbes Road. At sunset six days later they got their first view of the smoky city of Pittsburgh, nestled at the confluence of the Ohio, Monongahela and Allegheny Rivers. From Squirrel Hill they looked down on the Monongahela, crowded with dozens of ships belching plumes of black smoke into the atmosphere, already thick with soot and haze from the multitude of coal, glass, iron and steel factories hard at work all across the city.

In the early afternoon of the next day they walked through the streets of Pittsburgh, looking first for a place to stay. "Let's find the Catholic church," said Patrick. "That should put us in an Irish part of town."

They asked and got directions to St. Paul's at the corner of Grant and Fifth Streets, close to the south bank of the Allegheny. They walked through the clean neighborhood cramped with row houses and after two tries found a boardinghouse with one room left. Mr. Quinn, a small man with a round face and a bulbous, purple-veined nose, demanded a week's rent of seven dollars up front.

"Each week, in advance," he said. "And I'll have no trouble from the likes of you or you'll be out on your arses."

Donnie paid him and Quinn showed them to their room on the second floor. The bed was barely big enough for the three of them but they would make it work. A small table, one chair and an old chest of drawers with half the knobs missing, completed the furnishings.

Over the next week, they made the rounds to the shipwrights but the industry in the city was now constructing predominantly steam vessels. Donnie had no practical knowledge of steam and he was over qualified for any jobs available with those still making traditional sailing ships. He was willing to take the work but they were unwilling to hire him. Patrick and Jimmy were turned away as well.

They went to the iron works, blacksmiths, glass manufacturers and even store merchants but found nothing but rejection. After five days of searching, they saw a flyer advertising the need for laborers to work on the construction of an aqueduct over the Allegheny River. The previous one had been destroyed by an ice jam in February. The aqueduct was the terminus of the Mainline Canal which moved people and thousands of tons of freight into the city on a daily basis.

John Roebling, a German immigrant, had recently won the contract based on innovations he made manufacturing wire rope. He needed laborers urgently. All that traffic and commerce were at a standstill. The pay was six dollars and eighty cents a week for a twelve hour day and Sundays off, as good as railroad wages, and better than digging coal.

Roebling hired them on the spot. Their first job was with a crew clearing the remains of the old structure. Then they worked on repairing the seven stone piers and digging large, deep anchorage holes on each shore. The work was hard and monotonous.

Patrick didn't mind the work even though the pay wasn't going to get him anywhere anytime soon. He sent half of it to Ellen and, after food and rent, never had much left over. Donnie always paid Mr. Quinn and tried not to take Patrick's money. He had been promoted to a supervisory position and still had a good part of his savings left. "Save it, Patrick," he said. "I'm doing fine and you need it much more than I do."

Patrick refused at first but over time he let Donnie do it though he was careful to record how much he owed him. They worked all through the winter, weather permitting. Once the clearing and repairing of the piers was completed, Patrick and Jimmy were assigned the task of splicing, twisting, greasing and wrapping wire. It took a month for Patrick's hands to stop bleeding from the cuts that, even with gloves, ripped and shredded his skin. The cables were eleven hundred feet long and stretched across the Allegheny. By the end of April the project was nearing completion and time to decide what to do next.

Roebling had already secured another contract to construct a highway suspension bridge over the Monongahela River less than a mile away. They had the work if they wanted it. Jimmy was ready to move on and head west even though he hadn't been diligent about saving money. He liked drinking and gambling at cards too much.

"How much do you have?" asked Patrick one night at Shaughnessy's, their neighborhood tavern.

"Enough to get to Independence. I'll get work there on a wagon train. They need men to scout, move livestock and drive the wagons for those who need it. I'll find something."

"How about you, Patrick?" said Donnie. "Have you decided to stay on with Mr. Roebling?"

Patrick took a long swig of his beer before answering. He thought about bringing out the flyer from his pocket: an army recruiting poster he saw a week ago. One item on it had been gnawing at him ever since. It promised a hundred and sixty acres of land at the end of a five year enlistment. He put his hand in his pocket and fingered it but decided not to say anything. "Maybe," he said.

The aqueduct reopened a few weeks later, on May twenty-second. Tens of thousands of onlookers lined both sides of the river to witness the event. Pittsburgh was ready and in need of good news. A torrid fire six weeks earlier, had destroyed a third of the city, leaving only remnants of chimneys and walls in its wake. Today, two thousand tons of water would be let loose into the wooden trough supported by Roebling's wire rope system. If successful, stalled commerce would flow again and the city could get back on its feet.

Patrick stood proudly with Jimmy and the other workers at the river's edge. Bands on each shore played "Hail Columbia," "Yankee Doodle Dandy," and other popular tunes.

"I think most of these people are here to see it collapse," said Jimmy.

Patrick shook his head and smiled. "Ah, you have no faith, Jimmy." He held his breath as Roebling and the mayor of Pittsburgh moved to open the canal gate. The water burst through and when the first boat floated easily to the other side, wild, enthusiastic cheers reverberated from both sides of the river.

He punched Jimmy playfully on the arm. "We're part of this, cousin," he said.

"Does that mean you're staying on to build the next one?"

"I didn't say that."

Chapter Twenty-Three

Washington, D.C. August 1845

Jane commuted between New York and Washington D.C. for the first few months after Polk's inauguration. She wanted to be close to the decision makers in order to better form and express her opinions. The campaigns had been fiercely fought, full of lies and deceptions on both sides with the issue of slavery gaining momentum and widening fissures that were already causing irreparable cracks in the very foundation of the Union. But Polk and Jackson were right, the American people cared more about growing the country and the opportunities that would create. In a very close election, they elected James Polk as the eleventh president of the United States.

Today, Jane had meetings with Governor Marcy, whom she had not seen since he was selected by the president to be his Secretary of War, and Nicholas Trist who had recently been named Chief Clerk for Secretary Buchanan in the State Department. She walked up the steps of the Georgian style building on Seventeenth Street and Pennsylvania Avenue, and was escorted to Marcy's office by a fresh-faced army lieutenant.

He came around from his desk and took her hands in his. She sat down and they exchanged pleasantries before Jane bluntly asked, "Why is Mr. Polk provoking Mexico to war?"

Marcy stared at her for a moment, then said, "We still hope it can be avoided."

"Hmmm," said Jane. "He sent General Taylor into Texas. I see no better way to look one up than that. It's nothing more than poking a stick into a hornets nest."

"We're trying diplomacy to avoid it. I'll tell you about it but it must remain off the record, Jane. Can you agree to that?"

She waved her hand and nodded impatiently. "Yes, of course."

"The President has named John Slidell to be Minister to Mexico. It's a recess appointment and Mr. Polk wants it to remain a secret as long as possible."

"What will be his purpose?" said Jane.

"To peacefully resolve the border issue with Texas, and negotiate for the purchase of California and New Mexico."

"At what price?"

"He has the authority to offer twenty-five million dollars on his own but the president let it be known he would consider going as high as forty."

Jane let out a soft whistle. She was all for peaceful negotiations and that was a tremendous amount of money, but she assured Marcy it wouldn't work. "The overriding sentiment in Mexico City is for war," she said.

"We have sources that say they're willing to negotiate."

"I wouldn't believe that, Governor."

"Why not?"

"Any Mexican politician who is seen to be negotiating with the United States will be ousted the moment it's discovered. Their government is, as always, in chaos. The Mexicans generals and politicians are so busy battling each other there's no way they're prepared to fight anyone else. Nevertheless, Governor, I guarantee you they will."

"What would you suggest we do then, Jane?"

"I'd replace Slidell with my friend from Texas, William Cazneau. He's well connected and would strive to build a coalition of liberal republicans. There are many ready to declare their independence and establish the Republic of the Rio Grande in the north. He'd also make sure the money, which is indispensable, goes to the right individuals. And he'd have strongly advised against sending General Taylor into Texas."

"Texas requested that. To protect them from invasion. A very real threat don't you agree?"

"A lot of noise and saber rattling but as I've already said, the Mexicans *will* fight. They'll need little more than the provocation of our army in Texas."

Marcy took out his watch and flipped it open. Jane made a move to get up. "I know you're busy, William."

"Can you stay a bit longer? Someone is coming who would like a word with you."

"Will he be here soon? I have an appointment with Nicholas Trist. I want to congratulate him on his appointment as Chief Clerk."

"I'm sure that's not the only reason," said Marcy with a knowing look.

"Well, I do want to share my thoughts with regard to Mr. Cazneau and the republicans in Mexico."

Just then there was a knock at the door. "Ah, here he is," said Marcy.

At first Jane was shocked. She thought it was Andrew Jackson himself walking through the door but then remembered that was impossible since Old Hickory had just passed on in June. It was the venerable newspaper man, Thomas Ritchie. He did resemble Jackson with his white hair and angular features but he was not as tall or rawboned. She stood and took his outstretched hand.

"Miss Storm," he said. "An honor to meet you."

"It's my honor, Mr. Ritchie."

He motioned for her to sit back down and he took the chair next to her. "We appreciate the support you gave Mr. Polk during the election and like very much what you have written about Texas, especially your latest piece in *The Review*. That is your work is it not?"

Her article was an unsigned opinion letter in O'Sullivan's *Democratic Review*, but he knew full well it was hers. Texas had voted to accept annexation on July fourth and she argued that the country should now cease the acrimonious debate and welcome her with open arms. In the editorial, Jane coined the phrase that history would forever attribute to O'Sullivan.

"It was time," she wrote, "to join together and ensure that other nations, England and France in particular are stopped from thwarting our policies and hampering our power, limiting our greatness and checking the fulfillment of our manifest destiny to overspread the continent." *Manifest Destiny* became the rallying cry for a generation of Americans and the expression that would forever describe the unquenchable, quasi-religious quest for land and the subjugation of an entire continent.

"Miss Storm," said Ritchie. "As you might know, I've been given the privilege of overseeing the publication of *The Daily Union* by the president. I'm here to offer you a position with the paper."

Jane was both surprised and flattered but she knew instantly that she wouldn't accept. The regular income would be a benefit but working for one party's printed organ was not for her.

"Thank you, Mr. Ritchie. Very much. And please thank the president for me. But I must decline your offer."

Ritchie obviously expected a different answer. This was a real and rare opportunity, especially for a woman, but Jane had no concern over that. She saw the reaction in his eyes.

"I do appreciate it," she said. "Believe me. But I'm already finding fault with some of Mr. Polk's actions and I doubt there is any way in the world you'd allow me to state them in the *Union*."

Thomas Ritchie was not one to beg. He stood to leave. "No, Madam," said Ritchie. "That most certainly would not be tolerated." He nodded to Marcy. "Governor," he said before storming out.

"I suppose, Jane," said Marcy, "I shouldn't be surprised but I thought it would interest you. And you'd be a great asset to the party."

"Please don't take it that I don't value your help, William. But while I'm completely on board with annexation and expansion, I won't hold back when I believe things should be approached in a different manner."

She got up and he walked her to the door. "Thank you again, William. I would welcome an opportunity to interview Mr. Polk in person if you could schedule it."

"I'm working on it, Jane."

Chapter Twenty-Four

Pittsburgh, August 19, 1845

Jimmy didn't leave for Oregon right away. There was a problem getting their final wages. Roebling was strapped because he hadn't yet been completely compensated by the city for the aqueduct. He and Patrick worked on the new bridge until the money came in.

Two months later, Roebling was able to pay them and get them current for their wages on the new bridge. Jimmy quit that day. They each had three months pay in their pockets, eighty-two dollars. After Patrick paid Donnie the thirty dollars he owed him for food and back rent, he sent forty-five to Ellen. He was confident that much would be enough to get the family passage to Philadelphia.

Jimmy pestered him for a decision. The idea of enlisting in the army was never far from his mind and it was time he did something about it. He went to Fort Pitt to see the army recruiter. Sergeant Kilkenny, a tough, leather-faced veteran of the Seminole Wars, gave Patrick a quick look over when he walked into the small office. He pointed at the chair for him to sit and said, "So you're looking for adventure and glory, eh son?"

"Well, sir, I'm looking for land."

"Ah yes," said the sergeant, hearing Patrick's brogue. "That's a good deal now isn't it. Are you a citizen?"

"Not yet. I've only been in the country a little over a year."

"No problem. You'll be a full fledged, property owning American when you complete your enlistment. And it's almost certain they'll be waiving the five year waiting time to become a citizen for those who sign up to be a soldier. Can you read and write?"

"Yes."

"Good. The pay is seven dollars a month and you get a twelve dollar bonus for signing up. The bonus is paid when you get sworn in. The seven dollars will come to you every month on payday."

"When do I get the land?"

The sergeant let out a short laugh. "Not until you've fulfilled your five year obligation."

"Where will the land be?"

"That's something I wouldn't know. Don't concern yourself about that. One thing we have in this country is plenty of land."

"And that's guaranteed? The land I mean."

"By the full force of the United States government. It's right here on your enlistment paper. You said you could read, correct?"

Patrick looked it over. The pay, the bonus, the land allotment were all there. "I don't see anything about becoming a citizen."

"You can trust me on that," said the sergeant."

"What happens next?"

"You sign the paper. Report back here next Monday morning by nine a.m. A doctor will verify you're fit for service, then you'll be sworn in. We're shipping out for New Orleans the next day to join General Taylor. He'll be needing brave young men like yourself very soon."

"Is that when I get the bonus?"

"Yes, the paymaster will be here then with cold, hard cash."

Patrick picked up the papers and looked them over one more time. He knew his sister and parents wouldn't like it anymore than Jimmy would but it seemed the only way. Still, he wasn't completely sure. He bit his lower lip and said, "I'd like to think about it."

"What is there it think about?" said Kilkenny, clearly irritated. "There's the land, good pay and free room and board. You'll be seeing the beautiful country, and women, of Mexico and you'll come home to the gratitude and admiration of your countrymen."

"My countrymen," he thought, not realizing he said it out loud.

"Yes, your grateful countrymen."

Patrick looked over the paper again before finally taking up the pen and signing his name.

"Welcome to the United States Army, Private Ryan," said Kilkenny. "Be back here Monday and don't be late."

Patrick went to their room and wrote a letter to Ellen, telling her of his decision. He'd mail it after he got his bonus money. He didn't say anything to Jimmy or Donnie until Saturday when he met up with them at Shaughnessy's. When he got there they were sitting at their favorite spot opposite the end of the bar, under a faded painting of Pope Gregory XVI. Donnie grabbed three beers and sat them on the small table.

"Well, Patrick," said Jimmy. "What are you going to do? It' time for me to move on and I want you to come with me."

"Time for me to go too," said Donnie. "This all work and no play is killing me."

Patrick laughed. "No play? he said. "You're with a different lass every week."

"Another reason to leave this city. The women are closing in. One of them is threatening me with a visit from her brothers if I don't step up and make her my wife."

"Just one?" said Jimmy.

"Miss Elizabeth Brannon seems to think I've made her promises. If I don't escape soon, I might be forced into marriage, or else be found face down in the Allegheny River."

"Would you be exaggerating a wee bit, Donnie?" said Patrick.

"Have you seen Miss Brannon's brothers? They're the brutes who run the docks and collect debts for the gambling bosses. If you don't pay you're either permanently maimed or never heard from again."

Jimmy slammed his glass down on the table, spilling beer down its side. "Donnie," he said. "She's a Protestant! The Brannons are the leaders of the Belfast Boys. My God, what are you doing?"

"But she has the most beautiful brown eyes you've ever seen, Jimmy."

"Can't you just tell her it's over?" said Patrick. "Maybe she'll understand."

"Sure," said Donnie gesturing to the picture of the pope. "And then I'll go convince His Holiness to become a Presbyterian."

Jimmy directed his frustration at his cousin. "It's time you made up your mind, Patrick. Are you coming with me or not?"

"You know I can't. Things are getting worse back home. Ellen wrote me that more and more are going hungry and losing their homes. My parents are at my Uncle's house but he may be losing it soon as well. My brothers can't find work and at this point we don't know where they're living."

"You still don't have near enough money for a farm," said Jimmy. "I know you're tired of hearing it, but there's land for the taking out west."

Patrick pulled out the recruiting poster from his pocket and spread it on the table.

"What's this? said Jimmy. "Some kind of a joke?"

"It must be," said Donnie. "Nobody in there right mind would want to be a soldier. They're the dregs of society, too lazy or too stupid to make it in the world."

"Well, I'm not lazy," said Patrick. "Maybe I am too stupid."

"That's not what I meant," said Donnie. "But it's a stupid idea if you're actually thinking about it."

"I've already done it," said Patrick.

Donnie put his head in his hands. Jimmy stared at him in disbelief. "Don't do it," he finally said. The words came out thick and hoarse.

"I report in Monday morning. I'll get a hundred and sixty acres of land at the end of my enlistment."

"Dammit Patrick!" said Jimmy. The bar went silent. The bartender eyed them thinking there might be trouble. Jimmy lowered his voice and leaned in closer. "A war will make the riots look like a walk in the park. What good is a hundred and sixty acres if you don't live to collect it?"

"I have to take that chance."

"No you don't!"

Donnie tried to smooth things over. "Well then," he said. "We need to send you off properly, Patrick. There's nothing left to do but get roaring drunk on this fine Saturday evening."

Jimmy stared mutely at his cousin. Patrick felt like he was letting him down, like he'd let everyone else down. Right then, he had the urge to do exactly what Donnie suggested. He stood up to head to the bar and said, "I'll get us some drinks."

Jimmy put a hand on his arm to stop him. "No you won't," he said. "We'll not have you spending your money. Tonight's on us."

A short while later three girls who Donnie had previously invited arrived. "This is Bridget," said Donnie, pulling the prettiest of them closer to him, "and her friends, Margaret and Eileen."

Margaret sat next to Jimmy. They had apparently met before. She had black hair, blue eyes and mounds of creamy white flesh bulging from her plunging neckline. Jimmy was mesmerized.

Eileen had sandy blonde hair, freckles across her nose and a bored look on her face. Patrick stood up and pulled a chair out for her. She looked him over, giving him a halfhearted smile. "Nice to meet you," said Patrick.

The beer and whiskey worked its magic and soon they were laughing and talking, forgetting all about the army and what might lay ahead. Eileen loosened up and Patrick found her to be witty and fun. He even got up the courage to kiss her on the cheek. She acted surprised, then leaned in and kissed him right on the lips. He was thinking about what might happen next when he saw a strange look come over Donnie's face. He turned to see someone behind him at the edge of the table.

"Elizabeth!" said Donnie, with an attempted smile frozen in place.

The captivating and alluring Elizabeth Brannon stood there seething. The ivory skin of her face was flushed with red blotches and her eyes, as beautiful as Donnie said, were tinged a pinkish red. Her voice quivered when she spoke.

"Don't Elizabeth me you despicable deceiver."

Behind her were four men the size of oxen, the notorious Brannon brothers, each bigger and brawnier than the other. A jolt of fear erased much of the effects of the alcohol on Patrick. He watched Donnie slowly pull his arm off Bridget's shoulder. She wanted to challenge this interloper, but was too drunk to speak.

"You told me we'd go out tonight," said Elizabeth. "Yet here you are with this diseased tramp."

Eileen wasn't as impaired as her friend and she fired back. "Get lost, ya repulsive prig."

That was the last thing Patrick remembered. The Brannon boys waded into them and soon the brawl was out on the street. Patrick briefly held his own, landing two punches to the head of one of them but he never saw the blow coming that knocked him unconscious. He woke up, face down in a dim alley, his head feeling like it had been hit with a sledge hammer.

He sat up and tried to focus. Everything hurt as he got to his feet and slowly staggered his way back to their rooming house. When he turned onto the street he saw uniformed policeman in front of Quinn's place. He ducked back around the corner and watched the cops drag Donnie down the steps of the house, throw him in the back of the police wagon and pull away.

Fear and nausea churned in his stomach. He hadn't seen Jimmy and couldn't be sure he wasn't already in the back of the wagon. He decided to go to the house. Mr. Quinn met him as soon as he walked inside.

"You'd better not be found here, boyo," he said.

"What happened?"

"The coppers came looking for the three of ya. They were most interested in your cousin, for murder they're saying. But he wasn't here so they took young Donovan away."

"Murder?"

"Yes, and you surely picked the wrong person to kill. One of the Brannon boys it was. Jail might be the safest place now."

He went up to the room, grabbed his few belongings and put them in a cloth sack. He was heading out the front door when he heard Mr. Quinn behind him. "Ya owe me rent!"

"I'll get it to you, Mr. Quinn," he shouted.

He ran down the street not really knowing where to go. His head pounding with each step. Before he made it to the end of the block he stopped when he heard his name being called.

"Over here, Patrick."

He looked across the street and saw Jimmy halfway down a narrow walkway. He started towards him. "No," said Jimmy, holding up his hands. "Head towards the aqueduct."

The Allegheny River was just under a mile away. When he could see the aqueduct Jimmy caught up to him.

"They took Donnie to jail, Jimmy."

"I know."

"What happened?"

"It's bad, Patrick."

"Mr. Quinn said it was murder."

"It was an accident. I pulled out my revolver, to fire it in the air to break things up. My arm got hit as I was pulling the trigger and the gun exploded right in the chest of one of them. Donnie and I took off in different directions. I looked for you but couldn't see you anywhere."

"What are you going to do?" said Patrick.

"We've got to leave Pittsburgh right away."

"What about Donnie? We can't let him stay in jail."

"Are you saying I should turn myself in? I'll get no fair trial in this city. No, we have to leave."

"Jimmy, I'm in the army, remember? I report tomorrow."

"Jesus, I forgot."

Jimmy dropped to a sitting position and put his arms and head on his knees. Patrick noticed two men upriver moving their way in a hurry. He turned and looked the other way and saw three more coming just a fast.

He nudged Jimmy and pointed them out. "We have to go."

They took off running, through the streets of Pittsburgh. They found an abandoned stable off a side street and hurried inside. "They're obviously watching the docks," whispered Jimmy. "And I'm sure the railroad too. We'll have to stay here until it gets dark."

"Then what?" said Patrick.

"Well, you'll be getting out of this mess tomorrow. I don't know what I'm going to do."

"You can join the army with me."

Jimmy laughed then winced in pain. He rubbed his side. "I think I broke a rib. The army's the last place you'll ever find me."

Chapter Twenty-Five

They spent the night in the barn. Patrick woke before dawn, cold and stiff from sleeping on the ground. Jimmy was already awake, staring into the dark.

"I have to get back to Quinn's," he said. "I need to get what's left of my wages so I can make it to Missouri."

"I'll go with you," said Patrick.

"What time do you have to report in?"

"Not until nine. I have a few hours."

When they got within sight of the house they saw Daniel Brannon walk up the steps. They were obviously not leaving Quinn's unattended. It wouldn't be possible to retrieve his clothes, or his money, even if the Brannons hadn't already discovered it.

"They went around the corner and stopped in an alley. "Jimmy," said Patrick. "I'll be getting my bonus money this morning. You can pay me back when you strike it rich in Oregon."

"No, Patrick. I can't take your money."

"What else are you going to do? The police and the Brannons are likely watching every escape route out of the city. Take the twelve dollars. Pay me when you can."

"And I'll tell you again, and for the last time, I won't take your money. What the hell. Maybe I'll join up with you. We'll come back home heroes."

"I just want to come back and claim my land."

"Now I'll have land as well. We can combine plots and have one big farm. That doesn't sound too bad does it?"

"I never thought of you as a farmer," said Patrick.

"Nor did I. I'll let you and your da run it and I'll travel the world with the profits," said Jimmy. He slapped his cousin on the back, grimacing in pain when he did it. "Looks like it's my only choice at the present moment, so might as well make the best of it."

"What about Donnie," said Patrick.

Jimmy rubbed his ribs, thinking. "Bridget lives a few blocks away," he said. "Let's go see if she knows anything."

They waited at the corner where she lived, hoping to catch her on her way to work.

"I have to leave soon," said Patrick.

"Just a bit longer," said Jimmy.

Ten long minutes later she emerged and walked down the street in the opposite direction. Jimmy called out to her. "Bridget. Bridget!"

She stopped and whirled around. When she saw them she turned back the way she was going and picked up her pace.

"Bridget, please wait." Jimmy ran and caught her by the arm.

"Let go of me," she said with unrestrained rage. He did, then got in front of her. She tried to get past him but he blocked her.

"Get out of my way or I'll scream bloody murder."

"Please, Bridget. I just want to ask about Donnie. Have you heard any news? What's he being charged with?"

She glared at him and let out a short, angry laugh. "You mean other than the fact he's locked up for something you did?"

"My arm was hit when I tried to fire my gun in the air."

"Tell it to the judge, not me. But the police aren't your biggest problem. You killed Joey Brannon. His brothers, their gang, and everyone else for five square miles is searching for you."

"Do the police know it was me who fired the gun?"

"I told them. Margaret and Eileen told them."

"Could you go to the police station and find out if they're going to let him go?"

Bridget laughed derisively. "Faith, and why wouldn't I? The Brannons, who have a cousin or two on the force, would love to see me sobbing over him. No, I won't be doing that and if I were you I'd get out of here quick, and never come around again. I'll keep this to myself, why I don't know. Maybe because I despise the Brannons more than I hate myself for falling under the spell of a cad like your friend Donnie. Now leave me be."

She pushed past them. They watched her walk away. "I think he'll be fine," said Jimmy. "He's got witnesses. The police here can't be that corrupt that they would charge him with something he didn't do."

"I hope you're right," said Patrick.

"If I didn't believe it I'd turn myself in."

"I know you would, Jimmy. So, you're joining up with me? It's a five year enlistment. You know that right?"

"Yes. Five long years. If you can do it, cousin, so can I."

A ragged group of forty, poorly clad recruits milled about in front of Sergeant Kilkenny's office. Most were Irish immigrants but there was a handful of Germans as well. There were also a few who, like Jimmy, needed to escape the law, creditors, or some other kind of trouble.

The sergeant was quite different than the last time Patrick saw him.

No longer was he the friendly recruiter, painting a rosy picture of army life, its adventures, and the dark-eyed, brown-skinned women of Mexico. He was gruff and surly when he signed up Jimmy who was obviously not some newly arrived foreigner. When he asked why he was joining, Jimmy gave him a curt answer.

"To look after my cousin here."

Kilkenny didn't like Jimmy, or his attitude, but he didn't say anything other than to have him sign the enlistment paper and tell them both to follow him outside to the yard. Kilkenny then shouted for the entire group to fall in. Most had no idea what he meant and they shuffled about asking each other what to do.

The Germans didn't speak English, and most of the Irish couldn't comprehend the rapid American version the sergeant was speaking. A group of four soldiers waded into them with shouts and shoves. They cursed and pushed the recruits, physically putting them in four lines of ten. Jimmy got angry and spoke to Kilkenny.

"They don't understand, Captain."

"Keep your mouth shut. I'm a sergeant, boy, and you'll address me as such. All of you, line up in straight rows of ten. Now!"

Once they were in formation, Kilkenny led them in a single line to the door of the barracks. One by one the new soldiers went inside to be examined by the doctor, a disheveled, unshaven man with bloodshot eyes. They stripped off their clothes and were told to turn around. He looked them over, for what Patrick wasn't sure. Then they were each pricked with a lancet that inoculated them with a smallpox vaccination.

After the physical they were marched to the barber for a haircut. Then they all stood at attention and were told to answer "present" when a corporal named Brenner called out their names. Some didn't answer because they didn't understand his pronunciation of their names. Brenner called out "Mitcheeal Henragagun" and when no one answered, he shouted it again louder. The recruits looked around at each other.

Sergeant Kilkenny screamed "answer up!" and threatened to flog each and every one of them. Still nobody answered. He went to the corporal and snatched the roll sheet out of his hands. The name read Micheál Heneghan.

"Heneghan," he screamed.

A tall, reed thin man in his mid-twenties with slightly rounded shoulders raised his hand. "State your name," said Kilkenny.

"Me name is Meehawl Heneghan. It's Irish."

"I know what is," shouted Kilkenny. "From now on," he said. "You answer to Michael. You're in the U.S. Army now and not Meehawl anymore. Got it?"

"Yes, sir."

"Yes, Sergeant!" said Kilkenny.

"Yes, Sergeant," said Heneghan.

When all were accounted for, Kilkenny administered the oath to them as a group. They swore to defend the constitution against all enemies and to obey the orders of the President and their superior officers. Then they were formed once more into one long line and marched towards their barracks.

The recruits were issued gear, including a uniform with an extra fatigue jacket, a pair of boots, a blanket, knapsack and musket. It was well after midnight when they were marched to the wharf in their new, stiff, ill-fitting clothes. They boarded the steamship that would take them down the

Ohio river to Cairo, Illinois, where it joins the mighty Mississippi. They would stop there to pick up more new soldiers coming from Michigan before continuing down to New Orleans to join General Taylor.

They were sent topside and Patrick found a spot near the front of the ship, below and behind the pilots cabin. It provided a bit of cover underneath an overhang and some protection from the wind. He and Jimmy stowed their gear and and got as comfortable as possible. The ship would be taking off at dawn.

They woke to the rumbling of the steam engine vibrating the ship. The sun wasn't up yet and the horizon was a cloudless violet-gray. A thick mist hung over Fort Pitt which sits on a triangle of land at the convergence of the Allegheny and Monongahela Rivers where they merge into the Ohio River. The ship pulled away from the dock, black smoke swirling from its two smokestacks, and chugged into the murky waters of the Ohio.

Corporal Brenner shouted for them to get on their feet and into formation. Sergeant Kilkenny did not ship out with them. A Sergeant Adams did in his place. Once they were lined up, Adams called the roll and then each man was issued a ration of beans, biscuits and pork. They would be responsible for cooking their own food.

Patrick introduced himself around and got to know some of the other lads. He found Heneghan while he was bent over his fire cooking some beans and bacon.

"Good morning, Micheál, my name's Patrick."

"And a fine morning it is, Patrick."

"Where are you from?"

"Shanagarry," said Micheál, "in County Cork."

"I'm from Cork too," said Patrick. "Up north in Newtownshandrum.

How long have you been in the states?"

"Just six months. Got a job in the coal mines but it literally choked the life out of me. I signed up for the land."

"As did I," said Patrick. "What brought you to America?"

"We were evicted off our farm and there was no work anywhere. I fell in with some lads and got in trouble for robbing the redcoats of food and guns and had to run."

"Aye," said Patrick. "My family has been evicted as well. I'm hoping the money I send will get them here soon."

"Not soon enough, mate," said Micheál.

Patrick avoided the card games that occupied most of the men. He needed to send Ellen ten dollars in the letter he'd written when they got to Cairo. He spent his time reading and getting better acquainted with his new comrades.

The ship had paying customers on the lower deck who didn't appreciate being on board with immigrant soldiers. It was against the rules to go below but Jimmy did anyway and found a traveling salesman who sold him whiskey. Micheál purchased a bottle as well and came out of his quiet, reserved shell. He produced a fiddle and played rousing and merry tunes. Many of the lads danced jigs about the deck.

It turned out that Micheál could also sing like an angel. Along with the rest of them, Patrick was overcome with homesickness when he sang "The Wind That Shook The Barley." No one, not even Jimmy, could hold back the tears.

"While soft the wind blew down the glade
And shook the golden barley.

Twas hard the woeful words to frame
To break the ties that bound us
Twas harder still to bear the shame
Of foreign chains around us
And so I said, The mountain glen
I'll seek next morning early
And join the brave, United Men
While soft winds shook the barley.
While sad I kissed away her tears,
My fond arms 'round her flinging,
The foeman's shot burst on our ears,
From out the wildwood ringing, -
A bullet pierced my true love's side,
In life's young spring so early,
And on my breast in blood she died
While soft winds shook the barley!"

Chapter Twenty-Six

Cairo, Illinois, September 3, 1845

The steamer ran aground a few times in shallow water, delaying their arrival at Cairo. It took eight days to make it there. The men wished to go ashore to stretch their legs on solid ground and see the city. They were refused permission and ordered to remain on board. The new recruits from up north had not arrived but were expected at any time.

Jimmy and some others slipped off the boat under the cover of darkness. Patrick declined to go but was able to get ashore the next day by volunteering to cut and load firewood for the ship's engine. He stuffed the letter to Ellen in his pocket to mail if he got the chance. Jimmy hadn't come back to the ship and he was worried.

The boat from Michigan arrived later that day, bringing a group of fifty more recruits. Patrick leaned over the deck railing and watched as they got ready to board the ship. He couldn't help but notice the towering figure of one of them. He was a spectacle of a man; at six feet four inches tall, with a powerful body that was equally proportioned from head to toe. He had a full head of lush, black hair and a dusky-red, week-old beard. Even from far away he had a powerful, almost mythical presence.

His heart skipped a beat when he saw Jimmy move among the new arrivals, trying to mingle in without drawing notice. An officer observed him and started heading his way. Patrick was sure his cousin was about to be accosted until the booming voice of the big man called out to the lieutenant. He had noticed Jimmy too and was creating a diversion for him. The lieutenant went to the man, and Jimmy was able to blend in and sneak back on board with the group. A swelling of gratitude and admiration for this stranger came over Patrick.

Jimmy hadn't slept in two days and looked it. "I thought you might have headed west," said Patrick.

He scratched at his stubbled cheek and said, "Don't think I didn't consider it. But how could I leave you to fend off the Mexicans all by yourself?"

"You're lucky you didn't get caught," said Patrick. "You need to thank the man that helped you."

"Who's that?"

Patrick pointed him out on the other side of the deck, stacking his gear. "The tall one. An officer saw you and if he hadn't stopped him you'd be in real trouble."

"He looks like a behemoth," said Jimmy. "I'll thank him later, right now I need some rest. Were you able to go ashore and mail your letter?"

"I got off the boat for awhile with a work party but didn't get a chance to mail it. What were you doing?"

"I found a poker game and much better whiskey than what's on this broken down old bucket."

After the new men were settled in, Patrick went to thank the soldier who protected Jimmy. He'd learned his name was John Riley. He was leaning over the rail, reading a newspaper when Patrick approached. He looked to be around thirty and was as handsome as he was tall, with cerulean eyes that carried equal amounts of intensity and amusement. Though he was a private like the rest of them, it was as clear as day that here was a man better suited to giving orders than taking them. He shook his hand and became conscious of how small his was, lost in Riley's huge grip.

"You're welcome, Patrick," said Riley. "But your cousin should be more careful. When we get to a real post he won't be getting away with wandering off so easily."

Patrick shrugged and smiled. "Jimmy's not easy to control," he said. Then he asked John where he was from.

"Clifden, County Galway," said Riley. "It's been a long while since I've been home. I joined the British Army back in '38. I was assigned to an artillery unit. Saw action in Afghanistan in '39. I was home for a short while after that."

"I'm surprised," said Patrick.

"About what, lad?"

Patrick tilted his head and looked up into Riley's eyes. "That you'd fight for the British I guess."

Riley's lips tightened and he nodded. "There wasn't much choice. Jobs and food were always scarce. The pay was decent and I'll tell you this, lad, once I was in, I liked it. Most of them hated us Irish, until we fought side by side with them. I was decorated for bravery and promoted a few times before finally making sergeant."

John folded up his paper and held it up. "I need to pass this along," he said. "Will you walk with me?" They moved down the deck and Patrick noticed how all the Michigan boys made way for him and beamed when he acknowledged them. He handed the paper to a small, grizzled Irishman who was much older than all the rest of them, and said, "Pass it on to O'Shea when you're finished."

They continued strolling and Patrick asked him how he ended up in this army. "I was discharged in Canada a year ago. Went to Mackinac, Michigan to find work, maybe get some land. I have a wife and son back in

Clifden. I wanted to get settled and bring them over but I soon discovered I wasn't fit for working in a field or a factory. I like soldiering after all, and was told one could rise in rank in the American army."

He paused and looked closer at Patrick. "And what about you, lad. Where are you from and how is it you and I are together on this boat heading down to join General Zachary Taylor to fight Mexicans."

Patrick told him his story, including the Bible riots, losing his money, working on the aqueduct in Pittsburgh and his decision to join the army for the land.

"That's a lot for someone as young as yourself. How old you?"

"Nineteen this past July."

"Just a couple years younger than I was when I first signed up. You've experienced much more than I had by nineteen."

"I would much rather have stayed home with my family."

Riley's loud, rolling laugh broke through the throbbing of the engines and the murmur of conversations on the ship. It touched Patrick's heart with a lightness that he hadn't known for a long while.

"Wouldn't we all," said Riley. "But things keep getting worse in Ireland. Work is even harder to find now and the British are cracking down. They wanted to send me to a garrison in Dublin. Did you know there are more troops stationed in Ireland than anywhere else in the world, even India? They act as if it's an actual war. That's the main reason I left the army. It's one thing to fight infidels, quite another to crush your own people."

Riley was impressed by Patrick's participation in the riots. "You took a stand, lad. That's what we all have to do. You've had a taste of battle then haven't ya?"

Patrick wasn't sure how much of a stand he actually took. "I don't know," he said. "It felt like I was caught up in something I had no control over."

"Don't diminish it, Patrick. We need to stand up for ourselves and that's what you and your cousin did."

Riley exuded so much pride at being an Irishman that Patrick and the rest of the lads could't help but feel the same way. He was also well-informed. He understood where they were going and why. He said that they needed to be prepared. War with Mexico was inevitable. All of the men grew to respect and gravitate to him, except perhaps Jimmy. Later that evening when they were bedding down for the night Patrick told him about their conversation.

"I don't trust him," said Jimmy.

"Why on earth not?" said Patrick.

"They say he doesn't drink or gamble. What kind of soldier, or Irishman, is he?"

Patrick shook his head and laughed. Maybe Jimmy was intimidated. Many men were upon first meeting John Riley, even officers in the United States Army.

Chapter Twenty-Seven

New Orleans, September, 1845

The steamer arrived in New Orleans on Tuesday, September twenty-third. The men gathered along the ship's rail as it rounded a bend in the river and the city came into view. Hundreds of steamships, loading and unloading massive amounts of freight, cotton and livestock lined the shore. Most had dual smokestacks and they stood like a forest of tall, branchless trees, spitting smoke into the sky. In the distance beyond the shore, Patrick made out the three spirals of the Cathedral of Saint Louis in Jackson Square.

They cruised a few miles past the city and docked in view of the fort. They were marched the hundred yards to the New Orleans Barracks and went inside to claim their bunks and store their gear. The next morning they were officially formed into Company K of the Fifth Infantry.

General Taylor had moved the army to Corpus Christi, Texas. Company K would join them but no one knew exactly when. Their two new commanding officers had not arrived yet but were expected soon. Until then the days were filled with roll calls and work details from reveille at six in the morning until taps and lights out at nine o'clock.

Three days after their arrival torrential rains poured down and continued through Saturday, putting a stop to anything that took place outdoors. The men were restless with nothing more to do than write letters, play cards or just lay around talking. Micheál took out his fiddle and some of the boys danced and sang with him until Sergeant Adams arrived and put a stop to it. Patrick took the time to write Ellen a second letter and mail his bonus money.

On Sunday, the men were given the day off. The storm had dissipated, leaving large white and gray clouds drifting through the vivid blue sky like enormous sailing ships heading toward the Gulf of Mexico. Patrick wanted to see the city so he and Jimmy, and most of the others, requested passes. All were denied with no reason given.

"I'm going anyway," said Jimmy.

"I wouldn't, lad," said John Riley.

"Then don't," said Jimmy.

"I'll be joining you," said Micheál. "I can't stay confined in here any longer."

"Knowing Sergeant Adams," said Riley, "He may just charge you with desertion."

"Only if we get caught," said Jimmy. "Besides both he and Brenner are off drinking somewhere. We won't be seeing them for the rest of the day."

A half a dozen of them decided to go. After wrestling with the decision, Patrick chose not to heed John's warning. He was bored and thought he might go to the cathedral for Mass. Five of them left together, Patrick, Jimmy, Micheál, Liam McCartney and Fred Leahy. No one noticed or cared as they sauntered out of the barracks and off the post for the four mile walk to the center of the city.

It seemed that every race and culture of humanity walked freely along the streets of New Orleans. The styles of clothing and the variety of languages were a constant curiosity to Patrick's eyes and ears. Tantalizing aromas of unfamiliar foods drifted in the air, making his mouth water. He didn't want to spend any money but finally couldn't resist ordering a deep-fried french pastry called a beignet. It was filled with fruit and covered with powered sugar. He nearly moaned out loud at the first taste of it. He also had a rich cup of coffee mixed with milk, called café au lait.

Jimmy, Liam and Fred decided to sample the prostitutes who appeared like moths to the flame of young, naive soldiers walking the streets. Micheál went with Patrick to the cathedral. They took some friendly ridicule from the others but Patrick didn't care. New Orleans was a Catholic city after all and he had a longing for the ritual of the Mass which reminded him of home and family.

The St. Louis Cathedral catered to the French residents and when they asked for directions a kind woman told them there was a church they might like better, St. Patrick's, just a mile away near Lafayette Park. It was where the English speaking Irish and Americans in the city went to worship.

The church was tall and stately, with slender columns and one lofty bell tower. Inside, Patrick counted sixteen splendid stained glass windows. Behind the altar were three paintings, one of St. Patrick, one of Christ rising to heaven and the last of Jesus pulling St. Peter from the sea.

After Mass, they walked back to the French Quarter. It was late afternoon, time to head back to the barracks. They searched a bit for Jimmy and the others but soon gave it up. As they walked out of the Quarter, they heard a clanging sound of scraping metal and voices singing a hauntingly moving dirge. They turned a corner and came upon a line of twelve African men shackled together and shuffling along in an awful yet somehow dignified rhythm. Their brown, bare backs gleamed in the flaming orange-red of the setting sun.

A white overseer on a large black horse held a whip in his hand and shouted at them to pick up the pace. They did so while continuing to sing in a magnificent mingling of voices in every range from bass to baritone to tenor. Patrick couldn't understand the words but the sadness and pitiful beauty were hard to bear. He was sickened further when he witnessed, a few yards behind them, a group of women with little boys and girls, clapped in irons like the men.

They followed them for a few blocks until the slaves were stopped at an auction house where they would be caged until being put on display and sold like livestock. Patrick didn't think he could be shocked anymore than he already was but then he saw a shingle hanging over the door that read Thomas Ryan/Owner and Auctioneer. A deep and confusing shame came over him at the realization that an Irishman, who shared his own father's name, could be a buyer and seller of human flesh.

It was dark when they made it back to the barracks, undetected, a few hours before Jimmy and the others did. He sought out John Riley and told him what he saw.

"You wouldn't believe it. Young black men, along with innocent women and mere children, some who were not much more than infants, being marched to an auction house. And the auctioneer's name is Ryan, Thomas Ryan. That's my father's name. An Irishman, John. How could he do it?"

"Being Irish doesn't make one a saint, lad."

"I realize that but to chain and sell human beings...children."

"A horrible thing to be sure, Patrick. But you're not Thomas Ryan. He'll have to answer for it on Judgement Day."

"I can't get the picture of those poor people out of my head. Or the pitiful and glorious voices of the men chained and paraded through the streets. And no one besides us took any notice."

Chapter Twenty-Eight

The next morning, the men of Company K were rousted out of their beds in the dark of predawn by shouts and batons hitting the frames of their beds. Corporal Brenner and Sergeant Adams ordered them to dress and get outside immediately. They were going to meet their new officers. When they were in formation Patrick was appalled to see that the captain and his lieutenant each had their own personal black slaves with them.

Captain Stuart Saxon sat erect and stone-faced on a large gray horse. He was five feet seven inches tall but on his mount he appeared extremely intimidating and much larger than his actual height. He had black hair that extended from under his cap just over his collar. His thick eyebrows over small, deep set eyes so dark they too looked black, gave him a fierce and frightening appearance. His slave, whose name was Jeb, stood straight and motionless, holding tightly to the the horse's bridle. His eyes were fixed on a point above the heads of the soldiers, making sure he looked directly at no one.

Saxon hailed from Alabama and was a West Point man, class of '37. As an artillery officer he was suppressing his rage over being assigned to an infantry company. He had been assured they would ultimately be attached to an ordnance unit but in the meantime he had to swallow the insult and bide his time. He said nothing as his cold gaze swept over each and everyone of them. Patrick stood stock-still and stared straight ahead, trying to be invisible.

His adjutant, Second Lieutenant Anthony Graves, addressed the men. He was a small man, five feet five inches tall and fresh from the Academy. Everything about his physical appearance was slight. His skin was pale, his hair stringy. His attempt at a beard was a waste of time; he could only manage patches of whiskers along his jawline and an almost invisible mustache. He paraded about making noise and puffing out his chest, like a peacock trying to attract a mate.

Graves was from Nashville and would have everyone believe that he was, if not the nephew of his fellow Tennessean, James Polk, at least a cousin of some sort. He was not remotely related and had never met the president. The only connection he had was that his father had purchased his slave, along with a horse, from one of Polk's neighbors in Columbia, Tennessee.

"My name is Lieutenant Graves," he said in a high, effeminate voice. Laughter rippled through the company. Brenner and Adams rushed through the lines seeking the perpetrators. When no one was caught, Graves continued. He pointed at Saxon. "Our commanding officer is Captain Saxon. You are now part of Company K in the Second Brigade of the Fifth Infantry and belong to him. You will pay attention at all times, follow instructions, be respectful, and display complete obedience to any order given to you by a superior. Is that understood?"

There were an undertow of assent but Graves demanded more. "Is that understood," he screeched. "Repeat, sir, yes sir!"

Company K responded but it still wasn't good enough.

"Sir, yes sir," he said again, louder.

"Sir, yes sir," they shouted.

"We'll be moving out sometime in the next week for Corpus Christi and, soon after that we'll be teaching the greasy Mexicans not to pick a fight with Uncle Sam."

They remained in New Orleans ten more days. Lieutenant Graves had them fall in every morning at reveille. Anyone who didn't respond immediately, or loud enough, to his name being called was denied breakfast and ordered to remain at attention, in full gear, until the rest of the men had eaten. Although they were constantly berated for not speaking or understanding proper English, it was nearly impossible for any of them to understand the accent of their southerner superiors.

Graves slurred his words in a long, lazy drawl making even Patrick's last name sound unfamiliar. "Raayeeen," he called out and when Patrick didn't answer he was one of the first to miss breakfast. There were a lot more of them, Micheál included, when Graves butchered both his first and last names beyond all recognition. Jimmy joined them but he did it on purpose. Instead of replying "present" he responded with "here" in an insolent, mimicking drawl. Twice.

After breakfast they drilled and marched but never to Saxon's or Graves' satisfaction. Saxon continued sitting silently on his horse while Graves filled the air with his whining, demeaning profanity. He strutted back and forth calling them "useless Irish drunkards, papist scum, and stupid Mick bastards."

After every insult Patrick heard John Riley tell them in a low, even voice to remain calm. "Steady lads," he'd say. Later in the barracks he told them, "React and you lose. Stare straight ahead without emotion. It's on the battlefield that we'll show them our courage and fighting spirit. That'll be our way to respect and acceptance."

Patrick didn't know how long Jimmy would be able to take it. He boiled with anger at each insult and no doubt Saxon and Graves observed it. They noticed everything, including John Riley. How could they not? His size and stature alone were impossible to ignore.

Saxon took a special and immediate dislike to Riley. When he ordered Graves to inspect him closer, he could find nothing wrong. His shoes and buckles were polished, his musket was clean and ready, his uniform spotless. He looked every bit the military man and more like an officer than the two southern aristocrats. Saxon displayed no outward reaction at John's passing inspection but he had his lieutenant intensify his scrutiny on everyone else.

On the first Wednesday of October, The Fifth Infantry was informed they would ship out in two days. Company K was given the task of loading baggage and supplies on the chartered transport steamers. It was a welcome relief from the drill and harassment. On Friday morning the entire command stood ready, muskets at right shoulder arms. Their bayonets were fixed and shining like the roofs and amber-red domes of New Orleans reflecting the rising sun.

They marched down to the dock accompanied by the songs played by the regimental fife and drum band. Patrick didn't recognize any of them until they played "Yankee Doodle Dandy." He followed along in single file with the rest of his unit and boarded the steamer, *Alabama*. Company K found an open section on the lower deck and they settled in for the trip to Corpus Christi.

Chapter Twenty-Nine

Corpus Christi, Texas, October, 1845

It took two days to get to Aransas Bay where they disembarked on St. Joseph's Island. The boat couldn't make it over a sand bar so they had to jump in the chest-deep water and wade onshore. Some of the boys were desperately afraid of the water and rode piggy-back on a companion. Jimmy was one of them. Patrick had never known him to fear anything but Jimmy confessed with panic in his eyes that he couldn't swim.

"Get on my back," said Patrick. Jimmy got up and wrapped his arms and legs so tight around Patrick's waist and neck that he nearly strangled him. The waves gave him a bit of trouble and his legs wobbled, causing Jimmy to squeeze harder. "Not so tight," said Patrick. "Or we'll both be taking a swim." When the water was only ankle deep Jimmy got the courage to walk on his own.

A day and a half later they were transported by longboats to join Taylor's Army of Observation on the west side of Corpus Christi Bay. The encampment stretched out over a bluff on a two mile section of beach overlooking the water. It was a beautiful spot with mostly warm days, cool nights and a consistent, refreshing breeze.

Soon after they arrived the weather changed to frequent spells of icy cold with torrential storms accompanied by the fiercest lightning Patrick had ever seen. At times the thunderclaps convinced some of the troops that the Mexican Army was attacking.

With the change in weather came sickness. Tainted water, nearly spoiled meat, and poor sanitary conditions turned the camp to something more akin to a remote hospital. At one time or another at least a thousand of Taylor's five thousand troops were on sick call, suffering from diarrhea, jaundice, malaria, fever, influenza, scurvy and other unnamed or unknown ailments.

The Fifth Infantry's tents were at the far end of the camp. Patrick and Jimmy shared one while Micheál bunked with John. Also joining them were an abundance of scorpions, snakes, lizards and on the warm days, mosquitoes and more types of insects than were imaginable. On one afternoon alone, John and Micheál found three rattlesnakes inside the tent curled up in their blankets.

"Saint Patrick," said Micheál, "must have sent all the snakes here to Texas when he chased them out of dear old Ireland."

It was now Patrick's turn to face a fear he didn't know he had; a near hysterical fear of snakes. It stayed with him constantly. The slightest noise in the tent or outside in the brush sent him into a panic. But it soon took second place to the terror that increased rapidly from their very own slave masters, Saxon and Graves. It began in earnest the first morning in camp.

In formation long before the sun was up, Sergeant Adams and Corporal Brenner went in and out of the lines shrieking like wild animals. Those who did not have perfect posture, chins up and chests out, with a spotless uniform, were shoved roughly to the ground. Patrick's collar was slightly askew and he was one of the first ones to go down. While laying in the sandy dirt, Brenner kicked him in the head, cursed him as a "useless Mick" and then ordered him to his feet.

Saxon watched, unbending and unsmiling from the saddle of his horse. Patrick got slowly to his feet. He heard John Riley from behind him. "Don't give in to it, lad." He took a deep breath, spit the sand out of his mouth, and stood at a rigid attention with his eyes straight ahead and, somehow, kept control of himself.

Taylor's army remained at Corpus Christi from the middle of October until the next March. Like the weather, things went from bad to worse during those five months for the men of Company K. Not even John Riley was able to avoid the barbaric treatment from their commanders. It didn't matter that his performance was perfect and he was the very image of a soldier. One morning in early November he made a big mistake.

Neither Saxon nor Graves were well versed on infantry tactics. They struggled with having the troops execute even a simple flanking maneuver. Out on the parade field, when one made a wrong turn or bumped into the man behind him both officers went on a tirade. Riley decided to try and help. He had more experience as a soldier than almost any officer in the U.S. Army at the time. His voice rang out strong and clear from his place in the middle of the platoon.

"With all due respect, Captain," he said. "I can show the men the proper technique."

It was as if he'd hit Saxon in the face with the butt of his musket. He spurred his gray charger right into the column, sending men scrambling and sprawling, except for John who stood his ground with perfect military posture as the horse pulled to a halt, snout to nose with him. Saxon turned his mount slightly so he could look down on him.

"Who told you," he said, "to open your filthy Irish mouth."

"Begging your pardon, sir," said Riley. "It's just that I have a bit of knowledge with these maneuvers from my time..."

"I don't care a damn about your experience, private. Nor will I tolerate your insolence."

"My apologies..."

"Shut up!"

"Yes, sir."

"Lieutenant Graves," shouted Saxon. "Buck and gag this man."

Graves looked like one of the drummer boys next to Riley. Patrick thought, wished really, that John would just pick him up and toss him at Saxon and knock him on his arrogant ass. Instead he marched off to the side of the field without any complaint or comment.

The inhumane punishment of bucking and gagging was not sanctioned by the army. But that mattered little in Texas. General Taylor, Old Rough and Ready they called him, had a reputation for fairness and affection for and from his troops. But Patrick could never understand how he could condone this kind of treatment on his soldiers from the likes of Saxon and Graves. Either he didn't know, or didn't care to know.

The boys of Company K watched as John was forced to sit on the ground with his legs pulled up. Sergeant Adams slid a pole under his bent knees and tied his hands together in front of them so that his arms remained underneath the pole. His ankles were bound together and a rag was shoved into his mouth, secured with a rope tied at the back of his neck. Forced to remain in that position, pain sets in instantly and gradually grows to a hellish, unrelenting agony.

Riley was restrained that way for seven long hours. He was released when taps sounded. Patrick, Jimmy and Micheál went out to help him back to his tent. He needed assistance even to stand up. Patrick gave him a biscuit and a sip of the brackish camp water. John tried to eat but could only manage one bite. Jimmy had a little whiskey. He always seemed to have a little whiskey. "Take this John," he said as he held the bottle to his lips.

It was the one of the rare times anyone saw Riley drink strong spirits. He took a sip and coughed slightly, then beckoned for a little more. Jimmy held it up for him again. "Thanks, lad," he said, smiling faintly. Then he slipped off into an exhausted sleep. Patrick was astounded the next morning when, as usual, John Riley was the first one out of his tent and in formation looking as if nothing out of the ordinary had happened.

Despite his outward appearance, Riley was never the same after that day. There was nothing definite about it, just a lessening of encouragement and advice to the rest of the lads. It wasn't that he stopped trying to help, but he became somewhat distant and brooding from that point onward.

Jimmy's first trip to the guardhouse came on a warm morning when a button on his jacket wasn't fastened. In truth, he put forth a lazy, disrespectful manner as if he wanted to provoke them. He often let out a muffled, indistinct guffaw from somewhere in the middle of the formation when Graves gave a wrong or confusing command. One afternoon Saxon decided to punish everyone unless the perpetrator confessed. From his horse, his flinty eyes cold as steel, he threatened them in his gruff drawl that sounded as if he had stones in his throat.

"Ya'll will stand here, at attention, until the man who laughed comes forward. I don't care if you're here all night."

Jimmy stepped forward. "It was me, Captain, sir," he said, adding the unnecessary "sir" with dripping sarcasm. He never stood more erect as he marched to the front. Saxon drew his sword and Patrick believed he was going to run him through with it. Instead, he smacked him on his right cheek with the broad side, knocking him to his knees. A trickling stream of blood ran from the gash down off his chin into the sand.

"Sergeant Adams," said Saxon. "Buck and gag this papist pig."

161

Chapter Thirty

Corpus Christi, January-March, 1846

On December 29, 1845, President Polk signed the bill that accepted Texas into the Union as the twenty-eighth state. Two months later, on February 19, 1846, it became official. Nine years after declaring their independence from Mexico, Texas relinquished her sovereignty and became part of the Republic as a slave state.

War fever intensified on both sides of the border, as did the drilling, training, marching and other mundane duties like latrine digging and guard duty. After two months at Corpus Christi, Captain Saxon was able to get relief from the infantry training he abhorred. The Second Brigade would now receive artillery instruction.

John Riley would also be in his element but he knew better than to show his knowledge. Instead he assisted the others quietly, with whispers, nods and hand motions, to help them comprehend the commands. With his help, they picked up the this part of their training faster than they did the infantry maneuvers. It didn't matter to Captain Saxon. He found fault no matter how well they did.

Riley openly admired the ability and precision of the other artillery units under the supervision of Major Samuel Ringgold. He pointed out the speed with which they moved and positioned the glimmering bronze six pounders. He praised both the officers and the regular soldiers who could hitch and unhitch the field pieces to their teams of horses and place them in different firing position with seemingly effortless efficiency.

"Faith, Patrick," he said. "I'd like to be with those lads instead of stuck here with Saxon."

"But we're training in artillery now as well," said Patrick.

"That we are, lad. But these officers of ours are more concerned with breaking us than preparing us for combat."

"You think other officers are different?"

"Sure and I do. Men chafe under commanders they despise. You can see how those lads perform, with precision and enthusiasm. They're even proud of the powder stains on their uniforms."

Normally it took eight men to load, ram, point and aim the cannons. Each man had to concentrate on his task or risk bungling the whole process. It took hours of tedious effort and Company K often practiced with less than eight men in order to imitate battlefield conditions when members of the crew might be killed or wounded.

Even with John's help they struggled to meet Saxon's standards. Their mistakes sent the Captain's outrage to a higher level. Artillery was his specialty and his path to promotion. He would be damned if the men under his charge were anything but perfect. Jimmy became the main scapegoat.

On more than one occasion he was forced to "ride the horse." He had to sit all day on a raised narrow wooden beam with his hands bound behind his back and iron chains tied around his feet. No one could stay up long without falling and when Jimmy did, he was spat upon, kicked and hoisted back up. He refused to let them see him break. He responded to each and every occurrence with unhidden contempt.

"I look forward to our first battle," he told Patrick one night. "Bullets flying everywhere. No one will know if Saxon was killed by a Mexican or not."

On Sundays, Saxon forced Company K to attend Presbyterian

services conducted by a fellow officer from another battalion. When they asked to be excused because they were Catholic, he flatly refused and threatened to punish them for insubordination. But they did get free time on Sunday afternoons, when the officers made sure they had time for their own amusements of hunting, fishing, horse racing and card playing. They even built a theater to put on and act in their own plays.

Most Sunday afternoons Patrick rested, read or tried to write Ellen. Occasionally he went into Corpus Christi, known locally as Kinney's Ranch, which bordered their encampment. Before Taylor's troops arrived, it consisted of twenty or thirty small houses on a bluff covered with mesquite and evergreen shrubs with a view of Padre Island to the southeast. Now it had been turned into a ramshackle town of over a thousand camp followers.

Both Spanish and English were spoken among the gamblers, con artists, laundresses, prostitutes and peddlers of rotgut liquor who flocked to Kinney Ranch to feed off the American troops. Many were fluent in both languages, including a few priests who came to convince the Catholic soldiers that they were on the wrong side of the coming conflict.

Jimmy spent every spare moment at Kinney Ranch, often sneaking out after taps. He used what money he had on liquor, poker and whores. Many mornings he was either still drunk or suffering severely from his nights of excess. He wasn't the only one. When any of them swayed even a little bit during formations they were punished for drunkenness.

The penalty was to be forced to stand on a barrelhead where it was impossible, even for a sober man, to maintain his balance. The barrel inevitably teetered and when the culprit fell over, he was smacked with a sword or the stock of a musket and put back on it. He had to remain on the barrel for two hours, then off for an hour, then back on for two hours from reveille to taps.

It was a chilly night around their campfire when John first spoke openly of being on the wrong side. "I've been approached," he said, "by an itinerant priest. The Mexicans are remarkably aware of our situation and the abuse we suffer. They call us *Los Colorados* because there are so many redheads among us. He gave me this."

He passed around an open letter from a Mexican general named Mejia that encouraged them to become deserters. As Patrick read it his heart beat faster. It could have been addressed to him personally:

Irishmen! Listen to the words of your brothers, hear the accents of a Catholic people. Is religion no longer the strongest of human bonds? Can you fight by the side of those who put fire to your temples in Boston and Philadelphia? Did you witness such dreadful crimes and sacrileges without making a solemn vow to our Lord?

Why are you antagonistic to those who defend their country and your own God? Are Catholic Irishmen to be the destroyers of Catholic temples, the murderers of Catholic priests? Come over to us; you will be received under the laws of that truly Christian hospitality and good faith which Irish guests are entitled to obtain from a Catholic nation. May Mexicans and Irishmen, united by the sacred tie of religion and benevolence, form only one people.

Patrick didn't know what to think. "Surely, John," he said, "You're not thinking of going to the other side?"

"These Protestants can't wait," said Riley, "to seize Mexico's land, destroy the Church and extend the plague of slavery further south and west.

165

Is it right for us to fight for that?"

"But you'd be a traitor," said Patrick.

"A traitor to what?" said John. "You see how we're treated and yet they wish to use us against our Catholic brothers and sisters in Mexico? Believe me when I tell you that we're completely expendable. We'll be in the front lines as mere cannon fodder when the fighting starts."

The next morning, hundreds of the same flyer John showed them littered the camp as if they were blown in by the wind. No one, including Old Rough and Ready himself, could fail to take notice.

For the rest of their time in Corpus Christi, John didn't speak to Patrick about desertion again, knowing he was determined to see it through and get his land. But the letter did remain on Patrick's mind. The idea of running off occasionally comes to every hapless, homesick soldier during the long hours of drilling, discipline and loneliness. But how could he flee? As bad as things were and no matter what abuse they took or danger they encountered, he had a responsibility to get land and he wasn't going to fail yet again.

Right before they left Corpus Christi, Patrick was thrilled to receive a letter from Ellen. She was getting along fairly well, as were Aunt Mary and Uncle John, but the news from Ireland wasn't good. The potato crops were failing again and this time it appeared to be the worst anyone could remember. Staggering numbers of people were starving and losing their homes.

Ellen asked if there was any more money he could send. It was urgent to get their parents to America. Patrick was paid every two months and sometimes that was delayed. He was sending home ten out of the fourteen dollars he received and resolved to add two more dollars to that.

Chapter Thirty-One

Along the Rio Grande, March, 1846

It took a week for Taylor's four thousand man army to leave Corpus Christi. Just under a thousand were temporarily left behind, too sick to travel. Their journey would take them on a one hundred seventy-four mile march from Kinney Ranch to the left bank of the Rio Grande.

The day Company K departed was hot and dry with a strong wind that blew sand everywhere, blinding and choking the troops from their first step in the soft dirt. In some places their feet sank up to their ankles. Patrick's sixty-pound pack seemed twice as heavy as that, made worse by the diarrhea he could never quite recuperate from. Like many others, he also had recurrent fevers and splitting headaches. He did his best to ignore the pain and just keep putting one foot in front of the other.

The commander of the Fifth Infantry's Second brigade, Colonel McIntosh, drove his officers who in turn drove the men relentlessly, like reluctant cattle. Captain Saxon needed no encouragement. No one was allowed to stop until the entire brigade halted but many were so exhausted they couldn't help it. Jimmy faltered and Patrick stopped to help him. Saxon rode up and horsewhipped both of them around the neck and shoulders. "Stop again, Torpey," he said, "and I'll have you shot. You too, Ryan. Now move it!"

They didn't find water until late in the day and when they did the ranks broke and the men dove into the small lake like children seeing the ocean for the first time. Once refreshed, they proceeded a few more miles before camping the night in an open prairie surrounded by a grove of fragrant lavender shrubs with budding purple-blue flowers. The weather stayed hot over the next few days. The ground became firmer and better for marching but water was always a concern. Some days they marched over twenty parched miles before finding potable water.

They continued on a southwest course, going through plains abundant with purple lupine, bright red fireplant and puffs of white blooming flowers atop Spanish bayonet. After ten days out they reached a small river called the Arroyo Colorado. Excitement rushed through the troops when a group of fifty Mexican horsemen were spotted on the opposite bank.

Patrick saw them and heard what sounded like a hundred bugles blowing from behind them. He and every other soldier believed there were thousands of the enemy waiting just out of sight behind the opposite bank of the river. Two of the Mexican dragoons splashed across the river under a flag of truce and advised Taylor's second-in-command, General Worth, that they would fire on them if he attempted to cross it.

Worth would not be intimidated. He put his artillery in place and ordered the infantry to fix their bayonets and prepare to cross the swift moving river. Patrick's mouth was dry and his heart pounded so hard he thought it might burst right out of his chest. He expected at any moment to be shot and killed. Images of his parents came to him and along with the familiar, crushing thought that he had failed them.

The river was a hundred yards wide. It was only about knee high but, as instructed, Patrick held his musket high over his head and waded across. He looked for Jimmy and saw the fear in his eyes, as much from the water as the Mexicans. He watched General Worth spur his big black stallion into the water and charge boldly across. Patrick thought he was going to be shot out of his saddle.

When he reached the top of the opposite bank, General Worth waved his hat. When the men reached him they saw the company of cavalry galloping off. A loud cheer rose up as if they had just won a great battle. Many later claimed to be eager for a fight and upset that they did not get a chance to kill a dirty Mexican. Patrick felt nothing but a great wave of relief.

The weather remained warm and dry as they hiked on, more alert to the possibility of an attack. The country still contained vast open prairies, now edged with low, rolling hills. It seemed as if the rattlesnakes from Corpus Christi were part of their moving army. Patrick saw many scuttle off the trail and in his fear, believed every rustle in the bushes to be a rattler ready to strike.

Day after day they made their way in the boiling heat with little water. Along with the snakes, swarms of mosquitoes, flies and other blood thirsty insects harassed them relentlessly. The soft, sandy dirt had become extremely hard and hot. Patrick's pack got heavier with every mile and his feet and legs below the knees screamed at him with every step. Many simply fell to the ground, unable to get up.

Nothing entered Patrick's mind but the next step. He kept his eyes strained on the ground directly in front of him and willed his feet to move one at a time. The last few days of the journey became nothing more than a miserable blur.

The first thing General Taylor did when they reached the Rio Grande was erect a thirty foot pole at a sight where he would build a fort. The Second and Third Brigades stood at attention and the band played "Hail Columbia" while the American flag was raised. The provocative, unequivocal message was being sent to the Mexican Army, encamped and openly visible on the opposite shore in the town of Matamoros, that, disputed or not, this was American territory and they were here to defend it.

Construction on the earthen fort started immediately. Named Fort Texas, when finished it would be star shaped with six sides and a waterlessmoat around it, twenty feet wide and eight feet deep. The ten foot high and fifteen foot thick mud walls had redans at the top of each point for cannons to be placed on them. It would house five hundred men and its architect, Major Joseph Mansfield, assured Taylor it would withstand all the artillery fire the Mexicans could throw at it.

Taylor sent General Worth across the river in an attempt to negotiate. General Mejia refused to meet with him, sending his subordinate, General Vega in his stead. Taylor requested a peaceful settlement to the border dispute but it was emphatically rejected. It was assumed by both sides that the fighting would start very soon.

Company K set up camp on a bluff at a bend in the river. At that location, the Rio Grande was a hundred yards wide. At other spots it narrowed so much that Patrick thought he could easily throw a stone across to the other side. Matamoros was right there as clear as day, a half mile beyond the river's edge. It appeared to be a tranquil place with wide streets, clean white houses with red tile roofs and numerous church steeples.

The anticipation of battle intensified when two cavalry men out on patrol were captured. General Taylor ordered everyone to stay vigilant and to sleep with their muskets. A full scale attack could come at any moment.

From where their tents were set up, Patrick had a full view of Matamoros. He could see the townspeople going about their business and the many soldiers marching and parading about in their blue and red uniforms, their bayonets and brass buttons flashing and reflecting off the meandering river. Rumors spread regarding the enemy's strength and courage.

"I heard they have seven thousand troops," said John. "And more on the way."

"Sergeant Adams says there are ten thousand right now," said Patrick.

"I'm told they'll run before they fight," said Jimmy.

"I wouldn't believe that if I were you, lad," said John. "Many of their generals are experienced fighters with a European style army and we've got maybe four thousand men at the moment."

One thing was certain, there were a lot more soldiers on the Mexican side than there were on the American side. When their military bands weren't playing, Patrick heard the sweet sound of church bells. On their second morning he observed a priest leading a procession of local citizens as he blessed and splashed holy water on a line of cannons pointing right at him. It brought home that he was part of a Protestant army invading a Catholic country. What, he thought, would his father and brothers think of his being here?

Chapter Thirty-Two

Bravado continued to run rampant through the camp. Men with no battle experience whatsoever bragged about what they would do to the stupid, lazy Mexicans. A company of Texas Rangers was attached to the army. There would be more militia coming but for now they were the only volunteers with Taylor. Many of them had fought the Mexicans in the war for Texas independence and the years of bloody border conflict which followed.

Patrick overhead one Ranger assure everyone within earshot that he would get himself a "greaser scalp" to take home to his children. It was not something he wanted to admit, but Patrick was fearful and apprehensive about how he would hold up once the shooting started.

The attacks they believed were imminent did not take place. The two dragoons who had been captured were released a few days later and upon their return, told how they were treated graciously. They talked about the good food, the cultured officers and the beautiful women they met. Meanwhile, more and more Mexican soldiers preened and paraded on the opposite shore.

The women were the talk and fascination of the entire American army. Everyday they were seen doing laundry and bathing in the river. It was scandalously stimulating for the men, so many of them mere boys, miserably lonesome and thousands of miles from home. They hooted and hollered while the señoritas laughed, waved, swam and splashed about like beautiful mermaids, their bronze bodies naked from the waist up. "They're enjoying it as much as we are," said Jimmy.

The excessive punishment by Saxon actually increased now that they were on the banks of the Rio Grande, and desertions began to mount up. The bathing beauties were without doubt an added incentive to the rising tide of Irish lads disappearing into the night and swimming to the other side. With church bells ringing and sensuous young women cavorting in the water, it was an easy decision to make. Company K lost the most. Every other morning at roll call one or more were missing. It reflected poorly on Captain Saxon and completely infuriated him.

The desertions became a problem that General Taylor could not ignore. One morning the camp was littered with a sea of leaflets like the ones at Corpus Christi. How they got there, no one seemed to know. This one promised full Mexican citizenship and three hundred twenty acres of land if they would come over to their side.

After nine men deserted in one night, Old Rough and Ready gave orders for the sentries to shoot any man swimming across who did not obey the command to stop and return. The next morning Patrick, John, Jimmy and Micheál watched from the bluff and saw two boys from their company, Aidan Quinn and Robbie McVee, run to the shore and jump in. They swam furiously, but the current dragged them down past the main part of camp. A volley of muskets fired and Patrick saw the swimmers' arms and legs stop moving and their bodies drift lifelessly downstream.

When he heard the cheers congratulating the snipers on their kill, Patrick wanted to take up his musket and shoot them all. Jimmy couldn't believe what he was seeing. John rocked back and forth on the balls of his feet, his thick neck muscles bulging. "As far as I know," he said, "war has not been declared. Shooting a deserter when a country is not at war is a crime, pure and simple."

"Why," said Micheál, "should we fight for these people who so easily kill our own lads?"

"We shouldn't," said John.

Patrick was as angry as the rest of them but he couldn't let himself consider deserting. "You'll go and fight with the Mexicans?" he said.

"Perhaps," said John.

"I might too," said Jimmy. "Right now all I can think about is blowing Saxon and the rest of these bastards straight to hell."

"Jimmy," said Patrick. "You can't swim and you're deathly afraid of the water. They won't have to shoot you, you'll drown first."

"It's too dangerous right now," said John. "But when the time's right, lad, I'll not hesitate."

Later on, inside their tent after taps Jimmy and Patrick talked more about it. "I'm not risking my life for these Protestant swine," said Jimmy. "Think about it. It would be like marching with Lewis Levin and the nativists when they invaded Kensington."

"What about your ma and da?" said Patrick. "Don't you care about what they think? Don't you want to see them again?"

"All I know is that not only are we being treated worse than dogs, we're watching our friends being shot down."

Taylor posted extra guards and sentries around the camp, as much to keep his soldiers in as to keep the Mexicans out. Each evening, and some mornings, Patrick heard musket fire as men took the risk despite the danger. He couldn't help but admire those with so much courage to make the attempt under such conditions.

General Taylor never did discipline Saxon or any other officer who inflicted excessive punishment. But he did try to calm his immigrant soldiers. He issued an order that Catholics could not be forbidden from going to their own Sunday services if they were not required to be on duty.

Patrick thought it a feeble gesture. Where would they attend Mass anyway? There were no chaplains, Protestant or Catholic, with the army. But John Riley knew different. "The priest I met in Corpus Christi," he said, "is in Matamoros now. He says Mass at a hacienda not too far north of here."

Patrick didn't ask how he knew that. It didn't see how it mattered anyway. There was no chance that Saxon would allow them to go, orders or not from General Taylor. In the meantime, every enlisted man was put on shifts constructing the fort. When they weren't digging in the hole, or packing the dirt for the ten foot thick walls, Saxon made sure that Company K was drilling or performing guard duty.

Rumors abounded that the Mexicans had crossed the river and the men were repeatedly called out on general alarm during the night. They were told again to sleep with their muskets and be ready at a moments notice. But nothing happened other than the appearance of more and more cannons being placed on the opposite shore, as always with great religious ceremony and military pomp.

General Taylor's order to shoot to kill didn't stop the desertions. It did work to increase the anger of those who were being abused and mistreated. Now the Irish lads who attempted it waited until dark. On one night alone, thirty took to the river, including five more from Company K, and three African slaves. Patrick was glad to know they made it. He heard them calling from the other side, taunting their former officers and inviting their friends to join them.

More leaflets appeared, blowing like autumn leaves through the camp. This one was addressed to all the Europeans in Taylor's army, advising them that the nations of Europe condemned this attempt by

America to rob Mexico of more of its territory, and encouraging them again to come join them.

Just after sunset on a Tuesday of their third week on the Rio Grande Patrick heard gunshots from down by the river, followed by the long roll of drums calling the men to arms. Company K formed up and rushed to the shore. Instead of seeing the Mexican army charging across, Patrick saw the body of Charles Kelly, from his own platoon, bobble along in the current until he sank.

A cheer rose up from the officers and most of the men. Sorrow and rage nearly overwhelmed Patrick. Charles, only seventeen years old, was a good lad from up north in County Mayo who always talked about missing his dear mother. He looked over at John who slowly shook his head and turned away.

The next day some desperate soldier tried it in broad daylight. He made it all the way across. When he got to his feet on the other shore, a single shot fired from one of the snipers broke the morning stillness. An approving cheer applauded the shooter at the incredible 200 yard rifle shot that dropped the deserter. The man lay there until a group of Mexicans dragged him out of the water and buried him.

That put a complete stop to the daylight attempts. At night, it was a different matter. More and more eluded the guards, hid somewhere on the riverbank until the time was right and then plunged in. It became easier for them when Taylor ordered round the clock work on the fort. There was constant activity at all hours making it easier to slip off into the brush without being noticed.

Patrick tried to remain steady and prepare himself for what was to come. He continued to worry about how he would perform with bullets and cannon balls coming at him. He wrote to Ellen and included a letter for her to forward to their parents. He tried to keep it optimistic by telling them about the beautiful land he had seen and the amazing city of New Orleans, leaving out seeing the chained slaves and anything about their brutal officers. He apologized once again for how things had worked out but hoped all would be well once he got their land. He was saying goodbye without actually putting it into words.

Company K marched to the construction sight of Fort Texas early on a Friday morning and waited at attention for their work assignments. Today they would be down in the moat. They jumped into the waist-high pit and started digging. The weather had turned hotter. By mid-morning it was already ninety degrees yet Captain Saxon sat stiff and erect watching them from his horse with his uniform shirt buttoned all the way up. Next to him was Major Mansfield, the man in charge of constructing the fort. Saxon was speaking with the major but his voice was raised and his words obviously meant for the men.

"The jackass is the symbol of the Mexican," he proclaimed, " and it isn't the shamrock but the pig that is the emblem of the Irishman."

"They're not as smart as pigs," said Mansfield, taking his hat off and fanning himself. "But they make for easy target practice don't you think, Captain?"

"Maybe they believe the Pope will save them," said Saxon. Both of them laughed loudly. They kept at it, ridiculing the Virgin Mary, the saints, and the "papist pageantry" of the marching Mexicans across the river.

The men were shirtless and sweating in the boiling heat. Jimmy, who had indulged in too much whiskey again the night before, was not yet completely sober. He stopped for moment to swat at the insects and wipe his brow. He was leaning on his shovel when Saxon spotted him. "Torpey," he shouted. "Up here. Now!"

Jimmy didn't move a muscle. He acted as if he heard nothing at all before calmly going back to shoveling. "Sergeant Adams," screamed Saxon. "Bring that Mick drunkard to me this instant."

Corporal Brenner went down with Adams into the pit. Jimmy picked up his shovel and held it across his body. Patrick believed he was going to swing it at the first one to get to him. But when they got close, he simply smiled and dropped it. They took him out of the pit and when he was in front of Saxon, he spit on the ground.

"I've had enough of you, Torpey" said Saxon. Then he shouted to the rest of them. "Company K, fall in, now." They scrambled up the sides of the moat and stood at attention. Patrick's platoon was in front, closest to Saxon who had dismounted from his horse.

"Put him on his knees, Sergeant," said Saxon. "And tie his hands behind his back."

Saxon must have planned this beforehand because there was a small fire burning off to the side. He took three quick strides to it, picked up a branding iron with the letters HD on it and held it high for all of them to see. "This Irish piece of dung is an habitual drunkard," he said. "He's to be branded as such for all the world to see."

When Patrick realized what was about to be done a cold hatred settled in his guts. He saw nothing but the shining, evil snake eyes of Captain Saxon. John Riley put his huge hand on Patrick's shoulder and held him in place so he couldn't bolt forward and smash the captain's face to a bloody pulp.

Jimmy struggled to get up but it was futile. Brenner held on to his arms and Adams had him in a headlock, keeping him still as Saxon stood and looked down, smiling smugly. Slowly and deliberately he pressed the iron on Jimmy's forehead as if he was a piece of livestock. When the red hot metal made contact with Jimmy's skin, the hiss of it went through the ranks of Company K like a lightning strike.

Jimmy's shrieks could be heard throughout the camp, and no doubt by the Mexicans across the Rio Grande, as the letters proclaiming his crime were scorched into his forehead. The sickening, vile smell of burning flesh mixed with the hot desert air, and hit Patrick like a punch in the gut. He bent over and vomited. He wasn't the only one.

Chapter Thirty-Three

Fort Texas, April 12, 1846

Jimmy was hauled off to the guardhouse. When he returned to their tent the next morning, the wound on his forehead still raw and red, he said only one thing before collapsing onto his bed roll. "I'm going to kill him."

Later that day, Patrick heard band music and ringing church bells coming from Matamoros. He stepped out of his tent and watched a long parade of a thousand-plus soldiers being led by an officer on a white stallion. General Ampudia had arrived to take over as commander of the Mexican forces.

Ampudia sent General Taylor a written ultimatum to vacate the area and return to the other side of the Nueces River. Old Rough and Ready responded by ordering a blockade of the Rio Grande, cutting off the Mexican's main supply line. Ampudia considered it an overt act of war.

The next day was Sunday and Patrick was astonished when John showed him a pass he secured to attend mass at a local rancho. Saxon was on a reconnaissance mission for General Taylor and Graves was not on duty, apparently sleeping off a night of drinking and card playing. The officer of the day was the camp quartermaster, Lieutenant Sam Grant. He was a good officer from Ohio who had serious qualms about the war. He was also against slavery and had no love for Saxon or the way he treated his men.

He issued John the pass, following Taylor's decree that Catholics would be allowed to attend their own services. John then took Patrick, Micheál and two others, Timothy Leahy and Joe McCartney, to see Grant.

The weather had changed to heavy rain so all work and training were suspended. Lieutenant Grant issued each of them passes. Patrick hadn't been to church since New Orleans and very much wanted to go. He needed to cleanse his soul and receive holy communion should he not survive what was soon to come.

Jimmy was in no shape to go with them. His wound was still open and extremely painful. The five of them showed their passes to the sentry at the northern perimeter of the camp and walked off the compound. John was more upbeat than he'd been since that first day on the steamer in Cairo. They were slogging their way through the rain and mud to the hacienda, when he revealed his plan to Patrick.

"Micheál and I will not be returning to camp with you, Patrick," he said. "The padre I met in Corpus Christi is here. He's arranged for a boat to take us across the river once Mass is over. I'm to be made a lieutenant of artillery in the Mexican Army."

Patrick slipped slightly in the mud as he stopped in his tracks. He looked at Micheál, then back at John. He was shaken by how it was happening but not surprised. It was all but inevitable.

"I would like you to come with us," said John. "If it's in your heart to do so, but I understand if you cannot."

"We know your obligations, Patrick," said Micheál. "I'm alone in this life and have no one but myself to be responsible for. I've had enough of these nativists or Protestants or whatever they want to call themselves to justify their hatred. I'll be going with John."

"And you'll both fight against us?" said Patrick.

"We'll be defending our Mexican and Catholic brothers," said John. "I don't wish you or the rest of the lads any harm but, God help me, that's the way of war."

181

They walked on in silence with only the sound of raindrops and their boots sloshing in the mud. Patrick's conscience and his heart were with John Riley and the Mexicans but how would he ever be able to explain it to his family if he went with them?

"Jimmy is going to join us as well," said Micheál.

"What do you mean?" said Patrick.

"Once on the other side, I'll make arrangements for him," said John.

"Arrangements?"

"The padre has a ferryman upriver whose sole purpose is to transport the likes of us across."

"How long have you known of this?"

"Of the ferryman, just recently. But this has all been in the works since Corpus Christi. The priest had authorization to offer me the commission. I made up my mind to go before we marched to Matamoros but it was not possible until we arrived here."

It bothered Patrick that Jimmy hadn't confided in him about the plan. Jimmy was his blood kin and beyond that they had become as close as real brothers. There was a good chance they would soon be trying to kill each other. He had a hard time walking. His body was heavy, weighed down with feelings of doubt, loss and hopelessness.

John led the way to the hacienda of Jaime Aragon. His wife, Maureen, whose maiden name was Gallagher, had come to Texas from Dublin with her family in the early 1830s. Señora Aragon was a devout Catholic and angry at the American invasion and the fact that so many young boys from Ireland had been unwittingly drawn into the conflict. She was a sweet woman who welcomed Patrick and the rest of them as if they were her own long lost sons.

She showed them to a courtyard with four rows of benches facing a long wooden table covered with a clean, white linen cloth. On top of the cloth was a gold chalice. Behind the makeshift altar hung a large, rough wooden crucifix holding the suffering and dying Christ. Around the courtyard there were four portraits of saints, one of which was Saint Patrick. In the back of the courtyard was a beautiful statue of the Virgin of Guadalupe.

The five foot high statue was ensconced in the recessed area of an arch made of red brick. A planter filled with flowers and blooming cactus plants stretched the ten foot length of the structure. Vines of morning glory, with bursting buds of brilliant blue flowers spread up and around the walls of the arch. Freshly cut white and pink desert roses in terra cotta pots sat on the ledge of the planter, giving the shrine the feeling of a sacred, tranquil park.

The Virgin was painted with dark-skin and had Indian features. Her black hair was covered with a turquoise colored shawl that draped over her golden dress. Her hands were clasped together in prayer. Patrick stood admiring her when Señora Aragon came up behind him. "Isn't she beautiful?" she said.

"Yes, very much so."

"She's revered throughout the country as the divine protectress of Mexico," said Señora Aragon, "especially by the poorest of the poor. I've come to love and respect her as much myself. I spend many hours in prayer before her. She gives me great comfort."

Patrick nodded, not saying anything. The image of his mother came to him as he stood next to this woman who was about her age and had the same dark hair and brown eyes.

The rain was now a gentle drizzle as the benches were filling up, mostly with old Indian women. Señora Aragon pointed to the last row. "Please, sit," she said. "Padre Pancho will be starting soon."

Patrick had never been to Mass that wasn't held inside a real church but this setting gave him a powerful spiritual feeling. John and Micheál sat down next to him. He turned around for another look at the statue and saw a young woman approach the shrine. She placed a pot of flowers in front of the Virgin and rearranged the other ones already there. As she turned to find a place to sit their eyes met.

At the sight of her, Patrick's breathing became difficult and his pulse raced as if he had been running for his life. She was the most beautiful creature he had ever seen or imagined. Her flawless skin was the color of honey. She had silky black hair that glistened like a raven's plumage when the morning sun hits it. He was overcome with a feeling unlike one he'd ever known. He lost all awareness of where he was or what he was doing there. All he could do was stare at her, open-mouthed, as she finished her task and walked toward the front row of benches.

He became vaguely aware of John, Micheál and the rest of the congregation getting to their feet. He didn't get up. He couldn't. The señorita cast a demure sideways glance at him when she walked by. Her eyes were a deep brown, seemingly as dark as her hair and full of kindness, passion and tenderness. It was impossible for him to look away from her.

She smiled and Patrick thought she may have laughed at him. She had good reason. He gaped like a simpleton and was turned completely around while everyone else was on their feet paying attention to the priest. John elbowed him in the ribs and smiled, motioning with his head to the front.

A slender, black-haired priest in white vestments was standing with his back to them and his arms outstretched, facing the crucifix. Patrick tried to concentrate but it was impossible. He stared at the back of the señorita's head, covered with a pale blue silk shawl that draped down over her shoulders.

He heard the familiar latin liturgy but only as background noise. He hoped that she would turn her head one way or the other so he might see just a portion of her lovely face one more time. Only when the priest began his sermon was he able to look away from her and temporarily break the trance he was in.

The young, handsome priest had lean, angular features which spoke of Spanish blood. When he started talking it was in Spanish but then he switched to near-perfect English. "Welcome to our Irish friends who have joined us today. My name is Father Francisco Salinas, but everyone calls me Padre Pancho. I wish to speak directly to you soldiers…why have you invaded our country? Your president and his army wish to steal our lands and destroy our sacred religion. Who is it you serve? Those who mock the Pope, the Virgin Mother and all the saints? Those who enslave our fellow human beings and treat them like mere beasts of burden?"

Patrick thought about John and Micheál. They would be leaving with this priest and he would never see them again unless it was on the battlefield. An shiver went up his spine to the base of his neck and he listened more intently.

"Our heavenly Father who sent his son to die for our sins is the only master we have. I fear for your immortal souls. You are serving a misguided earthly lord, not the one true King. Consider what you're doing. God forgives all, but only if we repent and no longer sin."

185

His words hit Patrick hard. He had never known or cared much of the politics or the reasons the United States professed for being here. He thought of Jimmy's assertion that this war was nothing more than a bigger version of the Bible riots and he was now on the same side as the nativists. It sickened him to think of it that way and for the first time he was ashamed of the uniform he was wearing.

Padre Pancho finished his sermon. Patrick got in line with John, and Micheál to receive communion. It had always been a holy experience but this time he was distracted as he watched the beautiful señorita receive the wafer and walk piously back to her seat. He asked God to forgive him for being more concerned with the desire for her to glance his way again than he was for the condition of his immortal soul.

After he took the Eucharist in his mouth he bowed his head and turned to go back to his seat. He kept his head down but cast his eyes to the side to sneak a look at her. He couldn't help himself. He tripped slightly and saw a brief smile dance across her face. It immediately disappeared but the tingle that ran through his body had nothing to do with receiving the holy sacrament.

He didn't want the service to end. He didn't want to leave and he certainly didn't want to go back to camp. When it was over, John went up to speak with the priest. He and Micheál followed after him. John introduced them and as he shook hands, the señorita came up and stood next to him. He could hardly contain himself.

"This is my sister, Alicia," said the priest to the three of them.

She smiled and gave them a short curtsy. "*Mucho gusto*," she said. Then with just a bit of an accent, "Pleased to meet you."

Patrick didn't know what to do or say. Take her hand? Bow? No words came out of his mouth. There was a rushing in his ears that blotted out any sound. John and Micheál responded but he stood in a mute daze until he noticed they were all laughing at him, including Alicia. His face reddened and beads of perspiration broke out on his forehead. Just as he was about to find his voice, a commotion came from the corral on the other side of the courtyard.

Four mounted riders circled the hacienda, hooting and firing their pistols in the air. From their long hair and buckskin clothing Patrick knew they were Texas Rangers. Two of them charged their horses right into the courtyard, scattering those near the front and knocking over benches.

"What have we here?" shouted one of them. "This isn't a church, and yet look at all the false idols." He rode next to the picture of Saint Patrick and knocked it to the ground. Another one threw a lasso around the crucifix and pulled it down, overturning more benches. Patrick and the others had to jump out of the way and watch powerlessly, as the Rangers were armed with colt handguns and Bowie knives.

A third one rode his horse up to the shrine of the Virgin, swinging a rope above his head. He tossed it at the statue but missed. As he was about to throw it again, Alicia ran and put herself between the horse and the statue. "Don't touch her!" she screamed.

The Ranger laughed and said to the one who was apparently their leader, "Hey Seth, look at this little *greaserita*. A whore just like her 'virgin' mother." He threw his lasso and it slipped over Alicia's head and shoulders. Patrick, filled with instant fury, ran and leapt at the man, pulling him out of his saddle. They both tumbled to the ground. Patrick made it to his feet and pummeled him with every ounce of strength his rage produced. He meant to kill him and would have if the other Rangers hadn't rushed to his aid.

187

They yanked Patrick off him and began beating and whipping him. John and Micheál came to help and for a few moments there was a brawl. The other mounted Rangers pulled their pistols and it looked as if they were all about to be gunned down. Before they could shoot, a booming explosion was heard and everything stopped. Señor Aragon had fired a shotgun in the air. Out of nowhere a half-dozen armed Mexicans fighters appeared and trained their guns on the Rangers. Padre Pancho pulled out a long pistol from underneath his cassock.

"Enough!" shouted the priest. Then to the Rangers: "Leave this placenow. I won't be responsible for what happens if you don't."

They were surrounded and now outnumbered. The one called Seth rested his eyes on Patrick. "I'll remember you potato head. See you in camp." He walked his horse out of the courtyard and said, "Let's go boys."

They galloped off. Señor Aragon's men waited for a sign from him. It was obvious they wanted nothing more than to pursue them and give them what they deserved. Patrick had the same thought but Aragon just shook his head and his men slowly retreated from sight.

Chapter Thirty-Four

Patrick went over to Alicia who was still standing by the Virgin's statue. "Are you injured?" he asked.

"No, are you?"

"I'm fine."

He wanted to say more but once again he was unable to find the words. Her dark eyes flashed as she smiled, filling him with a joy he didn't know existed. They faced each other, both awkwardly silent, until she put a hand on his arm.

"What is your name, señor?"

"Patrick. Patrick Ryan from County Cork, Ireland." He had no idea why he included where he was from.

"*Muchas Gracias, Patricio*," she said.

"Si," said Padre Pancho who had come over to them with John and Micheál. "Thank you very much." Then he said to John, "We should go, Señor Riley."

"Yes, Padre," said John. "In a moment."

Patrick stood there trying to comprehend all that had happened and the fact that John and Micheál were leaving. John pulled out his pass and handed it to him.

"Give this to Jimmy," he said. "If he's up to it he may still be able to use it today."

Micheál pulled out his as well. "Perhaps someone else can use mine," he said.

"You're really going then," said Patrick.

John put both his powerful hands on Patrick's shoulders and looked down into his eyes. "It's the right thing for me, lad. I'll never be anything more than a private with the Americans and more importantly, we're on the wrong side. Look at what just happened. I need no more justification than that."

Patrick felt dizzy, like he was about to faint. He wanted to go with them and yet he couldn't. The only perfectly clear thought he had was that he wanted to remain in the presence of the stunning Alicia Salinas. Yet for all he knew, she saw him as a lovesick puppy to whom she was grateful but nothing more. He looked at her and their eyes locked together. In the deepest part of his soul he believed there was more to it than that. He heard the padre's voice as if from some far away place.

"You're not coming with us, Patricio?"

It took him a long minute before he answered. "Padre, I...I have a responsibility..."

"To more than your God and your Church?," said the priest.

"No. Yes. Forgive me, Father."

John stepped in. "He has his family back in Ireland to think of, Padre. Don't judge him too harshly."

The priest studied him closer. "No, of course not," he said. "We all have to follow our own conscience. But I must ask you to remain here for a while until we can get your friends across the river."

"He won't say anything, Padre," said John. "We can trust him."

"Very well, but stay a bit and have some of the delicious cake that Señora Aragon has prepared."

Patrick shook hands and embraced his two friends. He had to fight off tears. Leahy and McCartney came over. They would be going across the river too.

"Take care, Patrick," said Micheál. "I wish you were coming with us."

"Be safe, Micheál," said Patrick. "Perhaps we'll meet again one day when this is all over."

"I'll pray for it," said Micheál.

He watched them walk away, led by Padre Pancho, Señor Aragon and his armed men. As sorry as he was to see them go, the idea of staying with Alicia, even for a few minutes, was exhilarating. Señora Aragon came over holding a tray of small cakes. Alicia was still standing there, now looking reserved and somewhat nervous. Patrick found his voice. "You're not going with them, Alicia?"

"Not yet," she said. "I will stay here tonight, then go over to Matamoros in the morning. Will you sit with me for a moment?"

He wanted to tell her he would sit with her forever but he blushed and smiled as he took her outstretched hand. She took him to a bench under a large olive tree. The rain had stopped and the sun peeked through the clouds. They talked for more than an hour though it seemed liked only a minute. He told her about Jimmy, Ellen and his family in Ireland. He explained his reasons for not going with John and Micheál and she said she understood.

She told him that her mother died ten years ago and that her father, had been executed by government forces in 1840. He had joined with the Federalists who, like the Texans, had declared their independence and formed the short-lived Republic of the Rio Grande after Santa Anna abolished the Constitution and proclaimed himself dictator. He was captured and killed after a battle against Centralist forces. Their small ranchero in Saltillo was taken by the government.

Patrick was touched by her story. He took her hand in both of his. "I'm so sorry, Alicia."

"You haven't had an easy time either," she said.

"It's nothing compared to yours. How is it you ended up here?"

"After our father's death, I went to Mexico City to be with my brother. He was in his last year at the seminary. We have a cousin who is a secretary for the archbishop. I stayed with him for a while. Francisco was never one for pursuing an easy life or seeking privileges. He could have secured a position in some rich church in the capital with our cousin's connections but he wanted to help people. He was sent to Matamoros to cover a vast area where most of the flock are peons and indios."

"I have to ask," said Patrick. "After what happened to your father, why is it your brother is on the side of the Mexican government?"

"It is very complicated, Patricio. One would have to be blind not to see the excessive wealth and corruption in our country, the army and even the church. But he's a priest first and foremost. His concern is for the lowest among us. Right now your government and its army is our biggest threat. If you steal our land and destroy our religion we won't be able to change anything."

He wanted to tell her that it wasn't his government and that he had no desire to take anything from anybody. He wished only to take her in his arms. He also longed to tell her that he loved her but that would be insane. They had just met, there was a war about to explode, and fate had put them on opposite sides.

"You will not join us?" she said. Her voice was soft, sweet and enchanting.

"Not because I don't want to," he said.

"Then why, Patricio? You're a good man. I knew it the first moment I saw you. Do you think your mother and father would want you to be against us?"

Anger and confusion coursed through his veins, constricting his throat. He stood up. He had the urge to run, just run, fast and far away. Not to the Mexican side. Not back to camp. He wanted to pull her to him, kiss her and take her away from the army, the Church, his responsibilities. When he answered he shouted without meaning to.

"What am I to do then?" he said, the words tumbling out. "Abandon my family? Destroy all their hopes and dreams? Damn this war! Damn the Protestants, and the officers who have forced decent men to desert."

Alicia stood and faced him, smiling radiantly. She put her hands to his face and placed them tenderly on his cheeks. "You must do what is in your heart, Patricio. It's between you and God. I don't know what's happened here between us but I know I've never felt this way before. And, whether you know it or not, you're an open book, so easy to read. I could see immediately that there was something between us. Something that words can't define."

"Alicia, I have never felt this way before either. I didn't know it was possible. It's so strange. Like a part of me has been missing and now, here with you, I'm whole. How can that be when I've known you mere minutes? I don't want to leave you."

"Then come with us."

His head and shoulders slumped and he kept his eyes on the ground. "I can't. I just can't. My family is counting on me. I've already failed them more than once. I can't do it again. Can you forgive me?"

"I understand, Patricio, but I wish it were not so."

"I'm sorry, Alicia. More than you can know." He turned and started walking away before she saw his tears. She called out to him.

When he turned around she rushed to him. Their lips came together in a warm, moist kiss. She let go of him and ran to the the open arms of Señora Aragon who was watching and waiting for her from underneath the front arch of the hacienda. He hesitated a moment, hoping she would look at him one last time. When she didn't, he hung his head and made his way back to camp.

Chapter Thirty-Five

Patrick approached the sentry at the northern gate. The rain had started back up again in a light, steady shower. He reached into his pocket for his pass, wanting nothing more than to turn back around.

He had a duty to his family yet the padre's words rang to his core. Then the crushing thought came to him that he might cause the death of his friends, or worse, Alicia's. It may have been at that moment that he made up his mind. It wasn't a conscious decision yet. He had no plan. And he needed to be sure about what Jimmy was going to do.

When he got back to their tent, Jimmy was on his feet. He touched the raw, purple-red letters on his forehead and grimaced in pain. He was still wobbly and Patrick held his arm to steady him. "How are you?"

"My head is on fire and the pain behind my eyes feels like I'm being stabbed from the inside. But I would have felt better if you hadn't returned, Patrick."

"I couldn't leave you here by yourself."

Jimmy looked away. "I'm going to be leaving you."

"John told me."

"Why didn't you go with him then?"

"You know why, Jimmy."

"I think your da would understand and maybe even encourage you. I'm going. Then, by God, I'll light out for Oregon. Did John give you his pass?"

Patrick handed it to him "Are you sure this will work? It's getting late. Mass was at ten and that was hours ago."

"I'm hoping the guards don't know the reason for the pass, and that they don't know Jimmy Torpey from John Riley."

"You'd better hurry then."

"I will but first I have to take care of something." He bent down and pulled an eight-inch artillery shell from under his bedroll. It had a fuse six inches long attached to it. He held it out for Patrick to see.

"What are you going to do with that?" said Patrick.

Jimmy opened the flap of the tent and looked out. The rain had stopped again but there was a heavy mist in the air. "I'm going to make sure that Saxon is in his tent," said Jimmy. "Then I'll light the fuse and toss it in."

"Forget Saxon, Jimmy. You'll never get away with it. Just go."

Jimmy reached up and touched his wound. "Do you think I'll ever forget about this horrid scar burned on to my face? Or any of the other tortures Saxon got his pleasure from inflicting? No, I won't be forgetting any of it. And he'll have plenty of time in hell to remember me."

"Saxon was out on a mission today," said Patrick. "What if he doesn't return until after dark. How will you escape then? The pass will no longer be good."

"I'll wait. I'm not leaving until the remains of Stuart Saxon have to scraped off the inside of his tent. Not just to satisfy myself but also for Robert. These nativists are all the same and someone is finally going to pay. I've run from the law in Philadelphia and the Brannon brothers in Pittsburgh. I'll run again but not before getting revenge."

"Can you run? It looks as if you can hardly stand."

Jimmy put on his coat and shoved the shell inside and under his arm, holding it close to his ribs to keep it in place. "I'm a bit dizzy but once I start moving I'll be fine."

It was mid-afternoon and Patrick's stomach growled. The only thing he had eaten all day was one of Señora Aragon's cakes. "Why don't we go to one of the sutlers and get some food? You'll need to eat before you go and the walk will loosen up your muscles. That way we can see if Saxon is there without getting caught with that bulge under your coat."

Jimmy thought about it. He was weak and the food would do him good. "You must be hungry," he said, "if you're willing to pay those swindlers for food. I'll go with you. We'll just stroll by Saxon's tent on the way."

"Leave the shell," said Patrick. "You can always come back for it."

Jimmy patted it almost affectionately. "No, I'll hang on to it. For safe keeping."

"What if we run into an officer and you can't salute properly because you're carrying it?"

Jimmy knew he was right. He put the shell back under his bedroll. They walked through the long line of tents, heading for the small bluff where the camp followers and the sutlers were located. The officers' tents were a few rows over, at the other end of the company street. When they got to Saxon's, it looked as if he was back because Jeb was out front preparing a meal for him. From inside the tent they heard his rasping drawl yelling at his slave to hurry up.

"He's there," said Jimmy. Without another word, he went back to retrieve the shell. He moved without difficulty, his pain forgotten for the moment. Patrick kept walking slowly ahead, not wanting to be noticed. He went to the row behind Saxon's tent and walked back towards theirs just as Jimmy, was returning wearing a fiendish grin.

"Please, Jimmy, don't do it."

He didn't answer. Patrick followed him for a few yards until they got close to the rear of Saxon's tent. Jimmy paused and waved at him to get away. Patrick went around to the front and stopped a few yards away from Jeb who looked up from his cooking and nodded politely. The camp was coming back to life after the rain. Men were moving about and details were being called to go back down into the pit to continue constructing the fort. There was no doubt Jimmy would be seen, and caught.

Patrick was in a near panic. He knew he should get away from the area. He also realized that Jeb was probably going to be hurt in the blast. Patrick motioned for him to come away from the tent. He looked confused, not sure what to do. Patrick waved again, frantically, and Jeb, with a quick look over his shoulder started moving. Just then Lieutenant Graves appeared walking from the other direction. Patrick did an immediate about-face and took off in the opposite direction. The shell exploded.

A fireball erupted inside Saxon's tent. The heat of the blast warmed Patrick's back and neck. He turned and saw Jimmy running his way, nearly crashing right into Graves who was rushing towards the explosion. Jeb was on the ground, moving slowly and trying to get up. Soldiers came sprinting from every direction. Jimmy stumbled as he ran away from the inferno. Patrick caught him before he fell to the ground. As they regained their balance, Patrick saw Graves looking right at them. He yelled, "Stop those Irish bastards!"

The commotion from the shock and flames made it doubtful that anyone heard or understood what the lieutenant was saying. The first thought that came to most of the men was that the war had finally started. Patrick took a quick look back and saw Saxon emerged from the tent screaming, his back in flames. Graves got to him and pushed him to the ground where another officer smothered him with his coat.

They didn't wait around to see what happened next. At first they ran as fast as possible until Patrick realized they would create a lot less suspicion if they tried to act normally. He took hold of Jimmy's arm and said, "We need to walk."

"I have to go to our tent," said Jimmy.

"There's no time."

For a moment everything moved in a prolonged, dream-like slowness. Suddenly and almost as if planned, fellow soldiers from Company K grouped together around them. They had somehow assessed the situation and were providing cover. Officers and men alike rushed towards the explosion from every direction.

Patrick changed their pace to a quick walk and they were soon out of sight of the burning tent. Their mates from Company K stopped and formed a sort of wall behind them. Alicia's brown eyes and beautiful face flooded his mind with excitement at the idea of seeing her again. All thoughts of the army, Ireland, or land in America dissipated into thin air like the smoke over Saxon's tent.

They had to escape and he needed his head to be clear. They still had the passes but the camp and guards would be alerted as to what had happened. They couldn't risk it. "Let's head down by the river," he said. "We'll hide in the chaparral until we can figure out what to do next."

They didn't walk a straight line. Instead, with as deliberate an effort as possible, they maintained a casual, meandering motion. They went down a couple of tent-lined avenues of their infantry section until they got to the fringe of the camp. It was then that Patrick noticed Jeb trailing behind them. He caught up to them.

"You swimmin' da river, suh?" he asked.

Patrick certainly didn't need or want anymore complications. "No," he said. "My cousin can't swim."

"But you're running off," he said. "Take me with you."

Patrick didn't know what to do or say. He looked at Jimmy who just shrugged. It didn't matter much for them if Saxon was alive or dead. They would be pursued no matter what. He had no idea what punishment would be in store for a runaway slave but there was no time to argue.

"We won't stop you, Jeb, but you're on your own."

Chapter Thirty-Six

They waited until they were sure no one was watching and then dashed into the thick growth of thorn-sharp bushes and prickly pear, stopping fifteen feet in when they could make it no further. Patrick's pants were torn and all three of them were bleeding from scratches on their faces and arms.

The river would be watched and patrolled more heavily now. Snipers were probably getting in place, just waiting to see if they were foolish enough to try to get across. They huddled low to the ground in a small opening in the dense mesquite listening for any sound of a search party. They heard nothing but the river and shouts in the distance from the camp.

Jimmy smiled and said softly, "I did it Patrick. That son of a whore Saxon won't be tormenting anyone ever again."

"I hate to disappoint you, Jimmy, but he's still alive."

"That's not possible," he said. "The tent exploded in flames."

"I don't know if he'll live or not but I watched him come out of the tent. His back was on fire and they were smothering the flames with jackets. And Graves saw both of us."

"I saw him too," said Jeb. "He's a hard man to kill."

Jimmy was silent for a moment. Then he told Patrick in a low whisper that he was sorry. "It seems I've dragged you yet again into a terrible situation." Patrick didn't say anything. "You don't seem to be very upset by it," said Jimmy.

"Well," said Patrick. "Other than the fact that we're once more running for our lives, I'm not. John and Micheál are safely with the Mexicans. The priest from Corpus Christi helped them."

"I know all that," said Jimmy.

"The priest has a sister, and she's beautiful beyond words."

Jimmy started laughing. "Keep it down," hissed Patrick.

"You've come to this God forsaken place and you've fallen in love? The Lord does work in mysterious ways now doesn't he? Let's go collect her and make our way to Oregon."

"We have to make it out of here first," said Patrick.

They remained hidden in that spot until well past nightfall. More than a few times they heard footsteps and voices but never close enough to be discovered. The storm had passed and it was a moonless night. When they decided to move out, they crawled blindly through the underbrush, tearing their clothes further and ripping open new flesh.

Patrick led the way, keeping the sound of the river on his left. The pace was slow and painful. When the rushing Rio Grande got louder he motioned for them to stop and said, "I'll go see if I can tell where we are."

It was so dark he couldn't see his hand in front of his face. At the edge of the chaparral he heard the river maybe ten feet directly below. To the left, the dim lights of Matamoros lit up the dark sky. That convinced him they had come north and were on the right track. He crawled back into the underbrush.

"Do you know where we are?" said Jimmy.

"We're right above the river but I don't know how far we are from Aragon's place. It's on flat ground with a few rolling hills surrounding it, perhaps a mile from the river." He didn't say it but hoped that Alicia would still be there.

"We should go to the river," said Jimmy. "And follow it upstream."

Patrick didn't respond right away. He was thinking the same thing, even though there was a good chance patrols would be out along the shore.

Hopefully they were far enough away from the camp to avoid detection. Jeb had been silent the whole night but now he spoke.

"I can't be caught," he said. "Saxon will lynch me at the nearest tree."

"Maybe he died," said Jimmy.

"It don't make no difference," said Jeb. "No one will allow a slave to be spared once he's run off."

"Hell," said Jimmy. "We'll all be hanged if we're caught."

Patrick stayed silent. He couldn't see Jimmy's face but knew he was smiling when he said, "But the river's not where your girl is."

He was glad for the darkness which prevented them from seeing his flush of embarrassment. "If we get caught," continued Jimmy, "you'll never see her again anyway. The river is our best chance to escape."

He had to agree. They moved out, staying on the top of the bank and the fringe of the chaparral. After they had gone a few hundred yards the vegetation thinned out. The gray-yellow light of dawn allowed them to see the river below on their left and low hills off in the distance to the right.

They continued on slowly, seeing the river and shoreline bend to the west. Jeb pointed to a spot a half a mile up where the bank sloped down closer to the river's edge. The sun was just about to burst above the horizon. It was time to make a run for it.

"I'll go first," said Patrick. "No sense in all of us being shot if we're seen."

He ran hard and fast, half expecting a sniper to cut him down. He made it to where the bank was about three feet above the river. He jumped down and hit the sandy shore. He waited a moment with his back flat against the embankment. When no shots rang out, he stood and waved for

Jimmy to follow.

Jimmy was slower but made it without a problem and Patrick signaled Jeb to come on. When all three were safely sitting facing the river, Jimmy said, "Now what?"

"I'm thinking I should swim across and find help," said Patrick.

"We shouldn't split up now," said Jimmy. "You'll find your señorita and forget all about me."

Patrick smiled. "I should have left you to fend for yourself with the Brannon Brothers."

Jimmy let out a short laugh and said, "John told me there were Mexicans up and down the river who would help us. Let's keep going."

It was full daylight now. The sun sparkled and reflected a golden hue off the river. At the edge of the water they could see upstream for a few hundred yards. It looked like there was a series of inlets that they could get to and remain hidden.

"The current's too strong," said Jimmy. "I say we make a run for it. Get to another cove. We can go from one to the next until we find help."

Whatever they were going to do they had to do it now. "Then let's go," said Patrick.

He made the sign of the cross and then all three of them bolted up the shoreline. The first inlet was fifty yards away. Jeb was the fastest. Jimmy struggled and Patrick slowed down to help him. They were panting heavily when they made it there. The next cove was much further away, more than a hundred yards.

Just as they were about to run for it they heard voices. Patrick put his hand up to tell them not to move. He crept to the edge of the rock wall of the inlet and heard Spanish being spoken. He peeked around the edge and saw three men next to a small boat resting at the water's edge He told the others to stay put then took a deep breath and walked out into the open, holding his hands up near his ears. "Hola," he said.

They jumped and two of them pulled revolvers from under their serapes. "*Alto!*" commanded one of them.

Patrick raised his hands higher in the air. He recognized Jaime Aragon. "Señor Aragon," he said.

Aragon looked closer. A small smile appeared on his face."*Un Colorado*," he said.

Patrick gestured behind him and said, "*amigos*."

Jimmy and Jeb showed themselves. Señor Aragon nodded, pointed to the boat and said, "*vamanos*."

Chapter Thirty-Seven

Matamoros, Mexico, April 13, 1846

It was a quick ride to the Mexican side of the river. Señor Aragon took them directly to John Riley who was already fitted out in a lieutenant's uniform and the transformation was astonishing. His coat was dark blue with a stand up collar of crimson, embroidered with a yellow exploding bomb and gold epaulettes on his shoulders. The trousers were also blue with the crimson piping down the outside seams. His hat was a tall black shako topped with a red pompon.

Patrick was so affected by the change that he spontaneously saluted him. Lieutenant Riley beamed at the sight of him. He returned a crisp salute then nearly smothered him in a huge bear hug. Then he did the same thing to Jimmy. He took stock of Jeb without saying anything for a time.

"This is Jeb," said Patrick.

He stuck out his hand and Jeb took it. "Of course. Saxon's servant."

Jeb stood a bit straighter. He was a six inches shorter than John but he looked him straight in the eye. "Slave, suh, but never again."

"Will you join us then?"

"If you'll have me."

"We most certainly will. Welcome, Jeb." Then he returned his attention to Patrick and Jimmy.

"Ah," he said. "So good to have you here, lads. I must admit Patrick, I'm surprised to see you."

"He's not here to see you, John," said Jimmy.

John smiled at Patrick and said, "The beautiful Alicia."

Before Patrick could respond Jimmy said, "Are you a general already, John Riley? The Mexicans must truly be desperate."

John laughed loudly. "Not yet, Jimmy. But you never know now do you? Let's get you to the barracks. We're organizing a special battalion under the command of Captain Moreno."

Patrick wanted to find Alicia but things were happening rapidly and the impact of his actions descended upon him. He had ruined any chance of getting land in America and was now being hurried into the enemy's forces. The conviction he had evaporated into uncertainty that came upon him hard and fast. Would Alicia even want him? Welcome him?

He still had no money, no land, and no prospects for the future. He had only just met her and spent one brief hour in her presence. What if she didn't feel the same way about him? He swallowed his doubts and fears and said nothing. Jimmy, however, did not suppress his feelings.

"I don't think I'll be doing that, John," he said. "I'm done with drilling, marching and discipline. I'll be heading north as soon as I can."

Lieutenant Riley's mouth tightened and he rocked slightly back and forth before he spoke. "Even if you're lucky enough to get out of Matamoros and past the Americans, will you just take a leisurely stroll through the desert? If the guerrillas don't get you the Comanches will. They'd have your scalp before the sun goes down on the first day. I thought that you, out of all of us, would want to get some vengeance."

"Saxon tasted my vengeance," said Jimmy.

"Maybe," said Patrick. They told John what Jimmy did. "He was still alive the last time I saw him."

"Can't say that I blame you, Jimmy," said Riley. "But they'll be looking for you even more so now." He didn't wait for Jimmy to respond.

"Lads," he said. "Come with me to meet Captain Moreno. There are incentives to join besides teaching Saxon and the rest of them a lesson."

There was really nothing else for them to do. If Patrick was going to see Alicia again he would have to remain here. Jimmy truly had no other choice. Neither did Jeb but of the three of them, he was the one who was most anxious to join and fight.

They walked down a side street from the main plaza to the barracks. Around the corner was the Cathedral, the Church of Our Lady of Refuge. It had two tall bell towers on each side which had been destroyed in a violent hurricane a couple of years before and were not yet fully restored.

At the barracks they were received with shouts of welcome by some forty fellow deserters. The first to greet them was Micheál who was overjoyed to see Patrick. There were a few raised eyebrows at the sight of Jeb but he too was welcomed.

Patrick knew the lads from Company K and most of the others he recognized by sight. There were a couple Germans but the rest were immigrant Irishmen like him. Lieutenant Riley introduced them to a grim, paunchy sergeant and two corporals, none of whom spoke English.

They went to see Captain Moreno in his cramped office at the main entrance to the barracks. He was in his early thirties with an air of sophistication and a weary countenance which made him look older than his years. He was not happy about being given command of these deserters but was trying to make the best of it. He spoke English easily and welcomed them with practiced appreciation. He indicated for Jimmy and Patrick to take the two chairs opposite his desk. He called an aide to bring in another for Jeb. John remained standing by the door.

"Gentlemen," he said. "You've made the right decision. I have enlistment papers here for you to sign. You'll be awarded immediate Mexican citizenship and three hundred and twenty acres of fertile land upon completion of five years service."

Things were rushing forward at an uncontrollable pace. Patrick was a deserter and once he signed those papers he would also be a traitor. The land was twice as much as the American's offered, but it was in Mexico. What did he know of the country other than the disputed area they marched across to get to the Rio Grande? The Captain slid the papers across the table. They were written in English. The three of them studied them without saying anything.

After all that he'd gone through, Patrick was surprised that the land didn't seem to mean that much. He reckoned he could bring his family to Mexico despite that not being anyone's plan or dream. His mother wouldn't like it. But the truth of it was, he didn't do this for the land.

Captain Moreno's chair scraped the floor as he shifted impatiently. He sent a questioning look at Lieutenant Riley. John knew that both Patrick and Jimmy didn't truly want to be soldiers any longer and understood why. He put a hand on Patrick's shoulder.

"Sign the paper, lad," he said. "Take the land. It's what you've always wanted. And, you'll be respected and welcomed here wherever you go."

He hesitated a moment longer before taking up the quill and signing the paper. He slid it back over to the captain. Jimmy and Jeb still sat there staring at their documents.

"What are you going to do, Jimmy?" said John.

"Oh hell," said Jimmy. "It's worth it to get a chance to finish off Saxon, and Graves too. And three hundred twenty acres is nothing to scoff at. Might even find myself a little señorita like my cousin has."

Patrick stiffened and he shot a threatening glance at Jimmy. She was no mere peasant girl or camp follower. He let it go, realizing there was no harm meant. Jimmy signed his name. Lieutenant Riley turned to Jeb.

"Can you read, lad?"

"Some," he said. "But can't write much. I'll sign my mark if you'll give me a gun to kill as many of those white devils as possible."

John smiled, "Ah, you'll get more than that, Jeb. We'll give you a cannon so you can blast the slave breeders into oblivion."

Captain Moreno got out of his chair and the three new recruits stood up. He extended his hand. Patrick shook it first, then Jimmy and Jeb. "Welcome to the Mexican Army," he said.

Chapter Thirty-Eight

Back at the barracks they were issued uniforms similar in color and design to Lieutenant Riley's. The trousers were different, white canvas instead of blue, with a red stripe down the seam to indicate they were part of an artillery unit. They were given two different hats. The dress hat was the same as John's, a tall black shako topped with a pompon. The other was a soft visor-less field cap of dark blue cloth with red trim and a red tassel.

Lieutenant Riley formed up their new unit and marched them to a hotel in the main plaza which served as the headquarters of General Ampudia. The general strode out and marched back and forth in front of his new soldiers. The brass buttons and numerous medals on his uniform sent out shafts of light in the late morning sun. The general had broad shoulders, deep-set, lifeless eyes and a black mustache with a long white goatee.

Ampudia had a reputation for ruthless tactics against the Texans during and after their fight for independence. He had been an artillery officer at the Alamo and a vicious scourge along the border during that conflict. He was known as a cutthroat even against his own people. A few years prior he was sent to put down a rebellion in Yucatan and had the insurgents beheaded and their heads placed on pikes around the town square.

As he walked through the ranks inspecting them, Patrick saw Padre Pancho emerge from the hotel. The priest was to be Ampudia's translator. He went to the front of the formation where the general joined him. Lieutenant Riley strode to them and saluted Ampudia sharply. "As promised, Excellency," he said. "I have delivered capable men to serve under you. There will be more, but for now we have a good beginning."

Ampudia nodded while John spoke. He waited for the priest to translate. Then he spoke to the his new men in Spanish. When he paused, Padre Pancho told them that all of Mexico welcomed and thanked them for coming to the aid of the Church and their Catholic brothers and sisters. He promised fair treatment and the ability to rise in rank. He ended by saying they would soon push the *yanquis* back to the Nueces River and out of Mexico forever. A cheer rose from the men. General Ampudia looked them over one last time before turning and walking back into the hotel.

They were marched back to their quarters and told to be ready in two hours to begin training. Until then, they were free to get themselves settled and to look around the town. Patrick had only one thought in mind. He, Jimmy and Micheál were standing by their bunks when Lieutenant Riley joined them.

"I need to speak to Padre Pancho," said Patrick.

John, smiled knowingly. "I hope you don't wish to go to confession. I don't think he, or our Lord, will consider what you've done to be a sin. On the contrary."

Jimmy laughed. "No, John. Patrick wants to find out where the priest's pretty sister might be."

John winked at Patrick. "She's here, lad."

Patrick's heart skipped a beat. "You've seen her? Where is she?"

"She and her brother are dining with the General. I don't think it wise to interrupt them."

"I have to see her, John."

"You need to be patient. I do know this, she would like nothing more than to see you as well. She asked me many questions about you and was devastated you would not be joining us. I underestimated you, Patrick. I told

212

her you'd be staying with the Americans."

"Jimmy had something to do with it. But the truth is I would have found a way to see her again."

"He's been hit by a thunderbolt," said Jimmy.

John pointed out the window and said, "it appears she's set her cap for him as well." Patrick followed his hand and there she was, running towards their building.

"Alicia!" he shouted and darted for the door. Behind him, the three of them laughed as he ran off.

She saw him as soon as he pushed open the door of the barracks. They rushed to each other. Patrick wanted to laugh and cry at the same time. He wanted to tell her that he would never leave her side but all he could manage was to say her name over and over again. They embraced and then kissed right there on the street in front of God and everyone. Hanging out the bottom floor windows of the barracks were all the new Irish soldiers of Mexico, hooting and whistling.

"Patricio," she said, finding it hard to catch her breath. "I'm so happy you're here. I didn't dare hope and yet I couldn't help it. John Riley said you would not. But you did, Patricio. You came to me."

"And I won't leave you, Alicia. I want to be with you always, no matter what happens or where we end up."

She slipped her arm through his. "Walk with me," she said.

He was beside himself. They strolled through the clean, well laid out streets of Matamoros, holding each other close. He smelled the sweet fragrance of the lemon and orange trees, ripe with fruit, that were scattered through the town. There were two-story brick buildings with colorful flowers in boxes in the windows and rows of adobe houses. It seemed a prosperous town but at the edges were crude mud huts with thatched roofs where the poor eked out a living.

Townspeople and soldiers alike walked about, seemingly oblivious to the *yanquis* a few hundred yards across the river. Most greeted the couple with smiles of approval but Patrick did feel the stares of some officers who apparently disapproved or were jealous of this lowly Irish deserter with the stunning Alicia on his arm. He didn't care. At that moment he too lost all concern for the looming conflict.

When they reached the main plaza, they saw Padre Pancho coming their way. When he got closer he gave them both a big smile. "*Bueno*," he said. "I see you have decided to join us after all, Patricio."

"Yes, Father."

"My sister was very worried about you." Patrick blushed and didn't know what to say. "And look at her now," said the priest. "I've never before seen her this happy."

"I've never been this happy before either, Father."

"I would have guessed that, Patricio. Please, call me Francisco, or Pancho if you like. I feel we are to be as close as brothers you and I."

"Thank you, Pancho. Thank you very much."

Chapter Thirty-Nine

The deserters went to work training and drilling under the watchful eye of Lieutenant John Riley. They had to learn the military procedures and customs of a new, albeit less zealous army. War fever was just as rampant, if not more so, on this side of the Rio Grande. General Taylor, on the surface at least, was content to let his army prepare and wait in a state of provocation. The Mexican bands played patriotic songs incessantly while the *soldados* marched and officers paraded around in a flourish of boasting threats hurled across the river.

Lieutenant Riley insisted they no longer call him John in the presence of the other men. He was a fair and patient commander but a demanding taskmaster who would abide no laziness or foolishness. No one wanted to make a mistake and get dressed down by him. Patrick strived to make him proud. With their previous training, they were soon a more than passable artillery unit.

Those first days in Matamoros, Alicia and Patrick were able spend the evenings together. For Patrick, every second in her presence was magical. He also got to know his new comrades better, especially Jeb. His cot and Jeb's were next to each other and one night they talked long after lights out.

"Where are you from, Jeb?" asked Patrick.

"Jeb ain't my real name. That's my slave name."

"Oh?" said Patrick "What's your real name?"

"Henry. Henry Harris. I was born in Talbot County, Maryland, on the banks of the Chesapeake Bay. I don't know how old I truly am. Never knew my father. He was sold off before I was even a year old. I only saw my mother a handful of times, when she was allowed to come visit from where she lived, far across the county."

Patrick didn't know what to say. He didn't have to respond because Jeb went on talking.

"Maryland wasn't that bad," he said. "Mostly I did farm work. Had lots of different jobs; field hand, blacksmith, cook, and any task that needed doing. The threat of a beating was always there but if you kept your nose clean it could be avoided. On the Sabbath we had a little time for ourselves, after church services."

"How did you wind up with Saxon?" said Patrick.

"Have you heard of Mr. Frederick Douglass?"

"The escaped slave? He's written a book about his life I believe."

"That's him. A great and brave man, even back then in his youth. He got into some trouble with his owner. They didn't like that he'd learned to read. An educated negro is a dangerous negro who owners feared might rise up and kill them in their beds.

"But Fred never talked about any of that. He said we needed to know about freedom and that the promise of America wasn't just for white people. We met when he was sent to Mr. Covey's farm. My brother and I were on loan from our owner to Covey but Fred was sent there to be disciplined. Covey was known all over the area as the very best negro breaker."

"What't that?" asked Patrick, fearing that he already knew the answer.

"Owners with unruly slaves sent them to Covey. He would find the slightest reason and then whip 'em violently with the lash or that hickory cane he favored. One morning after he'd been there about six months, Fred refused to admit whatever it was he was accused of doing. Covey went after him with his cane and none of us could believe it when Fred reached his hand up, grabbed hold of that stick, and stopped him in his tracks.

"Fred absolutely refused to be hit. Even though he weren't full grown yet, he was a big, strong boy and Covey, try as he might couldn't strike him or wrestle that cane out of his grasp. They seemed frozen like that until Covey let go and charged at him. Fred, calm as could be, put one hand on his throat and held him at bay.

"Fred never struck a blow. All he did was prevent himself from receiving an unfair beating. We was all sure there was gonna be a lynchin' right then and there, but Covey backed off and screamed at us to get back to work. I guess he didn't want word to get out that this was one negro he couldn't tame. He mostly let Fred be from then on.

"Wasn't long after that, Fred started holding reading classes in the woods. At first my brother and I was afraid to go but he talked us into it. Covey and a few church elders got wind of it and jumped us one Sunday afternoon. We was studying from the Bible but that made no difference to any of them good Christian men. A week later my brother and I were sold off. I never saw or heard tell of him again and I only started hearing rumors about Fred escaping and getting famous much later on. I was sold south to Cap'n Saxon's father and shipped to his plantation in Alabama."

Patrick heard the snores of their bunkmates rise and fall throughout the barracks as he tried to think of something to say. "That's awful, Jeb...sorry, Henry."

"There was another slave name Henry on the Saxon plantation so they just told me I was to be Jeb from then on."

"Was he always so vicious and cruel?"

"He wasn't as mean then like he is now. That happened after he went into the army, when he got sent to Florida to fight the Seminoles. He was always angry at some slight or dispute with his superiors."

"So you were with him in Florida?"

"Yeah. He wanted a slave to go with him to tend to his needs and I was chosen. I had a wife and a baby girl by then and begged not to go but it was no use. I'm going back to find them even if it takes the rest of my life."

"I hope you do," said Patrick.

"And I hope your cousin succeeded in killing Saxon," said Henry.

"I don't know, it looked to me like he survived."

"Then maybe I'll get the chance to do it myself."

"You might have to fight Jimmy for that," said Patrick

Henry smiled in the dark. "Thanks for letting me come with you."

Patrick rolled over, pulled his blanket up and closed his eyes. "There's nothing to thank me for."

"Well, one thing's for sure. If he's alive, the Cap'n and the rest of them are going to be hearing from me. From you too, right?"

"Me too, Henry."

Chapter Forty

Along the Rio Grande, April 25 - May 3, 1846

Patrick wrote to Ellen. He struggled with the right words to tell her what he'd done. In the end he simply said that they were brutally abused by nativist officers and took matters into their own hands. He made sure to mention the three hundred and twenty acres, his Mexican citizenship, and that he would send money when he could. He then confessed that he had fallen in love. It rang hollow on the page but it was the best he could do. He asked her to forward the letter to their parents after she read it.

He was concerned about getting mail to Philadelphia but Alicia told him not to worry, the letter would get to its destination. She mailed it for him, using the return address of her cousin's residence in Mexico City. He felt lighter after it was sent and convinced himself that things would turn out for the best.

Within a couple days, Lieutenant Riley approached him about a promotion to corporal. He had never given a thought to rising in rank. From the moment he enlisted in Pittsburgh his only intention was to survive and claim his land. Taking him aside to discuss it, Riley said "I need someone the men respect, Patrick. And someone I can trust."

He was caught off guard and not sure what to say. "I don't know, John. What would my duties be?"

"Making sure the lads are on time, prepared and taking the training seriously. When the fighting starts, I'll need you to keep a cool head and ensure everyone stays focused on their assignments."

Patrick didn't say it out loud but he fretted again if he would have the courage when the time came? "The pay," said Riley, "Is twelve dollars a month. That's a significant increase."

He would be able to send more to Ellen and keep some for Alicia and himself. A promotion would be a step forward and he decided to accept it.

"Thank you, John," he said. "I hope I can live up to your expectations."

John put a hand on his shoulder. "I've no doubt you will, Patrick. And remember, in front of the lads, call me Lieutenant Riley."

Two weeks after they deserted, General Mariano Arista arrived to replace General Ampudia. He strutted into Matamoros with two thousand more troops, over half of which were cavalry outfitted in brilliant brass armor fitted over sky-blue jackets. Their helmets were also a polished brass with gleaming silver ornaments topped off with long horsehair plumes that fluttered in the breeze as they high-stepped their horses through the main plaza of Matamoros. General Ampudia could only smolder with resentment and salute as Arista flamboyantly took over his command.

Patrick was surprised by Arista's fair skin and the fact that his hair was a light red. He even had a few freckles and some of the men thought he might have Irish blood in him. He had spent time in both Florida and Cincinnati and was known to have respect for Americans. But that didn't soften his stance. He wanted nothing more than to be a hero and rid his country of the *yanquis*.

One of the first things Arista did was compose another broadside for Taylor's army in which he reiterated the promise of land and advancement for any immigrant soldiers who would join the Mexican side. The leaflets spread all over their old camp and were effective, as more men deserted every night.

The day after his arrival, Arista sent his cavalry across the Rio Grande a few miles upstream to disrupt the American supply line from Port Isabel. The cavalry commander, General Torrejon, surprised a scouting party, killing eleven and capturing sixty. A few days later, another force under a Major Quintero again crossed over and killed four Texas Rangers, taking four others as prisoners. General Taylor now had the justification he needed. First blood was drawn by the Mexicans on, disputed or not, American soil.

With every passing hour the anticipation of battle intensified. Patrick was officially given his corporal stripes. He had worked at every artillery position and now helped teach the men to improve their speed and efficiency. They were able to fire two to three times a minute but Lieutenant Riley wasn't satisfied. They needed to increase it to four or five times a minute.

Patrick told himself he was ready despite the growing fear in his gut as the thought of being blown to pieces became a very real possibility. Courage is a thing all men aspire to and there is no greater test than in war. He had never before thought about being heroic, but now it mattered. He wanted to be the best man he could in the eyes of his fellow soldiers, his commander and the woman he loved. More than anything though, he wanted to survive.

On May the first, three weeks after they deserted, Patrick, Jimmy and

Micheál watched in disbelief at what was happening on the opposite shore. It appeared that Taylor's entire army was packing up and moving out. Hundreds of wagons kicked up a giant dust cloud and thousands of men were seen marching away.

"Are they giving up?" said Micheál.

Lieutenant Riley joined them and took out his spyglass. He held it on Fort Texas for a long time. When he pushed in the glass he said "There are still soldiers inside and men and cannons on the parapets."

"Where are the rest of them going?" said Patrick.

"Taylor must be afraid for his supply line," said Riley. "He's most likely heading out to Port Isabel to insure its safety."

Patrick knew little of military strategy but it seemed to him a good time to attack. They did, but not until Arista sent a contingent of two thousand men and twenty artillery pieces across the river downstream at a place called Longoreno to surround Fort Texas. It took three entire days to ferry them all across the river due to a lack of boats.

At the first light of dawn after the infantry was on the other shore, their Mexican sergeant roused the men and marched them to a position behind a redoubt fifty yards from the river's edge. Lieutenant Riley was already there with his field glass trained on their target. "They've got four eighteen pounders," he said. "Along with a mortar and a number of six pounders. They can do a lot of damage to us and the city."

Patrick immediately thought of Alicia. They parted last night, knowing that today they would begin the attack. She promised to evacuate the city as soon as the shooting started. He needed to know where she would go.

"I'll be with the rest of the camp followers," she said. "In a place well beyond the town."

"I'll find you as soon as it's over," said Patrick holding on to her tightly. "Stay safe."

"I love you, Patricio." Her words soothed him but not enough to overcome the fear he had for her.

Lieutenant Riley continued studying the enemy through his scope. He let out a short grunt, almost a laugh, and handed Patrick the glass. He pointed at the fort. "The parapet on the far right," he said.

It took a minute to focus and locate what John wanted him to see. There, staring back through his own glass was Captain Stuart Saxon. His head was bandaged and his arm appeared to be in a sling but he was obviously in full command of the artillery there. Patrick looked for Jimmy. He was standing ready next to the cannon, rammer in hand. He raised his eyebrows at John and pointed the glass toward his cousin. John nodded his permission.

"Jimmy," he hollered, "come have a look."

Patrick handed gave him the glass. "The parapet on the far right."

Jimmy peered through the eyepiece. "Damn him," he said.

Patrick didn't know if Saxon actually saw or recognized them, but Jimmy turned around, bent over and dropped his trousers, revealing his very white bare ass. Not only did the Irish lads appreciate it, their new Mexican comrades did as well. They roared with laughter and raised their voices in a loud "*Viva Los Colorados*!"

Lieutenant Riley also smiled but moved to get the men under control. "Put your pants back on Jimmy. You'll need a bigger weapon than that to do Saxon in."

Chapter Forty-One

Matamoros, May 3 - May 5, 1846

They had thirty cannons lined up facing Fort Texas from three different directions. Patrick tried to quell his rising apprehension. He watched Lieutenant Riley move up and down the line, encouraging and inspecting the men and the cannons. He had the same expression and attitude as if they were out on the training field.

As they waited, the sweet, pungent smell of incense drifted through their ranks along with the low murmur of latin prayers. Patrick turned to see Padre Pancho followed by a long procession of women coming their way. Right behind her brother, he was horrified to see Alicia, her head bowed and her angelic face shrouded in a black lace mantilla. Pancho stopped at each artillery piece to bless it and the men manning it. When they reached him, Alicia came and they embraced. His concern for her turned to anger.

"What are you doing here, Alicia? You told me you'd find someplace out of danger."

"I will, but this must be done first."

"Please, Alicia, get away from here."

"Si, Patricio. Stay alive and come for me. I love you."

His voice cracked when he said, "I love you too. Now go!"

Patrick fought back tears watching the solemn group move on to the rest of the cannons. When they passed a heavy silence bore down upon all of them. Jimmy could not stand still. His body rocked back and forth but he looked ready. Micheál's eyes were closed, his head raised to the heavens as his lips moved in silent prayer. Henry's mouth was tight, his eyes blazed. He showed no emotion until he caught Patrick's eye and smiled in what appeared to be gratitude.

Lieutenant Riley stood tall, straight and fearless with his hand on the hilt of his sword. "Ready now, lads," he shouted. "Concentrate on your individual tasks just like we've done in training. This is where we get our vengeance."

The men cheered and then they heard Jimmy above the rest, "aim for that snake Saxon." Down the line came orders shouted in Spanish. Lieutenant Riley pulled his sword and held it high. He repeated the commands in English.

"To action!"

Patrick repeated the order and they all stood ready.

"Load!"

The men moved swiftly as a unit. Henry shoved the round ball down the muzzle and Jimmy rammed it in all the way. John Riley pointed his sword at Fort Texas.

"Fire!"

Before Patrick could repeat the order, the ground shook and his ears exploded with the boom of thirty cannons belching smoke and recoiling after launching their missiles. He was momentarily dazed but recovered and screamed "sponge!" It was doubtful anyone heard it. He couldn't even hear his own voice. It didn't matter. They knew their assignments. After the initial rush of fear, a strange calm came over him as he watched his men perform their duties. He gave up shouting and used the hand signals they had practiced.

After the first few shots the crew moved as one; loading, ramming, spongeing the muzzle to extinguish any lingering embers and then reloading another round. Lieutenant Riley was everywhere, encouraging and directing them to reposition the cannons for better effect. Patrick changed the elevation, re-sighted and gave the signal to continue firing. Choking black smoke filled the air making it impossible to see if they were having any effect on Fort Texas. Dirt and grime filled every pore, turning his skin coal black.

The American guns responded. A direct hit landed on a cannon a few yards to Patrick's left, tossing it and two men in the air like rag dolls. A severed arm, bones protruding from the bloody stump, came out of the sky and landed at his feet. Their shrieks somehow penetrated the screeching of the bursting shells. Even through the din, he heard them as clear as thunderclaps, and would forever. It was Dennis Conahan from County Kildare who was blown apart. He was a fine lad with carrot-red hair and a face full of freckles. Patrick was sickened by the sight, but there was no time to mourn or grieve.

The relentless firing went on for hours with only breaks to cool the cannons. The ringing in Patrick's ears didn't subside. They went back to work, not knowing if they were causing and damage or casualties. The aim of the Americans didn't improve after the initial hit that killed Conahan. The Irishmen were doing a good job of keeping them pinned down and forcing them to rush when they did fire.

Soon the enemy changed strategy. They heated their cannon balls in a furnace and shot over Riley's artillery, aiming instead for the town behind them. The heated balls were supposed to ignite the buildings of Matamoros but most weren't hot enough. Only a couple structures went up in flames and were extinguished without extensive damage. Patrick muttered a fervent prayer that Alicia was truly out of harms way.

They kept up the barrage all day and into the next. When they did halt the action, and the smoke cleared, they were able to see Fort Texas. There didn't appear to be any damage at all to it. Lieutenant Riley had them make adjustments so the balls made it up and over into the fort. Patrick knew there were underground shelters within the fort. He had helped dig them, and he doubted there were many casualties.

By evening time of the second day the shots coming back at them slowed down. "They're conserving ammunition," said Riley. "Hoping Taylor will be back soon." The word came down that they were to cease firing. It was time to rest and eat. Patrick went to John and begged to be allowed to go find Alicia. "I'm sorry, lad," he said. "I can't allow it. You need to stay here with the men."

His eyes were sore and burning. His ears had a constant ringing in them and with every breath he smelled and tasted smoke and gunpowder. There was so much dirt caked to his skin, he doubted he would ever be clean again. Above all else, he needed rest. He sat down, leaned against a rock and was asleep in an instant.

Chapter Forty-Two

Fort Texas, May 5 - May 9, 1846

The Americans stopped their intermittent shelling around midnight. It was still dark but Patrick was awake when Lieutenant Riley approached.

"Get the men formed up, Patrick."

"Where are we going?"

"Across the river," said Riley. "We need our guns closer. The infantry is going to make an assault on Fort Texas and we'll be providing cover."

They marched double time upstream, past the main road to Point Isabel. When they halted, they were about halfway to the spot where Patrick, Jimmy and Henry had crossed over. The moon was three quarters full but the clouds and the heavy brush gave them some cover. Four cannons had already been transported over and two more were on a flatboat moving across the water. Lieutenant Riley addressed them when they were on board their ferry.

"Lads, we have their fort surrounded. Our guns have been placed on the north-west side of the fort so we'll have better effect and be able to provide support when the fight begins. We'll commence firing at dawn, on my signal."

Standing in the boat, Patrick looked at his comrades with pride and affection. There were a few Mexicans among them but most were the young, Irish lads he'd been with since Pittsburgh. They had tasted battle together, forging a brotherhood that not even death could break.

The clouds drifted away revealing a gauzy, yellow-tinged sky. They took their positions a hundred yards from the fort. Patrick was able to see the guns and the silhouettes of a few men on the parapets. He asked Lieutenant Riley for his scope and saw once more the figure and face of Saxon peering at him through his own glass. It was then that Patrick was certain his former commander fully realized who it was shooting at him.

Despite being closer, their guns still did little damage to the earthen walls of the fort. In the late afternoon of Wednesday, the sixth, there was a formal break in the fighting. Patrick thought their long delayed infantry strike on the fort was finally about to begin. Instead, he watched a group of Mexican officers gallop up the dry moat to the entrance of the fort carrying a white flag.

The gates opened and three American officers rode out to meet them. Patrick didn't recognize any of them. The Mexicans demanded a full surrender; something every deserter knew was not going to happen. Saxon alone would fight to the death. In a matter of minutes the meeting broke up and when their officers dashed back to their lines, the order was given to resume firing.

Patrick and the rest of the men were tired, hungry and disappointed over the lack of success but they continued to function with mute, mechanical precision. General Arista reinforced them with more infantry units and four additional cannons but they were eight pounders and did nothing to improve their results. It was a standoff. The men grew increasingly restless. Lieutenant Riley was fuming. "We should have taken the fort days ago," he said.

"Why haven't we?" said Patrick.

"I have no idea. Our artillery is useless against those walls. We should be raining cannon balls down upon them while the infantry climbs up and over on ladders."

"We far outnumber them," said Patrick. "There can't be more than a few hundred men inside. What are we waiting for?"

Riley didn't say anything more other than to tell them to save their strength. They continued firing but it was sporadic, waiting until they saw movement on the parapets before taking a shot. The Americans were conserving their ammunition.

On Friday morning their infantry was withdrawn from around the fort. Lieutenant Riley paced back and forth trying to control himself. Patrick watched the troops march up the road toward Point Isabel and asked if they were going with them. John didn't stop walking, saying brusquely, "We've been ordered to remain here."

They continued their haphazard shelling, mostly it seemed to break up the boredom of standing around and watching. Later that afternoon they heard the distant sound of music. Patrick knew it was from their side because of all the horns. The Americans used mostly drums and bugles. The Mexicans loved a loud and showy presentation. They had an entire brass band in the conflict and it was them he heard. Moments later, the music was drowned out by the sound of musket and cannon fire.

"Sounds as if General Taylor has returned," said Riley. "Now is the time. Our soldiers know the terrain and the Americans won't have the fort to hide behind."

Patrick hoped he was right and that his former comrades would soon be running with their tails between their legs back to Corpus Christi. He was naive enough to think the war might be over then and there. His thoughts drifted to claiming his land and starting a happy life together with Alicia.

The roar and thunder of the battle to the north continued until close to sundown when all went quiet. Riley's lads lobbed shells at the fort but in the time between shots, the silence was ominous and eerie. Why hadn't they heard anything? Was Taylor in retreat? Where was their army?

The next morning came and went with no noise of the battle from the day before. The silence continued into the afternoon only broken by their half-hearted bombing of the fort. Around three o'clock, they briefly heard the band music again before it was drowned out by much closer sounds of explosions.

Less than an hour later, Patrick watched in horror as hundreds upon hundreds of *soldados* came stampeding towards him, weaponless and terror-stricken. He and his unit were nearly trampled, cannons and all, as the fleeing troops rushed down to the shoreline looking for boats to take them back across the Rio Grande. Seeing none, they plunged into the river and swam desperately for the other side. Cheers, along with musket fire, broke out from the parapets of Fort Texas.

Lieutenant Riley instantly ordered the cannons spiked and for them to get out of there. He didn't have to say it twice. None of them had any illusions as to what would happen if they were captured. Patrick ran like the rest of the Mexican Army. Fortunately, the ferries they had used were still there, out of sight a little further upstream. They made it safely across to Matamoros. Many others were not so lucky.

The current was ferocious that day and even those who could swim were taken by it. The river roiled and swirled with thrashing bodies as if a school of ravenous fish were feeding near the surface. Bodies floated by all day and into the next. Corpses that were caught and hung up in the rocks and tree limbs dislodged and drifted away as the river slowly receded. They twisted and turned as they went, making it seem like they were struggling and dying all over again.

Arista and his remaining troops eventually found their way across the river downstream but the casualty count was staggering: close to a thousand dead and at least that many wounded.

As soon as he got across, Patrick went looking for Alicia. He didn't ask permission. He went directly to the outskirts of town where the camp followers huddled. He searched frantically but she was nowhere to be found. He ran through the streets of Matamoros before finally finding her, caring for the wounded in a makeshift hospital in the main plaza. She saw him at the same time. Her eyes lit up and she smiled. He ran to her.

"Alicia, thank God."

"Patricio, you are alive."

They held on to each other in a desperate embrace. He didn't want to let go but she finally pulled back. She put both her hands on his filthy face and kissed him. "I was so worried," she said. "Have you seen Francisco?"

"No, I think he was with General Arista."

"Can you look for him? I must stay here with the wounded. There is very little we can do with only water and a few bandages but I can't leave them."

"Of course," he said. "I'll find him."

Patrick saw him down along the river bank, blessing the bodies of those that washed up on the shore. He was in some sort of trance and didn't see or hear him approach. Patrick called out to him but got no response. Pancho continued murmuring prayers, moving from one inert figure to the next. Patrick got closer and said his name again. Still no answer. When he was right behind him he put his hand on his arm. "Padre," he said softly. Pancho lurched and nearly fell over. Patrick grabbed him around the waist to steady him. The priest's eyes were glazed and he didn't recognize him.

Patrick shook him and said in a raised voice, "Pancho." Slowly he came to his senses. "So many dead, Patricio. So many of these poor men who were forced into this."

"Yes, I know," said Patrick. Come, Alicia is worried about you. There's no more you can do here.

He seemed to gain strength as they walked. Patrick let go of him and they went to Alicia. Pancho got control of himself and went right to work, encouraging those who seemed like they would survive, and performing the last rites on those who wouldn't.

Chapter Forty-Three

Matamoros, May 9-May 16, 1846

General Arista attempted to secure a truce but Taylor would have nothing but an unconditional surrender. That was never going to happen and so Lieutenant Riley and his men waited over a week for an attack that the Americans never mounted.

General Taylor was principled enough to care for the enemy wounded who were still on the other side of the Rio Grande. Truth be told, they were better off over there. The limited medical supplies of the Mexicans went first to the officers. The rest of the *soldados* were left to Alicia and the other camp women, who did the best they could to help and comfort them.

Patrick managed to see Alicia a few brief minutes each day before both being pulled away. She had so many wounded to care for and he was under pressure from Lieutenant Riley to keep the men ready and prevent them from getting completely discouraged. They had a talk inside Captain Moreno's office on a morning when the rest of their company was heading out for breakfast.

"We'll be marching out soon," said John.

Patrick was surprised. He thought they were going to stay and defend Matamoros. "Where to?" he asked.

"A place called Linares. We need to keep the lads ready."

"They're getting restless," said Patrick.

"Jimmy isn't helping with his constant drinking and complaining," said John. "Can you get him to restrain himself a wee bit?"

"I'll try, but it's never been easy with him."

"He's a good lad," said John. "He only needs a little more self control."

Patrick nodded in agreement. "One thing's for sure," he said. "Jimmy's a fighter and you can count on him when the bullets are flying."

"I saw it myself, Patrick. And you are too. But the rest of the lads look to both of you and if he's off getting drunk, well they'll easily fall into the same habit."

"I'll talk to him," said Patrick.

They marched out of Matamoros a few days later. They were ordered to leave all unnecessary baggage behind, including crates of ammunition and artillery, which they disabled. Like most commands in Patrick's new army, the orders only applied to the rank and file. The officers were allowed to bring whatever personal belongings they could manage.

If the Irish thought they were dispensable and mere cannon fodder to the Americans, the indios and peons who made up most of the Mexican troops were far less important to this army. They were in rags and the sandals they wore were mostly discarded after being soaked and destroyed in the river.

Even in defeat, the Irishmen were treated as celebrities by most of their superiors, who saw them as defenders of the Church and the nation of Mexico. Soon the officers were referring to the deserters as the Battalón de San Patricio, while their native soldiers were mere beasts of burden who could walk barefoot across the desert if need be. And they did.

The first day they only went four miles upriver in order to get away from the Americans and to make sure they weren't being pursued. Lieutenant Riley tried to keep them in some sort of order but the pace was difficult and the road rough and narrow. The line of troops and the nearly one thousand camp followers stretched for miles. They had very little water or food and after a few days it took on the appearance of a death march.

John had been correct, they were going to Linares, some two hundred miles south. Alicia told him she would be going there as well. She was to travel with General Arista and his staff. The general offered a horse for her and Pancho to share but he refused it, wanting to walk with the troops. Alicia wanted to walk too but both Arista and her brother convinced her to ride.

Patrick saw Alicia only two times during the arduous march. Once on the first night when she found him after they stopped and set up camp. Pancho came with her and they sat with Jimmy and Micheál around a small fire they were able to make with a few pieces of mesquite. "General Arista is going to take his cavalry and move out ahead of the rest of the army," said Alicia.

Patrick was torn. He wanted her to be as safe as possible, which would mean staying close to the high command but he also dreaded the thought of her not being nearby. He was also worried that the general was trying to win her favor. He had seen him smiling and leering at her and knew he wanted her to ride with him for more than just her safety.

"I want to stay with you," said Alicia. "Pancho, you take the horse and go with General Arista. I will walk with the rest of the women and cook for Señor Riley and Patricio."

Patrick wanted that more than anything but her well being was more important. "No, Alicia," he said. "Go with the general. Please. He can protect you much better than I can."

"I don't want to be safe, Patricio. I want to be with you."

236

"And I want to be with you. But I'd much rather you be with the general and his cavalry."

Patrick gave a pleading look at her brother. "Tell her, Pancho."

"Si, Alicia. It is better for you to go with the general. We'll be fine here. I will look after your Patricio."

"And who will look after you, *mi hermano*?"

"I will," said Patrick. "We'll look after each other, but only if you promise to go ahead."

Early the next afternoon she rode up and found him among the marching column. She dismounted and they walked together a short distance away to the side from the others. "I'm happy you're going," he said.

"I'm not, but I'll be waiting for you in Linares."

"I'll be counting the steps," he said.

They held each other and kissed furtively. She turned and got back on her horse. He watched her ride off. He was in the middle of the desert, tired, hungry, thirsty and running from the American Army yet at that moment he wondered how it was that such a beautiful, intelligent woman would even look at him, let alone love him? He put General Arista out of his mind as best he could.

The desert turned scorching hot. Patrick's eyes burned from the blinding glare of the sun and the grit and sand of the dusty trail. His mouth tasted of dirt and his lips were cracked and cut from lack of water. On the fourth day out, rain began to fall and they all rejoiced. The Mexicans shouted cries of *viva* up and down the long, straggling line. Patrick raised his eyes to the sky and let it rinse over him.

It wasn't long however before the blessed rain became a curse. It continued in torrents for a day and a half. The road turned into a quagmire.

Their feet sank nearly knee deep and the strength it took to take a single step was more than many could bear. Patrick saw men fall face first in the mud, unable to get up. He tried to help the ones he encountered but it took too much strength and he soon stopped trying or he too would have fallen, never to rise again.

When their food ran out, oxen were killed so that the men could have a little meat. With less oxen, more equipment was left behind, hidden behind and under clumps of brush. There was no wood to cook with so the meat was eaten raw. Patrick, like many, became ill almost immediately. The nausea and retching weakened them further but there was nothing to do but keep going.

The rain finally let up but the damage to their boots made them of little use. Patrick tied them around his feet in order to have at least some protection. He worried about Jimmy who lagged further and further behind. All his anger had turned inward. He was unresponsive to anything anyone said. He only stared straight ahead at the ground or off into the distant sky. Patrick tried to get him to talk.

"We'll be all right, Jimmy," he said.

"No we won't," said Jimmy. "We're dead men."

Chapter Forty-Four

Linares, Mexico, May 28 - July 6, 1846

Lieutenant Riley and Padre Pancho tried to keep up the spirits of all the men. John had a horse but was more often on foot, helping those who had stopped or fallen. He could be seen boosting someone on his last legs up on the horse and leading him along. Pancho gave constant words of support, prayer and gratitude for their sacrifice. He often took a heavy pack from one of them, shouldering it himself and taking the arm of the straggler. He had a reserve of strength and concern that Patrick and the rest of the San Patricios grew to admire and respect.

They finally got a supply of food and water at a large hacienda called Vaqueria. The owner graciously fed the entire army. It was only rice, beans and tortillas but it was delicious. After a punishing two weeks of averaging over twenty miles a day, they made it to another hacienda at Guadalupe. There they were resupplied with food and water.

They had lost almost a third of the army between their defeat and the march. Exhaustion, starvation, thirst, sickness, desertion and a few officer suicides reduced their ranks to scarcely a thousand men. The next day they marched into the small town of Linares. Patrick thought of nothing else but seeing Alicia.

He asked Lieutenant Riley for permission to find her. He gave it willingly but asked him to make it brief. Pancho went with him to Arista's camp. From there they were directed to the hospital where she was tending to the still numerous sick and wounded. Patrick was a repulsive sight, dirty and skeletal but her smile when she saw him made him feel like a king.

They stayed in Linares a little over a month. Long enough to have General Arista court-martialed for the defeats at Matamoros, known as the battles of Palo Alto and Resaca de la Palma. General Mejia, who replaced him as commander, determined that the Americans would next attack the city of Monterrey, the capital of the state of Nuevo Leon, eighty miles to the north. They would go there to confront them.

The time in Linares was spent licking their wounds and preparing for what might come next. Alicia and Patrick saw each other often but only for short periods of time. One afternoon following their daily drill, when the men were marching back to their tents Lieutenant Riley called to Patrick.

"Corporal Ryan."

Patrick went to him and saluted. "Yes, sir."

"Come with me to my tent please."

When they entered, John pulled out a large piece of paper and spread it across a trunk that doubled as a table. On it was a simple drawing but Patrick could easily see it was a picture of St. Patrick. In his left hand he held a key and in his right, a staff resting on a serpent. "What's this?" he said.

"I've designed a banner for us. The other side will have a harp and Mexico's coat of arms. I'll put Erin go Bragh in bold letters underneath that. What do you think?"

"It will make a fine flag."

"Will you ask Alicia to sew it for us?"

Patrick knew he could have asked her himself, or asked Padre Pancho, but it touched him that John thought he was the one to ask. "To be sure," he said.

"I'll pay for the materials of course. I doubt we can procure them here but perhaps in Monterrey. I like what they call us. We are indeed St. Patrick's Battalion."

"It's good, John" said Patrick. "The lads will like it too."

He took the drawing to Alicia and she loved it. She confirmed that there wasn't any silk available in Linares but she was able to sew a small version of it out of colored cloth. The people of Mexico called them by various names; *Los Colorados*, *Los Voluntarios Irlandeses*, but the one that stuck was *Los San Patricios*.

There were a few Germans and Dutch among them, and there was Henry as well, but the rest were from Ireland and it was from this point on that they were always referred to as the St. Patrick's Battalion. Soon all of Mexico knew and venerated them as the San Patricios. Even though it was a crude representation of what would become their inspirational banner, he could see and feel it's galvanizing effect.

"We'll find silk in Monterrey," said Alicia. "It will make a fine flag."

"Thank you, Alicia," said Lieutenant Riley when she showed it to him. "I want it to be as large as possible so the lads will always be able to see it and the *yanquis* won't be able to mistake who we are."

"I'll make it as big as I can," said Alicia. "With green, gold and white silk. It will be the most famous military flag in all of Mexico."

John smiled and slapped Patrick on the back. He was in his element; a soldier, a leader of men and a warrior ready for battle. He wasn't happy about their defeat, but believed they were on the right side of a holy war, defending an innocent people against an invading Protestant force. He was fighting not only for Catholic Mexico but also for Ireland. If he couldn't avenge the rape and pillage of their land by the English, he could make a stand here.

Patrick admired John Riley more than any man he ever knew, but he would never be like him. There was no satisfaction in any of this fighting for him. Lieutenant Riley would win fame and prestige on the battlefield. Of that Patrick was sure. But he only wanted it be over and to survive so he could start the rest of his life with Alicia and somehow find a way to fulfill the promise he made to his father.

Chapter Forty-Five

Monterrey, Mexico, July 12 - September 1, 1846

General Mejia marched his army out of Linares in early July. The terrain along the foothills of the Sierra Madre Oriental mountains was much different than the barren desert they had previously crossed. The rocky path was narrow and steep through treacherous ravines. The air turned crisp and thin and it took Patrick a while to get accustomed to it.

The troops were better supplied and the journey was shorter, only about a hundred miles. When they went through the pretty little town of Montemorelos located in a fertile valley filled with citrus trees on the eastern side of the mountains, cheering citizens lined the main road to greet them. By far, the loudest were directed at their band of deserters with shouts of "*Viva Los San Patricios*" filling them all with a sense of pride that none of them had yet earned. Lieutenant Riley beamed from his horse while every member of the San Patricios, Jimmy included, walked taller and straighter through the adoring crowd.

A few days later they arrived at Cadereyta Jimenez, twenty five miles south of Monterrey where the townspeople also gave them an enthusiastic reception. They remained there nine days before moving into Monterrey. Taylor's army was advancing towards them from the northeast and Mejia was determined to defeat them when they arrived.

Alicia and Pancho went ahead with the general and were with the first group to enter Monterrey. They were also going to make a visit to their home town of Saltillo some sixty miles west. They had an uncle with a small house there and family they wished to see. The padre had some business with the local bishop. Alicia didn't say what it was concerning other than it had to do with politics and the small ranch that had been their father's.

The city of Monterrey sits in a lush valley at the base of the Sierra Madre mountains. Large distinctive peaks tower over the city to the south and can be seen on three sides of the town. The air is cool and fresh. The fields were blooming with the sweet scent of oranges, figs and pomegranates when Patrick and the rest of the army arrived. The twelve thousand citizens were not pleased to see them but most greeted the soldiers with subdued warmth. They were obviously concerned for the safety of their city, their property and themselves.

The Santa Caterina river, clean and clear as crystal, flows on the south side of the mile long city. The streets are smooth and straight, the plazas large and spacious and the cathedral, with its richly-carved facade and elegant bell tower, is magnificent. Many of the houses are made from cut stone and there are small, picturesque cottages bordering the river with beautiful gardens and thick foliage. Patrick couldn't help but think that Monterrey looked like the perfect place to have a farm and raise a family.

Alicia and Pancho returned from Saltillo a week later. She moved into the house of a family friend, a former classmate of Pancho's, a lawyer who was away on business in Mexico City. The padre stayed with the army, in a tent like a common soldier.

General Mejia put the army to work fortifying the city. It was already a solid stronghold. The houses and buildings had flat-topped roofs, ideal for small batteries and snipers. On the western side of the city was a formidable hill known as Cerro Independencia. On the eastern end of the hill, directly overlooking the city, was a structure known as Obispado, the

Bishop's Palace. A small fort, Fortaleza Libertad, lay just to the north of Obispado.

On the south side of the river, was another hill, Cerro Federacion. Smaller, at four hundred feet high compared to eight hundred for Independencia, it also had a small redoubt at its eastern end called Fortaleza Soldado, Soldiers Fort. It had only one cannon and a handful of men there.

The main defensive point for the city was the Citadel; a monstrous fortress, built on the foundations of an unfinished cathedral. It sits a thousand yards north of the city in the middle of farmlands, giving it a clear field of fire. Its walls are thirty feet high, surrounded by a shorter, quadrangular, earthen wall with parapets all along it. This was where Mejia stationed the San Patricios.

At first they only had eight cannons but in time they would be reinforced to a total of thirty. From the Citadel the entire city could be covered, especially the Marín Road to the northeast, the route by which Taylor would be coming. It was a formidable position which gave confidence to Riley and his men.

Over the next few weeks, reinforcements and supplies arrived. It became known that General Ampudia would be returning. He had been named Commander in Chief of the entire Mexican Army and would replace Mejia. Ampudia was not well respected and many officers grumbled but there was nothing to do but accept it. When he arrived he brought five thousand reinforcements and money to pay the troops. For this alone his stock rose with the *soldados*.

Ampudia increased the efforts of fortifying the city. He forced the local bishop to allow him to store ammunition in the cathedral. El Teneria, the local tannery on the east end of the city, was turned into a fort and

Fortaleza del Diablo, the Devil's Fort, was strengthened with iron bars and more guns.

The citizens of the town who didn't evacuate pitched in, filling and placing sandbags on the roofs and bracing houses with bars, turning them into small, individual redoubts. They worked side by side with the soldiers, helping to repair and place cannons where they were most needed throughout the city.

When they weren't working, Lieutenant Riley drilled them over and over again. The San Patricios were becoming an efficient and experienced unit, ready and anxious to taste victory. Despite all the labor, their nights were mostly free. Patrick was able to spend precious time with Alicia. It was nearly two entire months that they waited for Taylor's force and it was the most wonderful time of Patrick's life.

He and Alicia went to dances, called fandangos, had long dinners at sidewalk cafes and walked together through the beautiful city of Monterrey. Music was everywhere; on the streets, in homes, at every military function and of course at the fandangos. Most of the music was from the beautiful stringed melody of guitars and violins but often there were brass horns and drums. The men singing were always in soaring harmony, sweet, mellow, and uplifting. There were a few sorrowful tunes but not many. Good times and good feelings far overshadowed any sadness or anticipation of war.

Patrick wasn't much of a dancer but he did his best. Alicia was amazing, twirling and moving in hypnotic rhythm. She always attracted a lot of attention but she made it clear to all that Patricio was her man. It wasn't long before they spoke of marriage. Sitting together in a small courtyard of a *pupusería* eating delicious tortillas stuffed with spicy pork and cheese, they held hands across the table in the fluttering candlelight.

246

"I have nothing to offer you, Alicia. If I survive, and if Mexico does as well, we'll have land to start a farm. But as of this moment I have only a few pesos in my pocket."

"I don't care about money, Patricio. I only want to be with you."

It was a sultry August night when they made love for the first time. They had been out dancing and drinking a few glasses of the local *pulque*, made from the juice of the agave plant. They strolled arm in arm back to her friend's home under a blanket of glittering stars. Their bodies were as warm as the summer evening and neither of them wanted the night to end.

They kissed passionately at the door, each unwilling to break their embrace. Patrick moved his lips lightly over her face, kissing her neck, her ears, her nose. He couldn't get enough of the touch and intoxicating, honeysuckle smell of her skin. His hands roamed from her waist to the small of her back. He leaned in, every inch of his body touching hers, pressing her flat against the wall. She let out a soft moan and pulled him even closer. He thought he should stop, break away, but he couldn't.

"I don't want to go," he whispered in her ear sending a long, sharp tingle from her neck down her spine.

"Patricio, we're not yet married."

"Forgive me, Alicia but who knows what's going to happen. The Americans might be here tomorrow and..."

She cupped her hand over his mouth so he wouldn't finish.

He leaned back and their eyes locked together, their breath quickened. They kissed again with a fervor that was now beyond either of their control. Alicia released one of her hands from his back, reached behind her, and silently opened the door. She smiled and put a finger to her lips.

"Quiet, Patricio."

They tiptoed up the stairs to her room, both giddy and lightheaded. They collapsed together on her small cot and struggled to remove each other's clothes, all the while kissing and touching newly revealed, burning flesh. When he saw and then touched her perfect, voluptuous breasts he nearly cried.

Neither of them had any experience and when he tried to enter her he was clumsy and so aroused it was almost too late. She reached down and guided him. It was over instantly for him in a convulsive spasm of overpowering, erotic ecstasy Their foreheads touched and they kissed and laughed at his inability to suppress the cries of his climax.

Moments later they were at it again, slower, and more deliberate. He found places to touch that made her writhe and groan and he was able to restrain his release until she clutched her nails into his back and trembled with the culmination of her orgasm. They continued throughout the magical night, rolling, exploring, touching and thrusting until they collapsed, entwined together, in a deep, sublime sleep.

Patrick awoke to the sound of a rooster crowing and shafts of sunlight leaking through the shutters. Alicia's back was against his stomach. He moved his hands softly up the contours of her legs and luscious round rump. She stirred, and turned around to face him with a shy smile that lit up her dark eyes and perfect face.

A gush of pleasure as strong as his carnal release surged through him. They kissed again and then made love one more time, slowly and tenderly. Afterwards, they curled up in each other's arms, reveling in the glow and afterglow of their love.

"Let's run away, Alicia."

"And where would we go, Patricio?"

"I don't know. Anywhere but here. My cousin always talks of Oregon."

She looked deep into his beautiful brown eyes she loved so much and held him tighter. "You would want me to leave my people and my country when we're the most vulnerable? When we're being invaded?"

"I want you to be out of danger. I want us to be together in a place where there's no war."

"I want that too, Patricio. But I cannot leave now. My brother needs me. These poor people who have no one but the Church need me as well. I can't do that."

"I did it."

"You left the Americans. They're not your people are they? If it was Ireland being invaded would you have left?"

He thought about it. "No," he said.

"Then think about what you're asking of me."

He let it go. Their die was cast and there was no escaping it. And at that moment he had to leave her. He was already late for morning formation and as lenient as Lieutenant Riley was with his corporal, he wouldn't like it.

"Then we'll see it through," he said. "I have to go now, Alicia."

"I know," she said.

"When can we get married?" he said.

"As soon as possible, Patricio. I will talk to my brother. He can arrange it."

They walked to the door. He held her close and they kissed one more time. "The sooner the better, Alicia. I love you."

Three days later, Tuesday, September first, Padre Pancho presided over their marriage ceremony at the Monterrey cathedral. Crates of ammunition lined the side aisles but they didn't care. John Riley stood up for him and Jimmy, Micheál and all the other lads from their band of deserters were there. Afterwards they had a party with food and music. Patrick wished his parents and brothers and sister could have been there to see it. He knew they would love Alicia and that she and Ellen would be great friends.

John gave Patrick two days leave which the newlyweds spent wrapped together in the clean linen sheets of the cot in her small bedroom, delirious in their love. She told him more about her family and of her time in Mexico City with her cousin who was on his way to being a bishop himself someday. He told her stories of his brothers and friends in Ireland and the spoke hopefully about their future. He confessed some of his doubts.

"You could have done much better than me, Alicia. I've seen how the men look at you, especially the rich officers."

She smiled. "But I do not love any of them, Patricio."

"I fear you've made a mistake," he said, and meant it.

She curled up closer in his arms and put her nose to his. "Don't speak of that again. We'll make it through these hard times. We will have a family. Perhaps a few little *colorados* to help you plant the fields eh?"

Chapter Forty-Six

Jane wrote repeatedly about the war while also publicly arguing for the rights of women. She organized a boycott on stores in New York that enabled women to gain employment as clerks for female customers. She helped found the Female Industrial Association and made speeches encouraging women to educate themselves, improve their skills and enter professions that paid more money than the ones deemed appropriate for women.

Her most powerful and popular columns however, consistently admonished Polk and his administration for provoking Mexico. It was true that she and Moses had a monetary interest in seeing the war end. They were part of a consortium to gain a land grant from Mexico across the Isthmus of Tehuantepec. If successful, they would be able to establish a transit connection for U.S. steamships operating on the Gulf of Mexico and the Pacific coast which would enhance both their financial situations.

While she was definitely concerned with personal gain, Jane passionately believed that the war should not be about conquest but about giving Mexicans the freedoms that could only be available if they were part of the United States. Texas was the model and, in her eyes and her columns, it could be achieved without unnecessary bloodshed. The people were ready and perfectly capable of self-government if only given the chance.

Sitting at her desk on the fifth floor of the offices of the *New York Sun* on Chatham Street in Manhattan, just a quarter of a mile from New York's City Hall, she and Moses came up with a plan. In addition to being the publisher of the *Sun*, Moses Beach was also the director of several New York banks. He had an idea to establish a national bank in Mexico with funds that he would supply.

"That's an excellent idea, Moses." said Jane. "The Church controls the finances and the government is in a never ending struggle to pry money from them. Right now they need to pay for the war and there's a constant battle going on between them. If they can find a way to end the war and become solvent they could establish credit and create new industries and a vibrant economy."

"But there's the problem," said Moses. "Will they stop fighting? What would it take?"

"There would have to be more than just a solid bank. The Texas border question needs to be resolved. California would have to be purchased at a respectable price."

"Who can we talk to, Jane?"

"A proposal like this would have to be authorized by the government and taken directly to Mexico City. The main goal must be a peaceful settlement to end the war."

"A peace plan?" said Moses.

"Yes, exactly," said Jane. She thought about it, staring out the window down on the crowded streets of Manhattan. "And I think you and I should be the ones to execute it. You have the money. I have the contacts and speak Spanish fluently."

Moses looked at her with a slight grin. He never ceased to be impressed by her quick mind and bold suggestions. "Can you get us an audience with Mr. Marcy?"

"I'll write him this instant."

Marcy received her letter and discussed it in a cabinet meeting. The president was not against it. He was determined to extend the country all the way to the Pacific Ocean, peacefully if possible but he was going to have California, no matter the cost. He told his Secretary of State, James Buchanan to meet with them.

Jane and Moses made the trip to Washington the last week of August. Their meeting was set for the afternoon of Tuesday, September the first. They arrived at the State building precisely at two p.m. and were shown into James Buchanan's elegantly furnished office.

Buchanan, six feet tall, his cravat slightly askew, rose from his cluttered desk and met them when they entered. His skin was almost pink and so smooth it looked as if he never had to shave. His eyes were two different colors; the right one brown, the left a light green. The brown one moved on its own, a wandering eye. As a result he tilted his head forward and to the side in conversation so that his good eye focused on whoever he was talking to. It gave the impression, real or not, that he was intensely interested in the person and what he or she had to say.

"Welcome, Mr. Beach, Miss Storm, or should I say Miss *Montgomery*. I appreciate your work. Most of it," he said with quick smile. "Please, sit."

They sat down in beautiful chairs upholstered in a gold brocade fabric. A matching settee took up one corner of the room. Buchanan went behind his lavishly carved red mahogany desk. It had drawers on both sides so two people could work opposite each other at the same time.

"Thank you for seeing us, Mr. Buchanan," said Moses.

"I must admit that I was not completely in favor of your visit but the president is intrigued by your proposal. Tell me more about it."

"We would like to be given diplomatic credentials to Mexico," said Moses. "Jane speaks the language and has numerous contacts within the government, the Church and with the British Consul there, Ewen MacKintosh. We feel there is an opportunity to end the conflict and establish a meaningful peace if Mexico can become financially independent of the Church. I have the resources to assist them in that regard."

"As I'm sure you know," said Buchanan, "we've been trying to negotiate a peace but the Mexicans won't even see our minister. How would you be able to do what he cannot?"

"I can meet with Mr. MacKintosh," said Jane. "We're investors in the Hargous Brothers of Philadelphia. They purchased the rights from his firm for transit over the Isthmus of Tehuantepec. He can put us in touch with high level government officials. I'll also be able to get letters of introduction to the Archbishops of both Puebla and Mexico City through my friend, Bishop Hughes of New York. I believe he has just been here to see you as well."

Buchanan tilted his head a little further forward towards Jane. "You're well informed I see. He too asked to go to Mexico to seek peace but the president declined to offer him the opportunity. Tell me, though, why would you think the British will help us? They worked vigorously to undermine the annexation of Texas. We know they offered military and financial aid to both Texas and Mexico."

"They realize," said Jane. "That that ship has sailed. They're more concerned now with stabilizing the Mexican government to prevent France or Spain from establishing a monarchy there. Also there's a matter of the substantial debt Mexico owes England. A National Bank would be able to assist with restitution."

Buchanan said nothing. He nodded his head slowly until Jane continued.

"Any peace," she said, "would have to have the blessing of the Church and be fair enough that the generals and politicians won't have their vanity slighted. And without a doubt there would need to be money to placate them."

Buchanan folded his arms across his chest and leaned back in his chair, debating with himself how much to tell his visitors. When he was ready he put his hands on the desk and cocked his head once more towards Jane. "We've been working with a representative of General Santa Anna."

Jane's attention sharpened. She glanced at Moses, then back at Buchanan, who went on. "We've authorized Santa Anna's passage from Cuba through our blockade in the Gulf. If he's not already in Veracruz, he will be soon, and after that, in Mexico City. In return he assures us that he will regain power and work for a peaceful end to the war.

"Also, the president has issued orders to General Scott to attack and seize Veracruz in a show of force that will assist Santa Anna in convincing his country to sue for peace. And if that doesn't happen, Scott will proceed forward and march to Mexico City."

When Jane spoke she tried to control herself. "That man," she said, referring to Santa Anna, "cannot be trusted. Even if he is able to resume power, he'll have to deal with the church and the fractured political factions. I believe we can do a better job or, at the least, help build a viable peace alliance especially with the banking proposition that Moses can offer."

"I don't know that I disagree with you, Miss Storm. Perhaps one strategy doesn't mean another can't also be employed. The president sent a request to Congress for two million dollars to provide for any expenditures required to end this conflict, specifically to grease the wheels with Santa Anna. Unfortunately Congressman Wilmot, a fellow Democrat from my home state of Pennsylvania I'm sorry to say, added a rider to the bill banning slavery in any territory we acquired from Mexico.

"The House passed it but the Senate refused and now Congress is adjourned. So we may indeed need you and Mr. Beach to help us. I will talk to Mr. Polk and he'll no doubt discuss it with the rest of the Cabinet. I can't promise anything. The president encourages and listens to everyone's opinion but in the end, he alone makes the decision."

Chapter Forty-Seven

Monterrey, Mexico, September 1846

The Americans were close; a mere hundred miles to the northeast in Camargo, along the Rio Grande. The work to shore up the defenses of Monterrey intensified. The roofs of homes became sniper nests. More citizens fled but those who remained were true patriots. They pitched in with all the work and armed themselves with whatever was available, including muskets, knives, rocks and pikes.

All leave was cancelled. It was sheer torture saying goodbye to Alicia. He demanded that she leave the city. She insisted on staying. Her place was with her husband, brother and the *soldados* who would surely need her when the fighting started.

"Alicia," he said. "Please. Go to Saltillo until the battle is over."

"No, Patricio. I would do anything for you, but this I cannot. Please, do not ask me again."

He sighed. They'd been through this before and he knew when her mind was made up. "Where will you stay?"

"Perhaps in the cathedral."

"No! The ammunition is there. One cannon ball and it will explode into a million pieces."

"Oh yes, I forgot." She thought for a moment. "There's a small church a few miles outside of town on the road to Saltillo. It's near the river. I'll go there to wait and pray."

It was useless to try to convince her otherwise. The Americans would be coming from the other side of the city so it was the best Patrick

257

could hope for. He took her in his arms. "I will see you again, Alicia."

"I have no doubt, Patricio. Before you go, I have some things for you."

She brought out a small bundle wrapped in brown paper. She untied the string, removed the paper and unraveled the banner. The vibrant emerald green and white silk and the image of St. Patrick stunned him with its artistry and beauty. She turned it over to the back side and it touched her to see how much the sight of it affected him. "It needs a little more work," she said. "The stitching on the edges has to be stronger and I wanted it to be much bigger, but for now it will have to do."

Her skill had brought John Riley's simple drawing to life. The harp and the coat of arms of Mexico were a golden yellow, as were the words Erin go Braugh and Libertad por la Republica Mexicana. On the other side, Saint Patrick in a lighter green, stood defiantly holding his key and shillelagh with his foot placed on a serpent over their San Patricios name. It was a moving and inspiring work of art.

"This is so beautiful, Alicia. John will love it as much as I do. So will the rest of the lads."

"It's nothing," she said.

"No, it's not nothing. It is the perfect symbol for who we are and what we're fighting for."

"Lieutenant Riley created it. I just sewed it."

"You've done much more than that, Alicia."

He had to get back. She repacked the flag and he got up to go. "And I have these," she said, handing him two letters. "My cousin in Mexico City received them and sent them to me."

Patrick's heart leapt when he saw the one addressed to him from

Ellen. The other was for Jimmy from Aunt Mary. He held them in his hand, nervous and hesitant. Alicia put a hand on his back and rubbed up and down, encouraging him to read his. He ripped it open, warmed by the sight of his sister's handwriting.

Dearest Patrick,

I am so relieved to hear that you are alive and, hopefully, still safe. We have been worried sick from news of the war. Aunt Mary and Uncle John are thankful to hear that Jimmy survives as well. None of us can grasp completely why you decided to join the Mexican Army though it does sound as though you were treated horribly. We believe this war is bad and continually pray for it to be over and that both of you will be returned to us.

And now Patrick, I have to give you the worst news. Mother and Da are both gone. The potato has failed again and this time it's more disastrous than ever before. Ma died from starvation and Da followed soon after. Aunt Josephine said it was as much from a broken heart as from a lack of food. I had sent them money but have no idea if they received it or what happened to it. Our brothers are roaming the countryside running from the law for stealing food. No one knows where they are or if they are still alive.

I so wish you were here with me Patrick. Aunt Mary and Nancy have been caring and considerate to me in my grief even though they mourn as well, especially Aunt Mary. But I long to have you here. I have never felt more alone or adrift, not even during our difficult journey to America. I love you Patrick and I miss you every minute of the day. Take care and please stay safe and survive. Give my love to Jimmy. Aunt Mary is writing him as well and I will include her letter in the same packet.

Your Loving Sister,

Ellen

Patrick stared at the letter, tears running down his face, staining the paper. He would never see his parents again; never feel the warm touch of his loving mother or the laughing, affection of his Da.

Alicia became distraught at his reaction."What is it,Patricio?"

He tried to tell her but couldn't form the words. She took the letter from his hand and read it herself. She guided his head to her lap and stroked his head, weeping silently with him.

Besides the suffocating grief, the conviction overwhelmed him that he was responsible. If he had done things the right way they would have already been in America and they would all be together. They wouldn't have died such a horrible, wretched death. He couldn't speak. He began to cry. Alicia tried her best to comfort him but the most she could do was hold him and say how sorry she was.

When he got back to his unit at the Citadel he gave Jimmy his letter and told him what happened to his parents. He knew exactly what Patrick was feeling.

"It isn't your fault," he said. "You know it isn't."

"He's right, lad," said John. "It's the fault of the British government, the English people and the Protestants who want to destroy all things Irish and Catholic."

"I lost our money," said Patrick. "It all went bad after that."

"No it didn't," said Jimmy. "It started long ago and came to a head when you arrived in Philadelphia. You had no control over any of it. No more than a ship at sea can control a tempest. You did the only thing you could do; weather it and survive."

"I don't know where they're buried," he said. His voice broke and his whole body convulsed. He covered his face with his hands. "I don't know what's happened to my brothers. I'll never see any of them again, Jimmy."

"You don't know that for sure. You're still alive, Patrick. Let's keep it that way. You have much to live for."

In his heart, Patrick knew it was true. So many of the lads had nothing and nobody. Most of them couldn't read or write and had no contact with their families back in Ireland. But it did nothing to remove his grief or guilt.

Later on, he showed their flag to John whose eyes filmed over at the site of it. "This far exceeds anything I could have hoped for," he said. "The men will gain strength from it and the Americans will learn to fear it. Gather the lads and we'll raise it up."

The St. Patrick's Battalion stood at attention as Corporal Ryan attached their banner to a rope and ran it up a long pole. They fired their cannons in a salute. The cheering from the San Patricio Battalion was heard throughout the city of Monterrey below them.

In his grief and the raising of their banner he didn't think to ask Jimmy about his letter. He talked to him about it that night, before they fell asleep.

"Ma and Da are carrying on," said Jimmy. "The house is probably finished by now but they won't open the store again. Brian and Jack are doing well, according to Ma. The good news is Donnie is back home and working at the shipyard again, so I don't have that on my conscience any longer. Ma doesn't say it, but deserting the army can't be something they're proud of. I've let them down and dragged you into all this trouble."

"What did you tell me about the ship in a tempest? We've done the best we could given the circumstances. We both need to survive Jimmy. We have to live on, make a better life."

"You do it, Patrick. You'll be making some Irish-Mexican babies. Maybe become a big rancher with lots of land. Ever since Robert was killed I've been driven only by anger and revenge. I'm surprised to still be alive but I won't make it much longer. It's inevitable."

"No it isn't. Maybe we'll both make it to Oregon. Damn it all Jimmy we've already walked enough miles through this cursed country to have made it there and back again. You'll see. One day this will be nothing more than a distant memory.

Chapter Forty-Eight

Monterrey, Mexico, September 19-25, 1846

The San Patricios did the best they could to take Patrick's mind off his loss. Led by Jimmy, who put on an uncharacteristic display of optimism, they teased him about being an old married man. Lieutenant Riley kept them all busy cleaning weapons and practicing their tasks.

As they surveyed the fields, the town and the road below the Citadel, Jimmy asked, "Do you think your Alicia would have given you a second look if old Donnie Donovan were here?"

Patrick smiled. "How do you think Donnie's doing? He must have made amends with his Da to be back working with him."

"Whatever it is," said Jimmy, "I'm sure there's a lady or two involved."

"Maybe he learned his lesson. Settled down and got married," said Patrick.

"I'll bet two months pay and both our three hundred sixty acres that didn't happen."

"You never know, Jimmy. Who would have thought we'd be in Monterrey Mexico, fighting Americans and that I'd be married to the most glorious girl in the world."

They were ready for the Americans, or so Patrick thought. Their total strength was now somewhere around ten thousand men: eight thousand regulars and the rest local militia. Besides the Citadel, they had four more excellent defensive positions around the city: the Bishop's Palace, Soldiers Fort on the other side of the river and the Tannery and Devil's Fort, both guarding the eastern entrance to the city. The streets were barricaded and the roofs of houses were manned and armed.

Taylor's army was in Marin, twenty-five miles away. The San Patricios stayed alert at their posts, vigilant for the first sign of the approaching enemy. They had time to reflect and talk. All were in high spirits with the hope that here was where the war would end. They heard rumors that Santa Anna had returned from exile and would soon be taking command of both the army and the country. Most of the officers and many of the common *soldados* were happy about it.

After two days of waiting atop the Citadel, Patrick spotted them. Lieutenant Riley used his glass and saw the large straw hat and the gray horse of Old Rough and Ready at the front of the long column. A unit of mounted Mexican lancers were out in front of the city as an advance guard. Patrick thought they would make a charge but they retreated and the Americans halted. Riley had them fire a few cannon shots and Taylor and his men backed out of range.

A company of horsemen decided to taunt them by riding in wide circles below the Citadel. They were within the range of their cannons, and John had them fire, but they were too fast. Patrick could tell they were Texas Rangers by their slouched hats and buckskin jackets. After a few passes they withdrew back into a very unmilitary-like formation behind Old Rough and Ready.

Mixed emotions of excitement and calm washed over Patrick. Their location was strong and secure, a fortress defending against a smaller invading force that they would surely decimate with their thirty cannons.

Nothing further happened that day, other than Taylor setting up camp at a beautiful spot called the Bosque de San Domingo. It was a favorite picnic area for the people of Monterrey, filled with bubbling springs and large shade trees of pecan, oak and Spanish moss.

The next afternoon the Americans split their force. A large group moved north and then west in an attempt to get behind the Citadel. Riley had them fire all thirty cannons but they were too far away, and soon out of sight. Ampudia sent men to reinforce the Bishop's Palace on the west end of the city. Lieutenant Riley remained confident, telling them that Taylor was making a big mistake. "He's dividing his army in the face of our superior numbers and position. It will be his undoing."

The waiting game continued and nerves frayed from the delay. Patrick's calm changed to impatience for the fighting to begin. At dawn the next morning sounds of gunfire came from the west. A strong squad of cavalry under the command of Colonel Juan Nejera engaged the attackers. With lances glistening in the morning sun, they charged. A dismounted force of Texas Rangers was ready and cut them down immediately with a scorching hail of bullets from their rifles and repeating Colt revolvers.

The Lancers regrouped and courageously charged again but met with the same results: innumerable casualties, including Nejera. The road was littered with the dead and dying bodies of men and horses as the survivors scattered to safety. The Americans now controlled the west end of the city and the supply road to Saltillo, and the fight had only just begun.

At the Citadel, Lieutenant Riley's attention was diverted back to the road below them. Taylor's men were moving forward, down the main highway as originally expected. The Americans fired first, lobbing mortars from long range but they were ineffective.

Riley waited until they were closer. It became clear that Taylor was attempting to seize both the Tannery and the Devils Fort. He gave the order to commence firing and the San Patricios poured cannon balls and grape down on them to support the Mexican defenders there. They cheered loudly when the Americans fled in retreat, leaving the mangled bodies of their dead and dying all around the two structures.

Their jubilation didn't last long. The Americans attacked again. When one company was driven away, another took its place. Patrick watched the swift movement of the artillery and though he couldn't make out the individuals, he knew that Saxon and Graves were down there doing great damage. No doubt they saw the green, white and gold banner of St. Patrick flapping defiantly in the stiff breeze and knew who they were up against as well. Riley had Patrick adjust their aim to try to take them out. They were not successful. By noon the *yanquis* had captured and were in control of the Tannery.

The enemy now advanced into the interior of the city, going from house to house in an effort to dislodge the rooftop snipers. The San Patricios were powerless, unable to shoot down on them for fear of injuring their own troops. It was exasperating to watch shots being traded on the street and across rooftops as darkness closed in on the smoke-shrouded city.

The weather turned icy cold and a freezing rain pelted down on the San Patricios. Captain Moreno huddled with Lieutenant Riley who then gathered the men under an overhang. "The Americans," he told them, "have control of Federal Hill," he said. "And have taken the Soldiers Fort on the south side of the river."

Patrick listened with mounting frustration. Jimmy couldn't hold his tongue. "How could they, John?" he said. Riley glared at him for violating his order not to use his first name in front of the men. He took a deep breath before he answered.

"They waded across the river and overwhelmed the defenders in hand to hand combat." What he didn't tell them was that the *soldados* once again panicked and ran. The Americans seized the few cannons there and now had them trained on the section of the city directly below them.

The night continued to be freezing cold and rainy. The next morning before daylight with frost covering the ground, the Americans on the west side advanced on Fort Liberty. They charged with fixed bayonets and routed the fifty Mexican defenders. When the sun burned off the heavy mist, Patrick clearly saw the American flag high on the pole of the fort.

Below them, Taylor sent more men to reinforce the Tannery. They dueled with Riley's artillery throughout the day but without much damage to either side. As the sun went down so came more rain, this time in blinding, torrential sheets.

Ampudia ordered everyone except the defenders of the Citadel to abandon the outer defenses and withdraw into and around the plaza. There were many who thought this was pure cowardice and spoke openly of mutiny. Ampudia threatened to execute anyone who disobeyed, forcing them to comply but the decision cast a demoralizing pall over the entire army.

Now four of their five solid defenses were in the hands of the Americans. Including the San Patricios, there were close to three hundred and eighty troops at the Citadel. They still had a commanding position while the rest of their army was huddled in an area of a few blocks in and around the main plaza. Right before dawn, the rain let up. Lieutenant Riley had them ready at their posts before the sun peeked through the cloudy horizon.

He shouted out when the enemy began their advance.

"This is it lads! Stop them now or they'll take the city."

The *yanqui* troops moved forward. The San Patricios worked smoothly, raining a barrage of grapeshot down upon them. But the Americans spread out swiftly, disappearing into houses and alleys. Under the cover of their artillery, they blew holes in the buildings and then secured the rooftops before moving on to the next house.

Unless the attackers were caught out in the open, it was impossible to determine where they actually were and how far they were advancing. It wasn't long before the *yanquis* had their own snipers on the housetops, dueling with Mexicans who were still bravely manning their posts on other roofs.

The same scene was repeated on the western side of the city. The Americans proceeded toward the main plaza, one house at a time. By the middle of the afternoon they were within two blocks of the cathedral where Ampudia was holed up. Patrick worried that at any moment he would see it erupt in a massive explosion from all the ammunition being stored inside. Sure enough, a cannon ball struck the clock tower and he held his breath. Thankfully, only the tower was destroyed.

Chapter Forty-Nine

Monterrey, September 25, 1846

When night came the artillery from the Citadel ceased firing. Early the next morning, two rounds from the enemy's biggest gun, a twenty-four pounder, screamed into the center of the plaza, just missing the Catheral. Within minutes, General Ampudia sent out a flag of truce and asked for a meeting with General Taylor. This time, not only were the officers incensed by another apparent surrender, so was every single San Patricio.

"We're done for," said Jimmy

"They'll tear us apart like jackals," said Micheál.

Patrick believed it as well. They were doomed. He watched Lieutenant Riley who had his field glass trained on the activity below. He couldn't tell exactly what was going on but they all recognized the parley flag.

"We picked the wrong side, cousin," said Jimmy. "I knew we should have just lit out for Oregon."

Right then Patrick was convinced he would never see Alicia again. If they weren't shot down like dogs, there would be a quick firing squad or a hanging. John Riley was no doubt thinking the same thing. He pushed in his scope, gritted his teeth and strode along the parapet not saying a word.

"These Mexican generals know more about surrendering than fighting," said Jimmy.

And surrender Ampudia did. While everyone denounced his cowardice, in retrospect he saved their lives. Taylor inexplicably agreed to an eight week armistice and agreed to allow the Mexican Army to march out of the city. Patrick couldn't believe it. Nor could Riley or the rest of the lads.

That afternoon, under the hate-filled glares of the American troops, the San Patricios filed out of the Citadel and walked down the long, descending path to join the rest of their forces in the the plaza. Not a man among them believed they would make it all the way there. Even without the brazen display of their flag, they were instantly recognized as the Irish deserters who had caused more damage and inflicted more casualties on them than any other Mexican unit during the fighting.

The soldiers who trained their muskets on them had to be restrained by their officers or they would surely have opened fire. Patrick held their banner high, walking proudly despite thinking he may be dead any second.

He was amazed when they made it to the plaza though he still doubted they would survive after they were forced to sit down in front of the cathedral. General Taylor never cared much for their welfare when they were members of his army so why would he care now? If he could easily look the other way then, he could do the same now, and let his soldiers have their revenge. Luckily, the American officers on horseback were strong in controlling their men. If it had been Saxon or Graves in command it would have been a different story.

Patrick considered it nothing short of a miracle when, the next morning, they marched out of Monterrey. They still had one more gauntlet to go through. Nearly the entire American army lined both sides of Saltillo Road to see them off. Again Patrick carried the flag and this time he saw familiar faces, most twisted in revulsion and loathing. The looks of hatred from those he had shared meals and stories with around a campfire gave him a momentary feeling of regret.

They were cursed and spat upon as they went by. Not a few rocks were thrown at them. There was a long, low growling of angry voices all along the road, punctuated by vehement shouts.

"Fuck you, Mick fucking traitors."

"Lucky Irish bastards...this time."

"Rot in hell you damn cowards."

"Worthless drunks."

As they passed the city walls, Patrick saw Captain Saxon and Lieutenant Graves on their horses. Saxon's eyes gleamed with undisguised loathing. Patrick raised his head, pushed back his shoulders and looked straight forward. Jimmy did no such thing. He looked Saxon right in the eye, gave him a big smile and shouted, "Top o' the morning, asshole. Better luck next time."

Some of the San Patricios snickered. Lieutenant Riley, riding his horse, gave his former captain a mock salute and they kept moving down the road, unscathed and away from Monterrey. When Saxon saw Henry marching among them, he couldn't control himself.

"That's my nigger!" he shouted.

He had to be restrained by a Colonel who placed his horse in front of Saxon's mount. He continued shouting as they passed him by. "I'll have him back before this is over." Patrick watched Henry. He walked straight and dignified, not giving Saxon a second glance.

When they neared the edge of the city, Patrick asked Riley if they were going to Saltillo. "Don't know, lad," he said.

"I've heard we're bound for Mexico City," said Micheál.

Patrick hoped that wasn't the case. "I have to find Alicia. She was supposed to be in a church along this road."

"We'll keep an eye out for her," said Riley.

"Wherever we're going," said Jimmy. "It's to our deaths."

"We'll get through this Jimmy," said Patrick.

"You think so? We've joined a lost cause, cousin. Don't you see? If there was any possible way I would flee."

"And do what? Go back to Saxon and Graves?"

"I'll go where I've always wanted to go."

"That would assure your prediction. You wouldn't make it ten miles before being caught or killed."

"I know, Patrick. That's why I continue putting one foot in front of the other like a dumb ox, forward to yet another defeat. We've been lucky so far. It won't hold."

"Maybe the war will be over after this," said Micheál. "How many more defeats can Mexico withstand?"

"Now wouldn't that be lovely," said Jimmy. "What do you think will happen to us then? The Americans will just forgive and forget?"

Lieutenant Riley rode up and informed them they were indeed heading for Saltillo.

"Any sign of Padre Pancho?" asked Patrick.

"Yes. He asked permission to stay behind in Monterrey to care for the wounded and dying. He said he would join us as soon as possible. He had no word on Alicia, Patrick. He asked me to look for her."

"We have to find her."

"We will, lad."

They passed by a church he was sure was the one Alicia had spoken of. She wasn't there although there was a group of women and children waiting for their men. They joined in behind the downcast, defeated army, swelling the already large number of camp followers and displaced citizens of Monterrey. John, true to his word, rode back and forth looking for and inquiring about Alicia. Each time he returned he gave Patrick a grim shake of his head.

It took four long days for Patrick and the rest of the Mexican army to travel the mere sixty miles to Saltillo. Alicia was there, waiting on the main road with the rest of the city to welcome the soldiers. He spotted her before she saw him and he broke formation and ran to her. "Thank God you're safe," he said as they embraced.

"I couldn't bear the thought of losing you, Patricio. Waiting in the church, then hearing the news of the defeat, we panicked and ran here to Saltillo. I'm so sorry."

"You've nothing to be sorry for. I'm here now and you're unharmed."

"Where is Francisco?" asked Alicia.

"He decided to stay in Monterrey to do what he can for those left behind."

She lowered her head and said a short prayer to the Virgin of Guadalupe for her brother.

They were able to spend only a brief time together before the army left after a few days for San Luis Potosi, three hundred miles to the south. General Santa Anna had indeed returned to power from his exile in Cuba. He ordered Ampudia to bring his forces to San Luis where he would be court-martialed for losing Monterrey to the *yanquis*.

"I'm going with you," said Alicia.

"You will not!"

Patrick was as startled as Alicia by the vehemence of his words. She started to protest but he cut her off, softening his voice this time. "Please stay here."

"But the Americans will surely come to Saltillo next," she said. "I want to be with you."

"And I with you, Alicia. A year from now, ten years from now."

She took his face in her hands. "*Esta bien, mi amor.* I'll go to Mexico City and stay with my cousin."

He wasn't so sure she would be safe anywhere but for now the war was far enough away from the capital that it seemed the best idea.

Chapter Fifty

San Luis Potosi, October, 1846 – January 1847

The journey to San Luis Potosi was through a flat, hard-packed desert with little vegetation other than cactus, mesquite and occasional clusters of stunted palm trees. It was a miserable trek without enough water or proper provisions. It took three weeks and again their ranks were depleted from sickness, exhaustion, and desertion. Many of the indios simply vanished into the empty and desolate landscape. No one made an attempt to stop or pursue them.

Patrick was more adapted now to the pace and rough terrain but the lack of good water and the long time between getting something to eat made it extremely difficult. They lost two of their wounded San Patricios along the way. Michael Burns from Dublin and Frances O'Toole from County Mayo both had wounds that festered. Their bandages were filthy and continued to leak blood. After two days on the trail they laid them to rest under a pile of rocks in the middle of the desert.

Micheál sang "The Minstrel Boy" and the rest of the lads bowed their heads in prayer. Patrick had grown accustomed to the bloody horror of war but that didn't ease his grief. He thought of their dear mothers who would never know what became of them.

They arrived in San Luis at the end of October. The great man himself was there. Santa Anna, who was calling himself, among other grandiose names, the Savior of the Nation, had taken control of the military and was ready to lead them to victory. His first order was to have General Ampudia arrested for his failure in Monterrey but the court-martial went nowhere. After escaping with their lives from Monterrey, there was a lack of agreement among the officers over his guilt.

Santa Anna ordered fortifications of the city, believing that Taylor was coming their way. They went to work digging trenches and building walls. When they weren't doing that, they continued with drilling and maneuvers. It was a week after their arrival when Lieutenant Riley was summoned by their commanding general for an audience. He took Patrick and Micheál with him and insisted they bring their banner.

In person, Santa Anna was an impressive man. He was five feet eight inches tall and somewhat thick around the middle but he had a presence and a compelling charm that the three of them noticed the moment he entered the room. His uniform glittered with medals, ribbons and gold epaulets. His thick dark hair was perfectly groomed and gleamed with a fragrant oil that smelled of mint. He had a few streaks of gray at the temples which added to his handsome face and aristocratic bearing. His penetrating eyes were a light gray color. He walked with a slight limp due to his artificial leg which replaced the real one he lost in a battle to expel the French from Veracruz during the Pastry War.

He smiled exuberantly as he walked towards them using his jeweled cane with its large golden eagle on the hilt. They saluted smartly. He returned it nonchalantly and extended his hand to John.

"Don Riley," he said. "I have heard much of your ability and bravery. I wanted to thank you in person for joining us and for bringing so many of your countrymen with you."

"Thank you, Exellency. May I present two of my best men."

"Of course, the famous San Patricios." He shook each of their hands, looking deeply into their eyes. John had Patrick unfurl the banner for him to see. "Ah, it is beautiful. I like very much the combination of Ireland and Mexico. Very well done. And I have no doubt it strikes fear into the hearts of the Americans, no?

"We do our best, Excellency," said Riley.

"So I am told," he said, laughing. "Come. Sit and talk with me awhile. We have much to discuss." They were brought a powerful drink called *mezcal* by one of the numerous, fawning colonels on the general's staff. Like the *pulque* they had in Monterrey, it too is made from the agave plant but with a much stronger taste and effect. Heat spread throughout Patrick's body after the first bitter sip.

"It's made locally here in San Luis," said Santa Anna. "I think it is the finest in all of Mexico. We have a saying. Let me see if I can translate it properly: 'For every ill, *mezcal*, and for every good as well.'"

He toasted them, they toasted him, and they all drank to Mexico and Ireland. The warmth spread from Patrick's head to his toes.

"Lieutenant Riley," said Santa Anna. "I have in mind the creation of a foreign legion as an official unit of our army. I would like you to command it."

John flushed, not from the alcohol but from finally being truly recognized for his abilities. "Of course, your Excellency," he said. "I am at your service."

"Very good. If I had a whole army of you and your Irishmen, the *gringos* would be back across the Rio Grande, licking their wounds and regretting their avaricious attempt to steal our lands."

"Thank you, General."

He pounded his cane twice and another colonel appeared with a small box. The General opened it and pulled out a set of epaulets and the bars of a first captain. "As of today you are promoted to Capitan."

John Riley beamed as Santa Anna pinned the bars on his collar and placed the epaulets on his shoulders. He saluted his new captain respectfully and then embraced him before the salute could be returned.

"I have to name a superior as the official commander of your San Patricios," he said. "Señor Moreno has been promoted to Major. He's a good soldier. It is unfortunate, but I must be concerned with petty jealousies of others. If you are seen as getting preference over one of our fine Mexican officers, well, that would cause problems. I'm sure you understand."

"Of course, Excellency. Thank you very much."

"It is nothing. You've earned it." He laughed and pounded John on his back. "I would make you a general if I could. All in good time, eh Capitan?"

Patrick and Micheál saluted their new captain and then shook his hand vigorously. No one deserved it more than he did.

"Now," said Santa Anna. "Let me have your banner. I will have the nuns at the convent here make you a larger one with finer silk. You are now officially El Batallón de San Patricio. We expect much from you and know you will recruit more of your Irish brothers to our side."

Patrick didn't want to give up Alicia's banner but there was nothing he could do. It did need to be larger but he wished he could have kept it for his own. He thought about asking for it to be returned with the new one but he remained silent. He handed it over to another colonel who had appeared out of nowhere.

"Thank you, General," said Captain Riley. "We won't disappoint you, or Mexico."

"Of this," he said. "I have no doubt."

He shook their hands again and said *"Gracias amigos,"* as they left.

They remained in San Luis Potosi for three months. Captain Riley made sure they stayed sharp and prepared but they did have free time. Patrick, attended a bullfight with Jimmy and group of other lads. It was a lavish, bloody affair full of ceremony and pageantry, but quite an experience watching a man stand in front of an angry, monstrous beast waving a cape. The arena was filled to capacity and when they were recognized as the San Patricios, the crowd stood and gave them a prolonged series of *vivas.*

They also went to a cock fight. Santa Anna, an avid participant in the sport with his own stable of fighting birds, invited their whole battalion so they couldn't refuse. Each contest was a fight to the death that Patrick found repugnant. Metal hooks were attached to the feet of the poor animals to insure as much blood letting as possible.

In the middle of January, they learned that the Americans were planning a second invasion from the east at Veracruz. Intelligence was received that a large portion of Taylor's troops in the north were being transferred to bolster that assault and therefore would not be coming south to attack.

Santa Anna, who had been to the capital and elected president for the ninth time, returned, determined to march them back to Monterrey and strike Taylor's weakened force. They were now a reinforced army of twenty-thousand, complete with a fearsome cavalry and enough artillery for the Savior of the Nation to finally drive the enemy in the north back to where they belonged.

Chapter Fifty-One

Mexico City, November 1846 to January, 1847

On November twenty-first, Secretary of State Buchanan issued Moses Beach and Jane Storm diplomatic instructions and identification as confidential agents to Mexico. They were authorized to meet with any government or church official they could to present Polk's Three Point Plan to end hostilities:

1. The United States would purchase, for a price to be determined, the disputed territory between the Nueces and Rio Grande Rivers plus California and all territory above twenty-six degrees latitude, which would include all of New Mexico.

2. All outstanding U.S. citizen claims against Mexico would be absorbed and paid by the American government.

3. The United States would restore all forts and buildings damaged in the war and no forced loans would be placed on the Mexican people.

As for the National Bank, Moses Beach was on his own to try and make that happen.

Jane, Moses and his daughter Drusilla took a steamer out of New York for Charleston South Carolina where they boarded a schooner for Cuba. They stayed in Havana a week before taking passage on a British mail ship to Veracruz, using passports provided them by the British Consulate in Cuba. They traveled in the guise of an English businessman and his family.

While in Havana they met with the Mexican Minister, Buenaventura Aroujo who gave them a letter of introduction to Vice-President Valentín

Goméz Farías asking him to consider their peace offering. Moses put the letter in his diplomatic pouch with the peace proposal and the fifty thousand dollars he was bringing in the hopes of establishing the bank.

The little British family arrived in the port city of Veracruz on the thirteenth of January. After being delayed two days by suspicious officials, they took a stage to Mexico City, traveling by way of the Old Spanish Highway through Jalapa instead of the direct but more dangerous National Road which was filled with bandidos and guerrillas. The two hundred and fifty mile trip took eleven days.

They stopped briefly in the picturesque city of Puebla to switch coaches and secure a letter from the local bishop, supporting their mission. Then they boarded a stage for the eighty mile trip to the capital. As they descended out of the mountains, Jane took in the beauty of the vast Valley of Mexico.

The spectacular, snow-capped volcanoes, Popocatépetl and Iztaccíhuatl were visible to the southeast. The rest of the plateau was surrounded by mountains and more snow covered volcanoes. The air was so clear that Jane imagined she could reach out and touch them. Lakes and meadows filled the landscape below. Villages, fields and gardens lined the edges of the two mile wide city, its skyline dominated by magnificent church spires and towers.

"Such a beautiful country," said Jane.

"Yes," said Moses. "And in so much need of help."

They secured rooms at the Gran Sociedad Hotel, two blocks west of the Constitution Plaza, known also as Zocalo. The rooms were adequate, though the mattresses had to be beaten to rid them of fleas. Drusilla immediately went to the bathhouse to freshen up. Jane sent a note to Ewen

MacKintosh at the British Consulate, announcing their arrival and asking him to set up a meeting with Archbishop Posada.

Santa Anna, true to his prediction, was back in power. Upon his election he vowed that his only purpose was to save and protect the nation. He turned over the running of the government to Farías and went to San Luis Potosi to prepare his army to attack the Americans still in the north.

Unstated in their peace strategy was that General Winfield Scott's attack on Veracruz would allow Santa Anna to make good on his promise of support. While he engaged Taylor's army a "crisis" would arise in the capital. The Savior of the People would be compelled to take control and have no recourse but to sue for peace in the face of civil discord and the superior American Army.

The afternoon after their arrival, Jane and Moses knocked on the rectory door of the Cathedral of the Assumption of the Blessed Virgin which extends across the entire northern side of Constitution Plaza. A smiling, unassuming nun opened the door and led them to small foyer. Within minutes a priest with an oval face that matched the shape of his body arrived to welcome them. He wore round, wire-rimmed glasses, the lenses of which made his eyes appear to be bulging. He smiled and bowed, extending his hands to both of them.

"My name," he said in perfect English, "is Padre Arturo Orellana. I'm the Bishop's personal secretary. He is very anxious to meet you. Please, follow me."

They went upstairs to a large library with two walls lined floor to ceiling with books. Portraits of saints were displayed on another wall, surrounding a large painting of the Virgin of Guadalupe. A rectangular table with eight empty chairs was in the center of the room.

"You're the first to arrive," said Padre Orellana. "The Bishop and our other guests will be here soon. Can I bring you something to drink? Sherry, tea or some of our delicious hot chocolate?"

"Oh, hot chocolate please," said Jane.

"Tea for me, Padre."

When he returned with their drinks he brought three men with him. Jane and Moses shook hands with Edward Thornton, a young attaché from the British Embassy, Bernardo Couto, a respected lawyer and former Minister of Justice, and Manuel Baranda, the current Minister of Foreign Relations.

"Mr. MacKintosh sends his regards," said Thornton. "He regrets that he cannot make this meeting. He asked me to invite you to stay at his home in Tacubaya where the accommodations will be much more to your satisfaction."

Jane and Moses exchanged glances. "Thank you," said Moses. "My daughter will be especially grateful."

"Excellent," said Thornton. "We'll send a carriage for you and your things."

They all stood when Bishop Posada swept into the room a few minutes later. His full-length black cassock was lined with purple piping and gold buttons down the front. He wore a purple skullcap and a large silver cross around his neck that extended almost down to the gold sash around his ample waist. Padre Orellana announced that he would be translating for the meeting.

"We are very worried," said Padre Orellana after waiting for the bishop to speak. "Your is still in the north and another force will soon be invading Veracruz. If they're successful there, they will undoubtedly march here to Mexico City and then we will be attacked from both directions. I fear for the safety of our people, our churches and our religion."

"We are here, Bishop," responded Jane. "To try to stop this madness between our countries. I too am Catholic and can assure you that my government has no intention of making war against our religion. President Polk is a Protestant, yet he has chosen me to represent him and to show he wants a fair and mutual agreement."

Bishop Posada studied Jane while she spoke. After Padre Orellana translated he said, "How do you intend to help us?"

Moses jumped in and went over the Three Point Plan and his banking proposal. He finished by saying, "We have assurances that General Santa Anna will work with us for peace."

"I don't know how much trust we can place in General Santa Anna," translated the priest. "But we, including these three gentlemen here, are in favor of your proposals and will assist however we can." Padre Orellana paused and then said on his own, "Rest assured, the bishop will not give Señor Farias the fifteen million pesos he is demanding of us for the war effort."

Bishop Posada stood and gathered his robes to leave. This time he spoke in broken English. "Please keep us informed."

Two days later, Jane, Moses and Drusila moved to the home of Ewen MacKintosh, the most influential European in all of Mexico. He had business and personal relationships with the powerful and wealthy, including General Santa Anna.

His carriage brought them to a grand house on a hillside in

Tacubaya, a small village of stately mansions, bordered by dilapidated huts where the impoverished eked out an existence. MacKintosh appeared from the rose garden in the back and gave them a wide smile as he came to welcome them.

He wore a tan shirt under a cream colored waistcoat and a brown, linen coat. He removed his straw hat as he approached, revealing a full head of collar-length silver and black hair. He spoke in the clipped cadence of a British diplomat.

"So good of you to come," he said, shaking all of their hands.

"Thank you," said Drusila, "for saving us from that dreadful hotel."

"You're quite welcome, madam. You'll be more comfortable here. Safer too. There's going to be trouble in the capital soon."

A tiny, old Mexican man with a deeply lined face appeared and showed them to their rooms. MacKintosh asked them to meet him in the garden for tea in thirty minutes.

Tea was served by a young señorita dressed as an English maid. Jane admired the delicate service made of Dresden china. The hand painted floral design beautifully complemented the gold trim on the cups and saucers. She took a drink of the burgundy colored tea that had a delicious hint of a fruit she couldn't quite place. Then she got right to the point. "What kind of trouble is it that you anticipate, Ewen?"

He hesitated a moment before answering. "Most likely some sort of military coup against Farias. Everything in this land revolves around crisis. General Santa Anna will use this one to his advantage and then we'll see if he's serious about making peace."

There was a pause in the conversation. Jane finished the last of her tea and nodded enthusiastically when the maid approached to refill her cup.

"What do *you* wish to see happen, Ewen?" she said.

MacKintosh smiled, appreciating her directness. "I, and my government, want Mexico to survive, to become stable and to thrive economically. And, quite frankly my dear, we don't want your country to seize the entire continent. We all want this war to end. And, under the right conditions, I believe General Santa Anna will support your initiative."

"Do you think that's what he will do?" said Jane

He let out a soft grunt. "No one knows what Santa Anna will do. I doubt even he does. The situation will dictate it and whichever way a fair wind blows, that's the direction he'll follow."

"Can you arrange a meeting with Señor Farias?" said Moses. "Maybe seeing him in person will help change his mind about peace."

"I'll try. And I'll do my best to assist in any way possible."

"We appreciate it, Ewen," said Jane, taking his hand. "And thank you again for your hospitality."

Chapter Fifty-Two

Battle of Buena Vista, February 21-24, 1847

The San Patricios marched out of San Luis Potosi to the cheers of the townspeople lining the streets who tossed garlands as the band played rousing songs. Their new banner fluttered grandly and the roar for *Los Irlandeses* was louder and more boisterous than for any other brigade.

Santa Anna led his twenty-thousand man force in extravagant style, riding in a red and gold carriage pulled by eight mules. Inside, he was accompanied by two young and beautiful señoritas. Mounted hussars surrounded his coach. They were elegantly arrayed with plumes, medals and ribbons, and their horses were decorated with dazzling silver saddles and harnesses.

It was another brutal march, back to where they were four months ago, only this time they had to contend with the winter's cold. There were thousands of new, conscripted recruits and, even though they were strong, tough indios, nothing could have prepared them for the back-breaking pace, the curse of dysentery, and the despair of being forcibly ripped from their homes and families for a cause they didn't understand or care about. Santa Anna would lose close to a third of his force to sickness, death and desertion on the way to meet General Taylor and his *yanquis*.

Believing after the defeat at Monterrey that the Americans would be coming south to attack the capital, all the wells and storage tanks had been destroyed along the route. Now that they were going back, there was no water to be found. Wood was also scarce. Those lucky enough to find any built small fires at night that drew crowds seeking some little bit of warmth.

On February twentieth, sixty miles outside of Saltillo, they finally found decent water and were supplied with a small amount of beans and tortillas. The next day it rained intermittently and the cold went right through Patrick's clothes, never allowing him to get warm or dry. When they camped that evening they were thirty miles away from the Americans who were at a place called Agua Nueva.

The next day word shot through the column that Taylor's army had pulled back to a section of mountains called La Angostura, The Narrows. Their supply base was a little behind them to the north at a hacienda called Buena Vista. Santa Anna perceived this as a retreat but their position was strong and they were well fed and rested, having marched merely a few miles compared to the three hundred by the Mexican Army.

The terrain was excellent for the defensive positions of the enemy. An immeasurable network of gullies, ravines, steep vertical hills and jagged cliffs provided protection that appeared impossible to penetrate. Taylor's troops were spread out, hidden in the gorges and behind redoubts they had made on a wide, flat plateau which was broken up in three sections with steep drop offs on all sides. He also had an artillery unit blocking the main road.

At Angostura Captain Riley found a good spot for their three biggest guns: two twenty-four pounders and one sixteen. It was on the rim of a ridge that had a commanding view of the plateau and the road from Saltillo that snaked through the tight canyon.

It took hours for Patrick and the men to pull the cast iron cannons up the steep hill, using both horses and back-breaking manpower. Their task would be to provide support and cover for both the plateau and General Blanco's infantry, forming up to confront the artillery unit blocking the road.

By the time they got the cannons in position, Santa Anna had already sent twelve hundred cavalry under General Miñón in a wide arc around the Americans' left. Their orders were to seize their supply depot at Buena Vista. Then he sent a note to General Taylor, advising him that he was outnumbered, surrounded and had an hour to surrender.

"Do you think they'll do it?" said Patrick.

Jimmy laughed derisively.

"They won't stop," said Captain Riley. "Until they're either at the gates of heaven or the gates of Mexico City. Stay ready, lads."

"Surely we have them this time," said Micheál.

"If we can get them out in the open," said Riley. "Our position is superior but be ready for a hard fight, lads."

General Blanco moved his infantry forward to attack. Patrick had the men load the cannons with canisters filled with musket balls. Captain Riley gave the signal and they began firing with rapid precision. The Americans answered back with their own cannons.

Blanco's infantry fought valiantly but were repelled after little more than an hour of combat. Now the American guns concentrated on the San Patricio's position and they traded fire until dark. Captain Riley lost half a dozen men but he was confident they inflicted much worse damage on the enemy.

General Ampudia, back in Santa Anna's good graces, had his command of two thousand troops troops scale a slender, unprotected ridge on the Americans' left. Enemy cavalry and infantry regiments were sent against them but the Mexicans drove them back and had them outflanked on that side. When it got dark, the shelling and the battle, except for random musket fire, ceased.

It rained during the night. The next morning the cold remained but the storm had stopped. It was bitingly brisk and clear. Reveille was blown separately from every brigade. Santa Anna meant to instill fear in the Americans with the size and strength of his army which, despite the losses getting there, was at least ten thousand men stronger than Taylor's.

Up on the hill, their San Patricio banner snapping sharply in the breeze, Patrick watched the Soldier of the People charge his big black stallion back and forth in front of the assembled troops. In his resplendent uniform and carrying a black flag that indicated no quarter would be given to the enemy, he didn't fail to inspire his men. The *vivas* echoed long and loud through the canyons making it seem their numbers were twice as many as they actually were.

When the battle resumed, General Ampudia had his men positioned on the San Patricios' right with two other battalions just to his left poised at the base of the plateau. Captain Riley ordered them to ready their cannons and wait for his command.

Ampudia moved his men forward. Enemy artillery opened up and many fell. The San Patricos were impatient to fire back. Patrick looked expectantly to John but they continued to wait. Finally the order came. The ground shook as they thundered holy hell down upon the *yanquis*. Captain Riley moved fluidly among them, his sword waving and pointing to change and direct their aim. They worked fast and with deadly effect.

Despite the smoke and haze below, it was clear that the enemy was being pushed back, helped by the wide gaps Riley and his Irishmen were opening in the enemy's lines. The Mexicans charged and the deserters cheered as a section of the enemy front turned and ran.

It wasn't long before the San Patricio became a target. Their barrage was devastating and the Americans needed to put them out of action. Mounted dragoons and a company of infantry moved up the hill towards them, getting to the base of their ridge. Patrick ordered the muzzles of his cannons lowered but they couldn't get them low enough to hit the attackers and they were about to be overrun.

Captain Riley sheathed his sword and grabbed a musket, ordering the rest of his men to do the same. Just in time, a company of infantry came to their rescue and drove the attackers back.

Artillery shells continued to come at them and they lost more men. One of Patrick's crew, Kieran Delaney, was blown to pieces right next to him. It was a ghastly sight but he couldn't stop to mourn or help him. There was nothing to be done in any case, except to say a quick prayer for God to take his soul to heaven. He continued with the work at hand as calmly and fearlessly as his commander while more bloodied and dismembered bodies littered the ground around him.

Ampudia's two battalions advanced onto the plateau and in a matter of minutes the enemy turned and stampeded in the opposite direction. Patrick saw General Taylor, sitting on his white horse in the distance, exhorting his men to turn around and fight. A group of reinforcements joined them and they did turn back. With a strong push they split the Mexican force in the middle and now the *soldados* were the ones scattering.

By nightfall, both sides held ground on the mesa without any clear advantage for either side. Captain Riley had his men continue firing until total darkness forced them to stop. Patrick was beyond exhaustion and collapsed against the nearest rock believing that tomorrow morning they would finally taste victory.

He was startled out of a troubled dream where he was trying, unsuccessfully, to save his brothers from British soldiers by Riley's strong hands shaking his shoulders. "Get up now, Patrick. We're moving out."

"Moving?" he said. It was completely dark as he tried to will himself awake. "Where are we going?"

"I don't know and I don't like it, but it's time to go."

Jimmy, Micheál and the rest of the lads were roused and all had the same question. Why were they retreating? Captain Riley had no answer and he was incensed. "We need to finish them off," he said. "One more strong push and we'll own the field."

John was not the only officer who was incredulous and furious. Many commanders had to be forced under pain of death to obey the order to vacate the field. Fires were lit all along the front to deceive the enemy into thinking they were still there as Santa Anna's army sullenly and quietly moved out.

Patrick stepped over the scattered bodies that were strewn across their path. He heard the moans of those not yet dead and the yipping of coyotes and feral dogs announcing the prospect of a voracious feast. Twenty-one San Patricios perished in the fighting at Buena Vista. In the midst of it the men were concerned only with performing their tasks and staying alive. Later, the memory of the dead and dying while he escaped would haunt Patrick for the rest of his days.

Before he left his army Santa Anna addressed them as valiant heroes. He would have no talk of defeat, telling them they had achieved glory that all of Mexico would celebrate. He displayed captured regimental flags and cannons as evidence. He then boarded his coach and, escorted by his elite guard, made a speedy retreat first to San Luis Potosi before going on to Mexico City.

Chapter Fifty-Three

Mexico City, February 27, 1847

Ewen MacKintosh did his best but Vice President Farias refused to see Moses. He and Jane continued to meet with representatives of the bishop, merchants, and moderate members of the Congress. They believed they were making progress and were optimistic that a settlement could eventually be reached. But Farias leaked to the press that they were American spies trying to incite treason and that was the beginning of the end of their mission.

The combative rhetoric between the three political factions, Farias's liberal Puros and their rival Moderados and Centralists intensified. On February twenty-seventh it flared into civil war on the streets of the capital.

Five National Guard Units loyal to Santa Anna refused an order from Farias to move out to Veracruz to defend against the American invasion. The rebels, largely affluent sons of doctors, lawyers and politicians, were called the Polkos for their love of the popular dance. They took over convents and other buildings around Constitution Plaza and began shelling the National Building and the University where Farias's troops had control.

Sporadic fighting continued in the streets for more than a week. During that time, Farias issued a ban on priests from preaching politics from the pulpit and prohibited public gatherings of more than eight people in the daytime, and three at night.

The revolt was poorly planned and lacked dedicated leadership. The Polkos themselves preferred fandangos and the good life to actual combat. Then came news from Santa Anna that his army had won a decisive battle against the Americans at Buena Vista. The Savior of the Nation sent word from the front that he condemned the uprising and sent some of his own troops to the city to restore order. This was the crisis Polk and Buchanan had anticipated but the fraudulent victory was not part of the plan.

With virtually no food or water, Santa Anna's depleted force made another lethal march across the desert back to San Luis Potosi. By the time they arrived they appeared to be an army of dead men; skeletons struggling just to remain upright. Many had ghastly grins on their faces from their skin being drawn so tight their teeth were constantly exposed. Believing Santa Anna's cries of triumph, the people gave them a victor's welcome.

To further burnish his deception, Santa Anna created the Angostura Cross of Honor to be presented to the brave heroes of the Battle of Buena Vista. Deservedly, all of the San Patricios were named as recipients and Captain Riley was promoted to the brevet rank of Major for his skill and courage on the battlefield. Major Moreno was made a colonel.

John had always sought this kind of recognition and while the accolades were justified, Patrick knew he would have preferred to earn them in a true victory and without the loss of so many good men. General Mejia made the presentation as Santa Anna left his army behind once more, this time to go the capital to quell the still boiling civil strife.

Newspapers were available in San Luis, both Mexican and a few American publications out of New Orleans. The Saint Patrick's Battalion was now the subject of an abundant number of articles and editorials. The nativist press in America showed them as loathsome and cowardly traitors, proof of the Catholic menace and fuel to their fire of revising the citizenship laws and stopping Irish immigration.

The Mexican publications lauded them as gallant heroes and defenders of their country and their faith. They were the best of the best and the tales of their bravery in battle, despite the concocted claims of victory, enhanced even more their national celebrity.

When Santa Anna entered the gates of Mexico City in the second week of March, he was hailed as a triumphant conqueror. He flaunted the captured American flags and proclaimed a great victory. A wave of patriotism spread like a prairie fire through the capital. All but the most ardent peace advocates got cold feet, perhaps because they believed that they really could defeat the *yanquis* or, just as likely, so as not to be labeled as traitors. National pride, for the moment, replaced party differences and with it came the final blow to Moses and Jane's peace efforts.

There were rumblings of what really happened at Buena Vista but the truth was still unknown. When he arrived, Santa Anna declared his support for Farias but that changed within days. The Moderados initiated a petition begging him to once again take control of the government, which he did with feigned reluctance.

His first order of business was to revoke the Farias demand for fifteen million pesos from the Church. In return, Bishop Posada had little choice but to approve a two million peso loan to the military. One of the very next things Santa Anna did was issue an order for Jane Storm and Moses Beach to appear before him. Ewen advised them of the summons.

"It's not an official warrant for your arrest," he said. "But I would treat it as such."

Jane let the words sink in. She was stunned and for the first time since coming to Mexico, felt real fear. Drusila was beside herself. "What are we to do, Father? We must escape." They both looked at Moses. He sat for a moment in silence before turning to MacKintosh. "Can you help us?" he asked.

Ewen's hand brushed down his cheek, fingering his long sideburn. "Of course," he said. "I can arrange a coach to get you to Puebla. From there it would be best to head north to Tampico where I believe your army is in full control. You should leave immediately. We can worry about your things later."

Jane wondered if all was lost or if there was something more to be done. "We should go to Veracruz and inform General Scott that as of now our mission has failed. He also needs to know who will be his allies. We have the names of those who want peace here, as well as those in Puebla and Veracruz. Maybe he can succeed where we haven't."

"It's too dangerous, Jane," said Moses. "If the fighting hasn't started there yet, it soon will."

"Dangerous, yes," said Jane. "But shouldn't we try? We owe it to our army and to the brave Mexicans who still desire an end to the bloodshed."

"I don't think Drusila can take much more. She's close to a nervous breakdown as it is."

"I'll go, Moses. You take her to Tampico. Get her home. I'll follow after I meet with General Scott."

"There's no guarantee you'll be able to get to him," said Moses. "It's a war zone after all."

"I'm willing to take that chance," said Jane. "We'll go to Puebla together and then split up there."

"I know someone who can assist you," said MacKintosh. "Joaquín Arriaga is a powerful warlord, a *caudillo*, who has his own small army. He holds no allegiance to any particular faction or party. I'll send a courier out to him and also give you a letter to take. He can provide an escort for you to Veracruz."

"Are you sure he'll do it?" said Jane.

"He's an old friend," said Ewen, "and he owes me a favor or two."

"How will I contact him?"

"Don't worry about that. He's a wanted man, a feared bandido, who fought with the Federalists in the fight for independence when they tried to establish the Republic of the Rio Grande. He hasn't, as of yet, joined in this war but could be of help to your army if called upon. If you don't see him in Puebla, don't make any inquiries about him. Board the stage for Veracruz anyway. He'll find you."

Chapter Fifty-Four

Antón Lizardo, Veracruz, March 21, 1847

Ewen provided them a coach and driver to get them to Puebla. Once there, Jane said goodbye to Moses and his daughter at the stage station. "I'll see Drusila safely on a ship to New Orleans," said Moses. "Then I'll join you in Veracruz."

"That's not necessary, Moses. Go on to Washington and inform Mr. Buchanan and the president of all that's happened."

"I feel like I'm abandoning you."

"Nonsense," said Jane. "Once I report to General Scott I'll follow you there."

The stage for Veracruz arrived two hours later. Jane boarded it, disappointed that Arriaga hadn't shown up. She sat across from a fat Mexican man and his sullen, equally fat wife. They ate tortillas and he spilled juice and beans on his already soiled shirt as he constantly leered at her with an oily smile. After three bumpy hours Jane was losing confidence that her escort would arrive. She stared out the window, trying to ignore the lecher across from her and his now snoring wife.

A shout came from the driver and he cracked his whip. The stage lurched and picked up speed. The Mexican's eyes widened. He pointed out the window and yelled, "bandidos!" Jane saw clouds of dirt and dozens of riders descending on them. Shots were fired in the air and the driver pulled on the reins. Jane's heart was in her throat with fear and a titillating hope that this was Joaquín Arriaga.

The stage stopped and the riders surrounded them. The fat man's

298

eyes looked as if they were about to pop out of his head. He fumbled at his pockets and pulled out a coin sack and thrust it to his wife, pointing to her chest. She shoved the money down her blouse where it was securely hidden between her large breasts.

A splendidly handsome rider cantered closer to the coach. Tall, with broad, muscular shoulders, he had pitch black hair and a mustache that extended down below the corners of his mouth. Ornate silver conchos decorated the straps and bridle of his magnificent chestnut stallion as well as his dusty but perfectly tailored black shirt and pants.

He dismounted and opened the coach door. The Mexican woman started screeching. "*Silencio!*" he commanded. Then he turned to Jane and smiled showing perfectly straight, sparkling white teeth. "Señorita Storm?"

"Yes...si, si," said Jane, trying to catch her breath.

He pulled off his hat, bowed slightly and said in English. "I am Joaquín Arriaga, at your service." He held out his hand for her to descend the coach.

"Thank you, Señor Arriaga," she said. "I was praying it was you."

He laughed. "I have brought an extra horse if you would like to ride. It will be faster but perhaps less comfortable than if you continue on in the coach, with us accompanying you of course."

She didn't have to think about it. Speed was of the essence, and the thought of riding across the plains with this dashing outlaw was thrilling. "Let's ride," she said.

Three days later they arrived at General Scott's field headquarters just days after his army, in unison with the navy under Commander David Conner, completed the first joint amphibious landing in American military history. Eight thousand troops landed on Collado Beach without the loss of one man. His command tent sat on a sandy strip of beach at a location known as Antón Lizardo.

Joaquín went alone with her the last two miles so as not to arouse the *yanquis*. A fierce norther was gathering force off the coast. Roiling black clouds mushroomed ominously in the distance and the wind grew stronger by the minute. They were met at the perimeter by nervous sentries who ordered them to dismount and after a brief confrontation, agreed to take her to see General Scott.

"Thank you, Joaquín," said Jane, taking his hand.

"I will wait to hear from you at our camp," said Arriaga. "If you need me again, just send word."

"I will but my plan is to go back to Washington."

"Good luck then," he said. "If things change, I am easy to contact. Just put out the word anywhere along the National Road and I will get the message."

She lingered a moment, watching him spur his mount and ride off swifter than the wind billowing at his back. She followed the sentry to Scott's tent and waited outside while he went in. She heard his irate voice and thought he might refuse to see her. She took out her diplomatic credentials and got ready to storm inside when the sentry reappeared and gestured impatiently for her to enter.

Winfield Scott had always been exceedingly conscious of his attire and military bearing, earning him the nickname Old Fuss and Feathers. His once chiseled features had turned into deep, sagging lines, a permanently furrowed brow and a face that displayed an air of perpetual disapproval. His imposing six foot two inch frame was now largely blubber but his concern for his appearance had not diminished with age or weight.

He looked up at Jane from his field desk where, in full dress uniform, he was studying maps and charts. He did nothing to disguise his annoyance at her presence. "Who are you madam?" he said. "And what in blazes are you doing in the middle of my battlefield."

She handed him her papers and said with sarcasm equal to his disdain, "A pleasure to meet you too, General. My name is Jane Storm and I have been sent to Mexico by the President to attempt a peaceful settlement to this war. I travelled here from the capital to inform you after things unraveled and we had to escape."

Scott huffed and studied her papers. He thrust them back at her. "I have not been made aware of any such mission," he said, looking her up and down. "Nor have I ever in all my days heard of a plenipotentiary in petticoats. Where is this Moses Beach who is named here?"

"His daughter took ill and he accompanied her to Tampico. We decided that I should come here to give you a full account of what transpired along with a list of potential Mexican allies."

"I have no time for what's happening in Mexico City unless you have word that they wish to surrender," he said. "Tell me what you have to report and be quick about it."

She relayed their experience in the capital and Bishop Posada's commitment to gaining peace. She told him about Joaquín Arriaga and his army that she was sure would assist if called upon. Then she gave him the names of peace supporters, secretly coded on a theater program in case it fell into the wrong hands.

"What am I to do with this?" he said.

"I would advise you to keep it and solicit their help when the time comes."

He tossed it on the end of his table amongst stacks of other papers, clearly unhappy at her impertinence. "You've completed your task, Miss Storm. Now I'd advise *you* to get yourself away from here. We are about to commence bombing."

As she turned to go, Scott shouted for his aide, a young second lieutenant named McClellan who immediately appeared. "Take this woman back to where she was found."

She stopped at the entrance to his tent. "I need to find transportation back to the states, General."

"That's not my concern. There are British ships still here. You seem to have a relationship with them, perhaps they can help you." With that he turned his attention back to his charts.

Chapter Fifty-Five

Battle of Cerro Gordo, April 17-18, 1847

Patrick's hope of the army being sent to Mexico City vanished when orders came to go east to stop Scott's advance. New "recruits" arrived to join them right before they marched the grueling four hundred miles to Jalapa. Hundreds of captured indios were brought in, yolked together like oxen so they could not escape. The Mexicans liked to boast about the absence of slavery in their country but they had no room to talk. These men were hunted down and herded like animals into the service of their country.

The route took them as close as fifty miles to the capital. Patrick wanted more than anything to cut and run to Alicia. He didn't speak of it to anyone, but Jimmy sensed it and John must have too. Jimmy was all for it. "From what I know," he said, "Mexico City is a large and populous. We can lose ourselves there until we find transportation somewhere out of the country."

"That's fine for you, Jimmy. Alicia won't leave."

"Not even for you?"

"I won't ask her."

"So you'll continue on this pilgrimage of death? Wouldn't it be better to escape and have a future with her?"

"Yes, it would but we've already talked about it. She won't leave her people under these conditions. Maybe when it's all over."

"Jesus, Mary and Joseph, Patrick! The Americans won't stop. They'll overrun this country and there will be no way out when that happens. Don't you see?"

"No, I don't. I see Alicia and I being together. And that's that."

"Well, all I see is dirt, dust and defeat as we slog off once more to our destruction."

"Then go, Jimmy. Please. Make for Oregon. I'll give you Alicia's address. Her cousin is an important priest. Maybe he can help you escape."

"And wouldn't that make me a fine friend and cousin. You've never left me so how can I leave you, and the rest of our poor misguided brothers?"

"Then, for the love of God, stop talking about it."

"Ah, but I can't do that either, Patrick. You have your beautiful Alicia. All I have is Oregon. Don't take that away from me."

The only thing to do was laugh, which they both did, as they continued the mindless plodding through more Mexican desert. A short time later, Major Riley made sure to have a talk with him.

"You're not thinking of doing anything foolish are you, lad?"

"You mean like joining the army, then deserting it to join an inferior one?"

John smiled without humor. "You know what I mean. We're beloved in this country but I doubt that General Santa Anna, or any other Mexican officer, would show mercy if one of us ran off."

"And what about you, John Riley? What would you do if I did such a thing?"

"I'd hate for it to come to that, Patrick. My duty is important to me, but not as important as you are. I believe we can stop the Americans. Even if they do get to the gates of the capital, the people will rise up with the army with whatever weapons they have."

"I hope you're right. No matter. I'll not be going anywhere until this is done and I can do so freely."

"That will happen, Patrick. We'll taste victory, you'll see. And once it's over we'll have our land our lives and our liberty."

They arrived in Jalapa in the first week of April. The city sits on the side of a hill at an elevation of four thousand feet, with lush tropical vegetation, magnificent rainbow-colored birds and many streams and rivers. Off to the south, Patrick saw the snow capped peak called Orizaba. On a clear day, with a spyglass, one could see the white sails of ships docked at Veracruz.

Scott's army was nearby, on its way to Jalapa as well after taking Veracruz. Santa Anna arrived and moved his troops south to a place called Cerro Gordo where the National Road tapers through a pass surrounded by craggy peaks. It appeared to be another strong position. The San Patricios were placed on the south side of the road, facing east. A small, swift river, the Rio del Plan was on their right.

Patrick planted their banner on one of three small cliffs below the summit of a large hill called El Telegrafo. Two other batteries were on cliffs next to them. Just to the north was a somewhat smaller hill called La Atalaya. In total the Mexicans had over thirty cannons tactically placed on the high ground. The only way the Americans could get to Jalapa was on this road which they had completely covered with more than enough firepower.

They waited with the confidence that the beguiling Santa Anna was invariably able to instill in his army. But, as their commander Colonel Moreno said later, God must surely be a *yanqui*. Somehow the Americans managed to cut a trail through trees, rocks and dense chaparral on their left flank. Santa Anna had left it unprotected, deeming it impassable. On the afternoon of April seventeenth, the enemy launched a surprise attack from there on La Atalaya.

Major Riley had the men turn their guns that way when their *soldados* were seen retreating down the hill towards Telegrafo. The Americans were in hot pursuit but between the San Patricio cannons and their force at the summit, the Mexicans had them in a vicious crossfire. The enemy's advance was stopped and they were pinned down, seeking protection in the gullies and among the boulders.

A blast of Mexican bugles signaled that their infantry was forming a counterattack to regain the hill. Major Riley gave the command to cease fire. Patrick saw the silver flash of bayonets being fixed and waited for the charge. It never came. The Americans had dragged a howitzer to the top of Atalaya and fired grapeshot, decimating the Mexican front ranks, and the whole line fell back.

The order came to resume shelling and the San Patricios continued relentlessly until dark, when all went quiet except for the haunting and all too familiar moans of the wounded and dying.

It turned uncommonly cold during the night. Tips of white frost clung to the chaparral when Patrick woke at dawn the next morning. Santa Anna knew this country. He had two haciendas close by and was adamant that the only way an army could get to Jalapa was by National Road below them. It could only be a very small, insignificant detachment that had gotten through the rough terrain on their left.

The San Patricios manned their station and were ready and anxious to inflict a punishing toll on the full force of the enemy when they appeared on the road. It began with artillery fire from Atalaya where the Americans had brought up two more cannons. From the sound, Patrick knew they were twenty-four pounders and they were raining terror down on Telegrafo.

Before long their position was targeted as well. They returned fire but without much success. It wasn't more than an hour before the *yanquis* spilled down Atalaya with blood-curdling screams and up the slope of Telegrafo. Patrick then witnessed once more the sight of *soldados* fleeing in panic.

Not only had the impregnable route on their left indeed been forged by Scott's engineers, a large contingent overran Santa Anna's command post at their rear in the village of Cerro Gordo. At the same time, the expected enemy force from the front was coming up the National Road. They were being ensnared in a trap with the river on their right and the enemy coming at them from the front and back.

White flags went up from units all around them. Major Riley shouted the order to cease fire and get out of there. Surrender for the deserters was not an option. The battle was no more than a couple hours old and they were running for their lives, just like the rest of the Mexican Army.

Patrick grabbed their banner and ran down the cliff and into a ravine on the river's edge. All discipline and order evaporated. Officers and lowly soldiers alike, threw down their weapons and raced off with the only thought being escape.

Santa Anna ran too. He was the first to leave. Just before the *yanquis* got to his camp at Cerro Gordo, he cut one of the mules from his carriage and rode away, leaving it and his men behind. Later, when his army wasn't getting paid, he said that thousands of pesos meant for payroll were left in his baggage and seized by the the enemy. They also "captured" one of his spare wooden legs. Newspapers in New Orleans reported that American soldiers paraded it around as a war prize and proof of The Savior of the People's cowardice.

Patrick made it down to the river and splashed through the pebbles and the shallow water until the sounds of the battle faded. He looked around for Jimmy and the rest of the lads. They were coming along from behind and up on the bank near the road with Major Riley further behind, helping the stragglers.

When they caught up to Patrick they all looked at their commander for what to do next. It was the only time he ever saw doubt on John Riley's face but it only lasted a moment. "We'll go to Jalapa," he said. "And decide what to do from there."

Hundreds more fleeing *soldados* joined them. They were a pathetic group making their way north with only the blackened, threadbare shirts on their backs. They had no order, no weapons and no hope. The sky filled with buzzards circling the battlefield for the banquet they were about to have. General Scott didn't pursue them. He had his hands full with the thousands of prisoners his army took, which included five Mexican generals.

Chapter Fifty-Six

Mexico City, May 14, 1847

When they got to Jalapa, Colonel Moreno was already there. He and Major Riley got them organized. The San Patricios lost another handful of men but no one was sure how many or if there would be more survivors coming along later. Their commanding general was nowhere to be found and it was determined that they wouldn't wait for him. There was no doubt that the Americans would be coming to occupy the town.

The decision was made to go to Puebla. They supplied themselves as best they could with a little water and beans and took off, constantly in fear of being caught defenseless in some mountain pass by the invincible *gringos*. They arrived in Puebla the first week in May and remained there for ten days.

Santa Anna, who had fled first to Orizaba from Cerro Gordo, was back in Mexico City. Major Riley informed his men that they would be moving out to the capital to join him. Patrick asked John for the use of his horse and permission to go ahead but he was refused.

"We'll travel as a unit," he said. "Once there you'll have time to see her, I promise you that."

When they reached the gates of the city a week later he was ready to defy any order if it meant he couldn't go to her. They were assigned to a barracks in an old monastery near Alameda Park with its tree-covered paths and marvelous fountains and statues. He laid down his gear and was heading out of the building when Major Riley called to him.

"Corporal Ryan."

He didn't want to answer. He had to find her. But John beat him to the door and blocked him with his mammoth figure. "Yes, Major." He said it in a way that indicated he was not going to be deterred.

"Don't you think," said John with a smile, "that a bath might be in order before you go see your sweetheart?"

He had been so dirty for so long he forgot what clean was. They had access to soap and water in Puebla but that was over two weeks ago. Patrick looked at himself and his clothes. He'd been much dirtier but his uniform was so stained and tattered it was about to fall off his cadaverous body. His hair was greasy, matted and looked more black than red. He realized that he must smell horribly. He had grown immune to the stench, not only of death and disease, but of himself and his fellow soldiers.

"You go wash up," said Riley. "I'll find a clean uniform somewhere. You can't go meet Alicia looking like that. She'll toss you over for a rich Mexican colonel."

It had been over eight months since he'd seen her though it seemed more like years. Doubt and fear crept into his mind and on to to his face. Jimmy and some of the lads laughed at the sight of him. "You'd better clean yourself up," said Micheál.

"Even the beggars in the street look more presentable than you," said Jimmy.

Their barracks were the nicest they'd ever had and there was a bath house just outside. Patrick hurried in and scrubbed off the muck and grime. John found a new uniform, complete with a dashing cap that had a red tassel. He looked like a new man.

The Major had Micheál go out and purchase flowers. He came back with a beautiful bouquet of pink and red roses. In his haste he was going to completely neglect bringing her anything. His mates shouted *vivas* as he rushed out of the building.

Finding Constitution Plaza and the cathedral was easy. It was a straight walk and less than two miles from the barracks. Patrick had seen many churches since coming to Mexico but this one was by far the largest and most impressive. He took no notice of it.

Soldiers, street vendors, politicians, priests and throngs of shoppers crowded the plaza. A line of poor people, the *leperos*, were on their knees waiting to get inside the cathedral. Many never stood up but made their way slowly, crawling on their knees. The disparity between them and the prosperity of the others might have been unsettling to Patrick if he didn't have his mind on one purpose.

He had the address of Alicia's cousin, Padre Orellana, but couldn't find the street. He tried asking directions but when he was able to make someone understand, he wasn't able to comprehend the answer. He decided to go to the cathedral's rectory where a small, smiling nun answered the door. She spoke no English. He tried asking for Señora Ryan but that got him nowhere. When he asked for Padre Orellana her face brightened.

"Si. Si. Un momento, señor."

She disappeared for a moment and then returned with a boy about ten years old. The nun nodded and gestured for him to follow the boy who was already walking off. Patrick hurried after him. They passed in front of the cathedral and he glanced up at the two giant bell towers. When he looked back panic seized him. The boy was gone. He broke into a run, nearly dropping the flowers searching for him. When he reached the end of the building there was still no sign of him.

"Señor," came a voice. Then again, "Señor!" Patrick looked to the left toward the middle of the plaza, then to the right down the street. He let out a sigh of relief when he saw the boy.

"*Por aqui*," he said, waving his hand.

Patrick made sure he didn't take his eyes off him again. They made a right turn down a small street which was no more than an alley. On their left, was a row of two story buildings that filled the entire block. About halfway down, his guide stopped and pointed to a door.

"*Es este, señor.*"

"*Gracias*," said Patrick.

"*De nada, señor*," he said and took off running.

Patrick stood there, roses in hand, looking at the door. For months all he could think about was this moment and now he was paralyzed with doubt and not a little fear. He had faced and overcome the savagery of battle but this was nothing like that. He wasn't the same person she had met at Matamoros. He'd seen and inflicted death and incomprehensible suffering. Would she still love him? How could she after what he'd been through and done? And he still had nothing but the hope of survival and the uncertain rewards from a country fighting a losing war.

The image and thought of her had sustained him through the worst possible difficulties and yet now he could not take another step forward to knock on her door. Out of the corner of his eye he saw a figure approach.

He turned as a priest in his black cassock and wide brimmed hat walked toward him. He was older than Patrick by about ten years and a couple of inches shorter. His large eyes were open and friendly behind round spectacles, and he was smiling. When he got close, Patrick was startled when he spoke his name

"Señor Ryan?"

He stared, dumbfounded, without answering. The priest spoke to him in English. "Are you Patrick?"

"Si. Yes. Yes, I'm Patrick."

"Welcome, Patrick. I am Padre Arturo Orellana, Alicia's cousin. Are you going to stand out here forever or knock on the door and make her a very happy young woman?"

Tears streamed down his cheeks. He brushed at them and banged on the door. He let a few seconds go by, his heart pounding in his ears, then knocked again, longer and louder. He shouted her name.

"Alicia! Alicia, it's me, Patricio!" He began to think she wasn't home. He looked at Padre Orellana who just kept smiling and nodding his head. He turned back to the door and as he raised his fist to knock again, it opened and there she was, even more exquisitely beautiful than he remembered.

"Patricio!" They fell into each other's arms. "Patricio. You've come. Praise God. You're alive." He had no words to say. They clung to one another crying and laughing tears of joy. He kissed her neck, her cheeks, her mouth, with a hunger he never had from the lack of food. They didn't move from the front door until they heard Padre Orellana from behind them.

"I think you two should go inside."

Chapter Fifty-Seven

Washington, D.C. May 14, 1847

After the successful siege of Veracruz was completed, Jane was transported off the British Man-of-War she had taken refuge on after meeting with General Scott. She found lodging at a convent in the city. She remained there for five days before being able to book passage on a merchant ship to New Orleans and then a steamer to New York. Moses was back by then as well but had not yet gone to Washington to make his report. He had pressing business and legal matters to attend to so Jane went by herself.

An army captain ushered her into the Secretary of War's office. He told her that Mr. Marcy would be there shortly. In a few minutes he arrived with Secretary of State, Buchanan. They greeted her warmly. Jane and Buchanan sat across from Marcy and she got right to it, starting with the details of her failed mission and her encounter with General Scott.

"I gave him a list of potential Mexican allies but he merely tossed it aside."

Marcy saw her irritation. "In his defense, Jane," he said. "He is conducting a military campaign."

"I understand," said Jane. "But what's the goal? To kill as many Mexicans as possible or to end the conflict and bring our system and freedoms to a welcoming people?"

Buchanan's hands were together up to his lips as if in prayer. He nodded for her to continue. She told them about the kind lieutenant who arranged for her to be taken to Collado Beach. There she sweet talked a sailor into taking her on his barge out to the harbor to seek passage on an

American merchant vessel, the *Indiana*. The captain demanded payment in U.S. dollars even to allow her to board his ship. She had only a few pesos and not enough anyway so she begged the sailor to take her to a British Man-of-War further out in the harbor with its Union Jack nearly ripping apart in the wailing wind of the building norther.

"The captain was not happy to see me but he had little choice since my escort was already steaming away back across the harbor. I spent the night with British evacuees from Veracruz in the mess area as the ship rolled and pitched. For a while we were all sure it was going to capsize. When the weather cleared the next afternoon I watched from the deck as General Scott bombarded a city filled with six thousand civilians."

"I read your dispatches," said Buchanan. They were printed in more than one newspaper," said Buchanan. "The president was disappointed that you revealed details of the peace mission."

"Mr. Polk should be more concerned with the wanton, and I believe uncalled for destruction of so many innocent lives."

"Scott had to think of his troops, Jane," said Marcy. "The Mexicans refused to surrender and the fever season was approaching. He needed to move his men out of the area without unnecessary casualties that using his infantry would have caused."

Jane nodded somewhat derisively and said, "I also criticized the Mexicans in my articles. For their complete lack of purpose or leadership, and Santa Anna's National Guard for betraying the peace effort."

"They don't appear to want to do anything but fight, Miss Storm," said Buchanan. Before she could respond he told her an envoy had been sent to join Scott. "Nicholas Trist has been named our official minister for peace with all powers to negotiate a settlement. It's likely he's already there. We hope that with the victory in Veracruz and Scott's approach to the capital that we can end it all before another major battle."

Jane raised an eyebrow in doubt. "Nicholas is a good choice," she said. "But Santa Anna has rallied a patriotic fervor across the nation and the peace advocates have gone silent. He'll have a very difficult task."

Buchanan leaned back in his chair in thought before saying, "Would you consider returning to assist Mr. Trist?"

She wasn't expecting that and didn't let them know that she was already thinking about going back, but on her own. Instead she asked, "In what capacity, Mr. Buchanan? General Scott will not give me the least bit of respect."

He glanced at Marcy who looked surprised at Buchanan's suggestion. Then he said, "Let me think more on it, Miss Storm. Right now the president is expecting you."

Marcy walked with her across the street to the president's residence, took her into his office and introduced her, then left them to meet in private. Mr. Polk was engrossed in paperwork when they arrived. He broke his attention, stood up and walked around his desk to shake her hand, his stern expression never changing.

She noticed that he was hollow-eyed and gaunt, much more so than in the likenesses of him she had seen. His gray hair swept back from his high forehead and hung down over his collar. He didn't look well. He was known to work incessantly and the rigors of the office and the war were apparent in his physical appearance.

"Please sit, Miss Storm," he said. "Tell me of your experiences in Mexico."

She sat and said, "thank you for seeing me, Mr. Polk." She hesitated at first, not quite sure where to begin. The president noticed it and asked, "Who did you make contact with in the capital?"

"We met with Archbishop Posada and various moderate and conservative congressmen. The British Consul, Ewen MacKintosh, was kind enough to put us up in his home and we had numerous discussions with him and his political contacts." We tried to get an audience with Vice President Farias but he refused, then told the press about us, telling them we were inciting treason.

President Polk listened intently, his pale, gray eyes boring into her with what she interpreted as complete indifference. When she finished he asked, "How would you assess the state of affairs in Mexico City?"

"In a word, sir, chaotic. Santa Anna's claims of victory at Buena Vista put him back in favor with the whole country. He has somehow retained his hold on power even after it became known that he removed his army in the middle of the night and General Taylor held the field. Mexico seems ready and willing to fight, to the finish I'm afraid."

Polk grimaced slightly as if something sour rose into his mouth. He motioned for her to go on. She briefed him on the botched Polka revolt and the fact that they had to flee when Santa Anna sought to have them arrested.

"Rather than follow through on any agreement he may have made to work for peace," continued Jane. "He marched his army east to engage General Scott, publicly vowing to die if necessary to save his country. You most likely know more than I about this but the Mexicans were routed at a place called Cerro Gordo."

"We received the reports," said the president. "General Scott is proceeding west and we believe is in Puebla by now."

"I met the bishop there," said Jane. "The city is not well protected and he's a strong supporter for peace. I doubt General Scott will have any trouble taking it."

Polk's expression didn't change. He stared at her impassively and she waited for him to say something. Finally he asked, "Is there anything else, Miss Storm?"

She felt her anger rise, not really knowing why. Perhaps it was the apparent indifference with which he received her information. Or the fact that she realized she was helpless to change or influence what was happening. "Only," she said, "I believe we haven't made proper use of the many influential and republican leaning citizens of Mexico."

She was about to go on but the president stood up, indicating the meeting was over. "Please give whatever more information you have to Mr. Marcy and we'll discuss it in our cabinet meeting." He didn't move from behind his desk. "Thank you for your efforts, Miss Storm," he said and sat back down and continued with his paperwork.

On her way out of his office, Jane made up her mind that she would go back to Mexico, by herself, as an independent reporter without attachment to any particular paper. And she would tell the truth about what she witnessed.

Chapter Fifty-Eight

Mexico City, June - August, 1847

Patrick stayed with Alicia for two days. They never left their apartment other than when she slipped out briefly to get them food. He would have stayed there forever if he could have but on the third day Major Riley showed up at the door.

"I can't cover for you any longer, lad," he said. "Colonel Moreno is insisting on your returning or he will report you as a deserter. It's time."

As they were leaving John reassured Alicia that Patrick would be able to return. "I'll make sure he has some time to be with you," he said. She gave him a big hug around the waist which is where she came up to on him. His face turned a crimson red. She laughed and said, *"Gracias, Don Riley."*

Alicia and Patrick did get to spend time together. Padre Orellana was gracious enough to move into another small apartment, so they could live two whole months as a married couple. When he wasn't drilling or cleaning and repairing weapons, they visited museums, ate at fine cantinas, and took evening strolls through the lush Alameda Park.

But more often than not they stayed home, made love, and talked about their future. She wouldn't allow him to doubt for one moment that they would have one. She always spoke as if nothing would get in their way; not war, politics, religion or money.

"This trouble will pass," she said. "We'll be together and have a family. I know it as sure as I know you are here with me right now."

He thought about telling her that everything he had done so far had been wrong. That he'd lost his family's money and abandoned his sister. That his failures had caused the death of his parents. But then he looked at her, held her close, and knew in his heart and soul that being with her, was where he was supposed to be. His guilt would remain close. He would never be able to completely erase it from his mind, but he didn't speak of it to her again. He needed to survive so they could both fulfill their dreams of a life and family together.

Santa Anna was fully back in power after taking over the presidency, resigning it, and then reneging on the resignation. It didn't seem to matter what he did. The country needed a leader and he was the only one who provided any hope of defeating the despised *yanquis*.

Soldiers and National Guardsmen were called in from all over the country and more peasants were forced into service. Santa Anna ordered church bells and old cannons to be confiscated and melted down and cast into new guns. At the same time he was overtly preparing to defend the capital, he was secretly trying to work a deal with the Americans.

Through Ewen MacKintosh, he demanded ten thousand U.S. dollars up front in return for his promise to open negotiations if General Scott agreed not to march on the capital. Once peace was achieved, the Savior of the Nation would require a personal payment of another million dollars.

General Scott and Nicholas Trist, both anxious to end the war, agreed to the initial payment, though both denied it later. They surreptitiously paid the ten thousand. Once the money was in hand, Santa Anna cut off any talk of peace and Scott, incensed but powerless to do anything about the deception, prepared to advance on Mexico City.

It took Jane six weeks to get back to Mexico. She landed in Veracruz on the twenty-sixth of June, still using her British passport. She was able to get a room at the same convent where she had stayed after the siege. She made discreet inquiries and found a priest who agreed to make contact with Joaquín Arriaga. Four days later, one of his men arrived and took her to his small hacienda some twenty miles away and well off the National Road.

Joaqín was surprised that she returned. They sat on a small patio under the arch of his house sipping *mezcal* and smoking cheroots. "It is very dangerous, Jane," he said. "More so now than when you were here before."

The air cooled and the setting sun turned the adobe walls of the patio a soft orange hue as Jane took in what he said. The effects of the cigar and the alcohol gave her a soothing feeling that matched the warm walls of the hacienda. She considered for a moment what drove her here. William Cazneau wanted to marry her and he had land in a lovely spot on the Rio Grande at a place called Eagles Pass. She could be sitting there with him right now, safe and comfortable.

She noticed Joaquín grinning, waiting for her to say something. "You were far away, Jane."

She laughed. The tip of the cigar reddened as she inhaled She blew out a long stream of white smoke. "I had to come back. I want America to grow but we have a responsibility to do it properly. And the people of Mexico should have the ability to decide for themselves what government they want. I feel it's my duty to let our citizens know what is actually happening here."

They sat silently, watching the sun slowly disappear. Then she said, "I need to get to Mexico City."

"We'll leave in the morning," said Joaquín. "You wish to go back to

Ewen's house in Tacubaya?"

"Yes, I'm hoping he'll take me in again. I haven't thought things through much more than that."

Joaquín saw her safely back to Tacubaya. Ewen welcomed them into his front parlor, clearly not expecting to see either of them. He offered rooms to both of them but Joaquín declined. He had many enemies in the capital and preferred the the hills and the company of his men anyway. He took his leave, telling Jane that if she needed him again to put out the word and he would find her.

After she freshened up, she met Ewen downstairs in his library where they sat and had brandy. "Are you still in the employ of your government?" he asked.

"No, I'm here on my own. I intend to send my reports back to the newspapers in the states if I can find a way."

"I have couriers who can get dispatches through to either Tampico or Veracruz and then on to a packet ship to New Orleans."

"Thank you, Ewen, for everything."

"You can stay here as long as you like, Jane" he said. "But your army will no doubt be here soon and it will no longer be safe. Unless, of course, things get resolved before then."

"What do you mean?"

"At General Santa Anna's request, I approached Nicholas Trist with peace feelers."

Jane flushed with anger. "He should have stuck with the original plan. All those lives on both sides at Cerro Gordo could have been spared."

Ewen nodded, taking a slow sip of his brandy. He placed the glass down on the side table by his chair. "I doubt anything would have turned out differently. You and Moses did your best."

She drank her brandy in silence. Ewen went on. "I think you'd be better off inside the city. The bishop's secretary can recommend someplace near the cathedral for you I'm sure. I refuse to believe the Mexican people will allow the city to be taken."

Three days later, Jane had an audience with the bishop. He was pleased to see her but expressed concern that she returned at such a perilous time. He had little hope, other than the tenuous belief that Santa Anna and his army would be able to repel the *yanqui hereticos*.

Despite her reassurances, he feared what would happen when the Americans arrived. It was now common knowledge that churches were looted and defiled and innocent civilians terrorized after Taylor's victory in Monterrey. He was convinced that if they weren't stopped, his majestic cathedral would be destroyed and sacked along with the city.

He asked if she was still empowered to make peace. She told him no, and then, without hesitation, he asked if she would be willing to act as one of his representatives if the opportunity arose. She told him that she did know the new U.S. peace envoy, and would be happy to act as an interpreter, messenger or in any other capacity.

He too thought it would be safer, at least for now, inside the city and insisted on putting her up in one of the apartments on the church grounds. The following Monday, she returned and Padre Orellana showed her to a small room around the corner from his own.

"It isn't much," said the padre. "But the bed is comfortable. There is a small desk as you can see and it is reasonably free of insects."

"It's more than I could have asked for," said Jane. "Thank you."

"Once you're settled in I'll introduce you to a few other bishops who will be good contacts. Oh, and my cousin will surely want to meet. She is married to a young Irishman. One of our famous San Patricios who I'm sure you've heard of."

The padre saw the surprise register on her face. She had of course heard of them though in her mind, infamous was the better description. With all her criticisms and doubts about the war, she was positive about one thing, traitors were the lowest of the low. She wasn't sure she wanted to meet this cousin but responded politely, "I look forward to it."

Chapter Fifty-Nine

On Sunday Jane attended Mass at the cathedral. As she walked in the twenty-five bells in the two towers rang out, reverberating throughout the city. She thought they must be able to be heard over the entire Valley of Mexico. Uniformed soldiers and officers filed in, mixing in and filling the pews with both the poor and affluent citizens of the capital.

The main altar is the most magnificent of all the fourteen chapels in the cathedral. The backdrop is made entirely of gold and adorned with statues and busts of numerous saints, including the Blessed Mother. The towering crucified Christ, made of a rich, dark brass, looms over the altar. The beauty and opulence, which the American Protestants found so abhorrent, filled Jane with a deep reverence and awe.

She looked down at the floor and noticed the dried, cracked wooden slats with irregular gaps in them that revealed and let through layers of dust and dirt. It made her think of Mexico, with its abundant, natural wealth and soaring possibilities yet plagued by a weak and crumbling foundation. She would find a way to use the example in one of her columns.

Padre Orellana was one of the priests distributing Holy Communion and when Jane took the wafer into her mouth, he gave her a benevolent smile. After the service she looked for him. He was standing with another priest, a beautiful young woman and a small group of soldiers. He saw her and waved for her to come over. As she approached she noticed that the fair-skinned soldiers, with more than one redhead, were more than likely some of the Irish deserters.

The padre broke off his conversation with the soldiers. "Señorita Storm," he said. "Let me introduce you to my cousins. He put his arm on the

325

other priest and said, "This is Padre Francisco Salinas and his sister, Alicia Salinas Ryan."

She shook both their hands. Alicia's face beamed with love and an innocent intelligence and Jane was instantly taken with her. They were both obviously *mestizos* which in the caste conscious society of Mexico indicated mixed European and indigenous ancestry. They each had the same luxuriant black hair and equally dark eyes. Alicia's were enhanced by long, perfect lashes. Her demeanor was modest and humble but her smile was as radiant as the Aztec sun.

"So good to meet you, Señorita Storm," said Alicia in English. "My cousin has told me all about you."

Before Jane could say anything, Padre Orellana announced, "And this is her husband, Corporal Patrick Ryan."

The young Irishman extended his hand and Jane shook it. He was taller than the rest of his fellow soldiers. She looked into his soft brown eyes, the color of which matched his wavy, mahogany red hair. A few freckles dotted his straight nose. He had a strong chin and when he smiled at her she felt a fondness she was not prepared for. "Good to meet you, Miss Storm," he said. "The rest of the boys here are in my battalion."

Jane acknowledged them all with a reserved smile, not ready to let go of her distaste for who they were. There were four of them and they all gave her a quick little salute. "We had better get back, lads," said Patrick. "The Major made me promise that we would return right after Mass."

Jane saw the crushed look on Alicia's face. Patrick took her hands in his and they kissed quickly. A piece of her coldness melted seeing how hopelessly in love they were and how much they hated parting.

When he was gone, Jane asked Alicia how they met. It was the first time she heard of the abusive treatment of the immigrant soldiers and it served to further thaw her disdain as well as increase her interest in their situation. It also fascinated her that romance could be found in the strangest time and place.

Padre Orellana interrupted her thoughts. She heard him say that the bishop wanted to see her. When she didn't answer right away, he asked, "Would Tuesday morning be convenient for you?"

"Yes, of course, Padre," she said.

"*Bueno*," he said. "We will see you at ten?"

"Very good," said Jane. Then to Alicia, "I look forward to seeing you again. Perhaps we could have lunch on Tuesday?"

Alicia smiled shyly. "I would like that very much, Señorita Storm."

"Please call me Jane, Alicia. I feel like we will be good friends."

"Thank you, Jane. I feel it as well."

Jane's meeting with Bishop Posada was brief. He asked for any news she had but there wasn't much to add since last week. She did tell him that she'd sent a note to Nicholas Trist but had not heard anything back yet. She also relayed the fact that Ewen Mackintosh had no further information on Santa Anna's peace feelers. The Bishop was already aware and apprised of that situation. Upon leaving, he asked her to keep him informed of any developments that came her way, which she promised to do.

Jane went to Alicia's apartment and from there they had lunch at a small sidewalk cafe in a far corner of Constitution Plaza. Over a light lunch of grilled chicken in a delicious tomatillo sauce they got to know each other better. Alicia was fascinated by Jane's background, travels and the fact that she was a writer of such merit.

Jane was impressed by Alicia's quiet strength and dedication to both her brother and her husband. She wanted to know more about Patrick and his band of deserters, and their renowned leader of whom there was so many conflicting reports and rumors.

"Have you met this Sergeant Riley who they say led them to desert?"

"Oh yes," said Alicia. "He's a major, not a sergeant, and definitely their leader. There is no doubt of that. Patrick idolizes him, as do the rest of his men. All of them were physically abused by their Protestant commanders. Patrick's cousin was actually branded on his forehead like an animal. His offense they said was drunkenness. And the *yanquis* call us barbarians."

Jane knew that harsh discipline was part of the army but thought it nothing more than needed preparations for war. She also knew that John Adams had protested the shooting of deserters in a speech on the floor of the House of Representatives. But she thought it was a small, isolated incident. She was, however, intrigued by the story of hundreds of immigrants not just deserting but forming their own unit and fighting for the enemy. "I would like to meet this Major Riley," she said. "Do you think you could arrange that?"

"It would be very difficult right now," said Alicia. "All leave has been cancelled and I don't even know when I will see Patricio again. I hope it is soon. I have something very important to tell him." Her face lit up with so much serenity that Jane had an inkling of what it might be.

"I have told no one else this, Jane. Not even my brother." She hesitated a moment more then said, "I am with child."

Jane felt a wave of tenderness for her as if she were her own sister.

"That's wonderful, Alicia. How far along are you?"

"Maybe two months. I'm not sure exactly. I can't wait to tell Patricio. He will be so pleased."

"I'm sure he will," said Jane. "And worried too I would think. Have you thought of going somewhere safer?"

"You sound just like Patricio. He will want me to do that but I cannot go. I won't leave him, or my brother."

Jane thought about Joaquín and his hacienda. He could get her away from here where she would away from danger. She saw Alicia's determination and decided not bring it up, at least not now. Instead she said, "Let me know if there is anything I can do for you."

"Thank you, Jane. Please don't mention it to my cousin or anyone else. I want Patricio to hear it from me."

"Of course, dear. Congratulations. I'm very happy for you. And for your handsome Irishman as well."

Chapter Sixty

Mexico City, August 8, 1847

The Americans were on their way. General Scott and his army had left Puebla and would soon be at the capital. A law had been passed making it a crime for anyone to negotiate for peace with the invaders, so no soldier, politician or clergyman in the capital publicly advocated for anything but full scale war.

John took pity on Patrick and allowed him to spend one last day and night with Alicia. It was Sunday and after attending Mass they had lunch at their favorite cafe. The city bustled and buzzed with apprehension. Some people were packing up and leaving, reminding Patrick of the riots in Kensington, but for the most part the attitude was one of defiant resistance. The citizens of the capital would make a stand, with stones and pikes if necessary.

When they finished eating, Alicia reached across the table and took both his hands in hers. "I have something to tell you, Patricio."

"You're going to leave the city as I asked?"

"And go where? It's too late to leave now anyway. No, I'll stay here and pray in the cathedral. I'll be safe."

"How can you be so sure? If Ampudia hadn't surrendered, the Americans would have blasted the church in Monterrey to rubble."

"They won't make it that far into the city. We will stop them this time."

"And if we don't?"

"I can't and won't believe that will happen. It's said that General

Scott will not attack our churches. He has attended Mass in Puebla and has ordered his officers to salute the priests."

"That may be true, but when the time comes he, and every one of his soldiers, will destroy anything in their path."

"This is where it ends, Patricio. One way or another."

"If we're defeated this time," said Patrick. "I won't survive. If I'm not killed in the battle, all of us will be executed."

"Do not say that again, Patricio. That cannot happen. You have to survive. You will survive. Not just for me, but for our little one."

He heard the words but they didn't get through to him. She raised her eyebrows and gave him an expectant look. He saw small tears form at the corners of her eyes and he returned her radiant smile but it still didn't register.

"Did you hear what I said, *mi amor*? We're going to have a baby."

The numbing blast of cannon fire had never stunned him more than when it finally became clear to him. Then he was flooded with an overpowering and incomprehensible ecstasy.

"A baby?" was all he could say.

"Si, Patricio. I'm pregnant."

He struggled for words, finally blurting out the only thing that came to mind. "Are you sure?"

She laughed. "Oh yes. I'm sure."

His elation turned to abject fear. "Then you must leave the city."

"No. We won't leave you alone. We'll be here when it's over so we can truly begin our lives together. It's God's plan. Don't you see?"

He didn't see anything but the need to protect her and their baby and his inability to do either. God's plan indeed. He hoped her faith was enough for both of them. He helped her from her chair and held her closely as they walked to the apartment. He hesitated to make love with her and she reassured him. "It's fine, Patricio. You will not hurt me."

"What about the baby?"

"He's safe and secure. You won't hurt him either."

"Him?" he said and she laughed again. He could barely contain his joyful amazement at the realization that this beautiful angel loved him. And now she was carrying his child. How was it possible that he could love her even more than he already did?

"Or her," said Alicia, giggling like a little girl herself. "Come, love me tonight, for as much as I trust in our Lord, one never knows for sure."

When he left her the next morning he kissed her gently on the lips one final time. She guided his head down to her slightly bulging belly and he kissed it as well. So much joy and dread all at the same time.

He was going to be a father. How he wished his own mother and father could be there to share in this. And his sister. His world might very soon be coming to an end but he was grinning like an idiot when he walked into the barracks.

"I'm sorry for being late, Major," he said.

"It doesn't appear that you truly are, Corporal Ryan."

"He looks as if he's had too much *pulque*," said Jimmy.

"Something much better than alcohol," he said. "I'm going to be a father. Alicia is pregnant."

John pounded him on the back. "Ah, that's terrific news, Patrick," he said, then announced it to the whole barracks. Jimmy, Micheál, Henry and the rest of the lads gathered around to congratulate him. All of a sudden a bottle appeared. From Jimmy no doubt. It was passed around until everyone had a sip. Even Colonel Moreno, stern-faced at first, shook Patrick's hand and took a drink. Then he gave a curt nod to Major Riley and things got serious.

"The *yanquis* are on the march, lads," said Riley. "Now we must defeat them, not just for Mexico and our own hides, but also for Patrick, Alicia and their blessed child."

The men cheered wildly. They would stop the invaders this time. A couple hours later, warning cannons were fired across the city announcing the arrival of the Americans into the Valley of Mexico.

Chapter Sixty-One

Mexico City, August 11 - 19, 1847

Brevet Major John Riley, tall and proud astride his black stallion, led the San Patricios into Constitution Plaza. The edges of the plaza, the side streets and all the buildings were filled with roaring crowds. On this day, no Mexican, citizen or soldier, believed that General Scott's small army would be able to take the city or conquer them as a nation.

The Savior of the People, in his most spectacular uniform, adorned with so many medals his jacket was hardly discernible, reviewed the troops. A hundred drums rattled and as many horns blasted as he saluted each battalion and brigade marching out to meet the enemy. Patrick strained and looked everywhere for a glimpse of Alicia. He knew she was in the crowd somewhere but could not locate her.

The San Patricios were sent to El Peñon, ten miles southeast of the city. They were positioned at a fort there on a hill, just a few miles west of Ayotla on the road where Scott's army was approaching. Major Riley brought new handbills Santa Anna himself had asked him to create in the continuing battle to win the hearts and minds of the immigrant soldiers and entice more of them to desert.

Patrick doubted if any would do so this late in the war. Jimmy said in a low voice, "Do you think any of them would change places with me?"

There were a few scattered laughs. "Don't let the Major hear you,"said Micheál.

"As if I care," said Jimmy. "He wouldn't be here either if the Americans had been the least bit ready to recognize his talents."

334

"We're all here now, Jimmy," said Patrick. "There's nothing more to be done except blow them back to where they belong."

"Spoken like a true Mexican," said Jimmy.

Is that what he was now? A loyal Mexican? *I'm an Irishman*, he thought. A Catholic, married to a beautiful Mexican girl, pregnant with my child. His constant guilt over his failures faded with the ironclad realization that they were his paramount responsibility. He would fight to the end and give his life to protect them.

Riley's flyers were tossed on the road outside the fort, to scatter with the breeze towards the advancing Americans. This one encouraged them to "abandon a slavish life with a nation who even in the moment of victory treats you with contumely and disgrace."

Patrick was surprised, and Jimmy was astonished, when a group of twelve more deserters shuffled down the road toward them. They had been recruited by priests in Puebla. Patrick's admiration for John Riley rose even higher. His example, battlefield exploits and rising fame were all a part of convincing his fellow Irishmen that they were indeed on the wrong side.

An army can only cross Mexico City's expansive highland valley, filled with lakes and marshes, during good weather. The rainy season was approaching and General Scott had to move his troops before the National Highway became bogged down and impassable. The road led right through their location at El Peñon. Major Riley got them in position at the fort. The San Patricios were ready.

Santa Anna arrived in El Peñon the next day, trailed by thousands of citizens, including camp followers, peddlers, vendors and hustlers. It had the air of a tremendous carnival procession. Did they not know what war was about? Patrick thought of all the men they had lost and the butchery and slaughter that lay ahead.

They should have known by now that the Americans would not do as Santa Anna predicted. Scott changed course and took a different route. He stopped a few miles down the road at Ayotla and over the next two days studied their stronghold. He turned his army south and then west around Lake Chalco and Lake Xochimilco toward the village of San Agustin. They would make their attack on the capital from the south.

Santa Anna repositioned his troops to the towns of San Ángel, Coyoacán and San Antonio all of which sat along the northern border of a five mile wide stone field called El Pedregal. No one was worried about the *yanquis* going through there. It was filled with ancient volcanic boulders, razor sharp lava rocks, thick trees and giant maguey plants, wet undergrowth and fast running creeks. Only coyotes, snakes and lizards could pass through it.

The San Patricios were sent back to their barracks to await further instructions. Patrick wanted to go see Alicia one more time but John wouldn't hear of it.

"Colonel Moreno would skin me alive, lad. We must remain together as a unit. No special privileges. Our new assignment will come any moment."

On Sunday, August fifteenth, a special Mass for the troops was said by the Archbishop. Colonel Moreno and Major Riley marched the San Patricios into the main chapel of the cathedral which was filled to capacity with bareheaded, kneeling soldiers and officers. Patrick could only comprehend a few of the Spanish words of the Bishop's sermon but he understood the warning that the *gringos hereticos* must be stopped at all costs or both Mexico and the Church would be destroyed.

It took over thirty minutes for all of them to receive Holy Communion. There were several priests there to help, including Padre Pancho who had returned from Monterrey. When they filed out after Mass, Patrick made the decision to sneak off to see Alicia. The apartment was just around the corner after all. He didn't care what the consequences might be. What could they do to him? Take away his corporal stripes? At that moment, he didn't care about his rank or any punishment.

As his battalion marched straight ahead, he made a right turn at the corner and kept on walking until he reached the apartment. He stayed only a few minutes. They held each other and prayed together for victory and an end to the war. When he got back to the barracks the Major gave him a stony stare but that was it.

Again they waited, and again the men wished for battle over the agonizing delay without the ability to go anywhere or do anything. Orders could come at any second. Three days later, on the eighteenth, the Americans set up camp at San Agustin. In addition to their ten thousand man force they had over a thousand wagons in their supply train.

The next morning Colonel Moreno received instructions to defend Churubusco, the giant stone-walled fortress which included the old Franciscan monastery and the church of San Diego with its large golden dome that crowned the entire compound.

At first their battalion was sent to the bridgehead on the Churubusco River just behind and to the east of the fortress but then they were moved back to reinforce the front of the monastery. Major Riley had cannons placed behind embrasures along the twelve foot high front wall with a full view of the two roads that converged at the bridge.

Though they were still known as the San Patricios, Santa Anna had reformed Riley's men into a combination of artillery and infantry, officially naming them Mexican Foreign Legion. Those in the infantry unit, lined the front and left sides, muskets ready and bayonets fixed. Patrick and the artillery group including, Jimmy, Micheál and Henry manned their seven cannons. It was a good position. The Americans had to come this way to advance into the city itself.

Seven miles southwest of them, on the other side of the Pedregal, General Valencia, a fat, obnoxious, heavy drinking rival of Santa Anna's, was entrenched near the village of Contreras. He had defied his commander's order to go to San Ángel and stay there. With five thousand men, two dozen cannons and the Pedregal to the east as a secure wall of defense, he was supremely confident he could hit Scott's flank if they came his way. When he received intelligence that the Americans were moving through the rocky terrain, he ridiculed the idea, saying "Not even birds can cross the Pedregal."

Santa Anna moved the rest of the army behind Churubusco and the river, spreading out mostly to the east. Just before two o'clock on Thursday afternoon Patrick heard cannon fire from the vicinity of Valencia's location. The Americans had again done the impossible. One of Scott's young engineers, Robert E. Lee, had somehow forged a path through the southwest corner of the Pedregal and the *yanquis* had gotten behind Valencia. The surprised general engaged them with his twenty-two pieces of artillery, temporarily holding the enemy at bay.

With three thousand troops, Santa Anna went to Valencia's aid. He was halted by another unit of Americans who had made their way through the lava fields and were now between him and his insubordinate general's left. They exchanged fire briefly before Santa Anna inexplicably stopped and pulled back to San Ángel. Later he retreated even further, leaving Valencia on his own. By nightfall rain ended, for the time being, the fighting at Contreras.

Chapter Sixty-Two

Battle of Churubusco, August 20, 1847

It rained all through the night as the San Patricios waited, wishing to be dry inside the monastery. Patrick and the others manning the cannons were lucky to be able to get some shelter under the tarps but it was cold and uncomfortable nevertheless. The thunder, lightning and the frigid, hammering rain seemed like a dress rehearsal for the impending battle.

The rain stopped with the dawn. The sound of renewed gunfire came from across the Pedregal. It lasted no more than twenty minutes. Valencia again defied Santa Anna by refusing to pull back from his position. He stayed put, holding on to the belief that he would have a great victory which would propel him, if not to the presidency, at least to unseat Santa Anna as commander in chief. With the Americans at the gates of Montezuma, the malignant disease of ambition and the thirst for power prevailed even over protection of the nation.

With an apparent change of heart, Santa Anna sent a brigade under General Rangel to go to Valencia's aid but by then it was too late. The rout was on. The Americans attacked from the rear and made short work of them. It was like shooting fish in a pond and those who weren't slaughtered or captured were fleeing in terror up the highway toward Churubusco and the San Patricios. The road, already soggy, turned into a muddy quagmire.

At the time Patrick didn't know anything more than a battle had started a few miles down the road to the west and, for whatever reason there was now a lull. Then he saw the forefront of a mob of *soldados*, stumbling and falling in the mud, running his way.

The other road, the Acapulco Highway, directly south of Churubusco, was guarded by Mexican troops at the small town of San Antonio, bordered on the west by the eastern edge of the Pedregal. But again the Americans found a way through it and got around the town. If they made it to the river and took the bridgehead, the monastery would be under attack from both the front and the left just behind the San Patricios.

The force at San Antonio pulled back to try and beat the *yanquis* to the bridge. They got there at the same time as Valencia's panicked troops. There were too many of them and the crossing got clogged with the frenzied attempt to get to the other side of the river.

For Patrick, the one constant in every battle was the sight of the Mexican Army stampeding away in fright. This time it was far worse for there would be no more battles if the Americans took the capital. The most he could wish for was Alicia's safety because it looked as if he and his fellow deserters would be fighting to the death to prevent them from taking the city.

He saw them coming. Hordes of navy blue coats moving up both roads right at them. The rain was gone and the sun beat down in all its indifferent glory. Their green and white banner fluttered valiantly above them. Patrick and his two cannons were at the corner of the wall, protecting the front and left sides of the monastery.

They had to hold Churubusco at all costs so that their army could get back across the river. Santa Anna had the bridgehead heavily fortified with three cannons and a regiment of battle hardened veterans but it was choked with a thousand *soldados* attempting to get over it.

Major Riley ordered them to hold their fire. The waiting was painful as the enemy came ever closer. They got to within a hundred yards and still

John held them back. When they were no more than sixty yards away Patrick heard the command.

"Fire!"

Even above the deafening roar of the cannons, the piercing shrieks and screams of both men and horses could be heard as grapeshot tore into the enemy, decimating their orderly charge. They clambered for protection in the high stalks of corn in the wet fields on both sides of the road. They fired their rifles from hiding spots and in short order, with a maddening display of discipline and courage, they had a few cannons set up on the waterlogged road.

Patrick changed their aim and his men fired at them. He recognized the big gray horse of Captain Saxon. He pointed him out to Jimmy. They sighted a cannon directly for him and blasted away. When the smoke lifted, Saxon had disappeared from view with the rest of his force but not before they inflicted great damage on the San Patricio infantrymen lining the monastery's parapet.

Patrick watched dozens of his comrades pitch over and fall lifeless off the wall. He screamed in fury and signaled to Jimmy, Micheál, Henry and the others to move quicker. But they were already working as fast as they possibly could.

Major Riley was a force all on his own. Completely indifferent to the bullets and grape coming his way, he moved up and down the line, encouraging the men and changing the direction of their cannons. With uncanny precision the San Patricios wiped the Americans and their cannons off the road and into the cornfields, causing chaos and destruction among their ranks.

The *yanquis* however were relentless and brave beyond belief. More and more of them appeared to take the place of the fallen and were able to get their cannons back into commission and continue shelling from the marshy cornfields. Patrick was sure that his former comrades knew exactly who was inflicting so much damage on them. How could they not with their banner waving brazenly in the sun.

Many of the Americans had the long rifles that were much more precise than muskets and they were picking off the deserters one at a time. But the lads kept at their tasks with focused discipline despite the whining bullets, crashing cannonballs and the dead bodies mounting up all around them.

Riley deliberately targeted any dark coated officer who made himself visible. His artillery, and his men, were as accurate as the snipers back at Matamoros who picked off the fleeing deserters swimming across the Rio Grande. The image came to Patrick of lifeless bodies bobbing down the river. Perhaps John was thinking the same thing. But revenge is for the victors. They had no time to concentrate on anything other than to keep their cannons firing.

The Americans kept coming. They always kept coming, like interminable, unrelenting waves pounding the shore. The San Patricios reacted when a small unit rose up and made a charge toward the bridgehead. Two blue bodies flew in the air as a twelve pound ball exploded right on top of them. The survivors scattered back amidst the corn stalks and into the ditches. The enemy was bogged down though it was hard to tell with the dense smoke shrouding the area. When it would lift or shift, Patrick was able to see the road which had turned from brown to red with flowing blood.

The battle continued for hours. Riley and his men were covered with black powder and grimy from sweat, mud and smoke. His infantrymen were running low on ammunition. Miraculously, a wagonload arrived but it was the wrong caliber for their muskets and therefore useless. They were replenished with ball and grape for their artillery, but cannons alone would not be enough.

As the ammunition ran low, their musket fire slackened. It did not go unnoticed. Seeing their opportunity, the Americans mounted another assault on the bridgehead, ignoring their casualties from John Riley's artillery which couldn't fire fast enough to stop them. They stormed through the twenty foot dike in front of the bridge and up and over to the breastworks. After a brief, bloody hand to hand struggle they took the bridge and in short order raised the stars and stripes high in the air. Then they turned the captured cannons on the monastery. Chunks of stone and shards of glass exploded and rained down on the remaining San Patricios.

Major Riley directed Patrick to turn his two cannons toward the bridge. It gave the Americans exactly what they needed to mount a full attack from the front. Their flying artillery got back on the road and now Churubusco was being assailed from two sides. Two San Patricio cannons were hit and destroyed within minutes of each other. A swarm of blue rose up from the fields on the left. They carried ladders and in no time were climbing the walls. What was left of Riley's infantry, could do nothing. They were completely out of ammunition. They waited courageously for the attack with bayonets fixed.

In unison, like the beating of a giant, ear-shattering drum, the Americans chanted "Over! Over! Over!" as they approached the wall. They came like savage barbarians, scaling the parapets, replacing their chant with wild, deranged screams while shooting and stabbing anyone in their path.

Patrick picked up a musket and swung it like a club as hard and fast as he could, but they were being overwhelmed. Someone raised a white cloth to surrender but Henry ran over and tore it down. They would not be taken alive if they could help it. Henry's body shuddered as it was rippled with bullets and he crumple to his death, still clutching the white flag.

A spark from a musket ball ignited the last of their powder supply. The wagon containing it exploded and three of their lads were engulfed in fire. One of them was Micheál who was screaming and writhing desperately. Patrick ran to him and began to drag him away from the inferno. A bullet crashed through his friend's forehead killing him instantly. His anguish wouldn't allow him to think of it then, but the bullet was a blessing. It saved Micheál from the unimaginable torment of burning to death.

Major Riley pushed and shoved his remaining men, yelling at them to retreat into the monastery. He grabbed their banner as they backed down a long corridor and through a door that spilled into a large assembly hall. They piled furniture they found there against the door. It was a futile effort. The *yanquis* crashed through it easily and poured in after them thrusting and stabbing with their bayonets. Another white flag appeared and this time Patrick grabbed it and threw it to the ground. He slipped and nearly fell on the stone floor, slick with blood from the fallen bodies.

The San Patricios were backed up against the wall. Patrick lost his musket but it no longer mattered. The Americans had bullets, bayonets, superior numbers and they were fueled by a madness for blood. Patrick noticed stairs at one corner of the courtyard and panicked men trying to get to them. It was the last thing he remembered before he was stabbed in the arm and then struck unconscious by a blow to the head.

Chapter Sixty-Three

When the shooting first started, Jane went to be with Alicia at her apartment. She was frantic over Patricio and her brother who had gone to be with his *soldados*. Jane made her some hot chocolate and tried to console her as sounds of cannons and faint musket fire could be heard from Valencia's position at Contreras. They talked about the baby and Jane asked what they might name him or her.

"I haven't thought much about that yet," said Alicia. "I know Patricio would like to remember his parents. I would like to do the same. We'll work it out when the time comes."

It was almost worse for Alicia when the noise of battle stopped. There was no information coming about what was happening. Jane stayed with her and they both spent a sleepless night. The next morning they heard the battle begin again and waited with the rest of the city for any news.

At noon the explosions resumed and it was clear that the Americans were closer. Alicia could not sit still. She paced the small apartment like a caged animal. They went out on the balcony where they could see clouds of smoke rising near Churubusco and the entrance to the city.

"I can't stay here," said Alicia.

"We can't go anywhere," said Jane. "It's too dangerous."

"I must go to the church and pray. It's the only thing I can do."

"I'll go with you," said Jane.

Alicia knelt down in a pew near the front of the chapel and began to recite the rosary. She said it low and fast as if the speed would send her prayers to God faster. Jane knelt next to her and said her own prayers. Inside the church they could not hear battle noises and now Jane was anxious.

Every so often she went outside to listen. The fighting continued but it didn't seem to be getting any nearer.

After a few hours the city fell into an ominous silence. Before too long, young boys came running through the plaza shouting that the war was over. Jane went back inside to tell Alicia. She was still kneeling and praying.

"Alicia, the battle is ended."

Alicia looked up and Jane saw the hope in her eyes.

"Have we won?"

"I don't know. But the fighting has stopped. I'm going to see the bishop. Maybe he know what's happening."

Patrick woke up to complete darkness not knowing if he was in heaven, hell or somewhere in between. He tried to open his eyes but they were sealed tight by sweat, smoke and grime. He moved and felt the pain in his arm and what seemed like the weight of a hundred stones on him. He recognized the clank of chains. *Surely I'm in hell,* he thought. Then came a whisper in the dark. "Patrick."

He wiped at his eyes and was able to unstick the lids a little. They burned and everything was a blur. "John?" he said.

"In the flesh."

"We're alive then?"

"Probably not for long, lad."

He forced open his eyes with his thumb and forefinger. It took some time to get them accustomed to the night. The searing pain in his arm intensified. His shirt was soaked with blood. He touched at the wound. The blood was already caking. He was relieved by that but then the full impact of their situation struck as his senses slowly returned. They were captured and would soon be dead.

Someone had dragged him to the wall with all the rest of the prisoners. He struggled to sit up and put his back against it. Major Riley was on his feet. He appeared to be wounded too but displayed a commanding and imposing presence even here, defiantly letting their captors know who he was. The Americans were screaming at them, almost with the same ferocity as when they were scaling the wall. Patrick set his mind to the fact that he was about to be killed. He prayed to God to take care of Alicia and their baby.

But an American captain, whose name they later learned was James Smith, prevented their assassination. He ended the fight just when they were about to be slaughtered. He put a white handkerchief on the tip of his bayonet and ordered his men to stop. He was a strong and brave officer and his soldiers must have respected him greatly to obey his command and not quench their thirst for vengeance. He prevented, for the time being, their mass execution.

Patrick was forced to his feet and herded with the rest of the captives out to an open courtyard. He saw the tall spires of the capital just a few miles away. There was no smoke or sounds of bombs or gunfire and a relief washed over him that perhaps it was finally all over. They had lost the war and the city, he thought, but Alicia would be spared. If that was the case, he could die a little easier.

Micheál and Henry were gone. At least they wouldn't face the gallows, or be bayoneted right there if Captain Smith could no longer hold his men back. The *yanquis* still wanted blood. He could see it in their faces and eyes. One look of indifference or unspoken approval from Smith and they would have massacred the traitors. But he was a good man and held firm.

Captain Smith had them tied together and they waited there not knowing what would happen next. Patrick looked for Jimmy but didn't see him. He couldn't tell how many of them were left but it was less than half of the two hundred of their battalion who were there at the start of the battle.

He assumed Jimmy was dead and his heart grieved. His cousin would never get to see Oregon after all. Their captors had seized their beloved banner and were parading around and waving it in a taunting manner. They threw it to the ground and stomped on it. One of them unhooked his pants and pissed on it. His fellow soldiers roared and cheered him loudly.

It rained again that night. The prisoners were left in the courtyard, out in the open, guarded by sentries who hoped for someone, anyone, to attempt an escape. Lightning lit them up and they were a ghastly sight. Patrick asked John if he knew what happened to Jimmy. "I saw him make for the stairs. He was running down them but I fear the worst. If he'd been captured they would have brought him here."

Poor Jimmy. Would Aunt Mary and Uncle John ever know of his fate? Would the army care enough to let them know about the death of a deserter, even if they could identify him? Patrick doubted it. They would only be keeping track of their own casualties.

His arm continued to throb but it wasn't serious. Just a gash above the elbow. John was also injured. He didn't remember how it happened but said his shoulder and collar bone were broken. The moaning of others more seriously wounded mixed with the wailing from the casualties still on road and in the fields below them, only to be drowned out every now and then by the roll of thunder. There would be no medical aid coming to them.

They remained in that courtyard for two nights. About a dozen more of their battalion were brought in, caught hiding near the river after escaping down the stairs. Jimmy wasn't among them. They did get food and water and eventually some bandages before being moved out of Churubusco.

In total there were eighty-five captured San Patricios. They were formed up in two columns and secured together by their own artillery drag ropes. Only the most severely wounded were put into wagons. One of them, Francis O'Connor, had both his legs blown off. Patrick couldn't fathom how he was still alive.

They filed out of the monastery like two lines of tethered oxen. Every American soldier along the way cursed, laughed or spat on them as they were paraded through the streets. One group of thirty-nine, including Patrick and John Riley, were taken to an abandoned adobe warehouse in San Ángel. The rest were confined in a similar building a few miles north in Tacubaya.

Chapter Sixty-Four

Bishop Posada met Jane dressed in a plain black cassock. He appeared both anxious and relieved. They spoke in Spanish. "The Americans have stopped the fighting," he said. "An armistice is being arranged and General Scott has agreed not to enter the city. This is very good news."

"Will Santa Anna agree to it?" said Jane.

"I'm sure he will, for the time being at least. I would like to send an emissary to Mr. Trist. Will you take a message to him, Jane?"

"Why, yes, Bishop. Do you know where he is?"

"Tacubaya. He's staying at Ewen MacKintosh's home."

"Will I be able to get through the lines?"

"I'll make my personal coach available to you and Padre Orellana will go with you. It will not be possible today but perhaps in a day or two when things calm down."

Three days later, after an armistice was agreed upon, Jane and Padre Orellana boarded the bishop's handsome coach with his coat of arms on the side. It was pulled by four stout, gray mules. They were stopped at the Churubusco bridge and it looked as if they were going to be turned back until an American major interrupted the sentry and asked what their business was.

"We're representing Bishop Posada," said Padre Orellana. "We have a message for Nicholas Trist. Will you let us pass?"

The major thought about it for a moment. General Scott had made it clear that citizens were to be allowed to move about the city and he was especially insistent that any member of the clergy be given the utmost respect. He looked Jane over and then the priest and allowed them through.

Ewen's courtyard was guarded by a small unit of soldiers. He was not currently there and the soldiers were not inclined to let them see Trist. She and Padre Orellana stepped down from the coach and she was about to try and force her way through when Nicholas appeared on the front porch. At forty-seven years old his full head of hair was graying and he was growing a beard which he didn't have the last time they met. He put a hand up over his eyes to block the sun. When he recognized her he was visibly shocked.

"Jane? Is that you? My God, how did you get here?"

The guard let her pass and they met at the foot of the stairs. "Nicholas, it's good to see you. I've come from Bishop Posada. This is Padre Orellana, his personal secretary. The bishop is anxious to know about the peace negotiations."

They went inside to one of the servant's rooms that Nicholas was using as his office. She relayed to him how and what she was doing there. He told her that General Scott had agreed to halt the hostilities and was ready to negotiate. They had only heard back from Santa Anna that he concurred and would be in contact. As of now, that was all there was to tell.

"Mr. MacKintosh," said Trist, "is attempting to put together a coalition. We would welcome the bishop's participation."

Jane had promised Alicia she would try find out anything she could about her Patricio. "Nicholas," she said. "Have you heard anything of the Irish deserters they call the Saint Patrick's Battalion? Padre Orellana's niece is married to one of them. His name is Patrick Ryan."

Trist was surprised by her question. "Yes, of course. Some are imprisoned here in Tacubaya. The others, along with their leader, Riley is his name, are in San Ángel."

"I must see Riley to find out if Patrick survived. Can you arrange it?"

Nicholas shook his head. "I don't think so, Jane. They're about to be court-martialed, if they're lucky enough to survive until then. General Scott is determined that they receive a fair hearing but the men are ready to take matters into their own hands I'm afraid."

"Please, Nicholas. Padre Orellana's niece is desperate for any word of her husband. Surely it can do no harm."

Trist kept shaking his head. He looked from the priest to Jane and reluctantly decided to agree. "All right. I'll get you a pass, but Jane, this is off the record. We have a lot of American reporters here and we're not allowing them access to the deserters. You have to promise me I won't see an article about them in the newspapers."

Jane did want to speak with John Riley and find out more about his band of Irish deserters, but she didn't think twice. "You have my word, Nicholas. Thank you."

The next day Jane went to the San Ángel warehouse where she showed her pass to the contemptuous sergeant before being allowed inside to meet with John Riley for the first time and to find out that Patrick Ryan was still alive.

Out of the eighty-five captured San Patricios, thirteen were not charged with desertion. They were either Mexican members of the Foreign Legion or European residents who had joined them after being conscripted. They were soon moved out to a different location with other prisoners of war. The court-martials for the forty-three San Patricios at Tacubaya began on

Monday, August twenty-third. The following Thursday the trials for John and Patrick's group of twenty-nine in San Ángel would begin.

Jane's pass continued to be valid and she returned to see Patrick on the day the proceedings started for his group. She spoke to him for nearly two hours while he told her his story. Before she had to leave she wanted to speak to John Riley. She promised Patrick she would return as soon as possible to retrieve the letters he was going to write to Alicia and his sister.

She found Riley writing his defense strategy with the pen and paper she'd brought both of them. "May I ask you some questions, Major?"

"I'm not going anywhere, Miss Storm," he said. "But I'm afraid I cannot offer you a chair."

"I don't mind sitting on the ground. She sat down next to him and asked him outright, "Why did you do it, Major Riley?"

"Do what madam? Leave an abusive Protestant army that was invading an innocent Catholic country? Join a people who would appreciate and reward my talents and abilities? Follow my religious convictions and my Irish heritage to prevent a land grabbing oppressor from conquering a weaker nation?"

"And you recruited others to follow you?" countered Jane. "Convincing them to join and fight with the enemy against their former comrades?"

"Some were comrades, to be sure, but their commanders were our tormentors. And the Mexican people and the Catholic Church may be your enemy. They are not mine."

"What do you mean tormentors?"

"You can interview each and everyone of these lads," he said. "You'll hear the same story of physical and mental torture that had nothing to do with military discipline and everything to do with a sadistic hatred of their race and religion."

"Did you not report them?" said Jane. "Surely something could have been done. Nearly fifty percent of our Army are Irish immigrants, yet they did not desert."

Riley let out a short, humorless snort.

"Not all were bad, but officers protect each other. Discipline is oftentimes harsh. I understand the need for it. But our West Point officers were infused with the hatred and bigotry of what you surely know as the nativist movement in your country. They made it their business to persecute these poor, ignorant lads who were not even given the right of citizenship."

"Will you use these abuse charges as your defense?"

Now Riley did laugh but immediately winced in pain from his broken shoulder. "And would you be telling the Pope that the Blessed Mary isn't the mother of Jesus? No, we all know our fate. We're using drunkenness and kidnapping as our defense but we know it's pointless. They want blood and revenge for our crimes."

"So you believe you're guilty?"

"I'm guilty of following my conscience. My religion and my rights as a human being were deliberately trampled. I saw this invasion of Mexico as the same thing, only against a whole country. Did I encourage others to come with me? Yes. And I'd do it again."

"You were promised land and an officer's commission?"

"There were inducements, just like in the American army; land and a signing bonus. I earned my officers rank based on experience and skill."

"They say you deliberately targeted individual officers with your cannons."

"Casualties are a part of war Miss Storm."

"Are you aware that those who want to see you punished the most are your fellow Irishmen who remained loyal?"

"I understand it. They did what they had to do, as did I. Perhaps they had commanders who were not brutal and vicious. I hold no anger against them for how they feel about me."

A guard shouted to her that it was time to leave. Jane thanked John and said she would be back.

"Better make it soon, Miss Storm. The lads and I have a date with the executioner."

Chapter Sixty-Five

The only question in anyone's mind was whether the traitors would be hanged or face a firing squad. The American military believed that being shot was the more noble punishment. It's quicker and less painful, but no San Patricio had believed they would get a trial let alone be afforded that consideration. Patrick just wanted it to be over and done with so Alicia's suffering wouldn't be prolonged.

Twelve officers sat on each of the two courts. The presiding officer at Tacubaya was Colonel John Garland. He would act as both the main prosecutor and defense counsel for the accused. This was the same for his counterpart, Colonel Bennet Riley at San Ángel. Colonel Riley was no relation to John Riley but he was an American born Irishman and a Catholic. General Scott was determined to create at least the appearance that no racial or religious bigotry would get in the way of justice being served.

By the time of his trial, John had a six page defense prepared. It was written more as a tall tale than anything else and he was actually having fun with it. His story was that he was kidnapped while at Mass and taken by Mexican Lancers across the Rio Grande. There he was brought before General Ampudia who tied him up and put him in the middle of the main plaza in Matamoros. He was given twenty minutes to either join them or be shot.

Abduction became a theme for most of the San Patricios, with drunkenness usually being cited as the cause of their being absent without permission. Intoxication was often given credence as a mitigating circumstance for desertion. Many men in the past had used it to have their punishment reduced and avoid a dishonorable discharge. While some of them were drunk when they fled, this of course was different, and irrelevant to the court since it was war time and they joined and fought with the enemy.

There were two informers used by both tribunals. They testified to seeing everyone of the deserters fighting at Churubusco. This countered the claims of some who said they either pretended to fire their muskets at the Americans or deliberately aimed over the heads so they wouldn't hurt anyone. The informers were immigrants to Mexico and had been conscripted in the Irish Foreign Legion after Santa Anna ordered all males into the military.

Both were with the battalion at the monastery. One, whose name was Thomas O'Connell, was from Ireland. The other was an Englishman named John Wilton. They obviously turned on the San Patricios to receive leniency. Both were paroled not long after the trials.

To Patrick's surprise, Pancho came to see him the day after Jane's visit. He rejoiced at the sight of his brother-in-law walking in the dim warehouse. He stood up and the two embraced. "It's good to see you, Pancho. I feared the worst."

"I was captured at Churubusco as well," said Pancho. "But General Scott paroled all priests the next day. Miss Storm gave me her pass but as of now it's not necessary. Scott has allowed us to have access to all our captured soldiers."

"How is Alicia? Is she holding up?"

"Yes, but she wishes to see you. She says you won't allow it."

Patrick's head and shoulders slumped. He stared at the ground before looking in Pancho's eyes. He physically ached for the sight and touch of her but couldn't allow it. "I don't want her here. I can't have her see me chained up like an animal."

Pancho put a hand on his shoulder. "Si, Patricio," he said. "But think of her as well."

"I am thinking of her." They were silent for a moment. Then Patrick said, "You'll take care of her won't you, Pancho? And our baby."

"Pancho couldn't speak at first. The words choked in his throat and his voice broke when he said, "Of course, Patricio. Have no doubt of that. I will protect them with my life."

Pancho stood to go. Patrick handed him three letters. "I've written Alicia," he said. "Also my sister and my aunt and uncle in Philadelphia. Will you take them and make sure they're sent?"

He nodded and put them in a fold in his cassock. He asked what he was going to do about his defense. "Will you plead not guilty?"

"Yes. I'll say I was taken against my will on my way back from Mass."

"Have you thought about pleading guilty and asking for mercy?"

"I won't give them the satisfaction. I'm not a citizen of the United States so how can I be a traitor to it? I'd gladly plead guilty to falling in love with one of the 'enemy' and of being loyal to her and our unborn baby. I'll put up a fight to the end, no matter how futile. Like the Mexican people I suppose."

Pancho tried again to get Patrick to agree to seeing Alicia. "She is desperate to see you, Patrick. I think we can get her here. General Scott seems serious about showing us that the Americans are not barbarians."

Patrick was visibly torn. Pancho looked into his eyes and saw the agonizing pain he was in. "Just think about it, Patricio. But not too long, eh?"

"I will," said Patrick in a nearly inaudible whisper.

Patrick remained in chains as each day more were taken out for their trials. All came back with little change in their expressions, knowing full well they were doomed. When his day arrived, two soldiers came for him. They unchained him and he was marched at gunpoint across the dirt road into the stuffy, windowless court room. Two lanterns, hung on opposite walls, providing only pale, yellow light.

He stood behind a desk next to the Judge Advocate, Colonel Riley. Twelve officers sat at a long table facing him. Each had a stack of papers, an ink well and a quill in front of him. Most were staring at him stone-faced but with obvious contempt. As his sight grew accustomed to the room he recognized one of them. It was none other than Lieutenant Graves whose eyes bore into him with unconcealed malice.

He was told to state his name, rank and date of enlistment. He gave his rank as corporal in the Mexican Army which didn't sit well with the judges. "Your rank in the American Army," said Colonel Riley.

"Private," he said.

"And your unit?" said Riley.

"Company K, Fifth Infantry."

"How do you plead?"

"Not guilty."

Graves let out a guttural laugh and Colonel Riley called for order. Then he asked Patrick if he had any objections to any of the judges. He had nothing to lose so he pointed to Lieutenant Graves. "Speak up," said Colonel Riley. "That one," said Patrick. "Lieutenant Graves."

"It's Captain Graves now, Ryan," said Graves.

Colonel Riley raised his voice and called for order once again. "What's your issue with him?" he asked.

"I knew him when I was under his command at Matamoros. He was vicious and abusive to my cousin, to me and to many others because of our race and our religion."

Simultaneous shouts of "Objection" came from the row of judges and again Colonel Riley called them to order. Then he asked Captain Graves if he knew Patrick. Graves got to his feet and stood behind his chair. Even in the dim light Patrick could see that his face was red and contorted. His hands gripped the back of his chair so tightly his knuckles whitened.

"This man," he said. "attempted to murder Captain Saxon right before he and his drunkard cousin deserted. He should hang for that even more so than for running away like the coward he is."

Colonel Riley ordered Patrick to be taken out of the room. He thought it was all over but they had him wait outside for a few minutes. When he was brought back in, Graves was gone and there was another officer in his place. He was told to state his case. One of the judges asked why he continued to fight with the enemy instead of trying to escape. He thought about telling them of Alicia but knew that would be foolish. Instead he stayed with his contrived story.

"I was afraid of being shot by the Mexicans for leaving, and shot by you Americans upon my return."

After his testimony he was told to sit down. They brought Thomas O'Connell in to testify. Patrick knew him by sight only. He was with them only a short time before Churubusco. He confirmed that Patrick was one of the San Patricios who manned two cannons in the battle.

After O'Connell was dismissed, Patrick was asked if he had anything more to say in his defense. When he said no he was taken out and walked back to the jail. As soon as they had put the chains on him, he was called to return to the court. He stood next to Colonel Riley and faced the judges. A captain named Ridgely stood up from his spot in the middle of the table with the verdict in his hand.

"Private Ryan," he said. This court finds you guilty of desertion and treason. You violated your oath to the Army and the Constitution of the United States of America. You joined the enemy and fought against the men and country you promised to support and defend. You are hereby sentenced to be hanged by the neck until you are dead."

Chapter Sixty-Six

Patrick was fully aware of what was coming but the words hit like an exploding shell. His legs didn't work properly and he had to be half dragged out of the building, all the time his mind tried to convince him it was all a very bad dream. He wanted Alicia. To see her, touch her, hold her close. He wanted her even more than deliverance from the humiliating and shameful death that was coming. One minute in her presence, he thought, and he could die in peace.

He gained some strength and control. He didn't want to show weakness to the other lads. Then he thought about what it would do to Alicia to see him like this. He wanted her to remember him when they first met. Or at her door in his new uniform, flowers in hand, unsteady at the mere sight of her. He wanted her to think about the first time they made love in Monterrey, and the last time a few short weeks ago. No, he thought, I can't let her come here.

Jane wasn't there when Patrick went for his trial but she visited later that day. He was sitting with his back against the far wall, his head in his hands just like the first time she came to see him. She went over and sat down next to him.

The prisoners still wore their filthy, blood-stained, uniforms but they had been allowed a small amount of soap and water to wash with before being taken to court. With his face free from dirt and grime, she saw how young and handsome he was with his beautiful mahogany red hair and kind eyes. She understood how Alicia fell so much in love with him. She knew the outcome but asked him anyway.

"What was the verdict?"

Patrick only let out a low, mocking sound from deep in his chest.

"Want to tell me about it?"

"There's nothing to tell, Miss Storm, other than the fact that I'm more convinced than ever that Alicia should not be allowed to come here. And please, whatever you do, don't allow her to witness my hanging."

"You can rest easy about that. She's already told me she could never do it."

Two days later John Riley was taken out to go before the judges. They had deliberately saved his trial for the last. He smiled and waved his six pages of testimony at his men. "It'll take them some time to sort through this," he said.

His trial did take longer than the others, close to three hours. He had asked for and was given the chance to call four character witnesses: two officers, a sergeant, and a corporal from other companies whose command he had briefly been under in Michigan. But it was all for naught. They brought him back to wait for the verdict, wearing his ever-present smile. As soon as he sat down after being put back in chains the guards returned for him.

"Riley! On your feet!"

"Well, lads," he said loudly. "I guess it only takes a few minutes to clear an innocent man now doesn't it."

There was subdued laughter. He was still smiling when he returned, not needing to tell anyone the outcome.

Jane continued being the conduit between the concerned Mexican citizens and the U.S. Army via Nicholas Trist. Bishop Posada gave her a letter addressed to General Scott, pleading for mercy for the beloved San Patricios. Through Trist she was able to get an audience with the general to present it to him. He was not pleased to see her again but did so because of his relationship with Trist. What started out with great animosity and indignation between them had turned into a warm, mutual respect. They both strongly desired a quick peace without further death or destruction.

As usual, Old Fuss and Feathers was the picture of military sophistication in his full dress uniform While they spoke his coat was being brushed and decorated with medals by an aide and he looked at the mirror more than he looked at Jane during their conversation. He glanced at the letter. This one was signed by the Archbishop, British merchants, affluent Mexican businessmen and many socially elite women.

"I'm afraid you've wasted your time, once again Miss Storm," he said.

"They beg you to spare the lives of the Irish Catholic deserters."

"I know what they want!" he thundered. "And I have an army and an entire country who want to see them swing by the neck."

"Most of them are ignorant boys," said Jane. "Who I'm told suffered greatly from barbaric commanders because they were Irish and Catholic."

"Thousands just like them, Miss Storm, never ran off or, more importantly, joined the ranks of the enemy. Their leader, I believe his name is O'Reilly, was responsible for countless casualties. *Our* boys need to see that justice is served and Madam, in this case, execution is the right and proper penalty. If I spared them it would not only be wrong, I would have a mutiny on my hands."

She didn't correct him on John Riley's name. It didn't matter, since he took offense at what she next said anyway. "I understand, General. But if you show mercy that might convince the Mexicans to work harder for peace."

With undisguised anger he said, "We've given these people one opportunity after another to choose peace over war. General Taylor let them off the hook in Monterrey and I could have sacked Puebla and done the same to the capital by now. Many of my officers, not to mention President Polk, are condemning me for not finishing them off immediately after Churubusco.

"And did you know," he continued, "that Santa Anna has demanded the release of these St. Patrick traitors as a requirement for peace? He's obviously stalling for time. I'm going to have to end this armistice and take the city by force. Many more good and brave young men will be lost as a result. The deserters will be given a fair trial and I will abide by the verdicts. Tell that to the Archbishop and all the ladies of this country who are so enamored with their Irishmen."

She realized there was no more to do or say. She stood, extended her hand and thanked him for his time. His face softened and he shook her hand courteously and, almost but not quite, apologetically.

"I promise you this, Miss Storm." he said. "I will personally review each and every case. Those men deserve what's coming to them but I want it done completely by the book. They're lucky they weren't assassinated when they were captured and I don't want it said that they were not given a fair hearing."

The condemned waited to hear when their sentences would be carried out. Pancho returned to talk to the men and hear the confessions of those who had the need. All the court-martials were completed by then and the cease fire would be officially terminated later that day. In the meantime General Scott was reviewing all the cases, one by one, just as he'd promised.

Riley wrote a letter to the British Embassy. He tried to convince them to intervene on his behalf citing the fact that he was a British citizen. He also had a letter for his son in Ireland, though he didn't know if he was in Clifden or even still alive.

Seeing Alicia became irrelevant for Patrick when the war resumed the next day. There would be no more access to the condemned deserters. The peace negotiations had turned into a farce, either purposely or through the Mexicans' inability to form a unified consensus. Santa Anna violated the agreement by bolstering his defenses and armaments.

American intelligence determined that metal was being melted down for cannon balls in a foundry at Molino Del Rey not more than a mile from Scott's headquarters in Tacubaya. There was a Mexican force assembled there and he ordered it attacked immediately upon the end of the armistice. It proved to be a brief and costly action, lasting less than two hours with extensive casualties. When they seized the foundry it was discovered that it was not being used to make munitions of any kind. After the battle there was another lull as both sides planned their next moves.

Chapter Sixty-Seven

General Scott had much on his plate yet he diligently reviewed every case. More requests for clemency flooded in to him from high-ranking Mexican government and military officials, foreign European ministers and members of the clergy, including another from the Archbishop. The General had been a lawyer many years before and he was a stickler for proper and legal military justice. He also wished to placate the Mexicans as much as possible in one last effort to convince them that peace could be had before more blood was spilled.

Out of all the trials, only two resulted in acquittals. A fifteen year old boy who was apparently retarded was one of them. The other had never officially joined the army. No enlistment or pay record could be found for him. Of the seventy others, two were sentenced to death by firing squad. On the eve of the executions, Scott's reviews and decisions were finalized but the full details were not made public until they were actually carried out.

Real information was hard to come by but rumors multiplied and spread throughout the capital. The most rampant one was that the Americans had decapitated John Riley and his head was speared on a pike and displayed at Churubusco. Mexicans from every level of society were convinced that the *yanquis* were capable of such cruelty even though General Scott did everything he could to declare that he would never allow something like that to happen under his command. Still, the rumor persisted and was believed by many.

Jane was able to meet with Nicholas Trist one more time. He had no further information on the struggle to attain peace but he did tell her that the first executions were to be held the next day in the Plaza of San Jacinto in

San Ángel. Then he gave her some news that she couldn't quite believe. John Riley had been given a reprieve. He would not be hanged. He had no word on the fate of any of the others so Jane decided not to tell anyone. She would go to the hangings and witness the executions herself.

After Molino Del Rey, the pause in the fighting allowed for what appeared to be every general in the American Army, along with their entire staffs, and thousands of regular soldiers to be present for the executions. The only one who wasn't there was Scott himself.

General Twiggs, thick-necked with white hair and a string of whiskers that covered his jowls and square jaw was given command of the executions. Fourteen years later he too would be condemned as a traitor by the U.S. Army after he seized a federal fort for the Confederates when the Civil War broke out.

It had rained nonstop throughout the night, ending just before dawn on the morning of September tenth. Patrick, unable to sleep, listened to the steady downpour that reminded him of the fierce squalls back home in Ireland. The soldiers came for them at first light. He heard the key in the lock and the voices of the guards yelling at them to get on their feet as if it were a paralyzing dream. He didn't think his body was capable of moving.

John Riley, even now, was a source of strength. "Time to go, lads," he said. "Let's show the bastards what brave Irishmen look like."

John extended his hand to Patrick. He took it and was pulled up on his feet. He had to force himself to take a step and when he did he pitched forward. He had the fleeting memory of getting off the ship in New York with his sister, followed by the thought that he failed to protect her like he'd failed in everything else.

The guards formed them into two lines, sixteen in one and seven, including John and Patrick, in the other. The remaining four were told to remain in the jail without being told why. They would soon learn that their demise would only be delayed. All of their hands were tied together in front of them. Most were in a daze and the soldiers had to push and shove them forward, out the door. Near the plaza, the cobblestone street was still wet from the night's rain. A few of them slipped and nearly fell over. Patrick wasn't the only one whose legs weren't working properly.

John Riley, striding confidently with his shoulders back just like he did in every battle, encouraged his men. "Steady, lads," he said. "It'll be over soon and we'll be in heaven with the angels."

Patrick gained some strength at the sight of his friend and hero and he too straightened up and tried to will himself to be brave. It was only a few blocks to the plaza and as they entered it he heard the long, peal of a hundred drums. The square was lined with a multitude of Mexican citizens, with many more huddled together on the roofs of buildings.

The line of sixteen prisoners was marched to an open grassy area a hundred yards off the plaza. Padre Pancho was there with four other priests, all of them dressed in full white vestments with gold trim. The deserters were halted in front of a monstrous, ghastly scaffold, forty feet long and fourteen feet high. Sixteen long ropes dangled from the crossbeam. Underneath were eight mule-drawn wagons with a Mexican driver seated and holding the reins on each of them. The priests went down the line of men, blessing them all and administering the last rites.

Jane had a clear view of the entire area from her place on the crowded front steps of the church of La Paroquia de San Jacinto. A chill shot up her spine when the long, slow drum roll pierced the somber air. She watched the prisoners being marched out to the gallows. Two were hauled up on the end of each wagon with the rough assistance of soldiers. They stood there with the nooses dangling above their heads, still dressed in their squalid Mexican uniforms. It was a wretched sight yet Jane was relieved, though apprehensive to see that neither Major Riley nor Corporal Ryan were among them.

Patrick didn't understand why he wasn't with those by the scaffold but thought it was only a matter of time before he was taken there. His group was marched into the center of the plaza, a short distance in front of the church. The steps of the church and the area immediately around it were filled with more citizens, mostly weeping women holding small wooden crosses high in the air or silently praying the rosary.

They were stopped in front of General Twiggs who was struggling to keep his unruly mount still. Off to the left, Patrick saw his old commanders, Saxon and Graves, sitting smugly on their horses in front of Company K. Twiggs held up his hand and the drumming ceased, replaced by a deathly stillness. In the silence, Patrick's mind flooded with a vivid vision of a laughing, running, red-headed boy with Alicia's dark eyes and sweet smile. It brought a sense of calm over him.

He watched his sixteen comrades being manhandled and thrust up under the ropes, two to each wagon. A soldier waited there for them and one by one their heads were covered with a white hood before the nooses were lowered and tightened around their necks. Seeing his friends like that, hooded and facing death in their squalid army uniforms was more than he could bear. He had to look away and prevent himself from retching.

When the sixteen were secured in place there was another long drum roll. A mounted captain rode up next to Twiggs and the drums stopped. The captain called for the soldiers present to stand at attention. Patrick was

371

intensely aware of every sound and movement. The slap of boots coming together and arms hitting their sides reverberated in his ears. The quiet that followed was broken only by the soft sobs of the women surrounding the church.

Twiggs got his horse under control and pulled out a scroll of paper. He unrolled it and addressed the throng.

"By the order of the Commanding General, Winfield Scott," shouted Twiggs, "the following men are to he hanged by the neck until dead for the crimes of desertion, treason and taking up arms against their own country."

Twiggs then read the names of the sixteen waiting on the wagons. When Patrick didn't hear his name, or John's, his attention sharpened. He gave a sidewards glance to John who made no movement or expression whatsoever. Twiggs continued.

"General Scott has further ordered that the remaining seven are to be whipped, branded and imprisoned for the crimes of desertion, treason and joining the enemy. The General has determined that since they deserted prior to the declaration of war, they are not deserving of a death sentence."

Patrick wasn't sure he heard it right. A current of surprise rippled through the Mexicans in attendance along with a rising roar of outrage from the soldiers and officers that mixed with a rush of blood and disbelief in Patrick's chest and head. He turned fully to face John who gave him one of his familiar smiles along with a wink of his eye.

When Twiggs finished, seven soldiers took hold of Patrick and the others and took them to a stand of trees near the church and tied each of them to one. They ripped their shirts, stripping them to the waist. Twiggs then announced they would receive fifty lashes and then be branded with a "D" so the world would forever know their crime.

Seven Mexican muleteers, brandishing eighteen inch long, knotted rawhide whips stepped forward to administer the floggings. General Twiggs had deemed the traitors unworthy of being whipped by American soldiers. Patrick still had difficulty understanding what was going on but all he could think of was that he just might get to see Alicia again.

The muleteers' whips snapped in unison with the first lashes sounding like the crack of lightning. Wide gashes opened on every back and blood splattered with each stroke. Their flesh became as bloody and raw as sides of mangled beef. Although he tried to endure it without showing pain, Patrick couldn't do it. He grunted and moaned with each slashing strike. He went in and out of consciousness but he didn't scream out. Neither did John Riley or the others. It was a show of strength and courage that belied their indictments as cowards.

General Twiggs in a display of malevolent vindictiveness, claimed to have lost count of the number of Riley's lashes. He ordered the muleteer to apply more, nine more to be exact. Jane with her close view from the church steps, didn't think any of them, let alone John Riley, would live through it. She learned later that Twiggs had offered a fifty dollar bonus, paid in gold, if Riley was killed during the whipping. John stayed upright longer than the others but eventually he slid down the tree in a heap.

When the whippings were over, buckets of water were thrown on the men and to nearly every one's amazement, all seven were revived. Seven soldiers went to a small fire and pulled out white-hot cattle branding irons in the shape of the letter "D." Three were to be stamped on the hip while the others, Riley, Patrick, John Daly and Thomas Cassaday were branded on their cheeks. None of them were able to conceal their suffering this time.

Jane heard the sizzle and smelled the awful stench of burning flesh.

She was happy that Alicia was not there to see it but thought she may have been able to hear the screams. They bellowed across the square and quite possibly could be heard as far away as Constitution Plaza.

Twiggs again showed a level of vengeance that was uncalled for, though it spoke for the outrage of most American soldiers. He rode over, dismounted, and inspected the "D" on John's face. He announced that it had been applied upside down. He ordered Riley branded once more on the other side. John screamed again and slumped into unconsciousness when the second iron crackled and hissed as it was rammed on to the other side of his face. Everyone thought that surely he had perished this time.

But John Riley was a man of incredible strength and endurance. More water was thrown on him and he was forced to his feet with the others. They had trouble staying upright, Riley most of all, so more soldiers came and held them on either side. They were dragged to the front of the gallows, followed solemnly by Padre Pancho and the other four priests. Patrick couldn't hold his head up straight, it rolled around as if he had no neck and he wasn't able to focus his vision or his attention on anything other than the incomprehensible pain that consumed him.

Another long drum roll signaled that the hangings were to begin. The priests moved from one wagon to the next, blessing the men one last time. The muleteers moved from the drivers seat and climbed up on the saddle-mule of each wagon. The animals were restless and braying. Twiggs issued the order and the carts lurched forward sending fifteen of the men to their deaths. One man, whose name was Dalton, suffered greatly. He writhed and thrashed in convulsive spasms, like a monstrous fish dying on a line. It took several long, horrifying minutes until he slowly choked to death.

The reprieved seven were then shoved to their knees. The same soldiers who branded them now approached with razors in hand. More soldiers came over to hold them down. Their heads were shaved in a manner that was more like a scalping. When it was finished they were yanked up, their heads ripped and bleeding like the mangled flesh on their back and issued one final order from Twiggs. They were required to dig graves for nine of the comrades.

Patrick couldn't even hold on to the shovel at first. He pitched over, his stomach hitting the end of the handle preventing him from going all the way down. He tried to focus but he fell more than once. Each time he was descended upon and manhandled up. Somehow he and the others completed their morbid task.

As his mind began to clear, the pain of putting his friends in their graves, right under the gallows, with the nooses still tight around their necks was worse than the physical agony he was in. Seven of the deceased had requested, and were given, a Catholic burial in consecrated ground. They were loaded in a wagon and taken to the church cemetery.

When it was finally over they were hauled off back to their jail. As they shuffled off a group of fifers piped out "The Rogues March." It sounded stridently light and airy but was a taunting tune after all, used to drum out disgraced soldiers from the army. There was no singing but every soldier present knew the refrain:

Poor old soldier, poor old soldier
Tarred and feathered and sent to hell
Because he wouldn't soldier well

It was a gruesome exhibition from start to finish. Part of Jane had believed they deserved a death sentence but after getting to know Patrick and Major Riley, and witnessing the punishments in person, her heart felt differently. Every Mexican she talked to believed them to be heroic martyrs. She couldn't go that far but they deserved a more honorable death than what they received. At that moment though, she thought only of Alicia and wanted to rush to tell her the news that her Patricio had been spared.

Chapter Sixty-Eight

The Final Hangings, September 13, 1847

Alicia wasn't at her apartment when Jane arrived there. She went to the cathedral and found her kneeling in the front pew, her hands clasped together on the railing and her head bowed and resting on them. She was crying quietly and didn't move when Jane spoke her name. She said it again. "Alicia dear."

She turned her tear-stained face. "Is it done?" she whispered.

Jane moved in and knelt next to her. She rested her hand in the middle of her back. "He has been spared."

It didn't register in her mind or on her face. "He was not hanged, Alicia. He was whipped and branded with a hot iron but Patrick lives, as does John Riley."

Alicia shook her head, trying to clear it and make sense of her words. "What are you saying? How is that possible? He was sentenced to die."

"He deserted before America officially declared war. It was a technicality that General Scott believed prevented him from giving some of them a death sentence."

"Patricio lives? He will not be executed?"

"Yes," said Jane. "I saw it all. Sixteen were hanged. Seven, including Patricio, were reprieved. After they received their punishments they were forced to bury nine of those who were executed, then they were marched back to their jail."

Alicia slumped forward. Jane went to hold her up, thinking she had fainted, until her body shuddered in sobbing spasms. After a few minutes, she leaned over and collapsed into Jane's arms, still shaking uncontrollably. When she regained some composure she turned and looked at Jane, tears streaming down her cheeks and her eyes shining. "God forgive me. I didn't even pray for his life, only that it be quick and painless."

"I know," said Jane, stroking the back of her head. "I know."

"Is he coming to me. Will he be freed?"

"Not yet. He and the others are to remain imprisoned. Hopefully only until the war is over."

"Can I see him? I must see him."

"Not now. The fighting will soon start again. I was lucky to make it out of San Ángel and it was difficult getting back into the city. But I don't think it will be much longer, one way or the other."

"Then he is not yet out of danger?"

"No he isn't. None of us are really. The next few days will tell. If your army can somehow defeat the Americans I don't know what might happen. He could actually be safer if Mexico falls. If Scott's army is defeated, his men might not abide by his decision and take their revenge anyway."

"I have to go to him."

"In time, Alicia. It's not possible now. Let's hope it's over soon and he remains safe."

They stayed and prayed for a while in the chapel. On the way back to her apartment Alicia remembered something. "I have some more good news," she said.

"What's that?"

"Patrick's cousin is also alive."

"Jimmy?" said Jane

"You know him?"

"Patrick told me about him," said Jane. "What happened? He said Jimmy died trying to escape from Churubusco."

"He hid in the cornfields and along the river. He made it to the church of Regina Coeli and was given sanctuary and a hiding place. The priest gave him a cassock and a wide brimmed hat and together they came here to me. The Archbishop has taken him in. He has a pallet in a small storage room deep in the basement of the cathedral"

"That is excellent news," said Jane. "Patricio will be very happy to hear it."

The four remaining San Patricios from the San Ángel jail were hanged the next day. It wasn't clear why their executions were not performed with the others, most likely it was due to not having enough mules and wagons available. Patrick, Major Riley and the others who were spared were forced to attend and dig their graves as well. Two days later, at the final hangings of the remaining thirty deserters they had to do it again.

The break in the fighting was over and Scott's army was again on the move, attacking Chapultepec Castle, the home of the Mexican Military Academy. Despite orders to stay out of the combat area, Jane decided she would witness the execution. Alicia insisted on going too. Jane tried to discourage her but she refused to take no for an answer.

"I'm going, Jane," she said. "With you or by myself. I must see Patricio, even if it's from a distance. I believe what you've told me but I need to see for myself that he's still alive."

"You don't want to see the hangings, Alicia," said Jane. "It's something you will never be able to forget. And Patricio may not even be there."

"I understand. If he isn't, I'll know he's still safe. If he is, maybe he will see me. I know it will give him strength."

General Scott reduced eight more sentences, confirming the death penalty for thirty of them. The executions were to take place at dawn on a small rise outside Mixcoac, a village just south of Tacubaya. From the scaffolds there was a clear view of the Chapultepec fortress and its grounds which encompassed three quarters of a mile and towered at the top of a two hundred foot hill just over a mile away. The Americans began shelling it the day before and would continue this day.

Jane and Alicia rose at four and started out. There were no passes or authorization allowed while the fighting persisted but they made their way through the city joining what resembled a religious pilgrimage. Hundreds of candle bearing women, from all classes of society, walked and prayed silently, mourning the martyrdom of their brave and holy Irishmen. The American soldiers didn't enforce their restrictions and allowed them through to the hanging site.

They reached Mixcoac as the sun broke the horizon. Jane was happy for Alicia's sake that they were not able to get close to the gallows. They stood in the middle of the somber throng a hundred yards from the hill where thirty nooses dangled from a long scaffold above fifteen wagons.

They watched the condemned men march out at bayonet point, their hands tied behind their backs. They were loaded up, two to a wagon, and one by one the nooses were pulled tight around their necks. Cannon and musket fire exploded in the distance as the Americans resumed the bombardment of Chapultepec.

The officer in charge of the hangings, Colonel William Harney, went into a vehement tirade as soon as the men were placed in the wagons. Neither Jane nor Alicia could hear his words but it became apparent that there was one rope without a prisoner under it. A mounted officer approached, spoke to the colonel briefly, then rode off.

A few minutes later he returned, followed by a small horse drawn cart carrying the last deserter, a man with no legs. It was Francis O'Connor. That he wasn't dead already defied logic, but he surely would be soon enough if left alone. Harney didn't care. His orders, he said, were to hang thirty men and he'd be damned if he didn't comply.

General Scott's choice of Colonel Harney to oversee these executions was one more deliberate statement to his army. He was a red-headed, Catholic Irishman who couldn't wait to send the deserters to their deaths. Scotts troops, were still furious that Riley and the others had escaped with their lives. Harney fully represented their hatred and thirst for retribution and he would inflict as much pain and humiliation as possible.

Harney's own men feared and loathed him. He was a disciplinarian in the manner of Saxon and Graves with a penchant for tying immigrant soldiers up by their thumbs. His command lost as many or more to desertion than even Saxon's and now he was going to make sure the traitors did not go tranquilly to their deaths. Most of the rank and file American soldiers were in complete support of his actions despite their lack of respect for him.

When O'Connor was placed on the wagon, his noose was lowered to accommodate his lack of legs. One of his irreverent Irish mates told him he would now be able to dance with them when they were at the end of their ropes. By then it was almost seven a.m. and all thirty were in place.

381

It was a warm day. The sun came out and beat down hard on them. Insects buzzed around, landing and crawling on their faces and exposed skin. It was a torture made worse by their hands being tied together and not being able to swat them away. There would be no white hoods covering the heads of this group.

The shelling of Chapultepec was in full force. Harney loudly proclaimed that the deserters would witness another American victory and the vision of the stars and stripes being raised before he sent them to hell. One of the condemned men raised his voice and said something. Jane didn't understand him but read an account later that he shouted to Harney, "If we won't be hung until your dirty old flag flies on the castle, Colonel, why then we'll be living to eat the goose that'll fatten on the grass of your own grave."

Harney dismounted and climbed up on to the wagon. He drew his sword and smacked the man on the mouth with the broad side of it. The man spit blood and a few teeth out yet he smiled broadly in Harney's face.

The morning dragged on, getting hotter by the minute. The crowd of onlookers remained silent. Alicia prayed with her rosary all the while looking for Patrick. Jane spotted Major Riley first. He always stuck out in a crowd. He stood tall, with unconquerable dignity, off to the side with Patricio and the others. She pointed them out to Alicia who burst into tears when she saw Patricio. He was too far off to get his attention so there was nothing to do but wait and watch. She would not be at ease until it was confirmed he would remain alive at the end of this day.

Musket fire echoed across the valley and the explosion of cannons moved the ground below them. The minutes crawled by as clouds of black smoke billowed over the castle. At nine o'clock the deserters had been standing there for three excruciating hours with their hands and feet bound and their necks chafing under the nooses. It was hard to make out anything in detail but Jane saw a flood of blue slowly but surely move up the cliff and over the walls of Chapultepec Castle.

The Americans continued scaling the walls of the fortress and everyone, including the prisoners, knew that it wouldn't be long now. A sober procession of five priests, Padre Pancho leading them once again, walked to the front of the gallows. Harney didn't stop them. He pulled out his telescope and trained it on the ramparts of Chapultepec. The noise from the battle suddenly subsided and all talking and praying stopped around them. A muted cheer was heard from the battlefield. The crowd watched the stars and stripes appear and flutter atop the highest tower of the castle clearly indicating the final defeat of Mexico.

Then a remarkable thing happened. The doomed men of El Batallón de San Patricio, ropes choking around their necks and about to be plunged into oblivion, raised a cheer of *vivas*. Jane was deeply moved by their bravery and insolent contempt right up to the bitter end.

Harney bawled out to the mule drivers and they flicked their whips. The fifteen wagons lurched forward and thirty bodies were launched in the air, swinging, kicking and banging into each other until all went limp and lifeless in the brilliant morning sun. An officer withdrew his sword and rode over to cut them down but Harney stopped him. His orders were to hang them, he said, not unhang them. With that he dismissed his troops. When they were gone, Alicia watched with sorrow and pity as Patrick and the others trudged over to take them down and perform their burial detail.

Chapter Sixty-Nine

Acordada Prison, Mexico City, September 20, 1847

Patrick and the surviving San Patricios were sent back to their warehouse jail. No visitors were allowed at first but soon General Scott gave priests permission to see the prisoners in his continuing effort to reassure all of Mexico and the world that he had no intention of harming their religion. Padre Pancho came to see them and assured Patrick that Alicia was fine and in no danger.

Two days later guards burst into the warehouse, shouting for them to get on their feet. Patrick immediately feared the worst. This time they would not survive. Major Riley rose to his full six foot four inch frame and confronted them. "What's this then?" he demanded.

"Shut up and line up," ordered a burly sergeant. "All of you."

Patrick and the others got up slowly. One by one all seven were fitted with eight pound iron collars locked tightly around their necks. The collars each had three, foot-long spikes on them. Then they were chained together and pushed outside. It took a moment for their eyes to adjust to the bright light of the morning sun. Except for John Riley, they were all afraid.

"What's happening," said John Daley

"They're going to kill us for sure this time," said Tom Cassaday.

Patrick remembered that Pancho told him of rumors that they might be transferred to a different jail. "We're being moved I think," he said, "To a real prison."

"Or marched to our death," said Daley.

"I doubt they would take the trouble to yoke us like this if that were the case," said Major Riley.

They were paraded through the streets, drawing sympathetic crowds as well as hateful stares from the American soldiers they encountered. Patrick remembered the slaves he'd seen in New Orleans being marched to auction. The difference was that the people here cared about them and their fate. He thought about Henry with a pang of grief for him, Jimmy, Micheál and all the other friends and comrades who were gone.

Five hundred Mexican prisoners of war were incarcerated in the main section of the two-story Acordada prison. The San Patricios were taken to a large cell on the second floor where an American sergeant and two privates guarded the door. Their chains were removed but the neck collars remained in place. Soon they were joined by those from Tacubaya whose sentences General Scott commuted.

Each morning all fifteen of them were tethered together again and sent out for a day of hard labor. Their shackles were removed while they repaired bridges, structures and removed debris from the war torn city. At the end of the day, the collars were put back on and they were marched back to the prison.

Within a few days the outrage from the citizens, the city government and the Mexican Peace Commission influenced Scott to order the barbarous collars removed. He also allowed virtually unlimited access to the deserters, further infuriating his troops. But he wanted a peace treaty and he wanted it soon. There was an election coming up and a victorious general who secured an enormous amount of conquered territory would almost be guaranteed the presidency.

With the restrictions lifted, Alicia came to see Patricio. She brought him clean clothes and some tamales. When she saw him she couldn't control her tears. Though he was dirty and unshaven she clung to him, never wanting to let go. He kissed her gently so as not to besmirch her beautiful face but she would have none of it. She pulled him closer and kissed his mouth, forehead and finally the raw, red scar on his cheek. "My poor Patricio," she whispered.

"I'm alive, Alicia. It's a miracle." He reached down and touched the growing bulge of her belly. "How's our little one? How are you?"

"We're both fine. What's going to happen now? When will you be freed?"

"I don't know. Our guards tell us we'll be taken to New Orleans and put in prison there. Others think we'll be let go once a treaty is done and the Americans leave. But I won't wait for that."

"What do you mean?"

He looked around before answering. Only one guard was inside, over by the door, but he didn't want anyone else to overhear them. Then he whispered to her, "I'm going to escape."

"But how?"

He put his finger to her lips. "I don't know yet but I can't stay here and wait for who knows what to happen. When I do, we'll need to leave the city."

She didn't say anything more. She was willing do anything he asked whether it meant leaving her country or becoming a fugitive in the mountains or the desert. When it was time to go she told him she would be back tomorrow, "With some of the pork, chili and rice you like so much."

He smiled and they kissed one last time. As she headed for the door she stopped and ran back to him. "Patricio! I almost forgot." The guard was watching now so she leaned in and told him in a low voice, "Your cousin,

Jimmy, he lives."

He was stunned and didn't believe what he was hearing. He took her shoulders in his hands and looked into her eyes. "Jimmy's alive?"

"Yes, Patricio. He escaped and made it to a church. The padre dressed him in priest garments and brought him to the cathedral where he's still in hiding."

It took a moment for him to grasp it. Then a smile lit up his face. "Jimmy, he said and laughed. "Dressed as a priest." It was at that moment that Patrick knew how he was going to attempt his escape from Acordada prison.

Pancho came by later that afternoon and Patrick told him his plan. They huddled in a corner. "I have to escape," he said.

Pancho nodded as if he was hearing a confession, then said "Is that wise, Patricio? There is much talk and negotiating going on. Wouldn't it be better to wait for peace? General Scott sentenced you to prison until the end of the war."

"I won't wait any longer. I can't. Soldiers have told us we won't be freed. We'll be taken to New Orleans and put in prison there. And even if they do let us go, who knows when that will be or what Santa Anna will do. I'm still a soldier in the Mexican Army after all."

Again the priest nodded. "There are three guards right outside the door, Patricio. And *yanqui* soldiers are stationed on nearly every corner. Not to mention all the guards on the first floor."

"Can you bring me one of your cassocks?" said Patrick. "And one of your large hats?"

A slight smile crept across Pancho's face. "I can do that. But then what? You'll still have to get past the guards and as I said, there are soldiers all around the city."

"Perhaps you or Alicia can bring some dye or grease for my hair to make it black. The hat will cover most of my face and hopefully my scar."

Pancho nodded. "So you'll just walk out of here?"

"Yes, God willing. As if I'm a simple padre leaving after caring for the prisoners."

"Is it worth the risk, Patricio? "If you're caught that would be the excuse they need to hang you like the others."

Patrick didn't hesitate. "Yes. It is. They may yet find a way to execute us anyway, or transport us back to America to waste away in some other prison where priests or wives are not given access."

"Does Alicia know about this?"

"I told her I was going to escape, but nothing more yet."

"Where will you go?"

"To the apartment at the cathedral first. After that, I don't know where or how. I was hoping you might help with that too."

Pancho looked around the room. It was twenty or so feet wide and thirty feet long. Large but not so big that the guards wouldn't easily notice a missing prisoner. He brought his attention back to Patrick. "When are you planning on doing it?"

"As soon as possible. I think it would be best to leave in the evening, after a day of labor. You could come as usual and bring the clothes. I'll leave while you stay behind for an hour or so until I can get far enough away."

"*Esta bien*, Patricio. Let me think more about it. But the apartment is not safe. The Americans are using the National Palace as their command post and they're as numerous there as bees around a hive."

Patrick nodded and said, "Thank you, Pancho, but please don't delay."

Padre Pancho made the sign of the cross over his brother-in-law and started toward the door.

"One more thing," said Patrick, a smile spreading on his face. "I'm told Jimmy is alive and hiding in the cathedral. We need to make sure he joins us."

Pancho nodded and smiled back. "So I've been told. I'll go see him," he said. The guard opened the door and took no notice of him as he walked down the long hall to the stairway, thinking that maybe it was a good plan. He'd make sure to wear his own shovel hat from now on when he visited.

Chapter Seventy

Pancho went directly to see his cousin, Arturo, to ask for his help. He found him at the small room he occupied while Alicia used his apartment. Arturo made them each a cup of tea and they sat at a table underneath a crucifix, where he told him of Patrick's plan.

"This must be kept secret," said Pancho. "There are spies everywhere."

"Si, Francisco. Don't worry. Where do they intend to go?"

"He doesn't know. I was thinking that Saltillo would be best. We have friends and family there who could help."

"But the American army still occupies the entire area," said Arturo. "And there are guerrillas all over the country in between. Perhaps he can hide in the apartment or the cathedral until the peace is settled."

"That could take months, maybe even a year at the pace they're going. And Santa Anna may rise up yet again and come back to try to regain the city. There are many who want to continue the fighting."

They were silent for a moment. "You know," said Arturo, "I have an uncle, my aunt's husband, who received a land grant in Alta California a few years ago. He has a rancho at a place called Castac. It's north of the Pueblo de Los Angeles."

"But the Americans have seized California," said Pancho.

"Yes but the territory is immense and sparsely populated. From what I understand they're only occupying the port cities."

"How would they get there?"

"We can smuggle them out in a mule train heading south for Acapulco. From there they can find transport up the coast. Perhaps our

British friends can arrange for a ship. There's been little ground fighting in the south so once they're away from the city there won't be any Americans along the road."

"*Yanqui* ships control the coast of Baja and Alta California do they not?"

"True," said Arturo. "But Acapulco is no threat to them. There's been little resistance and the fort there is in ruins. English and other merchant ships still sail freely. I think it's the safest route for them."

"Where would they have to land to get to this Castac? And how far would it be from there?"

"I'll find out for certain but I believe it would be San Diego where there's a mission, or San Pedro, and from there a journey of not much more than a hundred miles. We can provide them enough money to pay for any transportation they might need. The mission lands and property have been secularized and taken from the Bishop's control but there are still priests at the churches who can assist them."

"What will happen to your uncle's land when the Americans own California outright?"

"General Scott has gone out of his way to respect private property so maybe their government won't confiscate it. There are many ranchos in California. It would be hard to seize all of them without more fighting. But nothing can be predicted. You'll have to tell Patricio and Alicia of the risks and let them decide."

Pancho thought about his sister. Would it be better to wait until the child was born or go now when she was still able to travel? He wanted to be certain she was in agreement with her husband. He left Arturo and went directly around the corner to her apartment. Miss Storm was visiting with her. When he knocked at the door he heard them chatting lightheartedly with the knowledge that, for now, Patricio was safe.

Pancho smelled meat frying when his sister opened the door. She had a luminous smile on her face. "Francisco," she said. "You're just in time for dinner. Come, sit down. Did you see Patricio today?"

Jane was sitting at a table, chopping vegetables. She said hello and gave him a slight wave before she used her apron to wipe the burning tears out of her eyes caused by the onions she was cutting. Alicia went back to the small stove and stirred her simmering pork.

"I did," said Pancho. "He is well."

The two women looked at him, expecting him to say more. When he hesitated, Alicia was instantly worried.

"What is it, Francisco? Has something happened?"

"No, he's fine."

Jane was aware that he had something on his mind, something he wanted to say to his sister. "I should go," she said. She started to untie her apron but Alicia stopped her.

"Stay, Jane. We'll eat and then prepare plates for Patricio and Major Riley."

Jane glanced at Pancho and then back at Alicia. "I think your brother wishes to speak with you alone."

"Whatever there is to say, Francisco, you can say it in front of Jane. I trust her completely and you should too."

Pancho thought about it for a moment more before deciding to go ahead. "*Bien*," he said. Patricio told you he wishes to escape, yes?"

"Yes," said Alicia. "And Jane and I have talked about it. It seems he's told you as well."

"He has a plan. There are many details to work out but I wanted to know your feelings. It would mean you'll have to leave Mexico. Have you thought about that?"

"I have, *mi hermano*. I will go with him. Anywhere. He has suffered enough."

"And what if he's caught?"

"I'll pray that doesn't happen. Just like I've prayed for his safety, and yours, throughout this horrible war."

"He could remain hidden here," said Pancho. "Or somewhere else in the cathedral. Until the Americans leave."

Jane decided to say something. "Padre, there is no telling how long the peace process will take or if it will even be successful."

"He needs to be free," said Alicia. "We both do." Then she patted her stomach and smiled. "We all do."

"I've talked with Arturo," said Pancho. "He believes going south to Acapulco is the safest place to travel. Once there, you can catch a ship to California. His uncle has a large rancho where you'll be welcome. But it will be a long, difficult and dangerous journey."

"Francisco, I have traveled hundreds of miles to be with you, and then Patricio. I've been with the camp followers near the battlefields and have cared for the wounded and dying *soldados*. What could be more dangerous than that?"

"But you were not with child then?"

Alicia went to her brother and hugged him tightly. "We'll be fine, *Tio Pancho*. I am strong and so is our baby. But who will take care of you? I think you should come with us. Surely they need priests in California too."

The thought had never occurred to him. His work was in Mexico.

His people needed him. But he didn't say no. He kissed her on the top of the head and then looked into her eyes. "Then you agree? This is a good plan?"

"Yes," she said. She turned to Jane. "What do you think?"

"California is a boundless territory," she said. "It shouldn't be difficult to conceal yourselves and your identity there."

"Then it is decided," said Alicia. "When do we go?"

"Soon. Stay ready. When the time comes you'll have to go quickly."

Chapter Seventy-One

Cathedral Basement, Mexico City, September 27, 1847

Jimmy needed air, and to see the sun. More than that, he needed a drink. He'd been confined like a prisoner for nearly a month. The nun, Sister Maria, provided him with fresh clothes and regular meals that were delicious but she flatly refused to get him anything stronger than tea and appeared to be insulted when he offered her the few pesos he had if she would get him some *mezcal*.

He knew Americans were occupying the capital. He was able to understand Sister Maria when she indicated that the *yanqui soldados* were all over the plaza and the surrounding area of the cathedral. He'd heard the explosions and the distant sounds of skirmishes as enraged Mexicans waged guerrilla warfare from every corner of the city. That only lasted a few days before General Scott was able to force them into an uneasy submission.

He was elated when Padre Pancho came to see him. The nun led the priest down to the basement to the tiny room he occupied. "This one is driving us mad," she said. "He wants to know what's going on every minute of the day. Can you believe it, Padre, he even asked me to get him some *mezcal*."

Jimmy was just about at his breaking point when he heard the footsteps coming down the dark stairway. He rushed to Pancho and shook his hand, pumping it vigorously until the priest was able to get him to let go. "Padre," he said. "Have you come to get me out of here?" Jimmy kept going before Pancho could answer. "An American woman, came to see me. Said she was a friend of Alicia's and that Patrick survived. Is it true? Can it really be true?"

"He lives, Jimmy," said Pancho. "And so does John Riley."

Jimmy sank into his one chair and put his head in his hands. He looked up at the priest, his eyes wet. "I didn't dare believe it," he said.

"It's true, Jimmy. And we're planning his, and your, escape."

"When? Where are we going? How much longer do I have to remain in this cold basement?"

"We're working out the details but the plan is to get you to Alta California. That's all I can tell you now. You must be patient."

"I'll try, Padre. But I don't know how much longer I can stay here doing nothing. I need fresh air. Can't you and I go for a stroll like two priests contemplating Jesus? Isn't there a quiet neighborhood nearby where no one would take notice?"

Pancho moved toward the stairs to leave. "It's much too dangerous, Jimmy. Besides all the American soldiers, there are thieves and desperados roaming the streets who would be willing to murder you for being a *gringo* or turn you in to the army for a bottle of *mezcal*."

Jimmy sighed and nodded. He stood and took Pancho's hand in both of his with a firm, grateful grip. "Thank you, Padre. Speaking of *mezcal*. Do you think you could bring me a bottle? It's stifling down here and the sweet sister absolutely refuses to oblige me."

The priest smiled. "I'll see what I can do. But you must let go of this idea of leaving here until the time is right. It will happen soon."

"Not soon enough, Padre." As he disappeared up the stairs, Jimmy called after him, "And please, don't forget the *mezcal*."

When three days passed and Pancho hadn't returned, Jimmy couldn't take it anymore. There hadn't been any more sounds of violence from above for quite a while so he decided to risk it. He put on the cassock and pulled the shovel hat down over his forehead to cover the hideous scar. He went up the stairs quietly.

His first concern was the pesky nun. He got to the main chapel without being detected. There were a few peasants and a couple of wealthy old women kneeling in prayer. They took no notice of him, even though he neglected to genuflect and make the sign of the cross when he hurried by the crucifix above the altar.

He went to the side entrance and cracked open the heavy wooden door. A shaft of sunlight nearly blinded him and he closed it. He waited a minute, then pulled the hat down further, lowered his head and went out into the afternoon sun.

The street was off the main plaza and little more than an alley. He headed left, away from the square, breathing deeply and feeling the blessed sun warm his back. He had to prevent himself from stopping, turning around and removing his hat to let his face bask in it. He made two more turns, one right then one left, lifting his eyes to study landmarks so he could remember how to get back. There was a butcher shop with a red door at the first turn.

When he made the second turn he was on a wider dirt road lined with rundown shacks and small businesses. He raised his head slightly and saw that there were no soldiers, only small Mexican men balancing terra cotta pots filled with sweetmeats, and other food items on their heads. Women in faded shawls who looked like indios, their black hair tied up with ribbons, were gathered together with their baskets of vegetables and fruits, pausing to exchange news and gossip.

In a short while, he saw what he was looking for, a *pulqueria* with hanging beads for a door. He heard the faint strings of a guitar from inside.

He glanced around. When no one seemed to take notice, he pushed apart the beads and went inside.

It took some time getting used to the darkness. The guitar stopped and he could feel eyes on him. He stepped further inside and was able to make out the shape of the man behind the bar. Then he saw the guitar player, sitting alone in the corner and two other men together at a table in the middle of the small room.

They all stared at him. Not because it was that unusual for a priest to be in a *pulquería*. They knew right away that something was out of place with this priest. The bartender was instantly suspicious. In Spanish he said to the others, "What is this?"

Jimmy went to the bar. He lifted the brim of his hat slightly and looked the man in the eyes. "*Hola, Padre,*" said the bartender. He waited for Jimmy to respond.

Jimmy only spoke a few Spanish words but he knew how to order a drink. "*Pulque, por favor,*" he said.

The bartender poured the drink and slid it over with his left hand. With his right, he reached under the bar and pulled out a revolver. He pointed it at Jimmy's chest and thrust out his jaw, his mouth in a curled snarl. Then he said, "*Un gringo, no?*"

Jimmy froze. He was so concerned about Americans he hadn't considered that, right now, most Mexicans in the city would welcome the opportunity to kill any *yanqui*. He blurted out the first thing that came to his mind. He pointed a finger at his chest and said, "San Patricio."

A flicker of recognition crossed the bartender's face. He looked closer at Jimmy, now with interest instead of animosity. A wide smile broke out across his face showing a mouthful of yellow-stained teeth with a wide gap between the front two. The guitar player stayed where he was but the other two came up to the bar and looked him up and down, clearly curious about what he was doing there and why he was dressed as a priest. Everyone knew that most of the captured San Patricios had been hanged.

The three of them started talking all at once. Jimmy had no idea what they were saying but he knew he was in a friendly place. He pulled a few pesos from his pocket and slapped them on the bar. "*Gracias,*" he said.

The bartender shook his head, picked them up, said "*No, amigo,*" and handed them back to him.

The two men slapped him on the back and shook his hand. The guitar player came over, raised his glass and said "*Viva los San Patricios,*" and the others repeated it loudly.

Jimmy realized it wasn't a good idea to announce who he was, even in here. He put a finger to his lips and waved his hand up and down his cassock then moved his finger back and forth in front of him and they all got the message.

"*Si, Si,*" said the bartender. "*Silencio.*"

As soon as he finished his drink, another appeared. He tried to communicate with them and explain how he'd survived the battle but couldn't make them understand. He took off his hat and showed them his scar. He rubbed it and said *yanquis*. He gave up trying. It didn't matter anyway. He was welcomed and soon the invigorating effects of the alcohol took over.

His mood improved with each sip. Patrick was alive and with any luck, they would be getting away. His thoughts drifted to his nearly forgotten dream of Oregon. He stayed in the bar for a couple hours, until the sun was setting. He had to get back. He pulled out his pesos again and with gestures toward a bottle, asking to buy one to take with him. The bartender grinned, gave him the bottle and refused once more to take any money.

He walked to the beads at the door and in a brief panic, realized he didn't remember if he should turn left or right. He turned back to his new friends, raised his hands palms up and said, "cathedral?"

The bartender spoke to the guitar player who said, "*Si,*" and set aside his instrument. He put on his sombrero, came over and motioned for Jimmy to come with him. Jimmy waved at the bartender and said, "*Gracias, amigo.*"

It was dusk and the streets were alive after the day's siesta. Jimmy was loose and feeling good but careful enough to pull his hat down low. He hid the bottle under his arm, beneath the cassock, and kept his eyes on the guitar player's serape and sandals. He glanced up every now and then looking for any sign of soldiers.

Within minutes they were in Zocalo Plaza. The guitar player must have taken a different route because the cathedral was off to the right. They should have come up the alley to the side entrance if they had gone the way he had taken. The hair on his neck went up when he heard the unmistakable sound of marching boots and military commands in English. His guide stopped as the soldiers paraded right in front of them. He cursed under his breath.

He stood as still as a statue but wasn't able to refrain from taking a quick look. He tilted his head and looked out of the corner of his eye. The Americans were constantly on the alert for snipers or any sign of an attack from buildings or within crowds and so kept on high alert while moving through the city. At the exact moment that he looked up, Sergeant Adams, leading his old Company K, was looking right back at him. Jimmy lowered his head instantly and instinctively pulled on the brim of his hat. But it was too late.

Adams wasn't sure who he saw. But he recognized something in the strange-looking priest who was definitely not a Mexican. He called his troops to a halt. Jimmy was sober in a second. His heart raced. He saw the cathedral but he would have to get around Company K to get there.

"You there," hollered Adams.

At the sound of his voice, Jimmy took off. Running to the rear of the troops, he got around them and darted through the bustling plaza on a right angle to the church. He made it to the main entrance and burst through the doors.

Adams ran after him but by the time he got there Jimmy was already out of sight, running down the stairs to the basement. He searched through several of the chapels before giving up. He knew that face and after some reflection was reasonably sure it was the Irish deserter, the one named Torpey who had tried to kill Captain Saxon. When he got his men back to the barracks, he sought out Saxon who was now a brevet lieutenant colonel after receiving field promotions for bravery and distinguished conduct.

"Are you sure it was him?" said Saxon.

"Not completely, sir. Whoever it was, he wasn't a Mexican priest and he ran as soon as I called out to him."

Saxon went right to General Scotts headquarters at the National Palace. He wanted authority to search the cathedral but Scott refused. He would not anger the Bishop while the fragile negotiations for peace were going on. Saxon decided to go to the church to investigate the suspicious priest himself.

He sat in a pew in the middle of the main chapel, disgusted by the golden statues and the excessive images of false idols for every occasion or malady. He wanted to force his way into every corner of the building but knew that would anger his commanding general and not help his career, despite his battlefield prowess. Instead, he waited and watched.

After thirty minutes of no activity other than peasants coming in to pray, he left. He summoned Sergeant Adams and ordered him to place a guard at the church with instructions to look for a priest, any priest, who did not appear to be a Mexican. When days went by with no sighting of anyone suspicious, Saxon went to Acordada Prison to confront Torpey's cousin to find out if he knew anything.

Chapter Seventy-Two

Chapultepec Castle, October 11, 1847

Pancho recruited more priests, besides Arturo, to help with Patrick's escape. He had them make regular visits to the prisoners, telling them to always wear the same black cassocks and broad shovel hats. Often two or three were there at the same time. The guards complained of so many visitors but General Scott continued to allow unrestricted access.

He contacted the respected muleteer, Martín Mendoza. He was the one who had whipped John Riley at San Ángel. Despite the offer of gold from General Twiggs if Riley died, he had held back as much as possible with his strokes. He was filled with shame over his part in the affair and refused to take any money for helping Patrick. He vowed he would get them out of the city and safely to Acapulco. They would meet at the Church of Regina Coeli. It was a few blocks southwest of Constitution Plaza in a quiet neighborhood with little to no American presence.

The date was set for the escape. It would be Thursday, October the fourteenth. Alicia visited everyday leading up to it and Jane went as often as possible. She was busy with the Archbishop and citizen committees petitioning Trist and Scott but she had grown to care deeply for Alicia and wanted to help the young couple escape to a better life. She planned on being at the jail when Patrick made his escape to possibly create some additional diversion.

Alicia wanted to be there as well but they all thought it an unnecessary risk, especially Patrick. "Alicia," he said. "If things go wrong there could be violence. I won't jeopardize you or our baby. I'll come directly to you when I'm free."

She wanted to argue but realized it was for the best. "I'll meet you at the church," she said. "according to the plan."

Patrick had one important task before making his escape. He needed to tell John. For the first time he truly felt like a deserter, abandoning his friend, protector and leader. He wanted him to come with them but he would have to find a way to break out on his own. There was no way the two of them would be able to just walk out of the prison, especially someone the imposing size of Major John Riley. He waited until the Monday before he was to make the attempt to finally tell him.

They were sent out to the Chapultepec Castle to clear up debris from around the walls and grounds. It was midmorning when he finally got up the courage. They paused from loading another wheelbarrow with chunks of stone and wood. Patrick wiped his brow with his shirtsleeve and said, "I have something to tell you, John."

Riley rested his arms on the handle of his shovel. "I've been waiting to hear it, lad. It's been obvious you're planning something. You can't have been going to confession all those times you huddled in the corner with the padre."

He was about to tell John everything when he noticed a rider approaching out of the corner of his eye. A familiar fear shot through him when he recognized the rigid and unbending figure riding a big bay horse. "Look who's here," he said to Riley.

John looked up and made contact with the cold, black eyes of their former commander. A look of pure loathing came over Saxon's face. He turned to Patrick and said, "What do you think he wants?"

"Looks like we're about to find out," said Patrick.

Saxon spurred his horse over to the pile of stone and wood they were removing. At Acordada he had been informed where the prisoners were working for the day. Patrick and John stopped what they were doing and stood straight and defiant. Their guards were about to confront them when they saw the lieutenant colonel approach and signal them to back off.

John stepped forward and Saxon rode right up to him, not stopping until the bay's snout was touching Riley's chest. It reminded Patrick of the last time that happened back in Corpus Christi, right before John was bucked and gagged.

John gave him his biggest smile and said, "What brings you here on this fine day, Captain?"

Saxon ignored the insult, knowing full well that Riley saw the insignias of his new rank, but it was obvious he'd like nothing more than to unsheathe his saber and run him through with it.

"Out of the way, Riley," he said. "I'm not here to see you."

"What do you want then?" said John.

"Stand aside and keep your filthy Irish mouth shut. I'm here to speak to Ryan."

John stood his ground for a moment but there was nothing he could do but obey the order. No one would question the killing of a prisoner of war who threatened an officer. He went back to the pile of rubble and continued working.

Saxon turned his horse slightly and looked down on Patrick. "Where's your cousin, Ryan?" he said.

Patrick didn't know what to expect but it wasn't that. He hesitated, trying not to show any emotion. When he responded, he said, "He's dead. Along with your slave and every other lad from Company K who joined us."

"Where did he die?" said Saxon.

Patrick balled his fist, suppressing his anger. He supposed Saxon could strike him down or at the least make things worse for him and he couldn't have anything thwart his escape plans.

"At Churubusco, where we were captured."

Saxon studied him closer. "Did you see him fall. Did you see his body?"

"No," said Patrick. "I was stabbed and knocked unconscious. He was killed while trying to escape."

Saxon stared malevolently without saying a word or moving a muscle and Patrick almost believed he could read his thoughts. He held his gaze for a moment and then said, "Is that all, Captain?"

"I think you're lying, Ryan. I think Torpey lives and I believe I know where he's hiding. When I get him, he won't escape the noose this time, and perhaps neither will you. You're not out of this yet."

Patrick said nothing. Saxon narrowed his eyes even further waiting for Patrick to say something. When he didn't, Saxon pulled the reins tightly, turned his horse and galloped away.

Patrick watched him until a guard yelled at him to get back to work. He took his shovel and started pitching rocks angrily into the barrow. John didn't say anything. After a few minutes Patrick finally spoke. "He knows Jimmy's alive."

"Looks that way, lad," said John.

"How could he?"

"I don't know. Someone must have seen him."

"This could ruin everything," said Patrick.

"Don't you think it's time to tell me what you're up to?" said John.

"I'm getting out," said Patrick. "I have a plan."

"I hope it's a good one."

"I believe it is. I'm going to dress as a priest and walk out with other visitors Thursday evening."

"Just like that then?"

"Yes, if all goes well. Just like that."

"And where will you go?" said John.

"Jimmy and Alicia are going to meet me at a church. Padre Pancho has a muleteer who'll take us out of the city and to Acapulco with his mule train. From there, a ship to California."

"Need I remind you, Patrick. You're still a soldier in the Mexican Army. You enlisted for five years, remember?"

"Just like I enlisted in the American Army."

John nodded. A guard approached and they stopped talking. Patrick lifted the handles of the wheelbarrow and walked it to the edge of the wall, dumping the load down on to the large, growing pile of rocks and rubbish. When he returned he went back to shoveling and said, "Are you saying I should find Santa Anna and return to our unit?"

"We're still a battalion," said John. "The San Patricios have reformed under Santa Anna and he'll need men either to fight if the peace talks break down, or to maintain order when the Americans leave."

Patrick didn't say anything right away. There wasn't a chance in hell he would go back to the army, not unless he was forced at gunpoint. "I'll not be doing that, John," he said.

"Nor did I think you would. But it's something you must consider. Don't get caught by the Americans, or the Mexicans."

"Then you approve?"

"Aye. You're a brave man, Patrick, but you're not meant to be a soldier. And this war has been anything but honorable, on either side. You need to take care of your wife and child. I'd do the same in your position."

Patrick was surprised at the relief he felt. "I was hoping you might join us. Maybe you could find a way to escape too or come to California later on when this is all over."

John reached up and rubbed the scar on his right cheek. The scabs were almost gone but it was still purple and painful. He shook his head slowly. "I'm a soldier, Patrick. It's all I know and what I do best. I'll stay here and rejoin Santa Anna or whichever general takes his place." He let out a short laugh. "Who knows. I may make general one day myself."

"There would be no finer one, John, in any army."

"What can I do to help?"

"I was thinking you could divert the guards somehow."

"How about a lovely song," said John. "One like Micheál used to sing, eh? We'll get the lads together as you're making your way to the door. We'll give you a rousing rendition of "The Minstrel Boy." It would be a fitting sendoff don't you think?"

"Indeed it would, John."

Chapter Seventy-Three

Acordada Prison, October 14, 1847

Patrick was nervous marching back to the prison on Thursday. His stomach had been in a knot from the moment he woke up and now it was so bad he had trouble standing up straight. He had a hard time thinking of anything but all the things that could so easily go wrong. Padre Orellana, wearing his wide hat, was already there when they returned. Patrick rubbed his wrists when the chains were removed and tried to calm himself. He hoped this would be the last time he was ever shackled or imprisoned.

They had decided that Pancho would meet Alicia at her apartment and together they'd get Jimmy and go directly to the Church of Regina Coeli. Once Patrick got there, Mendoza the muleteer would come and escort the three of them to his house near the south entrance of the city. In the morning they would move out with his caravan of mules.

Jane arrived a short time later carrying a plate of tortillas. She was dressed in typical Mexican fashion, wearing a red and blue *rebozo*. Her dress had a very low neckline, revealing a good portion of her breasts which never failed to attract the attention of the guards. She acknowledged Patrick with a quick nod before mingling and talking with the other prisoners.

Two more priests wearing their shovel hats showed up a little later with two young women who also brought food. It was a few more than normal number of visitors but not enough to arouse concern. One guard stood inside by the door, indifferent to anything other than sneaking glances at the pretty señoritas. The other two remained out in the hall, playing cards as they normally did unless some officer happened to come by. Nothing seemed out of the ordinary.

At fifteen minutes before six, John went over to Patrick. There would be no handshake or display of sentiment. They had already said goodbye. "I'll have the lads move over," said John, "between you and the door so you can put on your priest clothes. Then we'll sing."

"Thank you, John. God bless you."

"Be safe, lad."

Tom Cassaday, John Daly and four others came over. Patrick went behind them near the back wall. Padre Orellana, holding his hat in his hand, joined him and brought out a folded cassock from under his robe. Patrick glanced at the guard who wasn't paying any attention and then he bent over and slipped on the cassock. His hands trembled buttoning it up.

Arturo then handed him a small container of grease. Patrick rubbed it in his hair and then added a thin layer over the red stubble on his face. He took the priest's hat and put it on, pulling it as low as possible. Then Arturo took off his glasses and handed them to him. "Put these on," he said. "It will help with the disguise."

At that point, John Riley shouted out, "Let's have a song, lads." A chorus of "ayes" came from the rest of the San Patricios. They came together in the center of the room.

The glasses made Patrick's slightly dizzy, intensifying the fearful nausea in his gut. He took a deep breath, nodded to John and then Padre Orellana. The Major sang the first verse alone. His stirring baritone voice filled the room.

"The Minstrel Boy to War is Gone.
In the Ranks of Death Ye may find Him."

Jane sauntered over in front of the singers. Padre Orellana walked over and joined her. Meanwhile the two señoritas moved near the guard on his left side. They smiled flirtatiously and moved their bodies slowly to the song that now the rest of the San Patricios were singing with Major John Riley. Padre Orellana made a show of smiling and blessing the singers. Jane clapped enthusiastically as she made her way to the door, motioning with her head to the guard that she was leaving.

Patrick pulled the hat as low as it would go over his right eye and then tilted his head that way. The blood pounded in his temples and his heart thumped so hard he thought it might be heard over the singing. When he was nearly to the door he turned to the men he had spent the last two years with under the most trying conditions. A calm come over him. He smiled at them all then he raised his right hand high above his head and made the sign of the cross.

Jane stopped to speak to the guard as he opened the door for her. He leaned in to hear her and perhaps get a closer look down her dress. "They sound like God's choir don't you think?" she said. He curled his lip and shook his head. Padre Orellana waited for Patrick to turn around. When he did, they went to the door together making sure Patrick was on his left side. They got past the guard without him noticing anything amiss.

In the hallway, Jane dropped the empty plate she was carrying and it broke in pieces on the floor. Arturo bent over to help her pick them up and one of the guards got out of his chair to help as well. The other one didn't even look at Patrick as he walked casually to the stairway. He paused for a moment, out of sight in the stairwell, until Padre Orellana caught up to him. He listened to his San Patricios still singing heartily as he and Arturo walked down and then out of the prison on to the streets of Mexico City.

411

"His Father's Sword he hath girded on,
With his Wild Harp slung along behind him;
Land of Song, the lays of the Warrior Bard,
May some day sound for Thee,
But his Harp belongs to the Brave and Free
And shall never Sound in Slavery!"

The song would never be far from his mind and in time he would sing it to his children and grandchildren when he told them the story of John Riley and the St. Patrick's Battalion.

The private assigned to watching the front entrance of the cathedral would rather have been on a work detail than on this unending monotony of looking for some phantom priest to appear. He paced back and forth in front of the church trying to stay alert. His shift would be up in half an hour when he could have a glass of whiskey with some of the boys and maybe write a letter to his sweetheart back in Ohio. He did notice the beautiful girl walk in the church with a tall, thin Mexican priest but didn't give them a second thought.

A few minutes later, Sergeant Adams came by with his relief, another reluctant private. They moved over to the corner of the building. "See anything," said Adams.

"No, Sergeant, nothing unusual."

As he was about to be dismissed, the private saw the señorita and priest come out with a second priest who most certainly wasn't Mexican. He pointed to them and said, "Not until now."

Adams recognized him immediately as the one he'd seen last time.

He still didn't know for sure it was Torpey but he wasn't about to take any chances. The three of of them were walking briskly in the opposite direction.

"Come with me," said Adams. "Both of you."

"But, Sergeant, I'm off duty."

"Not anymore, you're not."

They followed them from a short distance. Darkness was falling and lamplighters were out with their long ladders, lighting the turpentine street lamps of the city. Within fifteen minutes they watched the three of them walk up the short steps of a church and go inside. Adams told his men to keep watch. "Don't let them out of your sight. If they leave, follow them."

Adams went directly to Saxon and told him what happened.

"Was it Torpey?" he said.

"I'm pretty sure, but it was getting dark. Whoever it is, he and his accomplices are up to something."

"Gather up a few men and meet me back here. We'll find out what's going on."

Chapter Seventy-Four

Patrick was walking too fast as they left Acordada Prison.

"Slow down, Patricio," said Padre Orellana.

He wanted to run, like a retreating and panicked *soldado* but realized, like he did after Jimmy tried to kill Saxon, that they had to act as normal as possible. He slowed to a painful, unhurried pace. He also fought the impulse to look around. He did take Arturo's glasses off and give them back to him. "Now both of us can see," he said.

It was only a mile to Regina Coeli but it felt like ten. It was dusk when they arrived and Patrick forgot caution and ran the last few yards and up the steps. He threw open the doors and saw Alicia standing next to Jimmy. She rushed over and they held each other close. When Patrick raised his head and saw Jimmy smiling from ear to ear he couldn't help but do the same.

Alica stepped aside and the cousins hugged each other and laughed.

"You look much better as a priest than I do," said Jimmy.

"I prefer it to an army uniform," said Patrick.

"So do I," said Jimmy. Then he got serious. "What happens now?"

Patrick looked to Pancho and Arturo who were standing together in the center aisle.

"Señor Mendoza should be here any minute," said Pancho. Then he reached down to the pew and came up with an armful of clothes. "Put these on. If your escape has been discovered they'll be searching for a priest. With these you'll look like a couple of Mendoza's muleteers."

Patrick put on canvas pants and a long serape. Jimmy removed his cassock and did the same. Then Pancho gave them each a bandana and a sombrero. Alicia helped them tie the scarves on their heads.

When Saxon and Adams arrived at the church the guards reported that two more priests had come and gone inside. They seemed to be in a hurry but that was it. Saxon moved his men to the side of the building across the street and mulled over what to do. He wanted to break down the doors and charge inside but he was an officer in the United States Army, not a Texas Ranger, and General Scott would have him court-martialed if he invaded a church, even if he had good reason.

He sent Adams and three men to guard the back of the church. While he was thinking about his next move, two men with three mules approached in the flickering light of the lone street lamp on the corner. They stopped at the church steps and one man went inside.

As Alicia finished tying Patrick's bandana, the doors swung open and Manuel Mendoza walked in. He was a large man, not in height, but in every other way. His hands, his head, his shoulders and his bull-like torso indicated clearly that he was not a man to trifle with. He nodded to them and said, "Amigos." Then, in English, "Are you ready? We need to move out."

Alicia began to cry softly. She went to her cousin. "Thank you, Arturo, for everything."

He took her cheeks in his hands and kissed her forehead. "We'll miss you, Alicia. Very much. Write when you get to Castac."

"I will," she said. Then she went to her brother, standing with his arms at his side and a look of profound loss on his face. When she got to him she clutched him around the waist and buried her face into his chest, letting her tears stain his cassock. He enveloped her in his arms and rocked back and forth.

"Come with us, Francisco," she said, looking up at him.

He kissed her on both cheeks. "Not now, Alicia," he said. "Maybe in the future but I have to remain here, at least until this war is truly over. Let me know when you're settled, and tell me whether I have a niece or nephew."

Mendoza was anxious to go. "Now, señora, please." He had four more men with him besides the one holding the mules. They were positioned around the neighborhood like typical peasants loitering on the street except each of them carried two pistols under their blankets.

The group moved to the door and went out on the front steps. A slim sliver of the crescent moon was rising in the eastern sky. "I've brought mules for you to ride on," said Mendoza.

One of Mendoza's other men appeared. He hurried up the steps and spoke to him. Patrick heard the words *yanqui soldados* and saw the look of fear on Alicia's face.

Mendoza rushed down to his mules and opened one of the saddlebags. He brought out two pistols, ran back up the steps and gave them to Patrick and Jimmy. "Inside!" he said.

As soon as Mendoza got to them an all too familiar voice rang out from the darkness. "All of you, stay where you are."

They ignored the command, went inside and secured the door with a long piece of wood. Jimmy looked at Patrick in disbelief and said, "Was that Saxon?"

"It's him," said Patrick.

"How did he find us?" said Jimmy, though he instantly thought of Adams seeing him and knew that had to be it.

"I don't know how he found us here," said Patrick. "But he came to see me a few days ago. Said he knew you were alive."

"Damn him," said Jimmy.

Patrick stared at his cousin, seeing the guilt on his face, neither of them speaking until Jimmy said, "Adams saw me."

"When, Jimmy? How?"

Jimmy looked away, not able to say it to Patrick's face. "I snuck out to find a drink. I shouldn't have done it."

Patrick was too worried about Alicia and their situation to get angry. He spoke to Mendoza. "Can we go out the back?"

"Soldiers are there."

"How many?" said Patrick.

"Four, maybe five. I have men back there. We can rush them but we should do it right away."

Patrick shook his head. He couldn't risk Alicia getting shot.

"I've fouled things up again," said Jimmy. "Does he know you've escaped?"

"I don't know. I doubt he could have found that out already."

"I'll give myself up," said Jimmy.

Patrick wanted to tell him no, that they'd made it this far and somehow would find a way out. He thought that if they both surrendered without a fight at least Alicia would be spared. "I can't let you do it alone," he said.

"You can and you will," said Jimmy.

"Alicia's safety is all that matters," said Patrick.

"What matters is that you live too, Patrick. It's what your Da would want. You know he'd tell you that. The survival of your family, his family is what's important. Land and a farm was what he thought would insure that but in the end he'd want his seed to grow."

Patrick said nothing. The image of his father came to him and for the first time the shame of failure was gone, replaced by the absolute conviction that survival was all that mattered.

Alicia stood with her brother and cousin, fear and dread on her face and in her eyes. She came over and stood next to her husband. She didn't speak but it was clear she agreed with Jimmy.

"I'll tell Saxon I'll surrender once you're all safe and away from here," said Jimmy.

"What if he won't bargain?" said Patrick.

"I'm sure he will. It's me he wants."

They heard the noise of men on the steps of the church followed by a bang from the butt of a musket on the door. Then Saxon's voice again, "Open up Torpey or we'll come in and get you."

Jimmy went close to the door. "Back away, Saxon and I'll come out. But not before my friends are allowed to get away safely."

There was silence for a minute. The sound of retreating footsteps were heard and then Saxon said, "Send them out, hands where I can see them."

Alicia went to Jimmy and hugged him with all her might.

"You take care of him, Alicia."

"With my whole heart and soul," said Alicia.

Mendoza approached. "Can we trust this *gringo*?"

"We have no choice," said Patrick.

Patrick and Jimmy faced each other. "I told you I wouldn't make it out of this alive, cousin."

"They won't hang you for desertion," said Patrick. "And you didn't kill Saxon so if it's a fair trial you should only get prison time."

Jimmy took off the serape put his cassock back on. He put his gun in the sash around his waist, opened the door a crack and shouted, "they're coming out."

"Leave the pistol, Jimmy," said Patrick.

Jimmy gave him a sad smile and said, "Write my Ma and Da. Tell them how sorry I am."

"I will. Just surrender. Please."

Mendoza came to them and said, "It's time." He pulled the piece of wood halfway out so that he could slide it back if necessary. He opened the door a few inches and waited. Then he opened it all the way and went out first with his arms raised.

Patrick took hold of Alicia's hand and followed close behind them, the sombrero low on his head. Pancho and Arturo brought up the rear. Patrick took Alicia behind one of the mules and then went to the other side, making sure he was between her and the soldiers. The muleteer led them away.

When they were around the corner and out of sight Patrick called out for them to stop "Manuel," he said. "Where are the rest of your men?"

As soon as he asked, four men appeared brandishing their pistols. Patrick motioned for them to follow him. He went to the edge of the building, holding up his hand for them to wait. He saw Saxon and a group of soldiers standing in a line behind him.

Patrick took out his gun and said to Mendoza. "Maybe we can still save him."

"No señor," said Mendoza. "There are too many."

Patrick turned his attention back to Saxon as he called out to Jimmy. "Come out Torpey. Now!"

The door opened and Jimmy walked out.

"Hands up," shouted Saxon.

Jimmy went slowly down the steps, ignoring the command.

Saxon shouted again, "Put your hands up, Torpey!"

Patrick wanted to unload his gun on Saxon but knew if they started shooting Jimmy would surely be killed and most likely he and Alicia too. He watched his cousin move slowly toward Saxon, looking him in the eyes and smiling, just like he did when he walked out of the pit at Fort Texas, right before he was branded. Jimmy started to raise his hands. As he did so, he pulled the pistol out.

One of Saxon's men saw it and shouted, "He's got a gun!"

Jimmy broke into a run, right for Saxon. He raised the pistol and fired as he ran, hitting Saxon in the chest and then the throat. As their commander went down the soldiers shot in unison and Jimmy fell to his knees, his gun firing another shot in the air before he crashed face first onto the dirt road. Patrick shouted and was about to run to him but Mendoza grabbed him in both his arms and pulled him back.

"It's too late, amigo."

Patrick took one last look. Jimmy was laying next to Saxon who was on his back. Both of them were dead. Mendoza released him as Alicia rushed into his arms. "I'm so sorry, Patricio."

Patrick said nothing. He held Alicia close and turned his head toward Mendoza. They nodded to each other and the muleteer led the way down an alley and then on to a quiet side street. They walked to his house a few miles outside the city, near Tacubaya.

When they were bedding down, Mendoza came over and put a hand on Patrick's shoulder. "We leave first thing in the morning." He paused a moment and then said, "I'm sorry about your cousin. He's a very brave man."

Chapter Seventy-Five

Pancho and Arturo decided to spend the night at Mendoza's. In the morning, they said their final goodbyes, both promising they would see each other again some day. Arturo gave Patrick two letters.

"One is from Bishop Posada. It's addressed to any priest you may encounter. Along with the missions of San Gabriel Arcángel and San Fernando Rey there is a church in the Pueblo of Los Angeles where you may find assistance. The letter advises them to assist you in any way they can. The lands and property of all of the missions have been sold off but the churches there still have a priest and conduct services.

"Do not go to the San Diego mission. We've been informed that the American army has confiscated the grounds. We don't have any current information on San Fernando other than my uncle's rancho at Castac is about a two day ride on horseback north of it."

"Thank you, Padre," said Patrick.

"The final letter is for my uncle. His name is José María Covarrubias. At one time he was the mayor of the Pueblo de los Angeles so it should be easy to get into contact with someone who can take you to his rancho. I've already written him that you're coming but one never knows about the mail to California, especially during these hard times."

Pancho joined them. "I know you will protect my sister, Patricio."

"With my life, Pancho."

"Be cautious. Alta California is a vast territory but the Americans own it now. We know they control the ports and the main towns so those will be the most dangerous areas. You should be secure once you get to Castac."

Patrick nodded and said, "We'll get word to you when we arrive."

They shook hands. Pancho embraced his sister one last time and he and Arturo departed into the graying light of dawn.

Mendoza brought four men and six mules, loaded with fabric and leather goods, on the journey. Patrick and Alicia rode next to him in the lead. There were two roads to Acapulco. The more direct route went through Cuernavaca but he chose the slightly longer way through Cuautla. It was the safer of the two. There were less bandidos and though the Americans had seized Cuernavaca during the fighting, they had moved on to the capital. The two hundred thirty mile trip took fourteen days. A little slower than Mendoza would have normally travelled but he wanted to make things as easy as possible for Alicia.

After a few days on the trail, Patrick was finally able to relax somewhat. Until then he kept expecting the American cavalry to sweep down upon them. He grieved for Jimmy but all he had to do was look over at his lovely, pregnant wife and he was filled with hope and happiness. That didn't stop him from worrying about her. They still had a dangerous road ahead and he knew she was feeling weak and sickly despite her efforts to hide it.

She tried to put his mind at ease. "Patricio, have you forgotten how far I traveled with the army?"

"Yes, but you weren't pregnant then."

She gave him a loving smile. "You worry too much. We're fine."

Acapulco had once been a thriving seaport but ever since the Manila galleons stopped their voyages over twenty years ago it turned into a sleepy, insignificant town. The all but abandoned fortress of San Diego still looked over the tropical paradise with its safe harbor, protected from the open waters by small, lush islands backed by rugged granite cliffs.

Mendoza contacted Miguel Esparza, a local fisherman he knew who was also a smuggler and occasional privateer. He agreed to take them to Alta California as a favor to his friend. It was determined they would sail up the western coast of Baja rather than inside the Gulf of California where the U.S. Navy was active due to recent uprisings in La Paz, Guaymas and other hot spots.

Patrick thanked Mendoza. "I want to repay you," he said. "Padre Orellana has given us some money."

"No, I cannot accept it. You are a hero to my country, Señor Ryan and I will always be ashamed at my part in whipping Don Riley."

"What about Señor Esparza?"

"He won't take any money either. He's a skilled captain and will get you to the coast of Alta California. He said he'll have to determine whether to land in San Diego or San Pedro when you get close. You can trust him to get you safely on shore. After that, I'm afraid you will be on your own but it should be easy to find your way to one of the missions."

They shook hands. Alicia came up, stood on her toes and kissed Mendoza on the cheek and said, "*muchas gracias.*"

The muleteer stood there sheepishly for a moment before saying "*por nada, señora.*" Then Patrick and Alicia watched him walk over to his mount and lead his men and mules off.

Within the hour, Patrick and Alicia were rowed out to Esparza's three masted French Lugger he called *La Señorita*. It was a fast and dependable vessel, easy to land on or launch from a beach as the bow was designed to rise to the surf without taking on water or broaching. Esparza graciously allowed them to use his small but comfortable cabin. They stored their one small bag that contained a change of clothes for Alicia and the cassock and shovel hat Patrick used in his escape. Perhaps the disguise would be needed again.

The two of them went up on the deck. Patrick put his arm around his wife's shoulder and she put both of hers around his waist, resting her head on his chest. Together they watched the picturesque bay of Acapulco get smaller and smaller as Esparza and his crew of five able seamen set *La Señorita's* sails for the trip to California that would take them eleven days.

Alicia looked up at her husband. He put a hand on her belly and they kissed. They were both silent, saying nothing about the American Navy or what type of danger may lay ahead. They were filled with the simple contentment of finally and fully being together. Patrick thought about leaving his home and family in Ireland and understood what Alicia must be feeling as they looked upon the shores of Mexico for the last time. He also knew that she loved him and any regret she might have was overshadowed by the possibility of a real future they both believed would be theirs.

Epilogue

Rancho Castac, California, November, 1849

Patrick cantered his gray and white mustang into the corral and dismounted. He tied the horse up, took off his hat and used it to slap the dust off his chaps. He smoothed back his shoulder length hair, put the hat back on and headed for the main house.

Two years had passed since he and Alicia were rowed ashore on the beach of San Pedro where they secured a ride on an ox cart through the Pueblo de Los Angeles to the mission at San Fernando. From there they were provided a driver and a mule-drawn buckboard to take them up El Camino Viejo, the Old Road, over the rocky and treacherous San Fernando Pass and the rugged fifty-plus miles to Rancho Castac.

When they arrived at the long, rectangular adobe house of José and Anna Marie Covarrubias, they were welcomed and taken in as if they were blood relatives. Alicia went right to work, doing laundry and helping to cook for the family and the dozen *vaqueros* and numerous other ranch hands. Patrick thought she shouldn't be doing all that in her condition but she wouldn't listen. She continued helping until just before their son, James Francisco Ryan was born on March fourth, 1848.

The boy became the jewel and pet of the entire rancho. He had Patrick's red hair and Alicia's olive skin and dark eyes that were full of mischief and merriment. His father called him Jimmy. His mother did too, unless she was scolding him and then she called him *Jaime Francisco* in a stern but loving tone. The Indian and Mexican *vaqueros* called him Pancho, or Panchito. They couldn't get enough of his laughing, curious, exuberant

426

spirit. They took him on horseback rides, did rope tricks for him and let him run free through the bunkhouse.

Much had changed since they arrived. The American military took control of the California government after the Treaty of Guadalupe Hidalgo ended the war. Señor Covarrubias had recently returned from a constitutional convention in Monterey to set up a state government. It would be another year before California officially became a state. According to the the treaty, the Mexican land grants were to be protected but there were rumblings about the validity of many of them and proof of ownership would soon be required.

The biggest change however, was the discovery of gold. The tidal wave of immigrants and miners flooding the territory created a demand for beef in the north and prices soared. Castac, like the rest of the ranchos in southern California, experienced an unprecedented period of prosperity.

Patrick became a trusted, invaluable asset to Covarrubias. When they first arrived he was given minor tasks like caring for the horses and mules. Later he learned how to repair and make saddles as well as all types of other leatherwork and blacksmithing. Soon he was helping with the business side of the rancho which was growing and changing after the gold rush and the demand by the Americans for proof of the legality of the land grants.

When he wasn't busy otherwise, he loved being on horseback with the *vaqueros*, herding, driving and branding the cattle. He would never be able to ride as well as them. They seemed to have been born to the saddle. But he became a very good horseman, taking every opportunity to ride through the cool, rocky canyons, the pine studded high mountain country and the golden grassy meadows rimmed with magnificent white oaks, some forty feet around, that encompassed Rancho Castac.

Alicia was in the front yard, hanging clothes out to dry as he approached. She smiled and waved to him. Their second son, two-month old John Thomas Ryan, was asleep in a basket at her feet. Jimmy was with them and when he spotted his father he came running at full speed shouting "Papa." Patrick bent down to catch his beautiful boy as he leapt into his arms. He tossed him high in the air, laughing at his son's squeals of delight. He threw him up one more time then held him on his hip with one arm. He walked to his wife, put his other arm around her and kissed her. Jimmy squirmed and wiggled until his father let him loose. He and Alicia shook their heads and smiled as he ran off to chase some imaginary animal. Alicia put the last shirt on the line. She bent over and picked up their baby and together they walked to the house.

Acknowledgements

Many people have helped and encouraged me on the odyssey of this story. My children and grandchildren are my paramount inspiration. When I began writing seriously, my grandchildren were the only reasons that drove me to actually complete anything. This is my fourth novel and although it's not about him, my grandson, Nixon, was the book's inspiration. I wanted to write something that connected his Irish and Mexican ancestry. I'm half Irish and my daughter is married to a Mexican. In thinking about the two cultures I stumbled upon the story of the Irish Soldiers of Mexico and got hooked. I've used many of his father's family names, as well as some of mine to give it a flavor of his heritage. It's been a long and fascinating process and although Nixon isn't all that happy that "his" book isn't explicitly about him, I'm hoping that when he's old enough to read it, he'll appreciate his essential and fundamental part in the creation of it.

As for the actual writing, the first and foremost person I have to thank is my second ex-wife, Debbie Diehl. We weren't successful at marriage but we've been phenomenal as friends. She's read every word, more than once, and has been an unwavering, positive force of encouragement and motivation, steadfast in her reassurance that both the story and my capability to convey it were up to the task.

Patti Magness was the first person to read the initial draft of the story. She is the baby sister of my best friend, Tom. After he passed away suddenly and way too early in March of 2014, she and I began corresponding. She was kind enough to read and provide thoughtful and perceptive feedback on the very raw manuscript. Thank you, Patti.

My brother, Bruce, is a musician, singer and songwriter of except-tonal talent. I respect and admire his art and his opinion. I appreciate beyond words his consistent and enthusiastic support and advice. Who better to look at your work than your little brother? Only sixteen months apart, we not only competed vigorously from birth, we grew up in a family where finding fault was as unconscious as breathing. But he read and edited it meticulously with both love and a critical eye.

I'd also like to thank my friend, Cosmo DiCiocco, a skilled craftsman and builder homes, whose interest and curiosity about the subject matter, construction and process of writing never waned. We spent many evenings enjoying a little Irish Whiskey and great discussions about anything and everything. He's half Irish as well and we discovered that his maternal grandparents and mine both emigrated from County Cork in the 1890s. His intensely strong spiritual nature helped me better connect to the religious elements in the story.

I can't neglect Steve Owen. We've been friends since I was in the eighth grade and he was in Bruce's seventh grade class at Our Lady of the Valley elementary school. He is a poet with a kind, quiet, monastic makeup. Distance has limited our contact to long, gratifying phone conversations about old friends, good times, family, prayer, meditation, God, and writing, not necessarily in that order.

Not long after I began this project, I met Graham Heneghan and his wife Bev. We became great friends and I was pleasantly shocked to discover that Graham knew all about the Saint Patrick's Battalion. He's an Irishman himself and was fascinated by their leader, John Riley. His enthusiasm kept me going during rough stretches of frustration and self-doubt. Despite the fact that he regularly and mercilessly beats me in chess, I am eternally grateful for his positive and reassuring belief in the tale and my ability to tell it.

I also wish to thank Ann Howard Creel, an award-winning author and expert editor. I hired her to do a critique of my manuscript and her insightful suggestions and recommendations were invaluable. Her treatment gave me the confidence and energy to reach the finish line even though it forced me into some hard decisions.

There are a few others I want to mention, though I've never met or corresponded with any of them. The first book I read on the St. Patrick's Battalion is *The Rogue's March* by Peter F. Stevens. He brought to life John Riley and his *San Patricios* and started me on the path to discover more about them. *The Philadelphia Nativist Riots* by Kenneth W. Milano is an intensely researched and detailed account of the anti-Catholic riots that enveloped the city in 1844. I returned to it often for more information and it inspired me to make a trip back to my home town of Philadelphia to walk the streets where the mayhem took place. Finally, to Linda S. Hudson who wrote about Jane McManus Storm Cazneau in her marvelous book, *Mistress of Manifest Destiny*. Not only did she unearth and correct history's mistake of not crediting Jane with coining the phrase, Manifest Destiny, she brilliantly portrayed this extraordinary woman and her achievements. I'm not sure how it happened but Ms. Hudson opened the door for Jane to elbow her way into my story and refuse to be excluded even after I tried, unsuccessfully, to cut her out in an effort to make the book less lengthy. Though I've fictionalized parts about Jane in this tale, she deserves a story in her own right.

Last but certainly not least, to Gisele, a remarkable woman of great strength, kindness and passion. Thank you for your friendship, forgiveness and love.

Printed in Great Britain
by Amazon